PLAYBOOK

USA TODAY BESTSELLING AUTHOR

REBECCA JENSHAK

Rebecca Jenshak

www.rebeccajenshak.com

Cover Design by Lori Jackson Designs

Illustration by Sarah Jane

Editing by Margo Lipschultz

Proofreading by Sarah at All Encompassing Books and Rebecca at Fairest Reviews Editing Services

This is a work of fiction, created without use of AI technology. Any names, characters, places or incidents are products of the author's imagination and used in a fictitious manner. Any resemblance to actual people, places, or events is purely coincidental or fictional.

For Catherine.
Thank you for your friendship and for always being the best cheerleader. I'm sorry that there is no murder in this book, but at least the cover is pink!

AUTHOR'S NOTE

Thank you for purchasing Playbook. I hope you will enjoy Brogan & London's story.

Playbook utilizes American Sign Language throughout the story. ASL has its own syntax, grammar rules, and structure that is different from written and spoken English. There are varying thoughts on how to properly write sign language in fiction.

Most of the time my characters are signing and speaking at the same time. For those instances, I chose quote marks and italics. If the characters are not speaking as they sign, it is italicized only.

Additionally, I want to thank everyone who helped me in this process. I tried to write Archer with compassion and care, while remaining true to his journey. Any errors are mine and based on my experiences or those who I consulted with.

CHAPTER ONE
London

I hold my breath and adjust the packages in my hand to avoid the stench. When that doesn't work, I shuffle the red envelope that smells a lot like it was dipped in cheap perfume to the middle of the stack in the hopes of smothering the scent. I can't tell if I'm successful because the terrible smell is burned into my nostrils.

The line for the mail counter is out the door of the main lobby area and growing. Before I had a PO Box, I was completely oblivious to just how busy this place gets. Don't people know you can print postage at home now? Who would ever willingly stand in this line?

I guess me. But only because I need to talk to someone.

The room is filled with quiet whispers and heavy sighs. More than one person has commented on the smell as they've stepped up to the back of the line. The person directly behind me keeps inching backward, giving me a wide berth and shooting annoyed glances at me as they bury their nose in their shoulder.

I'm next up to be helped, thank god. I can't wait to drop these packages and get outside to breathe in the fresh air.

"I can help the next person in line." The woman behind the counter already sounds like she's had a long day. They opened an hour ago.

Rushing forward, I set my mail on the counter. "Hi."

She takes a step back and waves her hand. "I guess I don't need to ask if you're mailing any perfume today."

I'm pretty sure that's judgment on her face. I don't blame her. I'm judging the person whose mail this is too. Which is not me.

"I don't need to mail anything," I explain. "I just wanted to talk to someone about my PO Box."

Covering her nose with one hand, she moves tentatively back into position. It seems that is as much of an opening to continue as I'm going to get so I proceed.

"I am getting mail for whom I assume was the previous owner of the box."

"We have a bin where you can place items for previous box owners in the back corner." Her thin lips pull back in a sort of forced smile that doesn't feel the least bit friendly, but more like she's thrilled to move another person out of her line. "Next."

"No, wait." I glance back at the impatient person stepping toward me to take my spot and give them an apologetic smile, then back to the woman whose name tag reads, Beverly. "I have been doing that, but it's a lot. It's taking up my entire box. I actually talked to someone else last week and…"

Beverly doesn't look like she wants to deal with my problems today, so I stop talking. I'm going through a bit of a pessimistic phase so sometimes my words don't come out hopeful or cheery enough to win over friends and influence people. My roommate Alec calls me grumpy, but that's just a fun word people like to use. I am perfectly sunshine-y under the right circumstances. They've just been few and far between lately.

I divvy up the mail into two stacks. Mail addressed to me—a couple of envelopes that look like junk mail and a package I've been expecting with the most amazing red shoes inside—and everything else. Then, I motion in front of the stack *not* for me. "This is just from the last two days."

Today's bounty includes a dozen envelopes, two bubble mailers, and a small box. All of them addressed to Brogan Six.

Beverly arches a brow and picks up the one on top. It's a brown box, fairly small, and taped together with clear shipping tape stamped with little red hearts. It looks like it could be a Valentine's Day present, if it weren't August.

"I will take care of them," she says with a sigh and a begrudging look in her eye. Who said customer service was dead?

"Thank you. And is there any way to stop future packages from being put into my box? I'm the only person on the contract so if they aren't addressed to London Bennett, they aren't mine." I aim for a cheery tone, but I can tell I'm not winning any points with this woman by continuing to stand in her line and speak. No matter how friendly.

And I know it isn't her fault that the previous owner forgot to forward his mail, but it doesn't seem like that much to ask that the PO Box I pay for each month contains *my* mail.

In the two months I've had the box, it's always contained more mail for Brogan than for me, but it's gotten worse. This is the third time I've talked to someone. I'm sure they have bigger problems to solve, but it's annoying. My box isn't that large, so they put my packages in another box and leave the key in my small metal bin. It's twice as much effort. And sure, that's not really that big of a hassle, if the packages were actually for me.

They almost never are. And they're odd. His name is written in neat, loopy feminine penmanship in red or pink pens, covered in lipstick kisses or spritzed with perfume. Brogan Six is either a teenager with several pen pals or is having a dozen relationships with women by snail mail. An old-fashioned love affair. It's almost romantic. Except for the smell. I suppose if I were going to spray perfume on a love letter, I might be tempted to use my oldest, cheapest bottle. But now I know better. Only the expensive stuff for my future pen pal or nothing at all.

I have no idea when I might get to use that very important life lesson since the closest to a love letter I've written or received lately is the automated *thank you for your order* text I get every time I order DoorDash, but I'm tucking it away for the future.

"I'll see what I can do," Beverly says. It isn't the "It won't happen again" I hoped for, but it's something. She places the packages for Brogan behind her and then uses hand sanitizer. Good idea, Bev.

I shove my mail in my purse and thank her. My fingers are crossed that I won't be intercepting any more mail for my former box owner. How has he not realized he's no longer getting his mail? Maybe he was separated and moved out of his house, hence the need for a PO Box. He found some women to fill the void while he tried to win back his wife, and then she finally took him back and he moved back in and forgot all about his harem of pen pals.

It's a long shot, I know. My dad is in family law, so I know the statistics of married couples staying married. Or separating and then working it out. Still, I hold on to that image as I head to brunch with my sister.

I drive with the windows down, letting the hot air whip through my hair and remove the stench from the mail depot. Not a small sacrifice since it's already over ninety degrees outside. We've reached peak Arizona summer when the only pleasant time to be outside is when the sun is down.

At the restaurant, the hostess leads me out to a back patio where, to my surprise, my parents, sister, and her boyfriend, Ben, and his parents are all already sitting.

Sierra stands and rushes to greet me. "Lo Lo."

The familiar nickname she's used since we were kids makes me smile.

"I thought it was just us," I say, moving in to hug her. I wave at Ben over Sierra's shoulder and then the parents.

"I'm sorry. Ben has been wanting to get both of our families together and it finally lined up where everyone was free. Don't be mad." Sierra wraps her arms around me tightly, and all the tension from the morning and the post office debacle melts away. Sierra is goodness and light, and hugs from her always make me feel better. Even when she blindsides me with a family get-together. I could never stay mad at her.

"Oh." Sierra makes a choked sound and steps back. She scrunches up her nose. "New perfume?"

"What? No." I drop my face to the front of my dress to sniff. I don't smell anything. I mean, I can definitely still smell the perfume from the mail, but I thought it was just lingering in my nostrils—not on *me*.

My sister scrutinizes me carefully with amusement dancing in her blue eyes.

I groan. "I thought it would dissipate by now. You can really smell that?" I ask her, wondering how I'm going to de-stench myself. I don't have any spare clothes in my back seat. Maybe another spin in my car? I'll be soaked in sweat, which is arguably worse.

No, I take that back. This smell is horrid.

"Did you get accosted by the perfume spritzer at the mall?" Sierra moves another step away from me with a pained expression. Ben has moved from his seat to stand beside her and he wraps an arm around her waist, smiling at our interaction.

"I went to grab my mail before work," I grumble as I fan myself.

She waits a beat for more of an explanation. "And they were what? Fumigating the place with Chanel No. 5?"

As if Chanel could ever smell like *this*. This is more like those knockoff fragrance mists in the makeup aisle at a department store. The AXE body spray of women's scents. Only worse.

I reach into my purse for my makeup wipes. Maybe I can rub it off my skin.

"It's a long story and I'm starving." I start to move toward the table to take a seat, but my sweet little sister steps in front of me.

"What are you doing?" I ask, laughing and glancing at Ben. "I don't stink *that* bad."

Okay, maybe I do, but I'm too hungry to care.

"I need to tell you something." Sierra tips her head down, looking guilty.

"You mean something other than you turned our monthly brunch into a family get-together?" I smile at her. "It's fine, but if Mom and Dad start lecturing me about my job or ask when I'm going to 'find a nice boy like Ben,' I'm telling them about the time you snuck out and stole Dad's car when you were fifteen."

Her jaw drops. "You wouldn't?!"

No, I probably wouldn't, but I feel better just bringing it up.

Sierra is two years younger than me. I'm supposed to be the responsible one, the role model, leading by example and all that but I'm more like the cautionary tale to her happily ever after. She always had better grades and did better at sports and got along better with our parents. She didn't even have a bad hair phase in middle school.

She and Ben have been dating for over a year and she just started law school while nannying on the side. She's this wonderful, incredibly responsible, smart, twenty-two-year-old, following in our father's footsteps.

She's annoyingly perfect. I adore her more than anyone in the world though so it's hard to hold it against her.

"I need a cocktail." I sigh.

"On it." Ben turns toward the bar.

Sierra gives me another smile steeped in nerves.

"I'm fine," I assure her.

"Okay, but you might not be when I tell you the rest."

"The rest of what?" I feel my brows pinch together and the start of a headache.

"Ben's family is here."

"I can see that." I smile at her, then look past my sister to where Ben's parents are sitting side-by-side at the table. A little closer than most couples and smiling more. They always look so in love. "I like Ben's parents," I tell her. "It's fine. Really. I promise to go easy on the bottomless mimosas."

"Not just his parents," she says slowly.

It takes my muddled brain a moment for her words to sink in.

"Who else is joining—" My question is cut off when a familiar dark head steps up behind my sister.

Sierra glances back at him, then whispers to me, "Please be nice."

White-hot anger spreads through me as I come face-to-face with my ex-boyfriend for the first time in two years.

"Hey, Lo." He puts one hand in his pocket and keeps a foot of distance between us, but it still feels too close. He's in a black dress shirt and pants like he's heading to the office instead of brunch in the scorching heat. Always immaculately put together no matter the cost. I forgot that about him—or at least pushed it from my mind.

"Chris." I force his name between gritted teeth.

Ben steps forward and thrusts a glass of something in my hand. I down it quickly. Champagne. It feels all wrong for this moment. I glance quickly at the table and all eyes are on us. Our parents have the decency to look away, but Sierra and Ben keep staring with anxious, hopeful expressions.

"I'm going to head to the bar and grab another drink," I say to no one in particular.

I breathe a sigh of relief after I slump onto a bar stool and order a Bloody Mary, but it's short-lived when Chris comes to stand in the spot next to me and sets his phone down on the bar like he's planning on staying awhile.

When my drink comes, he hands his card over to the bartender to pay for it and asks for the same thing.

"Thanks," I say begrudgingly, then as dryly as possible add, "This totally makes up for the last time I saw you."

In bed with another woman.

As only Chris can do, he ignores my remark and leans against the bar. Cool and casual. "So, how've you been?"

I want to roll my eyes at his question. How have I been? Like we're old friends catching up instead of exes who vowed never to speak to one another again. Or I vowed it anyway.

"Well, I was fine until you crashed my favorite Saturday of the month," I say with fake cheer. No sense in pretending like I'm happy to see him. He knows I'm not.

He cranes his neck around and a look of disgust crosses his face before he rears back. "Oh, wow. Someone here smells like they bathed in bad cologne."

My cheeks heat. Perfect. The first time I see the lying, cheating spawn of Satan, I smell and have windblown hair. Not that it matters. I don't have any dream scenarios that include him seeing me and wishing he hadn't let me get away.

"Oh shit," he says, reading the embarrassment on my face. "Is that you?"

His lips quirk up in amusement.

"What are you doing here?" I ask, teeth gritted.

"Ben asked me to be here," he says by way of explanation. For all his terrible qualities, I know he's good to Ben, so that's something.

While I'm debating on what to say or do—tossing my drink at him would just waste a perfectly good Bloody Mary—Chris tries to engage again.

"So who is the guy?" he asks.

"The guy?" He's not making any sense, and I'm seconds from telling him to get lost, but then I spot Sierra out of the corner of my eye. I can manage a civil conversation for her. Just this once.

"You only ever wore perfume at the beginning of our relationship. Kind of like dressing up or making any effort at all with your appearance." The way he says it all so even-toned, like that's not the most asshole thing he's said (and he's said a lot of asshole things), is truly mind-blowing.

"All you need to know is that he's better than you in every way," I say sweetly.

With a disbelieving smirk, he brings his drink to his lips. "Really? Ben said you were still *very* single."

I have absolutely no problem with my single status—most of the time. But faced with the ex-boyfriend from hell, I suddenly don't want him to feel sorry for me or think it's in any way related to him. So I lie.

"It's new. I haven't even told my family yet, but he is so wonderful and the sex…" I lift my shoulders and let my head fall to the side in what I hope is a dreamy, stupidly-in-love expression.

His posture relaxes almost as if he's relived. Like he was worried that I was still hung up on him. As if. I don't feel great about lying—even to him. But it's not like we're going to run into each other again any time soon. I just need to make it through this brunch.

"Really?" He seems surprised, which honestly stings a little. "I thought you were going to live alone in a house filled with cats because men were evil."

He's paraphrasing from the things I yelled at him when we broke up.

"I said you were evil. Not all men. How's Chrissy?"

"Christina," he says, mouth tightening.

"Right. My bad. It was hard to keep up with all the women you were sleeping with while we were together."

"I'm dating someone new. Her name is Gretchen. It's serious."

"Serious," I repeat the word. "So then you're not allowed to sleep around or just like *some* sleeping around?" I lean forward like I'm super interested and not at all wishing he'd move far away so I never have to worry about running into him again.

Once again, he ignores me. "I'm glad you're dating again, Lo. New relationships look good on you." His smarmy gaze trails over me and I feel sick. "Maybe try a different perfume though. You smell like your great-aunt Doreen."

I slide off the barstool to head back to the table. I take a seat next to Sierra, and Chris drops into the seat next to Ben. I glare at him and he smiles back.

Sierra takes my hand and squeezes it. "Are you okay?" she asks quietly.

"Yeah, of course."

She looks so happy at my answer that I feel a twinge of guilt at how much she was obviously stressing about me running into Chris. My earlier frustrations that she blindsided me today ease. When Ben asked her out a little more than a year ago, she called me to make sure it was okay. And I'm the one who told her to go for it. I always liked Chris's family, especially Ben.

I force another smile and mutter where she can't hear, "I'm having brunch with the devil, but I'm just peachy."

"Now that everyone is here, we have an announcement." Sierra looks to Ben as her boyfriend stands with a mimosa in hand. He looks so happy. So does Sierra.

Ben clears his throat and then looks lovingly down at my little sister. "I asked Sierra to marry me, and she said yes! We're getting married!"

CHAPTER TWO
Brogan

I drop down to the ground, heart pounding and out of breath.

"What are you doing, rookie?" My teammate, Cody St. James, peers down at me with an amused expression on his face.

He's sweating and panting a little, but otherwise he looks like he could run all day long. I have no idea how he's standing.

"Just catching my breath," I wheeze out. My throat burns from sucking in hot air.

Laughing, he holds out a hand. "Never let them see you down."

He tips his head to the rest of our position group finishing up running cone drills. We're all teammates, but each other's competition too.

It takes all my might to get to my feet. I've been pushing harder than I even knew was possible since joining the Mavericks.

Once I'm upright, Cody grins. "Nice job, Six. You're looking good out there."

His words spark a jolt of pride through me. "Thanks."

"Now smile pretty, your favorite reporter is here." He claps me on the shoulder, almost sending me back to the ground.

I glance to where the crowd of media is gathered. And sure enough, Billy Boone is glaring at me from the fifty-yard line.

Two more teammates, Tripp and Merrick, jog up to us as we're slowly making our way off the field.

"Looks like you're still on Boone's shit list, rookie," Tripp says, grinning. "Seen his girlfriend lately?"

"It was his fiancée." Merrick cocks a brow as his mouth pulls into a smirk at my expense.

"Absolutely not. And I didn't know that she was in a relationship," I say for what is probably the hundredth time. If I had, I wouldn't have slept with her. I might not have vetted my hookup well enough, but I'm not out trying to be that guy.

"Well, whatever. He's still pissed," Tripp mutters as we get closer. "If I were you, I'd avoid him. Make a beeline for the locker room before he can pull you into another interview."

Probably not a terrible idea. The last time I talked with him, he spent twenty minutes going on and on about all the mistakes I made in my first pre-season game without asking me a single question. By the time he was done, *I* was half-convinced the Mavericks should cut me.

The guy is an asshole with a grudge, but he knows his football.

"I can't keep avoiding him all season," I tell them. Also, I really don't want to have an enemy so soon into my professional football career. Especially not one that gets paid to write articles about me.

"It's your funeral," Merrick calls after me as I veer off to approach Billy.

The stone-faced reporter's brows rise as he notices me coming toward him. He can't be more than a handful of years older than me, but he has this air of pretentious sophistication about him. He's always carrying around a legal pad and scribbling on it. Scribbles that are probably outlining my mistakes.

I force my smile a little bigger. I'm borderline beaming at the guy, hoping it deflects him from any thoughts of me and his ex naked. We're never going to be friends, but maybe we can put this whole thing behind us.

"Hey, Billy," I say with a friendliness that he does not reciprocate in his expression.

He crosses his arms over his chest, still clutching that notepad.

"Six?" My name comes out of his mouth more question than greeting.

"How are we looking?" I ask.

He hesitates like he's deciding if he's going to humor me before he says, "Cody looks sharp, as always, defense is tight, and your fellow Valley U teammate, Archer Holland, is one to watch if he can keep his injuries from sidelining him."

A spark of pride lights up inside of me for Archer. I play it cool, though, because if this guy knew he was more than just a fellow teammate, that he's the best friend I've ever had and is by my definition a brother, he might let that cloud his judgment of his performance too. I can handle his hate, but I won't stand for anyone taking shots at Archer.

Actually, come to think of it, I'm surprised ole Billy Boone doesn't already know. Maybe he isn't as good of a reporter as he thinks.

"I agree," I say instead. And I hope what he hears is, *See? We have common ground.*

"I know what you're doing." His lips press into a thin line.

"Making small talk?" And hoping he stops thinking of me as the guy who slept with his ex and goes back to thinking of me as just another football player that he doesn't want to destroy with words.

"You want to talk?"

It feels like a trap, but I nod.

"Fine, let's talk about how you're sleeping your way around town and making a mockery of the team."

A strangled sound works its way up my throat. "I didn't know, man."

"You rookie players are all the same. You think the rules don't apply to you now that you have a little bit of money and women are throwing themselves at you."

"So you agree that she threw herself at me?"

His face reddens. Oops. Not the right thing to say, apparently.

"I know the rules apply to me." I don't even know what rules we're talking about. A gentleman's code? Whoops. On him for assuming I was a gentleman, then.

"Word of advice, focus more on football than getting laid. Or don't, it'll be fun to watch your demise."

"You mean write about it?" I ask. He's already written a few things calling my skills and longevity into question.

"I'd rather cover high school football than write another word about you—good or bad." With that he stalks off.

I blow out a breath, then laugh. "So that's a no to grabbing drinks later?" I yell after him.

He flips me off without looking back.

"Why would you try to talk to him?" Archer asks as we sit at our new favorite lunch spot, downing our one cheat meal of the week: burgers and fries.

I swallow down a large bite and shake my head. It isn't very loud in the restaurant, but I still want to make sure he can easily read my lips. Archer has a profound hearing loss. If it's too loud or there are a lot of people, I sign for him or lean in closer too. "I really thought we could put it behind us. Does he really want to be with somebody that's screwing other guys behind his back?"

Arch shrugs his shoulders.

"He should be thanking me."

At that comment, my buddy throws his head back. He covers his mouth with his forearm as he tries to chew his food while he laughs at me.

By the time he calms down enough to speak, I'm smiling just from watching him cackle at me.

"Fine," I say. "I get why he's pissed, but I'm not a bad guy."

Archer's expression softens. "Of course you're not. You're just a good guy with terrible taste in women."

I nod and consider his words. "She was pretty hot though."

He shakes his head at me and drops the last of his burger onto the plate. "That's your problem."

"My problem is that I like good-looking women?"

"No, it's that it's your *only* criteria."

"That's not true," I say automatically.

"There was the girl you brought home from the grocery store. She stayed for two days and you had to basically kick her out to get her to leave. The realtor you slept with during our tour of the apartment." He grimaces.

"I didn't expect her to drop to her knees either, but I wasn't about to stop her." Who turns down a Tuesday afternoon blow job? No one.

"And then the bartender who, if I remember correctly, stole all our toilet paper on her way out."

"Okay. I get your point."

"Are you sure? Because I could keep going."

"Don't come at me like you haven't been doing your share of hooking up since we moved up here." Archer and I were drafted by the Mavericks and moved the hour north from Valley to Lake City after graduation. It's been chaotic and amazing, and yes, I've enjoyed the newfound attention that's come from being a professional football player. But so has he.

"The difference is my hookups aren't making headlines."

"Only because I accidentally hooked up with Boone's fiancée. Something *she* should have mentioned." I feel like everyone keeps forgetting that point.

"Or maybe you should have thought to ask."

He's not wrong, but we didn't do a lot of talking.

"Well, whatever the reason, you need to be careful. Coach did not look happy today when he talked to Boone after you." Archer grimaces.

"It'll be fine," I insist. "You worry too much. You're turning into Hendrick."

Archer scoffs at the mention of his oldest brother. "I am not. Take it back."

"I wonder what they're up to." The hardest part of moving up here has been leaving the Holland family. Archer and his three brothers are the only family I've ever known. I miss them. We talk weekly, but everyone has their own thing going on.

Hendrick got married this summer, and he and his wife Jane are enjoying the newlywed life, Knox is in the middle of the motocross season, and Flynn is enjoying the summer before he goes off to college.

"I talked to Knox this morning. He and Flynn are leaving tomorrow for Houston."

"Really? Already?" Damn, it seems like just yesterday summer started, and now the youngest Holland brother is going off to college.

"They're gonna make a week-long road trip of it. They're stopping at White Sands National Park, then spending a couple of days in Austin before they head to Houston."

I nod thoughtfully. I know it's dumb, but I feel a small pang of disappointment that I'm finding out via Archer and didn't hear from either Knox or Flynn. It isn't that I think it was intentional, but it's moments like this that remind me I'm not really one of them, even if they feel like brothers.

"Knox said to tell you not to get kicked off the team for being an idiot."

"He would know," I chirp back. Knox is the surliest of the brothers and last year he got into it with a teammate and got booted from his motocross team. "At least if I get kicked off, it'll be for something a lot more fun."

"Oh great," Archer says, chewing. "That's really reassuring, man."

CHAPTER THREE
London

An hour after the longest brunch of all time, I'm sitting on the treadmill in the middle of my living room with a bottle of vodka in my lap.

That's how Alec finds me. He crosses the room, eyeing me carefully.

"Bad day?" he asks, taking the vodka from me and chugging it like the frat boy he once was before handing it back. My roommate is dressed in a suit that is tailored to perfection. His dark hair still looks as good as it did this morning when he left and his hazel eyes are framed with long, thick lashes that any girl would kill for. Sometimes I forget that under this meticulously styled business exterior he's just a big ole party boy.

"That's impressive," I say, drinking another much smaller sip.

"I prefer it on ice with a lemon, but something tells me that's not the kind of happy hour we're having tonight."

"She's engaged," I say, still too shocked to put any feeling behind the words. "And he has a girlfriend."

"Whoever they are, do they know they're in two very different relationships?"

"No." I give my head a shake to clear it. "Sierra. Sierra is engaged. She and Ben are getting married."

"Oh," Alec says with a contemplative look. "That's great. Or maybe not, judging by how much vodka is gone from this bottle. Wait. I got it. The ex has a girlfriend."

"You figured that out way too easily." It doesn't escape my notice that Alec doesn't use Chris's name. He never does.

"Not my first time walking in on a girl spiraling over an ex-boyfriend."

"I'm not spiraling over him," I say quickly.

Alec lifts one brow and has that look on his face like he's about to serve me with many points to argue my last statement.

"Okay, not just over him." I realize that everything about this situation—finding me sitting on the treadmill in my tank top and leggings, tennis shoes next to me where I kicked them off, with a bottle of vodka—does give off *not over the ex* vibes.

I had planned to come home and run off the weirdness of brunch, but I slipped in my ear buds and turned on my workout playlist and before the very first song ended, I was replaying the day, getting all riled up all over again about Chris and how much of an asshole he still is. I was becoming a safety hazard. So I stopped and started drinking.

"He's dating a model."

"Ha!" Alec throws his head back and laughs. "Of course he is."

He says nothing else as he goes into the kitchen, gets two

glasses and fills them with ice. He comes back and sits on the floor in front of me.

He pours us each a glass, then sets the now near-empty bottle behind him, out of my reach, and holds up his glass. "To the model skank."

"She's not a skank." I take the other glass and swallow a big gulp. It burns and I cough. "Also, I don't love calling women skanks."

"Can you just be a petty bitch for a minute?"

That pulls a laugh out of me. "She graduated with a Masters in Social Work and volunteers at the food bank twice a week. Oh, and she was a competitive runner in college."

Both of Alec's brows shoot up. "I don't even want to know how you know so much about this woman. Have you been stalking her online since you got home?"

"His mom was all too happy to brag about 'Chris's lovely new girlfriend.' She never liked me for him."

Like *I* was the problem.

She thought I was too indecisive and lacking ambition. I *was* indecisive but I take offense to the other thing. I only lacked ambition because I was getting a degree for a job that wasn't the right fit for me. Once I found something I was passionate about, that changed. Or maybe I just desperately need to tell myself that. I'm a people pleaser and I hate knowing she thinks I'm not good enough for her son. Even if I don't want him back.

"I like your ex less with every new detail I learn. He should have stopped his mom from hyping up his new girl in front of you. Full stop. That's not cool."

I shrug. The whole thing was awkward. I'm not giving Chris a pass—I never give him a pass—but there's no good way to interact with your ex and his family. His dad had the decency to look a little embarrassed on my behalf, but I did my best to seem indifferent. What do I care if he's dating a smart, kind model who can run the four hundred in under two minutes? He is not my business anymore.

"Yeah, well, it doesn't matter. I hope they are very happy together."

"No, you don't."

"No, I don't, but only because he's the worst." I take another sip. "He's going to be my brother-in-law."

"Technically, he'll be Sierra's brother-in-law."

I groan. "How am I going to avoid him forever as planned?"

"Easy. Come home with me for all future holidays."

"Tempting," I say with a smile because I know he'd let me tag along with him any time I wanted. "Also, can we talk about the other thing? Because he's not why I'm upset."

Alec looks like he's fighting a retort, so I add, "*Really.* He's not. He's still awful and smug and all the things I remembered, but my little sister is getting *married.*"

"I thought you liked Ben."

"I do. I love Ben. Aside from being Chris's brother, he's basically perfect. But don't you think they're kind of young? She just turned twenty-two. And it's fast. They're planning the wedding for late October."

Alec doesn't seem to follow because his facial expression doesn't shift into the shock and judgment that I'm waiting for.

"That's less than three months away."

"I guess that's a little fast. Is she pregnant?"

"No. She was drinking at brunch. I think they're just that in love."

"Okay." He laughs softly. "So they won't have their pick of venue or DJ. None of this sounds like cause for worry."

"I don't want her to rush into anything and then have regrets. That's all." I mean, how well do you really know a person after dating for only a year? It took me twice that long to figure out Chris was bad news.

He nods thoughtfully. "If I've learned anything from dating women for twenty-five years now, it's that you can't change their minds if they're set on something."

"You started dating when you were in diapers?"

"You'd be surprised how young I was," he says.

I snort. I actually wouldn't be. Alec has the kind of charm and charisma that speaks of years of wooing the opposite sex. "And that's all you've learned?"

"That and to always say no when asked if any article of clothing makes you look fat." He smiles proudly, then that expression softens. "You can't stop her from marrying the guy she loves just because you're scared he might turn into his brother one day. And, hey, if he does, you know a great divorce lawyer. Two by then, if she graduates on schedule."

I scowl at my roommate, then take another drink of straight vodka. It still burns and I grimace. I'm more of a hard seltzer or mixed drink girl, but Alec loves his vodka and always keeps us stocked.

"Come on. Enough moping around. I know just the place to take weddings and ex-boyfriends off your mind." Alec takes the glass from my lips and pulls it away carefully. "Go get ready."

"I'm not up for people-ing tonight."

"You always say that. It'll be fun, and I'm not taking no for an answer." He stands and takes our glasses and the vodka to the kitchen. I lie back on the treadmill. It smells like rubber and dust. Gross. But I don't move.

The next thing I know, Alec is standing over me, grabbing my hands, and pulling me up to my feet. The room spins a little.

With a laugh, Alec steadies me by placing both hands on my shoulders.

"Change of plans. I'm taking you to dinner. We need to soak up some of the alcohol in your system."

"What was the other plan?"

"Drinks with some people from the station."

Alec and I work together at a local news station. I'm a graphic designer and he does the morning weather. He's way higher up on the social ladder at work, well really everywhere. He has friends at work; I have colleagues. I'm the only woman in my department and going out with them always feels a little forced and awkward. Whereas Alec has a wide variety of people that adore him and are always inviting him out.

"You don't need any more booze. You need a night of dancing and mingling with hot strangers. Chris is an idiot and frankly, you could do way better."

"I told him I was seeing someone." One side of my mouth lifts in a grin. "He was baiting me and the next thing I knew…it just popped out. And he looked so relieved, like he was glad that I wasn't waiting around for him."

"Maybe he wants you to be happy now that he's found his model do-gooder girlfriend. He could be a changed man." The smile Alec gives me tells me he doesn't believe that.

"I am happy. And I sort of have someone."

Alec cocks his head to the side.

"Luke," I remind him.

At the mention of my occasional, no-frills hookup, Alec shoots me a disapproving smirk that makes him look like trouble.

"What? Are you going to tell me it doesn't count because it's just sex?"

"I would never utter the words 'just sex,' but come on, Luke? That guy is not for you."

"So he lives with three other guys and his job sucks and he smells a little like garlic even first thing in the morning." With every word I say, Alec's expression just gets smugger. "He is a nice guy and we have fun together."

Or we did. He started seeing someone else recently and they must be getting more serious because I haven't heard from him in at least two weeks.

"The bar is so low I don't even know what to do with you." He pats me on the top of the head.

He's not wrong, but dating is exhausting and I'm already busy. Luke is all the effort I can manage right now. However, a night out sounds fun. "I did get new shoes today."

"Perfect. As long as they aren't sneakers, put them on and let's do this night up right. The first step to turning around any bad day is moping." Alec looks me up and down. "Now that we've checked that off the list, it's time to move on to partying to forget."

That's not my style, it's his, but for one night I think I can get on board, so I nod.

"Are you good?" he asks. "Really? Is this a Paige-level crisis?"

Paige is my best friend in the whole world so I did consider texting her after brunch, but I knew she'd be busy. Plus I just kind of wanted to wallow for a bit. "It's Saturday."

"And on Saturdays she's not available for crises?" he asks quizzically.

"Sex Saturday. They never make plans after five. I think they even turn their phones off."

"I'm sorry, what?"

Oops. I don't think that's something I should have shared. I shake my head like I'm not going to tell him.

"London Renee Bennett, tell me right this instant."

A laugh bubbles up and loosens my chest. "They reserve Saturday nights for sex."

He thinks. He thinks way too hard. Paige is going to kill me for telling him.

"I can get behind blocking out an entire night for sex, but every Saturday? And does that mean only Saturdays?"

"I've already said too much. She's unavailable but I'm fine." Then I plaster on a big smile and say as enthusiastically as I can, "Let's go dance with sweaty strangers!"

One side of his mouth lifts and he finally backs away. "I'm going to make myself a drink for the shower. You want anything? A coffee perhaps?"

Feeling better than I have all day, I follow him into our kitchen. It's my favorite part of the apartment. It's not a big space, but the island is cozy and the cabinets all have glass fronts. Alec doesn't cook, but he did a nice job organizing everything. His style is very minimalist and clean – lots of whites and grays. I could stand for a little more color, but since I moved in after he'd already decorated everything, I choose to think of it as a bougie Airbnb or hotel.

"No thanks." I grab the scissors out of a drawer and cut the tape on one of the packages I picked up today. My mood lifts considerably as I pull the shoe box out of the bigger box, and even more so when I take off the lid and peel back the tissue paper.

I lift one shoe out of the box and smile. I don't think I've ever owned a pair of red shoes before, but something about these said *pick me.*

Alec eyes them, brows lifted, and nods in approval as he cuts a wedge of lemon for his drink. "Well, all right now. Those are some seriously sexy shoes."

My stomach swoops with a little bubble of excitement. I know that going out and partying tonight isn't going to take away the sting of Sierra's engagement to my ex's brother. Tomorrow I'll be back to obsessing about it, but tonight...tonight I choose great shoes and great company.

"What's that other box?" my roommate asks, resting one hip against the counter.

I set the shoe down and frown at the package. I was in a haze at the post office, fueled with rage over getting another boxful of Brogan's mail.

I pick up the pink bubble mailer. The label is dirty and I can't make out the sender information. Actually, the whole front looks like it was dragged behind a pack mule across the country. My PO Box number is just visible under streaks of brown and black. It's light and flat.

"I have no idea," I say, tearing it open. I peer inside with a frown and then reach in and pull out...panties. Lacy, red panties.

"I didn't order—" I start, and then drop them, backing away with a lurch. I bring my hand up to my mouth and then recoil because that hand just touched someone's dirty underwear.

"What?" Alec asks. He eyes the panties with humor. "They match your new shoes."

He makes like he's going to pick them up and I shout, "Don't!"

"What's the big deal?" He lifts them up with one finger.

"They're not mine. Someone must have sent them to that guy… the one that had my PO Box before me."

"Damn. Really?" He sounds impressed instead of disgusted. Then he laughs like this is the funniest thing that's ever happened.

I roll my eyes and step forward and snatch them out of his hand, then quickly drop them into the trash. While I wash my hands with a whole lot of soap and very hot water, Alec continues to investigate the package the panties came in like he's hoping there's more.

"You didn't say he was getting dirty lingerie."

"I never open the packages," I say, but now that he's mentioned it, I wonder what else was in all those boxes and large envelopes that have been shoved into my mailbox.

"Why not?"

"You mean aside from it being a felony?" I wipe my hands off on a towel, then consider washing them again. "What kind of guy gets used panties in the mail?"

"A lucky one." Alec grins wide.

The great thing about going anywhere with Alec is that he knows everyone. It's one of the perks, and I've found via my roommate that there are many, of being on TV. People recognize him everywhere we go. They should. His face is on the side of several billboards around town. And even if our peers aren't exactly his target viewers, being the local weatherman is a fascinating job. People want to meet him, and they're interested in hearing about his work.

Alec is as personable and friendly in real life as he appears on TV, and the perks of his job often extend to me when I'm with him so I'm not complaining.

Like at the restaurant, we were led past a line of people waiting for a table straight to one in the back that they reserve for last-minute high-profile guests.

High-profile. The thought makes me want to snort. This is the same guy whose diet consists mostly of Kraft macaroni and cheese. Which made it especially funny tonight when the chef came out to say hello and asked how the food was. I think he was expecting more than the one-word "Excellent" response he got. But he sent over dessert after so maybe he wasn't too offended by our lack of proper foodie adjectives.

By the time we make it to Gaga, the hottest club in town, I'm full and happy and ready to do exactly what Alec planned for us—drink and dance with hot strangers.

The second we step into the door of the club, he runs into a girl who works for the local football team, the Mavericks. Or used to work for them. I missed the details, but we're welcomed into the VIP area and I quickly find myself standing around, not quite part of the conversation.

Someone is celebrating a birthday, judging by the balloons and number of champagne bottles I've seen brought up in the thirty minutes we've been here.

We're on the fringe of the VIP area, but I watch the people coming and going. Girls in short, sexy dresses and big guys that are probably football players. Most of them are dressed more casually than the girls, but many are wearing diamonds around their neck and wrists in that way pro athletes always do. Do they just run out of things to buy or did they always wish for a necklace that weighs five pounds?

I don't really follow sports, much to Alec's dismay. He played tennis and soccer all through high school and part of college, and because of his job, he's always in the know about local sports teams.

The club itself is nice. I came one other time with Alec, but we only stayed for one drink because his girlfriend at the time found out that my very friendly roommate had slept with the bartender. Not while they were together or anything, but Vickie (the ex) still wouldn't stay anywhere near, and I quote, "that fucking whore."

The VIP area is on the second level of the club. Plush black sofas and chairs are scattered around, and crystal chandeliers hang from the ceiling. Music pumps up from the dance floor below, but it's quiet enough to talk if you yell or stand close enough.

Alec nudges me, pulling me back into the conversation he's having with Laura, the one with the in with the Mavericks.

She smiles and leans closer to speak directly to me. "My friends are in the back corner. Do you want to come have a seat with us?"

Alec waits for my approval. He's good about always looking out for me since I'm not as social as he is.

"Actually, I'm going to walk around, maybe hit the dance floor."

"Do you want me to come with you?" Alec offers.

"No, I'll be fine." I wave him off. These new shoes are a smidge too tight and my feet already hurt. Plus, I recognize the look Alec is giving Laura. He likes her and is hoping she'll be coming home with us later.

I only make it as far as the bar before Alec rejoins me.

"I told you I was fine," I tell him. "Where's Laura?"

"VIP." He settles in next to me. "I told her I was coming to check on you and she got all misty-eyed. Girls love my caring, sensitive side."

I hum my disapproval at being used to pick up women. Not that he really needs a hook, I suppose. And he is caring and sensitive, so I guess it isn't like he's lying to get them into bed. Just playing the part a little too well.

He orders our drinks and before I know it, he's found someone else he knows. He tries to keep me in the conversation but it's too loud and too packed. Once I have my drink in hand, I fall back, people-watching.

Downstairs isn't quite as interesting as VIP and it's not long before I'm scanning the area we were just at. The girls are all gorgeous. The guys too. Even the ones that aren't that cute, still look cute. It must be some sort of professional athlete magic.

My gaze snags on one in particular. Tall, actually one of the tallest, which is saying something, muscular, but not the freaky kind that looks like they wouldn't fit through a doorway. While most of the other guys are in jeans and T-shirts, he has on a white button-down with short sleeves rolled up to show off his big biceps. There's something else about him though. He has a nice smile and warm eyes, and he's animated. While he talks, everyone around him is giving him their full attention. I can't hear him from here, I can barely hear Alec standing next to me, but as this guy talks, I find myself smiling in response to his facial expressions and wild hand motions.

When Alec is finally done making friends, we cheers, down our drinks, and then head to the dance floor.

Alec is a good-looking guy and he's super fun, but there's never been anything but friendship between us. Maybe it's because when I met him I was still a mess over Chris and had no interest in any guy, or maybe it's because shortly after that we started living together and we knew it would be too awkward if we crossed that line. Whatever the reason, I'm thankful we can dance and have fun. I can be completely myself without worrying. I know he'll look after me and he knows I'll do the same for him.

After we've danced to several songs, never leaving each other's side to make good on our dance with strangers' plan, we head back to the bar. Alec leans over after he orders our drinks. "I'm gonna hit the bathroom. Be right back."

I manage to snag a spot at the bar that isn't crowded and set my drink down. I pull my hair off my neck to cool down and get sucked into the conversation of the two girls standing next to me. They are facing each other, wide-eyed and grinning, in that typical girl-talk pose that makes me miss my best friend. I hope she's having fabulous sex tonight.

"I don't even care that he probably wouldn't remember my name tomorrow morning," the girl closest to me says. She has long brown hair that touches her ass and almost the hem of her skirt.

The other girl has short blonde hair. They're proof that opposites attract and that you can be hot with any hair color or length because they're both gorgeous. "I gave him my number."

"What? When?"

"I wrote it on a napkin and handed it to him while you were buying our drinks."

"What did he do? What did he say?" Her long brown hair swishes around her back and I get a whiff of her shampoo. It's nice.

"He just said, 'thanks.' Do you think he'll call?"

"If he has any sense at all."

The blonde makes a face that's somewhere between hopeful and nervous, lifts one hand in the air to show her fingers crossed, and then they both peer not so discretely at the other side of the bar.

I follow their gazes to the guy they're talking about. It's the guy from VIP, the one in the white shirt. From far away he was handsome, but up close this guy is in a whole other league.

His shoulders are broad and he's at least a foot taller than anyone else nearby. His brown hair has a mind of its own. One curl flops around his forehead as he chats and talks. He doesn't run his fingers through it or try to tame it in any way. And I get the sense that's not because he's unaware, but because he just doesn't care.

I'm still vaguely listening to the girls chattering on about him when one of them says, "God, I can't even imagine what it'd be like to spend one night with Brogan Six."

The name registers with a sense of alarm. I'm certain I must have misheard them. But I keep listening to see if they'll repeat it.

"I heard he had a threesome with that sports reporter and his fiancée."

"I heard it was the fiancée and one of her friends."

I feel like I'm listening to an episode of a really good reality dating show or a really bad daytime soap opera.

"Excuse me," I interrupt. I'm unable to hold myself back a second longer. Their heads swivel to me. "Did you say Brogan Six is here?"

Instantly I feel silly. There's no way that could be who they said. I mean, what kind of name is Brogan Six, anyway? I assumed it was some kind of pseudonym.

They glance at each other before returning their gazes to me, then nod in unison.

"That guy…" I tip my head toward him. "The one in the white shirt with the…" I gesture to my biceps and then to my hair. "Is Brogan Six?" I enunciate his name carefully.

"Don't you recognize him?" the brunette asks in disbelief. "He's only the hottest football player on the entire Mavericks team."

They look to me like they expect me to say more. I shake my head, then go back to sipping my drink.

Alec is taking a long time to get back. He probably ran into someone else he knows. I try to focus on my drink and not stare across the bar, but it's futile.

Brogan Six.

He's real and he's *here*.

I don't know what exactly I was picturing my mysterious former box owner would look like, but this isn't it.

He's young and attractive—too attractive to need to carry on long-distance relationships with dozens of women. Seriously, what the hell?

God, of course. I see all of his interactions differently now that I know who he is. The way he smiles as pretty women approach him, the lingering hug he gives another woman. He's a total player. Player isn't even the right word. He's a creep. He could get any girl he wants, but apparently, that isn't good enough. He needs to string them along via snail mail too?

The longer I watch him, the angrier I get.

All of it has me wanting to give this guy a piece of my mind. And you know what? Fuck it. It's been a day and this guy made me smell like old lady perfume on top of it. In fact, my purse still stinks. It'll never be the same.

Alec finally returns, sidling up to the bar beside me. He takes his drink.

"What'd I miss?" He studies my expression, one side of his mouth crooking up. I can't imagine what my face is saying right now, but it can't be good because he asks, "Are you okay?"

"Fine. I just saw someone I need to talk to." I thrust the rest of my drink toward him, so I won't be tempted to toss it in Brogan Six's face.

CHAPTER FOUR
Brogan

There's a gorgeous brunette staring at me from across the bar.

I noticed her on the dance floor earlier, but she was dancing with some guy so I thought she was taken. I am happy to have been wrong. She has this whole hot girl glare thing going on. I dig it. It's making it hard to concentrate on the woman next to me who has been telling me about her dog, which she named Brogan. I can't decide if that's a compliment or not but the way she's touching my arm, I think yes.

Another woman wraps her arms around me from behind, pulling my attention away from everyone else. I can tell it's Georgia by the pear-scented lotion she's always wearing.

"Come dance with me," she shouts over the noise of the club.

"I'll be out in a few. I want to finish my drink first," I tell her, looking over my shoulder and lifting my beer to show her I just got a fresh one.

The girl that was standing next to me bumps into her and shoots her a dirty look. "Excuse me, but I was talking to him."

Georgia flashes me a smile, then gives the girl the same one. Not letting go of me, she says, "Honey, no need to get the claws out. He's not taking me home tonight."

The other girl does seem to relax some at that knowledge. It's a new thing having women fight over me. I hooked up often enough before, but I wasn't that guy that had a trail of women following me around. I don't hate it, but sometimes it does feel odd. It's hard to distinguish whether they're actually interested in me or just in sex with a pro football player. I know, I know. What a sob story. Trust me, I'll dry my tears in one of these girls' tits later tonight. It's not that I expect sympathy, it's just weird.

"Excuse me," I say to the woman with the dog, then I angle my body toward Georgia.

Georgia from Savannah, Georgia. She's one of the first people I met when I moved here. Archer and I were at a bar near our first apartment—a small place that the team rented for us while we found permanent lodging. She marched up to me, asked me to buy her a drink, and then we spent all night drinking and getting to know each other.

"I can't believe you're leaving," I say to her.

We weren't ever official or anything, but for about a month we were inseparable. We partied and hooked up. She was a shot girl at a popular spot and knew lots of people. Guys were always giving her invites to big parties and events around town. That's how I met a lot of people—through Georgia. I have her to thank for the attention I've gotten off the field. She took me to parties where I met important people around the city, and with each event I made more and more contacts. At one of those events I met a woman casting for an underwear model and that's when things really took a turn.

Suddenly my face, and body, were everywhere. I was Brogan Six—sexiest new NFL player. Also weird. I don't quite understand how it all snowballed the way it did, but I know I owe Georgia a lot. We fell out of our situationship the same way we fell in, easy and uncomplicated. I got busy with team stuff and she moved on to someone new. She's not any more ready to settle down with one person than I am.

"I know." She sticks her bottom lip out and her Southern accent sounds more pronounced when she adds, "I can't believe this is the last time we're going to see each other."

"Yeah, me neither," I tell her honestly. We were never destined for anything serious, but I'm sad to be losing a friend here. "What does Georgia have that Arizona doesn't?"

"My family," she says, sighing dramatically. "My parents are going to cut me off soon if I don't move back and start learning the family business so I can take it over someday."

She wrinkles her nose, but a pang of something close to jealousy hits me. What would it be like to have family across the country, begging me to move back, and wanting to gift me something like an entire business? Don't get me wrong, I know the Holland brothers miss me in their own way and they'd do anything for me, but it's just not the same. There's this sense of tradition and generational belonging that I can't help but wonder, what would it be like to have that?

She moves an inch closer. The other girl leaves with a huff and I decide naming a pet after me might be a compliment but it's also a little bit creepy.

Georgia laughs as she watches her go. Her black hair bounces around her shoulders.

I wrap one finger around a curl. "Are you sure you don't want to stay over one last time? For old time's sake?"

"My flight is super early tomorrow. Besides, if I am going to show up at the airport on no sleep, I sort of had my heart set on Merrick being the one keeping me awake all night." She tips her head toward my teammate. Maybe other people would be offended by her honesty, but that's just not how Georgia and I have ever been together.

"Yeah?" I am surprised that of all my teammates, it's Merrick she has her eye on. He's a quiet guy who doesn't love going out. He's actually a nice guy, but he's got resting asshole face.

"Yeah, he's got this whole serious, angry vibe about him. I really want to see him come undone."

I laugh under my breath. "I'm going to fucking miss you."

She grins. "Me too. I'm the OG Six girl. It's the end of an era."

"OG Six girl?" I question, one brow rising.

"Yeah, like Ursula Andress, the original Bond girl. Not Bond's first lover, but the first after he became Bond, ya know?"

It's a strange comparison, but I understand her logic.

I glance over my shoulder to where Merrick is standing, hanging back from some other teammates, looking miserable.

"Yo, Thomas."

His bored gaze slowly moves to mine and he gives me a chin lift as he steps toward me. In the commotion I notice the brunette woman from across the bar is now standing a few feet from me. Her piercing green gaze is focused on me. I give her a half smile that she does not reciprocate. But she keeps staring. I can usually read signals pretty well, but I'm not sure if she wants to fuck me or tell me how much I suck. It's an odd thing, but I do get the occasional football fan who can't resist telling me that I'm overhyped or shouldn't have been a second-round pick or whatever other grievance they've found in my professional career.

"What's up?" Merrick asks, drawing my attention away from the pretty brunette.

"You have any plans later?" I ask him.

"Going home and going to bed," he says like he isn't sure why he came in the first place. I'm not sure why he did either. But Georgia practically preens beside me.

"Well, before you run off, Sleeping Beauty, have you met Georgia?"

The girl at my side steps in front of me and extends a hand to him. "Hi. I'm Georgia."

He stares at her hand a beat before taking it. Georgia takes another step closer. "I'm a big fan. I went to a small community college, but I followed my home state college football. I was at that bowl game where you made that great block against Alabama."

I smother a laugh. I don't know if she realizes it or not, but it's about the only thing she could have said to him to get his attention. He doesn't care for people that much, but he loves football. In fact, I think the only time I've ever heard him utter more than a few words at a time was when he told me about that game.

He stands there, mouth gaping open.

"Let's dance," she tells him and takes his arm. He lets her lead him away like he's in a daze.

"She is going to eat him alive," Cody says, stepping up to fill the space Georgia vacated.

"Nah. Well, maybe, but he'll enjoy it."

He nods, then motions to the VIP area. A lot of the guys have abandoned it, leaving it to Georgia's friends. They've turned it into their own personal dance floor, even with Georgia down here. "You went to an awful lot of trouble tonight for a chick that you're never going to see again and who is now going home with another dude. I don't know if you're the nicest guy I know or the dumbest."

I laugh it off. I booked out the VIP area for her goodbye party. I didn't do it expecting her to go home with me. I just wanted to send her off right as a thank you for all she's done.

My phone buzzes in my pocket. I pull it out and then frown at the same number that's been messaging me daily for weeks.

UNKNOWN

> Hey, it's Sabrina again. I don't know if
> you're getting my texts, but—

I stop reading and press delete. I should block the number, but some twisted part of me wonders how long she'll keep it up.

The guys around me are busy drinking and chatting up girls. Archer and the girl he's been seeing, Wren, are hugging one another. Everyone is having a good time. Except Cody. He hangs back like he doesn't want to be here any more than Merrick does. Or did. He looks pretty cozy now.

"I'm surprised you made it out tonight," I tell him, sliding my phone back into my pocket.

"Someone had to make sure things didn't get out of hand."

"Oh, relax. Have a drink, talk to some girls. We don't have practice until ten tomorrow." I get the bartender's attention. "Can I get ten shots of Fireball?"

Cody groans next to me. "Promise me you will not show up late and hungover."

He really needs to chill. "I'll be fine."

"Don't bullshit me. I was just like you my rookie season."

Well, that makes me pause. Cody is only a few years older than me, but he acts like he's about a hundred. "What the hell happened to you?"

His jaw hardens. "I grew up. You'll do the same if you want to keep yourself from getting cut or traded before the first game. You're young and talented, but eventually all the partying and fucking around will catch up to you. This job is hard and there are a million other guys who'd kill to be in your shoes. Right now, Coach is watching everyone closely, trying to decide who is going to make it and who isn't."

"Coach loves me." I don't know if that's true, but I know he cares more about my performance on the field than the rest of it.

"Everybody loves you when you're on top. But when your slipups start to affect your game, those same people will be asking for your head. If you ask me, Georgia leaving will be good for you. She's as wild and crazy as you. Her socialite ways have gotten you a lot of attention and I'm sure that's been fun, but it's taken your mind off football. If you're going to date, you need to find someone that understands your schedule and won't ask you to make sacrifices. Not now. It's too early in your career to let anything steal your focus."

Cody St. James is a beast. I look up to him on the field and I hope to have a career like his but come on. It's not like I've been flaking or my performance has been in any way impacted. I killed it at camp, and aside from Billy Boone, everyone from local fans to reporters have been excited about what I bring to the Mavericks.

So I laugh off his words. "It's Saturday night, St. James. Can we loosen up on the doom and gloom pep talks?"

Damn. Maybe I need to see if Georgia has room in her bed for one more grumpy football player. They both need to lighten up.

The bartender finishes pouring the shots and I take them four at a time, handing the drinks out to people around me. That's when I notice the brunette with the hot glare has moved closer. Or she's trying to. It's packed in here and the bar area is especially difficult to maneuver around.

She looks a little frazzled, a lot on edge, like she's had a bad night. For some reason I find myself wanting to know why. Even if it's something I've done. I could apologize to her all night long.

I give Cody the rest of the shots. "Take two of these and try to have a good time."

Then I move past him, cutting through my teammates to get to the girl. As I get closer, she aims a smile at me that feels…wrong. She's gorgeous but the way she's looking at me has a prick of unease spreading through me.

"Are you Brogan Six?"

"Hey," I say to her. "Have we met?"

"Definitely not."

Her smile falls. *Welcome back, sexy glare.* Her posture straightens, and she holds her head high as she regards me.

I extend a hand to her. "Nice to meet you. I'm Brogan. What's your name?"

She eyes it, hesitating for a beat, but then slips her small palm into my much bigger one. Electricity zaps through me. I don't know if she feels it or not, but she pulls her hand back quickly like she's been electrocuted.

"*You're* Brogan Six?" she asks again.

It feels like a trap. Like whatever her reason is for asking, I don't want to be him.

"I think so?" This chick has me sweating it. She has these big green eyes with long dark lashes that seem like they're piercing into my soul...and she does not appear happy with what she sees inside.

"Lo..." The guy that was dancing with her earlier steps up behind her. "Are you okay?"

His expression is concerned as he keeps staring at her. When she doesn't tear her gaze from me, he glances my way. It's a quick, dismissive glance at first. Then he does a double take.

"Perfect," she snaps finally, giving her friend—or maybe boyfriend, judging by the way he's protectively standing with his body angled between us—a quick glance before she steps forward.

Her head tips back so she can hold my gaze. She's at least a foot shorter than me, but she doesn't seem intimidated in the least. I let my stare roam over her body now that she's close. She's even more gorgeous than I thought. Long, dark hair that flows down past her shoulders. Her curves are accentuated by the tight black dress she's wearing and those curves are kicking. But her eyes are what hold me captive. The green is so distinct, so bright.

There are hot women all over this club, but she's...I don't know. I can't even think thoughts right now.

"Can I buy you a drink?" I ask because I have no clue what's going on, but I need one of those shots I just gave away to clear my head.

"No, thanks." Her expression hardens. "Did you used to have a

PO Box on Market Street? Number 148?"

Wait, what?

"Yeah." The word leaves my lips slowly as I ponder this turn in conversation. "How did you know that?"

The guy mutters something that sounds a lot like, "Oh shit."

"Because it's *my* box number now."

"No way." I smile, but when she doesn't reciprocate, I reconsider. I guess that's not a happy coincidence.

"Leaving aside the fact that you didn't have the decency to forward your mail, do you have any idea the kind of packages I have to sift through every day?" The horrified look on her face makes me wince.

I finally see where this is going, and yeah…it doesn't make me look great.

"Can I buy you a drink? We can go somewhere to talk." I half turn toward the bar. I definitely need a shot. Three or four in fact.

"I'll take a vodka and soda," the guy says.

She scoffs at him and elbows him in the side.

"I'm a big fan," he says to me finally, stepping forward and holding out a hand. "Alec Macormick. I work at Channel 3, and this is London Bennett."

"Alec," the girl hisses. *London.*

I like her name. I like her. She's all fiery and not afraid to walk across a bar and call out a guy she doesn't even know. I respect it.

Alec clears his throat and stands tall, letting his hand fall back to his side. "Was a big fan."

"Is everything okay?" Cody steps up beside me. He's a grumpy asshole, but he has my back and it's obvious something is going down. I spot Archer eyeing up the situation as well.

"Fine," I tell him.

"No, it isn't fine," London says, shifting her weight and drawing my attention back to her hot as fuck red shoes.

I drop my voice. "I am sorry about the mail. I forgot about the PO Box."

"You forgot?!"

All right, not the right thing to say.

"I'm sorry." Short and concise. Say less, Brogan.

She closes her eyes and shakes her head. It makes her long brown hair fall over her shoulders. "I don't need you to be sorry about the used panties stuffed into my mailbox every day; I just need you to make it stop. Maybe you could let your girlfriends know you've moved?"

"I don't have a girlfriend," I say dumbly. Did she say used panties? Yikes. Things have really escalated.

"Just hundreds of women with whom you engage in kinky mail play?"

"Kinky mail play?" I mouth the words, barely whispering. I hold my hands out. "I think you've got the wrong idea."

Cody cackles beside me and suddenly more people are listening in. I think I catch one person with their phone out recording. Perfect. Billy Boone will have a field day with this.

"Look, I'm not interested in what gets you off or whatever explanation you're about to make up on the spot now. Your secret is safe with me, just for the love of god please keep it out of my box."

And with that, she turns on her sexy red heels and stalks off.

I don't know what the hell just happened, but I am undone.

CHAPTER FIVE
London

"**O**h my gosh." Paige is folded over with laughter. I sip my wine, a resigned smile tugging at my lips. Tuesday night happy hour with my best friend is exactly what I needed. I feel lighter than I have in days.

"Shut up, it's not that funny."

"You yelled at *this* guy." She holds up her phone and aims the screen at me. A picture of Brogan in his Mavericks uniform stares back at me. He's holding his helmet in one hand, and his brown hair is sweaty and pushed away from his face. He's ridiculously good-looking. I'd think this photo couldn't possibly be real if I hadn't seen him in person.

Three days have passed and I still feel an odd mix of pride for standing up for myself and embarrassment for yelling at a local hero. Or at least that's what Alec called him after he we left the club.

"I'm sure that he's already forgotten about the whole interaction." And it's not like I'm ever going to run into him again.

"Of course he has women sending him their used panties, I mean look at the guy."

"Oh, I've seen him."

"Better or worse-looking in person?" She sets her phone in her lap and leans forward.

An image of Brogan flashes in my mind. The look on his face as I yelled at him, the way his shirt pulled across his broad shoulders, the warm brown of his eyes. He's photogenic in pictures (I spent the night after the incident looking him up and scrolling through every picture I could find), but in person, he just has something about him that makes him larger than life, irresistible even.

"Better," I admit finally. "Probably the hottest person I've ever seen in real life."

"Oh, really?" Her voice trails off in a tone I know too well. That voice has set me up on numerous blind dates and once convinced me to sign up for a dating app.

"He's a professional football player and underwear model," I say. "And I yelled at him."

"You're hot. He'd be so lucky to let you yell at him again."

Something only a true best friend would say.

Thankfully she drops it and asks, "What are you doing the rest of the night? Do you want to grab dinner or do a little shoe shopping?"

"I can't. I gotta work."

"You just left work," she says, one brow cocked.

"Illustration jobs have picked up. I'm booked through the month." I try to brush it off, but in true best friend fashion, she latches right onto it.

"Lo, that's amazing. I'm so happy for you. You are so talented. I've told you a million times that you should be doing that full-time instead of wasting away at that stuffy news station. Have I not told you that? I framed the drawing you did of me and Pat at our wedding."

Her excitement is the encouragement I didn't realize I needed.

"Get your parents out of your head," she says with a stern look. I hadn't been thinking of them, but now I am. They don't think my freelance work is a "real job." They think I need a stable, steady job with benefits and a corporate ladder to climb. Part of it is just that they're still salty I didn't go to law school like planned. But after two years you'd think they'd be over it.

"Thanks. I need that stuffy job to pay the bills though. I don't know if I'll ever make enough from the side projects to do it full-time, but it feels good to be creative."

My job at the news station is fine. I do graphic design for the website and social media pages, but there isn't a lot of room for creativity. I have specific colors and fonts I can use so that it's all cohesive and branded.

My freelance clients have a broad range of needs and wants. I get a lot of portrait requests, character art, and right now I'm even working on an illustration for a fantasy book cover.

"Well, I'm proud of you. And you know I will blast your information to all my clients. Do you have some business cards I can hand out during open houses? They're all still using paper."

Paige works for her family's estate sale business. She organizes and hosts estate sales for clients to sell off household items to prepare for the house to be rented or sold. We met in college. She studied interior design, even though she already knew she was going to work for the family business. Her husband, Pat, works there too. He does a lot of the heavy lifting, moving furniture around to stage for the sale and then delivering it after it's sold.

"I don't think that's exactly my target audience," I tell her.

"These old people have money to spend," she says, leaning back in her chair. "Last weekend I sold a fifty-piece basket collection for over five thousand dollars. Baskets! Who needs five grand worth of baskets?"

I snort a laugh. "What do you even do with that many baskets?"

"No idea, but I'd bet they're also looking for portraits of cats and dogs, maybe the grandkids."

"Perhaps cats and dogs in baskets?" I tease.

"Definitely." She laughs. "I am happy to pimp you out as the official Stephenson Family Estate Sale company artist."

"And I love you for that, but I'm okay. Truly. A few of my clients have already booked more projects with me later in the year. I know there will be slow months with only word of mouth marketing, but I don't have enough hours to spare anyway. Slow and steady is just fine with me."

"All right, but just say the word." She eyes me closely like she wants to make sure I'm not pushing her away when I really need a life raft.

Maybe I'm being stubborn, but I want to do it on my own with clients that I connect with. It's all been mostly referral so far and that's allowed me to build slowly. Cats in baskets isn't a bad fallback plan though.

"All right, well, I am going to do some shopping for Pat and my's vacation."

I groan. "Don't go."

She'll be gone the weekend of Sierra's engagement party, and I really wish Paige could be my plus one. Maybe it wouldn't be so awful with her to help me suffer through.

"You should just come with us. Tell your family that as my maid of honor, you're required to be there for the honeymoon. Besides, this is just Sierra's first wedding. I'm sure there will be others."

I laugh, something loosening in my chest at everything she just said. Even if I know it's not true. Or I hope it's not.

"I am not going on your honeymoon with you. I love you, but I draw the line at a threesome."

She snorts. "It's hardly a honeymoon when our wedding was almost three months ago. We've banged a lot of the newlywedded-ness out of our systems."

I seriously doubt that. I've seen how handsy they are even after being together for three years before getting married earlier this spring.

"Speaking of..." I slink down in my seat. "I may have let sex Saturday slip to Alec."

She laughs instead of shooting daggers at me, but still I feel bad.

"I'm sorry. I was drunk and spiraling..."

"It's fine. Everyone should schedule sex. I like to guarantee an orgasm once a week."

I can hardly argue with that.

"So you're not coming to the beach with us?" she asks, knowing the answer.

"I have to be at the engagement party. She's my sister," I say. And as worried as I am about it all happening so fast, I wouldn't miss it. "Plus, I'm not letting Chris get off that easily. He'd think I was hiding from him because I'm still obsessed with him or something."

"I don't know. Not showing up could be a real power move."

"He's too egotistical to see it that way."

"Fuck him," she says, and I arch a brow. Paige rarely cusses. "Seriously," she continues. "He was lucky your standards were so low in college. You deserve so much better."

I laugh again and nod my head in agreement, but my throat tightens. It isn't that I think she's wrong. I've accepted that Chris is an asshole and not the amazing guy I believed him to be during our relationship. I was young and in love. Stupid love.

Paige stands. "All right. I'm gonna go."

She pushes the strap of her purse over her shoulder and steps toward me. "Love you, Lo. Text me later and let's hang out this weekend. Should we hit the club?"

I glare at her, then wrap my arms around my friend. "I'm never going back there again."

On the way home from happy hour, I stop to get my mail. I brace myself as I turn the key but when I open the small, metal box it's empty, or nearly empty. I pull out the two envelopes – both perfume and lipstick-free. I double-check because it feels too good to be true, but yep, both are for me.

Today must be a slow mail day for Brogan's harem. And then my eye catches on the sender's name written in the upper left-hand corner on one of the envelopes. *Brogan Six.*

I glance around, half-expecting him to jump out at me, but I'm alone. I close and lock my mailbox and then carefully open the letter. His handwriting is small and neat and fills only about a quarter of the page.

> Dear London,
>
> Nice to meet you Saturday night. I'm sorry about the mail mix-up. It should be taken care of now, and your box should be free of my panty kink. If you run into any more problems, let me know.
>
> I really am sorry, and I think you got the wrong idea about me. Can I make it up to you?
>
> Brogan

CHAPTER SIX
London

Friday morning I'm in a staff meeting, struggling to keep my eyes open. Once a month we have these big department-wide meetings with management and members of the executive team. It always feels a little like they whisk in totally unprepared and hurried, as if this is just one of many meetings on the docket for the day and we're clearly not the most important.

My boss, Wayne, is standing in front of the conference room going over all the projects we're currently working on.

"And finally, the T-shirt design for the picnic next month." On the large screen in front of us, the mock-up of the shirt displays.

One of my coworkers, Shane, glances over at me and smiles. The whole team pitched concepts to Wayne, but he picked mine. A surprise since he hadn't shared that with me or anyone else as far as I know.

My design is simple, really. It says Channel 3 in the same style and font that is used on all the branding, but I made the inside of the letters a red and white checkered design to fit the whole picnic theme.

I'm pretty proud of it actually. I don't get to use a lot of creativity on the other projects I'm given. It's all consistency and following the style guide.

I glance around the table to gauge the reaction of management, and they're all smiling and nodding. Not in a super excited way, but in what I like to think of as the executive nod of approval. It screams "that'll do."

The VP of our department is perhaps the most impressed. She sits forward and turns her gaze to the three other executives. "I think it's quite good. Any objections?"

There are none, and I allow myself to feel a little excitement. The entire company is going to be wearing T-shirts I designed. It's sadly the coolest thing that's happened since I started working here.

"Great job, Wayne." She beams at my boss. "You have a wonderful eye for design."

My cheeks heat with the compliment she doesn't even realize she's giving me, and I wait for Wayne to correct her assumption that he did it.

He doesn't.

"Thanks," he says instead. "I thought it had a nice, simple but sophisticated, fun feel to it."

That's exactly what I had said to him when I submitted it.

The meeting adjourns and everyone is quick to leave. I hang back to talk to my boss. When he sees it's just the two of us, he offers me a small smile. There's no hint of remorse on his face or even embarrassment like I would expect from someone who just publicly claimed my work as theirs.

"You went with my design," I say, trying to keep my calm.

"Yeah. They loved it."

"Why didn't you correct them when they assumed you came up with it?"

"Ah, you know how the executives are," he says, casually gathering up his laptop and notebook. "It looks better for the whole team if it comes from me."

"But it didn't come from you."

"You work for me, so in a way, it did."

I don't know what to say or even feel. I'm angry and hurt. I feel betrayed, but then silly because it's just a dumb shirt design.

He starts to walk out of the room, but turns with his hand on the doorknob. "Oh, and I've been meaning to talk to you about your raise." Wayne's mouth turns down at the corners. "Human Resources has put a freeze on raises company-wide. I'm sorry."

After work, I swing by to get my mail and have another letter from Brogan. I must have read the last one a dozen times. Did I spend an embarrassing amount of time wondering how he wanted to make it up to me? Yes. But there was no way I was replying. I don't want to be another woman sending him embarrassing mail.

London,

I don't know if you got my last letter. Someone should really invent read receipts. Anyway, I feel really bad about not forwarding my mail sooner. Also, I'm not really into collecting *panties—used or clean. How about dinner or drinks this weekend?*

Brogan

His number is scrawled along the bottom. Dear god, the man gave me his phone number. Does he really think I'm going to call him up like he's just some normal guy? I try to picture what it would be like to go out to dinner with Brogan, and laugh. It's too ludicrous to even imagine.

I stuff the letter into my purse and head home. Alec has been gone all week to some big weatherman conference or something, so I order takeout and pour myself a glass of wine.

I flip through the channels while I eat and drink. I have a few new projects that I need to work on, but I've found that I'm able to be more creative if I take a couple hours break between jobs to reset.

There's nothing good on and I'm about to turn off the TV when I see his face. Brogan. His and several other Mavericks players' team photos are lined up, and the sports announcers talk about their expectations for the season.

I pull out his letters from my purse and reread them. They're sort of oddly sweet. He does seem sincere in his apology. He's just misguided in thinking I need him to take me out like I'm some sort of fan. I feel like I'm getting a pity invite or something. Or worse, he's just trying to have sex with me. I don't need a relationship or anything serious from a guy, but I don't think I'm cut out for casual with a guy who is used to women throwing themselves at him. I know guys like that. They're only interested until they feel like they've "won."

Either way, something tells me he's going to keep sending me letters until I make it very clear that we're all good and that I'm absolutely not sleeping with him.

That's the only rationale I can come up with when I find myself pulling out a piece of paper and writing him back.

> Dear Brogan,
> I received your letters. Consider this your read receipt. My box being panty and perfume-free is all I need, so thanks, but no thanks to the dinner or drinks. Might I suggest you invite one of your other pen pals?
> London

It's the weirdest letter I've written in my entire life, but I don't take time to rewrite it. Instead I fold it and rummage around until I find a stray envelope that probably went with a greeting card I never sent. Once it's addressed and stamped, I feel better. Sayonara, Brogan Six.

The following Tuesday, I get another letter. My surprise and annoyance quickly turn to amusement as I read. He's funny. I don't remember that about him.

> Dear London,
> Would you believe me if I said I've never written back to any of them? Well, none that sent panties. There are occasionally other types of mail I get. Just the other day I got a letter from Conner in Missouri. He said he was my biggest fan, so I sent him a jersey and a

signed photo. Wait. Does that make me sound cringe? I hope not, but honestly sometimes it feels cringe. It's still weird to me that people want my autograph.

Anyway, I know you said it was fine but I feel like I need to make it up to you. Since I've forwarded the mail, I've gotten an idea of what you were dealing with and I'd say that deserves a drink or maybe I should just buy you an entire winery? Let me know.

Brogan

✉

Brogan,

An entire winery, wow. Okay, fine. I want that. In case there aren't any good wineries looking to sell, I sent something along. Now we're even.

P.S. It's a little cringe, but also nice? Please tell me the signed photo was from your underwear modeling ads?

London

✉

By Friday, I'm opening my mailbox with so much anticipation and excitement hoping for another letter. I'm enjoying this letter war entirely too much. I don't know what that says about me, but when

I spot his now familiar handwriting, I am downright giddy. He's different than he seemed in person. Though to be fair, I didn't give him a lot of room to say much when we talked at the bar.

London,

What kind of pervert do you take me for? Actually, don't answer that. I definitely didn't send a child a picture of me with a sock stuffed in my underwear.

Speaking of underwear, I was delighted that you sent along your grandmother's. I can only assume that's who these belong to? I haven't seen good quality white cotton like this since my second-grade teacher came back from a bathroom break with her skirt tucked into her underwear.

No, I'm afraid we still aren't good. I'll keep an eye out for wineries for sale. Do you prefer something small—a hillside mom and pop, multi-generational operation where college kids go on the weekend to get drunk—or something more upscale where people dressed in suits say things like "this has a hint of oak!"?

In the meantime, I'm sending tickets to assuage my guilt. Hopefully that's not also cringe. If it is, then sell them and buy yourself a nice bottle of red. At least then I'll have bought you the drink I owe you.

Brogan

"I can't believe you talked me into this," I mutter to Alec, and then give my apologies to everyone already sitting in their seats as we shuffle past them to the center of the row. We're late. We were in line for drinks at kickoff, and now that we're finally down here, people are leaning right and left to see around us.

I'm still clutching the tickets in my hand. Honestly, I keep waiting for someone to stop us and tell us the tickets are fake or we messed up the seat numbers.

"I can't believe I had to talk you into this." Alec sits first. His eyes are big, taking it all in, and his smile is huge. "These seats are incredible."

"We're so close," I say, stomach flipping. The Mavericks players not on the field are in front of us, their blue and red uniforms lined up down the sideline. Look, I know Brogan Six isn't going to run by on the field and happen to look over at the fifty-yard line to check if I'm here, but we're close enough that he could. And that makes me nervous. I didn't want to accept the tickets, but once Alec found out, he wouldn't hear of me not using them.

He had his own selfish reasons, of course. He's a huge sports fan and turning down good seats to a game is like blasphemy.

"I could spit on the field," he says.

We're ten rows up, so yes, technically he probably could, but at the risk of hitting someone.

"Please don't." I let my gaze roam over all the blue jerseys. I don't even know what position Brogan plays or what number he is, so looking for him in the sea of blue feels futile.

Alec chuckles and then leans back, taking a drink of his beer. "Do you think if you get more mail for him, he'll get you more tickets? I mean, it's not such a bad trade. You bring him his used panties and I get to go to games for free."

"Whatever plan you're concocting, don't. I am here because I'm a fabulous roommate, but don't push it."

Alec's warm laughter continues.

I've only been to one other game, several years ago with Chris. Our seats were so high up. This is a completely different experience. Like Alec, he's a big fan. He'd be so jealous of me right now.

"There he is." Alec nudges me.

Since I'd been thinking of Chris, that's who I'm looking for, but instead it's Brogan Six I find.

My face grows warm as I stare at him. He jogs off the field with his helmet dangling from one hand. He's not smiling like he was at the club. Instead he has a serious, almost stoic expression. He's still the hottest person I've seen in real life.

Brogan turns, giving us his back. I smirk when I see his name and number. Six is number six. Cute.

My nerves settle by halftime. I stop worrying about being spotted, though I'm not sure why I was worried in the first place. Not once has Brogan looked up in the crowd for me. He gave me the tickets as an apology, and I accepted. Nothing else needs to transpire between us. We are even.

Though, admittedly, I am enjoying his letters and might even miss them. He's funny and a little self-deprecating, and there's just something about receiving a handwritten letter. I might need to get a pen pal. Do people still do that? Probably not twenty-four-year-old women.

Not quite as exciting for him, I'd imagine, since he receives approximately one million a day.

Alec keeps me updated on the game. I know the basics, as in a touchdown is worth six points and a field goal is worth three, but the yardage and whether or not a play is good is harder for me to grasp.

I eat my weight in buttery popcorn and then wash it down with too many beers. In the last minute of the game, I'm buzzed and happy and into it with the crowd as the Mavericks try to take back the lead. They're down by three points, lined up at the sixty-yard line on a third down. I continue to be bad at keeping track of the downs, but Alec is currently whispering, "Third down, boys, come on."

We all get to our feet as the ball is snapped. The quarterback surveys the field. My eye is drawn to Brogan. During the course of the game, I've learned that he is a tight end. He runs, pushes people around, and tries to get open for the ball and some other things that Alec said, but I stopped listening after he started going on about how it's an important position with a lot of responsibility.

When I find him, he's down the field with defenders in front and back of him. I glance away to see if anyone else is open, but the other team is doing a good job on defense—something I also got from Alec.

The crowd gasps when the quarterback gets rushed and is forced to throw a long pass down the field. Then everyone goes quiet as the ball sails toward Brogan.

"That's the game," some guy in front of us says and then groans. He takes off his Mavericks hat and whips it down to his side as he starts for the aisle.

Brogan jumps into the air, both of the defenders do the same, but the Mavericks rookie's hands reach just above theirs, and somehow he comes down with the ball.

He's hit on either side and the three of them crash to the ground in a tangle of limbs, but when the referee raises both hands indicating a touchdown, the stadium goes nuts.

"Holy shit!" Alec yells, jumping. He turns to me, then quickly back to the field.

Brogan stands with the ball and then does a backflip in celebration. His teammates run to him, and all the while Mavericks fans are still screaming their heads off. Me and Alec included.

It feels like it takes us forever to get out of the stadium. My beer buzz is nearly gone by the time the Uber pulls up to our apartment.

Alec downs Advil and a glass of water before heading to bed. I have no idea how he manages on so little sleep. He has to be at the station by four for hair and makeup.

I should go to sleep too, but I'm too wired. After I wash my face and brush my teeth, I sit down on my bed with my laptop. My ears still ring from the noise of the game. I check email, then scroll through reels for a while. Eventually though, I'm too antsy to even sit still.

I get up and go to my desk. The letters from Brogan are stacked next to my laptop. I pick up one and reread it. Then do the same with the others. Writing letters is an intimate thing. Even when you don't exchange any personal information, it still tells you so much about the person. Like, he's considerate and cares about his young fans. He's witty, and I like his sense of humor. Writing to him, I let myself get caught up in the fun. I got caught up in *him*. But he's a professional athlete with literally thousands, if not millions, of fans.

I wonder if he knew I was there. Can he check that the tickets were used? I roll my bottom lip behind my teeth as I think.

It would be rude not to at least let him know I accepted his apology tickets. Grabbing my phone, I type in his number and save it to my contacts. I have Brogan Six's number. It sends a little rush through me even if I never plan to use it again.

ME

> thank you for the tickets. We are now officially 100% even.

> It was a great game. Nice catch.

I hit send, then reconsider everything I wrote. Nice catch? Is that what you're supposed to say to someone when they get a touchdown? I have no clue. Oh shit, I realize he doesn't have my number.

ME

> It's London by the way.

CHAPTER SEVEN
Brogan

"That was the luckiest fucking throw I've ever seen," Hendrick says as we sit around the bar. He has one arm around his wife, Jane, and the other is draped on the table, fingers around the beer bottle.

Knox and his girlfriend, Avery, are across from them, and Archer and I sit at the ends. They all drove up for the first home game of the season. It was a trip knowing they were in the stands tonight. Sure, they came to lots of our college games, but this was different. It was special. Family making time for family.

I glance at Archer to see if he feels that too, but I can't read his expression tonight. He's not even trying to keep up with the conversation like normal. Because of his hearing loss, he usually watches closely to read lips or we sign for him. But he's not watching for either. He's been battling an ankle sprain all week and didn't get the minutes he wanted tonight. I think he's disappointed, but it's just the first game. There will be lots of opportunities for him.

"The throw was lucky, but the catch was all skill. I've got good hands," I say with a smirk, signing too, just in case Archer looks up.

The entire table laughs. Knox rolls his eyes. *"I didn't think your ego could get any bigger. Guess I was wrong."*

"A nationwide underwear ad will do that to a guy." Jane leans forward on her elbows, but angles her face so Archer can read her lips. "Tell the truth, did they make you stuff your crotch?"

"You cannot ask other guys about the size of their dick, wife," Hendrick says, then to me, "Don't answer that."

I keep my mouth shut until he looks away and then mouth to Jane, "All me."

She giggles good-naturedly. She's about as interested in my dick as Hendrick is, but she's fun. I miss her. I miss all of them.

"How's Flynn?" I ask. It's his first week of college classes. It feels weird without him here.

"Good," Knox answers. *"Or that's his standard answer when I ask anyway."*

Baby Holland has never been that talkative, which I'm sure is annoying the shit out of Knox now that they're a thousand miles apart.

"Yo, Ave. Did you catch that backflip in the end zone?" I ask Knox's girlfriend, and then take a long gulp of my beer. I swear it tastes better tonight after catching the game-winning touchdown.

"I sure did," she says, smiling. Her blue eyes sparkle with pride.

She's a gymnast, and when I got drafted by the Mavericks, I asked for some tips on perfecting my touchdown celebration. It was between a backflip and a little dance I choreographed myself. I guess my dance moves left something to be desired.

My phone is buzzing in my pocket. It has been nonstop since we got here.

"I'm gonna grab another beer. Anyone else ready for another?" I ask, glancing around the group.

Archer is the only one that raises his hand, and I slip off to the bar to get our drinks. While I wait, I pull out my phone.

UNKNOWN

Hey, it's Sabrina again...

That uneasy feeling claws up my spine. What the hell does this girl want? Her texts, what I've read of them, don't read flirty, but I have no idea why else she'd be so insistent to talk to me.

Not for the first time, I consider replying and asking...shit, I don't even know what. Who are you? How'd you get this number? What do you want?

It probably doesn't say a lot about me that I assume it's something bad. Since I got drafted, nearly all random emails, calls, texts, and even snail mail have been bad news.

Sure, a few friends from high school have reached out to say congrats or ask for tickets to a game. That, I don't mind. It's the people who I know don't give a shit about me and still think they deserve something from me that make it hard to trust some random stranger reaching out to chat.

I close out of the text from Sabrina and navigate to another unknown text as the bartender hands me my beers.

"On the house," he says. "Great game tonight."

"Thanks, man." I dip my head to him in appreciation and shove all the cash in my wallet in the tip jar. I used to bartend back in Valley while finishing college. It was a cool job. I liked chatting up people and the energy on a busy night when The Tipsy Rose was the place to be.

I'd say I miss it, but nothing is as cool as getting paid to play football.

As I carry the beers back to the table in one hand, I return my focus to my phone. I stop in my tracks as I read the two texts from London.

I damn near trip over my chair as I reread them, shuffling back to my seat.

"Walk much?" Knox asks dryly, catching my chair before it topples over.

"Shit, sorry."

My smile grows as I take a seat.

When I finally look up, everyone is staring at me.

I slide Archer his beer and he shoots me a puzzled look. "Georgia?"

I'm glad to see him engaging in conversation a little even if he still looks bummed. *"No. You remember that chick from the club?"*

"The one who thought you were buying used panties?"

"One and the same," I say with a wince.

"Gross, really?" Jane asks with a look of horror on her face.

"I don't," I clarify. Then I explain the situation with the PO Box. I got it after the underwear ads started popping up. I started getting a lot of mail and didn't love the idea of people having my real address. Archer and I had a good laugh over a few of the letters from women who asked for a lock of my hair or detailed out the things they'd like to do to me (or me do to them), but then I just stopped opening it. It was too much.

Arch and I moved shortly after and I closed the PO Box and

started using my agent's address on my website and other public sites. He forwards a few things. Letters from kids that want autographs or who say that I'm their hero. I hadn't given the rest of it much thought since then. Until London.

"Wait." Avery holds up a hand. *"People send you their dirty panties?"*

"Oh yeah." Arch answers for me. "And that's not even the weirdest thing. One woman photoshopped images of them together. It was pretty convincing."

"That's weirder than crusty undies?" Jane asks. *"I've received some strange fan mail, but that's just nasty."*

Jane was a child TV star. She has this amazing voice and a flair for the dramatic.

"They were naked photos," Arch says, one side of his mouth pulling up in a smile.

"Oh, that's creepy." Knox shakes his head and grimaces. He pulls Avery closer to him. It still catches me by surprise sometimes when I see him all lovey-dovey. I never thought he'd fall so hard for a girl, but Avery is perfect for him. She takes no shit, and Knox…gives a lot of shit.

"Why is she texting you?" Jane asks, bringing me back to the texts on my phone.

"I sent her tickets to the game as an apology."

"Smooth, bro." Hendrick nods his approval, grinning.

"Yeah, well, I didn't think she was there. I looked for her right before the game started and didn't see her, but she texted to thank me for the tickets and said nice game."

"Is she hot?" Jane asks.

"He wouldn't have sent her tickets if she weren't," Knox pipes up.

"*That's not true. I felt bad.*" I still do. I messed up by not forwarding my mail and I wanted to own that. Also, I really don't like being on anyone's shit list. Not Billy Boones' and especially not hers.

"*She's hot,*" Archer confirms.

I glare at him. I didn't tell him I thought she was hot, so those are his words. I feel a little hit of jealousy, which is absurd. She's about as interested in me as Jane is in my dick size. At least according to her letters.

But still…she came tonight and she texted.

"*What does she look like? I need a visual,*" Avery says.

Knox laughs. "*Are you tired of me, princess?*"

"*What? No, of course not. I just need to live vicariously through other people now that I'm off the market.*" She refocuses her attention on me. "*Hair color?*"

"*Brunette,*" Archer answers.

"*Dark brown, just a hint of red to it,*" I clarify. Brunette sounds too boring to describe anything about London.

"*Long or short?*" Avery is leaning forward, taking in all my answers.

"*Long-ish.*" *It came down past her tits* is on the tip of my tongue. Instead, I motion to about where it hung.

"Eyes?"

Hendrick laughs. "*Do you have a picture? Might be easier.*"

"*Sorry I didn't think to snap one while she was yelling at me. And her eyes were this stunning shade of green. Like a four-leaf clover.*"

"*Like grass? Her eyes were the color of grass?*" Knox smirks.

I flip him off. "*It was the first thing I thought of.*"

"*Maybe don't use that line on her. Or do. It's fun when girls turn you down."* He turns to Avery. *"Your eyes are the color of the sky on a sunny day."*

He's clearly making fun of me so I continue to flip him off.

Avery shakes her head. *"All I heard him say was that her eyes were stunning."*

"Back up," Hendrick says. *"She yelled at you?"*

"Oh yeah, she gave him an earful," Archer says, and I swear he sounds a little too happy about it. I think he enjoyed it more than I did. And I fully enjoyed staring at her perfect face while she chewed me out. But I've enjoyed her letters even more. She's feisty as hell. I swear I can hear her voice when I read her words.

All the attention suddenly has me hoping for a subject change. *"Anyway, how are things with you guys? How's the bar?"*

Hendrick waits a beat like maybe he wants to keep pressing me but relents finally. *"The bar is doing great."*

"We hung your jerseys up on the wall in the game room." Jane beams at Archer and then me.

"Awww. I'm touched." Arch holds his pointer and middle finger out in half a heart and Jane does the same, bringing her fingers to his.

We spend the next hour catching up. Hendrick wants to make sure we're being smart with our money and not blowing it all on dumb shit. In truth, I haven't spent that much. I bought a truck and some things for the apartment. The only stupid thing I've done was giving a chunk to my parents. They reached out after the draft. I hadn't been in contact with them in years and I knew they were only talking to me to get some of my signing money, but I guess I hoped it would be different if I made a gesture of good will. That was fucking dumb. I didn't do anything wrong that should have required me to make a gesture. I don't think. Unless being a kid who wants his parents to want him is something to apologize for.

Not a word since I sent the money, but I know they cashed the check.

Archer bought a ridiculously expensive sound system and also got a vehicle. We probably could have done with one between the two of us since we work and live together. We shared one all through high school and college, but it was fun to pick out matching trucks. His is silver and mine is black. Everything else is identical.

Knox fills us in on how he's spending the motocross off-season and praises Avery, telling us about how she's going to dominate again this year. And Jane tells us about some upcoming concerts she's going to do with pop star Penelope Hart.

I glance around the table in awe. If you'd told me as a kid that this would be my life, sitting around a table with a former pro baller, a famous TV actress, a motocross rider and his Olympic gymnast girlfriend, with my best friend and fellow professional football player...I would have looked at you like you were out of your mind.

By the time the conversation starts to die off, it's after midnight and Knox says they should head back to Valley.

"You're welcome to crash with us tonight," I tell him. "I can take the couch. We just got a new sectional big enough for an orgy."

"And with that, I think I choose sleeping in my own bed tonight," Knox says.

"We'll be back next month for the Seahawks game," Hendrick says. "Take care of yourself. You've got a long career ahead of you. Proud of you."

"Thanks." My throat tightens.

I hug each of them goodbye, and Archer does the same.

We catch a ride back to our apartment. It feels too quiet after the excitement of the night. I grab another beer from the fridge and head for the couch. Arch joins me. He lets his head fall back, exhaustion lining his face.

"How's the ankle?" I ask him. I nudge him to get his attention. He took out his hearing aids as soon as we got home. I sign the words and speak them again.

"Good," he says but then winces as he lifts his right leg and settles it on the coffee table in front of him.

"You want an ice pack?"

I start to stand, but he shakes me off. *"Nah.* I'll grab one before I head to bed."

A little of my buddy's usual happy smile returns. "That was some fucking game, huh?"

"Yeah, it really was."

Silence falls between us. Arch is the only person in the world that I can sit like this with, not saying a word and feeling totally at ease. It'd actually feel stranger sitting in silence by myself than with him.

"I should head to bed," he says finally. "What time are you heading to the field tomorrow?"

We don't have practice until eleven, but we usually go an hour or two early if we have any meetings or sessions with trainers. I don't have any of that tomorrow, but I know he needs to see the trainer for his ankle.

"I'll ride over with you. I could use some time on the massage table."

"All right." He stands and chugs the rest of his beer. I listen to him throw the bottle in the recycling, grab an ice pack from the freezer, and then head off to his room.

I stay on the couch, finally pulling my phone out of my pocket. I go straight to London's texts, rereading them, then programming her number in my phone.

It's late, but I decide to text back.

ME

Thanks. Were you at the game? I looked for you during the pre-game warm up but I didn't see you.

I rest my phone on my chest and close my eyes. A vision of her long hair and pretty green eyes—definitely the color of grass—sits in my mind. When a text buzzes a few seconds later, my eyes fly open.

LONDON

Yeah. We were a few minutes late getting to our seats. The beer line is no joke.

We. She brought someone. I should have assumed that. I gave her two tickets after all.

ME

Does your boyfriend like football?

I'm clearly fishing for information, but she doesn't call me on it.

LONDON

No boyfriend, but my roommate—you met him at the club—is a huge fan. I think he's hoping I continue to get your mail so you'll keep sending tickets.

The guy that was with her that night at the club. Alec something or other. He does the weather for one of the local TV stations.

> **ME**
> Has any more of my mail slipped through?

> **LONDON**
> Missing a few pairs of panties?

> **ME**
> Definitely not.

I'm not a germaphobe, but the smell of pussy is only sexy when I'm naked with a chick.

> **LONDON**
> No, I haven't received any more of your mail. My box does still smell like old lady perfume though.

> **ME**
> Dang. I forgot to spritz a little cologne on the letters I sent. Clearly I'm an amateur. Ah well, there's always next time.

> **LONDON**
> Next time?

> **ME**
> Well, yeah, it was kind of fun sending snail mail. I had to buy stamps and everything.

LONDON

You really know how to have a good time.

ME

You have no idea.

LONDON

Actually, I think I do. I've seen your mail.

I'm smiling at the screen. This is more fun than the letters. I like her dry humor, and I can practically see those green eyes piercing into me.

ME

Did you go out after the game? Do you have other roommates?

I'm happy to know there isn't a boyfriend. Although now I'm questioning why she keeps turning me down, then.

LONDON

No, we came back home. And just the one. Is this an interrogation?

Damn, she's feisty. I'm glad my memories of her were accurate. In person, in her letters, and over text, she just does something for me.

ME

No, just friendly conversation. I live with my brother.

LONDON

How does he feel about your panty collection?

ME

I don't sniff and tell.

LONDON

Gross lol

There's a pause in the conversation. I wander around the apartment. I still can't believe I live here. It's a long way from the shithole I grew up in before I moved in with the Hollands.

Archer's room is quiet. I should go to bed. We have practice tomorrow and a day full of film and meetings. But I don't want to stop talking to London.

ME

Are you a night owl?

LONDON

Sort of. I work at night sometimes.

ME

You're working tonight after the game? What do you do?

I'm firing questions at her so fast, I'm probably freaking her right the hell out, but I can't stop.

LONDON

> I'm a graphic designer. I work at Channel 3 but do some freelance on the side. That's what I'm working on tonight, but I think I'm about to call it. My lines are starting to get wonky.

ME

> That's cool. Can I see?

LONDON

> You want to see my work? You don't even know what it is.

ME

> Definitely. Doesn't matter.

Minutes tick by and I don't think she's going to do it, but then an image comes through. It's a drawing of...me. The back of me in my uniform. It looks so much like me that I'm wondering if she traced it from something. But then I see my right hand. Instead of a football, I'm holding a pair of red panties.

My head falls back and I laugh.

LONDON

> What do you think? New logo for your website?

ME

> You drew this?

LONDON

I sketched it while we were talking. I was working on a fantasy book cover before.

ME

You do book covers?

Damn, this girl just gets more interesting.

LONDON

Sometimes.

ME

What are you doing tomorrow night? Some buddies are having a party. You should come with me.

I want to see her again. I can't believe she was at the game and I didn't even see her.

LONDON

Like drop by or go *with* you?

ME

With me, like a date or something.

LONDON

And disappoint all your fans? *gasp*

ME

I think you got the wrong idea about me. I'm really not like that.

LONDON

Says the guy with more panties than me.

ME

Come out with me and let me prove it to you.

I stare at the screen, waiting for her reply. It's minutes before it comes.

LONDON

Sorry, not interested.

CHAPTER EIGHT
Brogan

Coach is pissed, Archer signs without speaking.

I nod my agreement as I chug water and try to catch my breath at the same time. I'm sweating out the shots from last night. I don't know if it's my imagination or if I can actually still smell the tequila leaving my body.

One of the other rookies got cut yesterday and we went out last night to cheer him up. I hadn't meant to stay as long as I did, or drink as much. But I felt for the guy. He worked as hard as the rest of us and then poof, it was all just gone.

Like I'm gonna be if I don't manage to find a second wind during the last thirty minutes of practice.

Showing up late was my first fuckup of the day. Archer normally would have woken me in time if I overslept, but he had to be here earlier than me so he assumed I had alarms set. Which I did. A dozen of them. But then I forgot to plug in my phone before I fell asleep.

Coach isn't an idiot. He knows why I'm late and dragging ass, and he's just riding me even harder. We jumped right into a scrimmage this morning and he's got the best defensive men coming after me hard. I have to show him I can take it.

"Six! You're so slow off the snap, my granddaughter could tackle you."

Nobody laughs, but I catch Cody's disapproving gaze. *Fuck.*

"Sorry, Coach," I manage to wheeze out.

"Don't be sorry. Get your ass to bed at a decent time tonight. Goddamn rookies partying all fucking night," he mumbles. "All right, men." His deep voice bellows. "Let's stop there."

Oh thank God. My shoulders relax.

"Everyone to the end zone for sprint and stride intervals." He lifts his right hand and points with an open palm like a ref would.

There's a collective groan, but we all hurry to obey. Our conditioning coach walks behind us with a whistle to lead the drill and Coach heads off the field. But as he does, I swear he looks right at me like he wants me to know this is all my doing.

After practice I hit the training room and do some stretching and roll out my calves. One of the new trainers, Libby, spots me as she passes by the room and then doubles back to come say hi. She and a few of the other trainers were with us last night. I can't remember how late she stayed, but she doesn't look like it was as late as I did.

"Tough practice?" she asks as she moves closer.

"Brutal," I admit, standing. "I think I finally sweated out all the tequila though."

Her laughter makes my headache worse. "You should have left with me. I told you that you'd regret it."

Right. Now I remember. She tried to get me to leave with her last night. I'm not sure if she was looking out for me or asking to get naked, but now as she rests a hand on my forearm and then glides it up to my bicep, I think it's pretty clear.

Libby takes a step closer, and the smell of her perfume hits my nose, making my stomach roil. It also makes me think of London and her claim that all my admirers wear cheap, old lady perfume.

I smile, and Libby must take that as an invitation because the next thing I know she's rising up on her toes and pressing her mouth to mine.

Worth noting, I stink. I haven't even showered yet, and as previously mentioned, I sweated out a bottle of tequila.

I'm too shocked to reciprocate or do anything. The next thing I know someone nearby is clearing their throat, and I come to my senses.

Libby steps back, taking her scent with her, and it clears my head enough that I look to the doorway where Cody and Coach are standing.

Fuck me.

Libby flushes and then scurries off. Wish I could do the same.

I open my mouth to tell my coach that it wasn't what it looked like, but he holds up a hand to stop me.

I don't know if it's expressly against the rules to hook up with someone that works here, but I never would. A second longer and I would have stopped her. I think I would have anyway.

"Six, is your dick going to keep causing problems for you this season?" Coach asks, hands on his hips.

"No, sir."

"I've cut a lot of talented young players that couldn't keep their head when they got to the league. I hope you won't be the next."

I swallow thickly. Before I can comment, he turns and leaves. His sneakers squeak down the hallway. Cody walks into the room while I sit down on a weight bench. I feel like I might throw up all over again.

"Seriously, rookie?"

"She hit on me. What was I supposed to do? I'm a likable guy. I know you aren't familiar with that," I tease. He cuts me a glare that proves my point. Women don't hit on him because he's a wall of indifference.

"You could start with not kissing her in the middle of the freaking weight room, maybe?"

"She kissed me." I groan.

"Coach doesn't give a shit about your excuses. You need to get it together before he decides you're a liability."

With those sweet, charming words, he leaves me too.

I take a minute to collect myself and then head to the locker room. Archer is waiting for me.

"You cool?" he asks.

I nod. "Yeah."

"You want to grab lunch?"

My stomach twists and growls at the same time. "Yeah, but something light."

"So no tequila shots?" He bites his bottom lip as he fights a smile.

Fucker.

"You're lucky that Wren was with you or you would have been

shit-faced too." He took this new girl he's been seeing out for the second time in a week. I think that's a record. She seems cool enough. She's hot and nice and all that, I'm just not sure she's as into my buddy as she is hanging out with professional athletes.

But Arch isn't an idiot. If he's cool with that, then so am I. And it kept his ass out of trouble last night so there's that.

"Maybe I need a girlfriend," I say, feeling about a hundred years old. I could have ducked out early, spent the night in my bed with a gorgeous woman. Archer might be on to something.

He laughs loudly, head falling back as he shuts his locker. "That's funny."

Shouldering his bag, he pauses as I stand there staring at him. One brow rises. "You're serious?"

"Well, I was, but your reaction is offensive. I could have a girlfriend."

"You haven't had a girlfriend since high school and that lasted, what, two months?"

"That's because you're my one true love," I tell him, joking but also not. I've never met anyone that I like spending time with more than Archer. Casual has always been the best compromise because, well, sex. I love my buddy, but I don't want to fuck him.

"Same, but I'm not going out with you."

"You'd be so lucky," I tell him.

"Speaking of chicks, whatever happened with that girl from the club you invited to the game? London."

"We texted back and forth the other night, but I think the whole women sending panties to me through the mail thing scared her off."

"No?" He gasps dramatically. Fucker. His lips curl into a smile.

"Wren has some friends. Want me to ask her to set something up? We could double-date."

"Nah." I shake it off. "I'll be fine. I just need to stay out of trouble."

How hard could that be?

CHAPTER NINE
London

"**A**re you sure you don't mind?" Sierra's eyes are big with genuine concern as she clutches our mother's old wedding dress to her chest.

When we were little and would play dress up, Sierra always gravitated toward the strapless white princess dress. I preferred our old Halloween costumes. I'm not sure what hidden meaning that points to about our characters or personalities, but I know it means that the dress has always been hers.

"I'm positive," I tell her sincerely. "It's yours. It always looked better on you anyway."

"I can save it for you after my wedding," she offers.

"Nah. That's okay. If I ever get married, I think I want to go and pick out my own dress."

"Oh, not me. When I close my eyes and picture walking down the aisle, the only thing I imagine is this dress."

"Then it's definitely yours." I smile at her. "You're going to look perfect."

She stands and holds the dress up in front of her. She looks so much like our mom that it really does seem like it was made for her. Both she and Mom are several inches taller than me with dark blonde hair and bright blue eyes.

We're at our parents' house in their room. I'm sitting on the bed while Sierra rifles through the old oak chest with all the wedding stuff and some other sentimental mementos like our baby blankets and Dad's old letterman jacket. Neither of them are here. They're off with friends for a weekend in Pine Top.

"Oh, I meant to ask. Do you think you can help me pick out invitations? There is so little time and I want it all to be amazing."

"I will help however you need."

My little sister beams. I've been waiting for an opportunity to talk to her about everything. Namely, how quickly this is happening. I hate to be the one to ruin this happy moment, but I'll hate myself if I don't say something.

"You know, it might be easier to get it all together if you wait until next summer."

She glances over her shoulder at me, dress still held up in front of her. It's not anger or frustration in her gaze, but disappointment.

I stand and move toward her. "What's the rush?"

"I love him. So much it physically hurts sometimes."

I snort a laugh, but she pushes on. "He's the absolute love of my life. I can't wait a year to marry him. I want to be his wife now. I'm ready, Lo Lo."

"You're sure?" A weird sensation swirls in my stomach. My little sister is getting married. It feels like yesterday she was tagging along behind me and letting me watch out for her, and now she's leaping ahead of me to this place where I haven't the first clue how to protect her or even if I need to.

"Yes." Her smile stretches wider. "Besides, Mom and Dad already had this same talk with me. It might seem quick to you guys, but I've known he was the one since our first date. So can you please just be excited for me?"

The one? Their first date? Love of her life? I'm speechless, which she takes as me still not being sold.

"Please, Lo?"

"Of course." I take her hand and squeeze it. "I'm always on your side, you know that."

Her smile widens.

"Just promise me one thing."

"What?"

"If at any point you decide that you want to back out, you'll tell me."

Her laughter is light and airy, like she can't fathom the idea. She gives my hand another squeeze and then drops it. "I promise. Now promise *me* something."

She sets the wedding dress down carefully in the open trunk.

"What?" Now I'm nervous with the way she's looking at me.

"Promise not to kill Chris between now and the ceremony."

Whatever I might have expected her to say, that wasn't it. I can't help it. I laugh.

"I'm serious," she says, fighting a smile. "I know how awful he was to you, and I will always hate him a little for it, but he's Ben's brother. It's inevitable that you two are going to see each other, and I want to make sure you're going to be okay. I need you, but he's family now too."

My lip curls all on its own. I'd nearly blocked out that pesky detail. Chris family. Ugh. No thank you.

"I promise not to kill him before the ceremony." I make no promises about after.

"Thank you." She lunges forward and hugs me tightly, then springs back just as quickly. "I told Ben it would all be fine. You've both moved on. He's dating someone, *you're* dating someone."

The way she says the last part like she's in on some secret makes me pause. And then I remember. Oh shit.

"Why didn't you tell me?" she asks, then smiles. "I had to find out from Ben. Chris told him. Since when do you tell Chris more than me?"

"I don't…" My words trail off. For a moment I consider telling her the truth, but she's looking at me so hopefully. And I don't want my lie to get back to Chris.

"It's new." I look away from her and try to play it off. I'm going to have to break up with my pretend boyfriend before Mom demands I bring him around for dinner.

"Like how long? Is it that finance guy Paige set you up with at her wedding?"

"No." God no. That guy was so boring. We only went out once and he referred to my illustration work as "my little hobby" three times in the span of two hours. If I wanted to be insulted over dinner I would have just gone with my parents.

"Is it that guy Luke that you booty call sometimes?"

My jaw drops. I have definitely never told her about Luke. I may have texted him a few times while we were out though.

"Does anyone say booty call anymore?"

"You're deflecting."

"No, it's not Luke. He started seeing someone else. I think it's getting serious."

"Serious as in he no longer needs his booty call?"

I glower at her, and then because I know she isn't going to drop it say, "It's new and not even worth talking about yet."

"Are you kidding? I'm about to be a married woman. I'm going to need to live all the dating drama through you."

"I like my life drama-free."

"Will you bring him to the engagement party?" Her eyes light up with the idea.

"No." I shake my head adamantly.

"Why not?" Whine slips into her tone. "I want to meet him. What's his name?"

"I just told you it's not worth talking about." My face grows warm. I look anywhere but at her because I just know it has to be obvious that I am lying through my teeth.

"Give me something. Come on." Those big blue eyes widen, and she tips her head down.

"Don't give me that sweet puppy dog face. It won't work this time."

"I think you should bring him."

"The engagement party is about you and Ben. I'm not bringing some guy who might turn out to be a real loser and ruin the night for you."

She laughs and then gives me a pitying look. Apparently, even my imaginary dates are shit.

After leaving my parents' house, I swing by to get my mail. It's been another week free of Brogan's fan mail. The perfume smell is almost gone. *Almost.*

I pull out a few envelopes, pausing when I see another from Brogan. After our back-and-forth texting last weekend, I haven't heard from him again and really didn't expect to. He asked me out and I said no. Have I regretted it? A little, but I know it's for the best. There's no world in which going out with him ends well for me. He's not the kind of guy you have a one-night stand with and then just move on. Where do you go after Brogan Six? I'd be ruined for all other guys. Of that, I am certain.

Still, my heart flutters in my chest at the sight of his penmanship scrawled across the paper.

> London,
> You're my lucky charm.
> Brogan

And folded inside, two more tickets to tonight's game that starts in…two hours. His lucky charm? I snort. The man is full of lines.

On my way out to my car, I text him.

ME

> Thank you for the tickets. I can't use them tonight, but wishing you good luck!

There. Short, sweet, to the point. And I used an exclamation point so it doesn't come off unappreciative.

Only a few seconds pass before a reply pops up.

BROGAN

> Why not? I need my lucky charm there. Plus I thought about it and box seat tickets felt like the only way to truly apologize. That and the winery, of course. We're closing on it next week.

At this point, I'm not even sure he's kidding.

I check the tickets again. Dear god, the man sent tickets to a private box. Is he for real? Shaking my head, I tap out a response.

ME

Wow. That was really not necessary. Seriously, apology accepted. We exchanged panties. We're all good.

I go to put away my phone, but another reply comes in. This man doesn't give up.

BROGAN

Come to the game anyway.

ME

I can't.

BROGAN

Why not?

ME

Because I don't even really like football and I don't think any of my friends are free tonight to come with me.

Sitting in a private box by myself sounds a little pathetic. So does admitting it to him. Paige is gone, Alec has plans, Luke and I haven't talked in a few weeks. Maybe if I hit him up, he'd go with me, but it feels wrong to invite him when another guy gave me the tickets. And anyone else I might ask is going to have so many questions on why Brogan Six is sending me box seat tickets.

BROGAN

Sidestepping the 'I don't really like football' comment. Did you ask Alec?

ME

He has a date.

BROGAN

Did you show him the tickets?

I laugh out loud. Yeah, if Alec found out I turned down box seats at a Mavericks game, he'd murder me. But I know he has plans tonight.

I don't understand why Brogan keeps trying so hard to make things solid. It's oddly endearing and more than a little frustrating. Especially when I'm trying my hardest to remember that I am one of many, *many* women he's probably talking to at this very moment. He has this way of making me feel special, but I'm sure he has that effect on everyone. I mean, come on, *I'm* his lucky charm? Doubtful.

ME

He has plans.

BROGAN

Yeah, with you to the Mavericks game.

ME

Fine. I will ask him, but I'm only coming if he's free.

BROGAN

He'll be free. Enjoy the game.

CHAPTER TEN
London

"I can't believe I agreed to this," I say as Alec hands me a beer. "Again."

"You got something out of it." He sets his beer between his legs and rubs his hands together as he scans the field like a kid at his first monster truck rally.

I brighten at the reminder. Alec let me drive us tonight in his Porsche. It's his baby. His parents gave it to him as a college graduation present.

I think I got a gift card to Target for my graduation, so I guess I can understand why he spent the entire ride to the stadium with one hand on the dash and the other leaning toward me like he was preparing to take the wheel at any sign of danger.

I am a good driver, thank you, but I might have gone a little faster than I would have in my own vehicle. What? I had to get the full experience.

It's halftime and the teams are starting to come back from the locker rooms. We're so far up that the players look like little dots on the field. We have our own private bar and there's free food and a TV so we can actually see what's going on if we want.

Alec is in heaven. It makes me feel a little less awkward about the whole thing. I still can't believe Brogan sent me box seat tickets. Who does that? It truly doesn't make any sense to me why he is going to such lengths to apologize. It doesn't track with everything else I know about him.

He's a professional athlete who gets bags of fan mail each week. What the hell does he care if there's one woman out there that doesn't like him? Actually, maybe it does track. The man's ego just can't handle me not falling all over myself to get with him.

I keep telling myself this because him wanting me to be here for any other reason is just too hard to wrap my brain around.

My phone buzzes in my lap and I look down at the screen. Surprise makes me sit tall when I see Brogan's name. I hold it up for Alec to see.

He arches a brow in question. "Somebody stole his phone maybe?"

"And decided to call *me*?"

My roommate shrugs. "Are you going to answer it?"

I don't get the chance before it stops, but then a second later it buzzes again.

"What the heck?" I mutter to myself as I stare at his name flashing on the screen. I am so thrown off that I do the only thing I can think of—I answer it. Then I don't say anything. There's background noise and some heavy breathing. And then, "London?"

"Hi." The word sounds strange, hesitant.

Alec is watching me with amusement.

"How's it going?" Brogan asks, more carefree than I would have imagined. Although to be honest, I have no idea what I would have imagined. Why the heck is he calling me?

"Umm...fine." I stand and look down at the field. Does he have his cell phone out on the sideline? "Where are you?"

"In the locker room."

"Your team is on the field."

"Well, that answers my next question," he says, and I can hear a little of the exhaustion in his voice. "I'm glad you came."

"I did it for the snacks."

His deep chuckle makes my stomach do a weird flip.

"Come have a drink with me after the game?" he asks, a hint of that cocky tone mixed with a charming plea.

A short laugh escapes my lips before I can stop it. "You do not owe me anything else. We're good. Beyond good."

"Good, but that's not why I asked."

"I'm not hooking up with you," I deadpan.

"I said *drink*." He enunciates the word.

"Don't you have somewhere you need to be right now?"

"Yeah. I do as a matter of fact. If I don't get out there soon, Coach is likely to bench my ass."

But he doesn't hang up like a sane person.

"What is he saying?" Alec asks, looking more entertained by the second.

I move the end of the phone away from my mouth. "He wants me to have a drink with him after the game."

"Say yes," he says immediately and loud enough that Brogan hears.

"See? Even Alec thinks it's a good idea. Come on, one drink. I'm not so bad."

"I think that's debatable."

Another deep chuckle. "I'm not hanging up until you say yes."

A whistle blows on the field. I don't know why I'm panicking—it's his ass on the line, but suddenly I feel a frantic need to put an end to this phone call so he can get back to the game.

"Can we talk about this later maybe?"

"Nope." He lets the p pop, and I swear I can tell he's grinning.

The man is missing a few brain cells I think. Alec's expression is starting to look concerned. Like Brogan *should* be.

"Fine. I'll go," I say, almost instantly regretting it.

He doesn't immediately respond, and I wonder for a second if he's played some cruel joke on me and is going to laugh and then shout, *"Just kidding!"*

But he doesn't. He asks, "Really? You're not just saying yes to get rid of me?"

That is exactly why I agreed.

"She'll be there!" Alec yells from beside me.

"I don't want to force you," Brogan continues.

I groan. "I will be there. *One* drink."

"Awesome. I gotta go. I'm texting you the address."

"Maybe do that after the game," I suggest. My heart flutters with excitement. Or maybe I'm having early signs of a panic attack. Yeah, that's probably it.

"Right." He laughs and then the background noise gets louder. "Gotta go. See you soon."

The Mavericks win the game and Brogan had several nice catches that had the crowd on their feet, but I couldn't enjoy the second half because I was a nervous wreck. Am I really going to meet up with Brogan Six at some bar? Given everything I know about him, it feels like a bad idea.

As if he's reading my thoughts, Alec bumps my elbow. "It's just a drink."

"With a guy that I barely know, and the things I do know about him include some pretty major red flags."

"Live a little, Lo. When's the last time you went out with someone new? Luke doesn't count."

I level him with a glare.

He laughs at me, not all intimidated. "I will go with you, if you want."

"You just want to hang out with the Mavericks."

"Duh. Of course I do. Why don't _you_?"

"He's a total player."

"Allegedly."

"I looked him up." He's been tagged in photos with so many different women. He is enjoying the life of a rookie athlete, for sure. That's great for him, but I don't have to willingly throw myself in front of his wild party train. I have more self-preservation than that.

"It doesn't have to be a big thing." It's apparent in his expression and tone he really believes that. Such a guy way to look at it. "Give yourself one night. Forget about that asswipe Chris, boring Luke, and everything else and go have fun."

At the mention of Chris, I want to immediately deny that I have spent any amount of time since the engagement announcement thinking of him. But that would be a lie. Mostly, I've been imagining him tripping and falling into the cake at the reception or having an embarrassing diarrhea accident. Sierra said not to kill him, but she didn't say I couldn't drop Ex-Lax into his drink.

"Going home and polishing off the last of the Riesling sounds more fun."

"I polished that off last night."

"You bitch," I say to him.

"You're twenty-four, not a hundred and four. There's still someone great out there for you."

"Brogan Six?"

"No, probably not. But it starts with saying yes. And I'll be on standby if you need a quick out. Text me."

"I can't tell if you're pushing me so hard because you really think I should go or because he's a Mavericks player."

"A little of both," he admits honestly. "But I don't know. He's gone to an awful lot of trouble to apologize and get you to go out with him. Maybe it could be something."

I do not have those same delusions, but I figure the sooner I go and have a drink with him, the sooner Brogan will realize we're not going to be getting naked. Ever.

The bar is not far from our apartment, so Alec drops me off on his way.

"Text me if you need anything and before you head home so I know you're safe." A slow grin spreads across his face. "Or if you aren't coming home, let me know that too."

"I'm coming home."

"We'll see."

Rolling my eyes, I don't bother arguing with him. I get out of the car and wave as Alec drives off. But there is a little spark of excitement as I walk up to the bar. I push it away, telling myself it has nothing to do with Brogan. Sure, he's the hottest guy I've ever met, and yeah, the idea of kissing him isn't exactly gross. But I'm not cut out for one-night stands. I like getting to know a person, going on dates, and all those beginning relationship milestones. Kisses turned into making out, then sex. Even if the relationship isn't going the distance, I still like the buildup and tension before having sex. Even Luke and I had that and we were totally using each other for sex.

Noise blasts my ears as soon as I pull the door open. It's packed in here. There are tables spread out around the space and the bar is in the middle along the back wall.

I step out of the doorway and move slowly toward the bar as I look around for Brogan. My nerves ramp up as I get farther into the crowded bar. I sidestep groups of people huddling together, talking and laughing, taking shots and holding drinks.

He's here. I know he is. He texted and said as much about ten minutes ago while Alec and I were getting In-N-Out and chowing down in the parking lot. Nothing beats In-N-Out. Not even the free food and drinks at the game.

Stopping, I turn in a circle to look for him. I lift up onto my toes and get an extra inch to my height. And then I hear him. Or I hear a loud group of guys, and swivel around to find him in the center of them.

Brogan is standing at the bar with three guys who I assume are his teammates. I move forward, watching him.

He's in jeans and a gray T-shirt that stretches across his broad chest and back.

If I had forgotten how good-looking he is—and I haven't—I'd be struck with it all over again. He has this charm and aura about him. He gets better looking the longer you look at him. It's his smile and this carefree approachability. He draws people in.

I know because I find myself walking toward him without ever making a conscious decision to do so.

Yes, I came here to meet up with him, but I think there was a small part of me that didn't truly believe I'd go through with it even after I walked in and spotted him.

Just like the last time I saw him, it's not easy to get to him. The area around the bar is filled with people and many have gravitated toward Brogan and his teammates.

I angle my body to squeeze past a group of girls forming a line, as if they're the wall protecting any other females from getting to the hot football players. One of them shoots me a dirty look as I pass by.

My breathing picks up along with my heart rate as I get close enough that I can clearly hear his deep voice. His laughter is a big, boisterous noise that holds nothing back.

Out of the corner of my eye, I spot someone else approaching him at the same time as me. The woman moves at a much faster pace than me. Boldly, she stalks right up to him. They exchange words. Him leaning down and her tipping her face up to speak only to him.

My steps falter. It feels like a bad time to go up to him, even if he did invite me, so I wait. Brogan nods his head and smiles as the woman stops talking, then Brogan leans over the bar to ask something of the bartender. It all happens quickly, but my anxiety spikes as I stand alone, uncertain of my next move.

The bartender hands over a shot of something to Brogan. I assume he's just buying the woman a drink, but when he passes it over to her, she settles it between her cleavage. And then the guys all around him cheer and holler as she tips her chest up to him. He runs a hand along his jaw, that ever present playful grin on his face. I'm not sure he's going to do it, but then she reaches up and grabs that gorgeous head of hair of his and buries his head in her breasts.

Judging by the hoots and laughter, he took the shot, but I march up to the bar, ignoring them completely. It's funny in a *what else did I expect from a guy who is getting panties sent to him* kind of way. I knew this was his life but seeing it eight feet in front of me is a whole other thing. And I know that getting involved, even for one drink, is not for me.

"Can I get a shot of tequila?" I yell over the noise.

A large body knocks into me.

"Oh shit, sorry," he says. His hands go to my waist as he steadies me. Those dark brown eyes meet mine and a slow smile spreads across his face. "London. You made it."

"Yep. Here I am," I say cheerily, stepping out of his hold. His busty friend is nowhere to be seen. "Just in time to see your no-hands shot-taking abilities."

His mouth draws into a line. He has a great mouth with full lips and straight, white teeth. "I'm sorry about that. She came up to me and—"

"Don't care." I hold up a hand so he doesn't try to continue. "Look, it's fine. Actually, no. It's not fine. I don't know why I said that." A frenzied laugh escapes from my lips. "What kind of guy asks a girl to meet him for a drink and then decides to do a few body shots while he waits?"

I give him a full second to answer, but he must not know what to say. There really is nothing to say. I shouldn't have come and we both know it.

"God, you really are good. You got me a little with the whole halftime call bit. Do you do that often? It's perfect. Don't change a thing."

The bartender sets my shot in front of me.

"Thanks," I say, then tip my head toward Brogan. "This is on him."

I toss the drink back, ignoring the burn all the way down my throat. The liquor coats my insides with a rush of warmth. I will not cough and ruin this. "Thanks for the drink. We're absolutely even now."

I turn on my heel to head for the exit, brushing past him. I hear him calling my name, but I'm small and weave through people quickly to put distance between us. I finally cough and blow out a breath that feels like fire. Tequila was a bad choice. I'm full of those tonight.

I'm almost to the door when a familiar head of perfectly gelled hair walks through it. I'm so surprised to see him that it actually takes a few seconds for my brain to catch up. I suck in a breath as Chris stops and scans the bar, much like I had when I walked in.

I sidestep to hide behind a group of guys, peeking out to make sure I haven't been spotted. And then I see her. Chris's girlfriend.

She's nearly as tall as him, with long blonde hair and perfect features. She has that bored, beautiful expression on her face, the kind that fills the pages of magazines. My stomach twists and I feel an odd sense of jealousy even though I'd never want Chris back in a million years. It still hurts to see him moved on with this gorgeous woman when I haven't.

Admitting it sucks. The end of our relationship devastated me and though I've healed the hurt and realized I'm better off, I haven't taken the next steps out of fear. I never want to feel the way I did then ever again.

I must stare at him too long from my hiding spot because Chris's gaze flicks in my direction and we lock eyes. I squeak and duck fast behind the group, knocking into one guy who gives me a peculiar look when he sees me hunkering down and using him as a shield.

"Sorry," I mutter, and then stick my head out again hoping Chris didn't really see me. We lock eyes again. Dammit.

His brow is furrowed as he speaks to his girlfriend and then they walk in my direction. Oh no. No, no, no.

Of all the bars, Chris just had to be at this one tonight.

Panicked, I look around the bar. Brogan is five feet to my right, scanning over the crowd for me. And Chris is getting closer.

"I swear I saw her," I hear him saying.

I consider sprinting past both of them out the door, but I'm not confident I won't trip and fall or add some other humiliating bit to this night. I glance back at Brogan and groan.

Fuck my life.

I pick the lesser of two evils, moving to my right and making myself visible to Brogan. His expression relaxes when he spots me and he hurries over.

"I'm sorry," he says immediately. "That sucked. You're right about all of it. I shouldn't have done it. She asked me to buy her a drink, I didn't think she was going to shove my face into her boobs."

"Yeah, yeah, yeah. It's fine." I sidestep him and then move behind him, putting his massive body between me and the last place I saw Chris.

"What is going on?" He lifts his hands to his sides and tries to turn, but I clutch his shirt. His back is muscular and his waist trim. He smells like cedar and something else…citrus maybe.

"Nothing. Just, uh, could you walk toward the door." Maybe I can still get out of here without speaking to my ex. I have nothing nice to say and I promised Sierra I wouldn't kill him.

"I can't quite hear you." He tries again to turn.

I open my mouth to repeat myself, but then it happens.

"Lo?" The deep voice from behind me sends ice down my spine. Since I haven't mastered my disappearing act, I let go of Brogan and turn slowly.

CHAPTER ELEVEN
Brogan

"**C**hris? Oh my gosh." Her words come out all high-pitched and breathy.

I turn and look at the woman next to me. I barely know London, but I can tell she's one hundred percent putting on an act. Gone is the fiery woman that told me off and instead she's faking politeness. The question is why.

I try to shake off the weird turn of events of the past few minutes and focus on the couple in front of us. The man is a few inches shorter than me, with dark hair and an air of importance and sophistication about him. I catalog him quickly as a total prick who thinks he's God's gift, but it's the way his stare lingers on London that pulls it all together for me.

She's slept with this prick. Dated him maybe? He's definitely looking at her in a way that tells me he wants me to know he's had her already. Correction, he's a grade A prick.

"I thought you saw me. You looked right at me," the guy, Chris, says. He doesn't like being ignored. What a shock.

"Sorry, no. I didn't see you." She leans into me and rests a hand on my stomach.

I have no idea what's happening or what to do, but my arm just sort of naturally wraps around her waist. She fits against me nicely.

Chris's stare locks on my hand resting against her hip.

"So this must be him," he says. "This is the guy you just started seeing."

If we had just started seeing each other, I think it'd still be an awkward thing for him to toss out so casually, but as it is, I'm a) taken aback and b) wondering why she agreed to have a drink with me when she's not single or why she yelled at me over the body shot when she's got someone else.

I'm also pissed I missed my window. She was single just last week.

London's eyes widen and she tries to pull away from me, but there's a crowd around us and she can't get far.

"Oh, uh…" She trails off like she isn't sure if she should introduce me. She probably doesn't want to, but it's getting awkward. Well, more awkward.

Stepping forward, but not letting go of her, I extend the other hand. "Hey, what's up, man? I'm Brogan."

Chris studies it for a moment before shaking my hand. "You play for the Mavericks."

"Yeah, that's right. Are you a fan?" I ask even though he's wearing a Mavericks shirt under his jacket.

"Oh my gosh," the girl next to him finally speaks up. "We were just at the game. No way!"

"My company had some free tickets," Chris says quickly. He looks to London. "This is the guy you're dating? Brogan Six?"

"Umm..." She trails off, then smashes her lips together like she doesn't trust her voice.

Chris looks to me like he wants my verification.

I can feel her body stiffen against me. It's all coming together now. Or at least enough to know whatever lie she's wrapped up in hangs on my response.

"Aren't you going to introduce me to your friends, sweetheart?" I ask her.

She looks up at me with a flare of shock that slowly dissipates into a calm resolve. Her lips curve into a smile and she turns her head to stare at the guy standing in front of us.

"This is Chris. We went to high school together," she says.

"We *dated*," Chris says, like I didn't already have that figured out by the possessive way he's eyeing my hand draped over her hip.

"I'm Gretchen," the girl pipes up. She looks to London. "You're Sierra's sister, right?"

"That's right," London says. "Have you and Sierra met?"

"No, not yet, but Ben talks about her nonstop."

I feel Chris's stare still hard on me.

"Can I get you guys something to drink?" I ask.

"No. Thanks. We're gonna head out."

"We are?" Gretchen asks.

I can practically feel London's relief.

"Yeah. I think we should try that new bar down the street."

"Well, hey, it was good to meet you. Any friend of my London is a friend of mine." I extend my hand a second time, forcing him to shake it again. I might squeeze a little extra hard too, just to fuck with him. I don't know what's gone down between these two but it's easy to be team London when the other side is this prick.

"I'll see you next weekend," Chris says to her, then, as if it just occurred to him, he asks me, "Are you coming to the engagement party?"

"Wouldn't miss it," I say without missing a beat and then I wink at him just for kicks. I don't usually try to piss people off, but this guy is making it too easy and too much fucking fun.

He tugs his girlfriend away and they head straight for the door to leave. London slumps beside me and lets out a breath.

"Thank you," she says.

"No problem, sweetheart," I say, using the endearment that had rolled off my tongue so easily in front of her ex. I'm not mad, in fact I rather enjoyed it, but I am curious. "What the hell was that about?"

"Nothing. Absolutely nothing." She smiles. Sort of. It's kind of a grimace. "Well, this was fun, but I'm going to go home and smother myself with a pillow now." She starts to walk off, but I grab her hand and she slingshots back to me. A tingle spreads up my arm.

"You're not getting off that easily."

"Can't we just call us even? You can go back to doing body shots and I can go home and forget this all happened."

"It's been a strange night for sure." I try a smile on her. She doesn't seem pissed anymore, more like shell-shocked. "Stay. Just for a little while. It'll give your douche ex enough time to get to his next stop and you won't risk running into him on your escape route."

She finally nods. "One drink and then I need this day to end."

After getting our drinks, I lead her to a table in the bar away from my teammates. I get the sense that whatever she has to say, she doesn't want an audience.

She takes a long pull from the beer bottle before setting it down. I'm across from her, watching her and waiting for her to speak. She fiddles with the label on the beer, pulling at a corner.

She doesn't meet my gaze as she says, "That was my ex-boyfriend."

"Oh, I know. He made sure I knew."

She looks up. Those dark green eyes lock on me. "It's a long story."

"I've got all night."

I'm not sure she's going to say any more at first. She sits across from me, picking at the beer label, seemingly lost in her own thoughts. I'm content just to stare at her. I'd forgotten just how gorgeous she is. That thick, long brown hair, the contrast of her inky black lashes against her skin, and the way her top lip flips up, giving her mouth this puckered look like she's just been kissed.

"We broke up a couple of years ago, but that's only the second time I've seen him since then. The first time was last weekend when I lied and told him I was dating someone. Sorry for getting you involved."

Am I relieved she's not actually dating someone? Yes, yes I am. "Why'd you lie?"

"Pride?" She shrugs. "I knew he was dating someone else and I didn't want him to think I was hung up on him or anything."

That makes sense, but it seems like a lot of effort for some douchebag that doesn't deserve any of her thoughts or attention.

"I never expected to need to prove it, but then he walked into the bar as I was trying to escape you and I didn't know what to do."

"I'm thrilled I seemed like the better option."

"Well, I didn't expect him to think we're together." She laughs. "Can you imagine?"

I can, actually. Or at least some heavy making out.

"In hindsight, I probably should have just told him you were a friend and that the guy I was dating was meeting up with me later."

"He wouldn't have believed that."

"No?"

"No guy is letting you out of his sight at a bar and he's definitely going with you to meet up with another guy."

Her cheeks take on a light-pink blush.

"Who's getting married?"

"My sister," she says, "is marrying his brother."

My brows rise. Damn. That's sticky.

"Yeah," she says as if reading my thoughts. "They started dating shortly after Chris and I broke up. I'd successfully avoided him until they announced their engagement. They're getting married in a few months so suddenly there are all these parties and plans, and I guess I'm not going to be able to avoid him forever like I'd originally planned."

I never understood how two people who used to date or cared about each other could come to a point where they'd need to avoid each other. It's beyond the feelings I've ever had for someone, I guess. But I can read the pain on her face and I feel for her, even if I don't think that asshole is worth it.

She blows out a breath and gives me a smile that doesn't seem all that happy. "Thank you for going along with it tonight. I guess he's going to figure out that I was lying soon enough." She laughs.

"I probably should have thrown myself at someone a little less high-profile."

"Right," I say, thinking. It wouldn't take a lot of research to find pictures of me with another girl as recently as tonight. An image of the woman who asked me to take a shot out of her cleavage comes to mind. "Yeah, I guess so."

We fall quiet. She keeps picking at that label, and I look up toward the bar where my teammates are still hanging out. Cody glances over at the same time and I can tell he's assessing the situation. His words from earlier this week come to mind and an idea forms slowly.

"Or maybe there's a way we can help each other."

Her head lifts and the question is on her face before she asks, "How?"

"I have started to get a bit of a reputation."

One brow cocks and her lips twist into a smirk.

"I know, I know," I say. "I'm not trying to say it isn't deserved, but my performance on the field is being questioned now because of it and I can't have that."

"Maybe you should stop taking body shots at the bar."

"She pulled my head into her cleavage."

"Or stop calling women during the game."

I wince. Yeah, Coach wasn't happy that I was almost late. I just had to make sure she didn't run off again. It felt like my last chance.

Fuck. Maybe my dick is still getting me into trouble. Which gives me all the more reason to convince her of my grand plan.

"Just hear me out."

She leans forward, elbows resting on the table.

"Let's just keep telling people we're together. You can let the prick ex think we're dating for as long as you need."

"What do you get out of it?"

"The same thing." I motion with my head to the bar. "If they think I've settled down, then they'll get off my back, and hopefully my coaches will too."

She looks at me like she thinks I'm joking. Her lips turn up at the corners and she opens her mouth as if to speak, but then stops herself.

The longer I think about it, the more I'm certain it's a great idea.

"How would we pull that off?" she asks.

"Simple." I shrug one shoulder.

"The second you hook up with another girl, they'll all know."

"All right. Good point." I tap my hands on the table as I think. Lying low isn't such a bad plan. Especially as the season is ramping up. I don't want my game on the field to be overshadowed by anything else. "So I won't hook up with anyone else."

"Anyone *else*?" she repeats. "I'm not hooking up with you."

"That isn't what I meant." Though it doesn't sound so terrible. My gaze drops to her mouth. "The season is about to get hectic anyway, so how hard could it be to make people believe I've settled down and become a one-woman man?"

She huffs out a short laugh. Her green eyes shine bright with disbelief. "You're serious?"

"Absolutely."

"No one will ever believe we are dating."

"Chris did."

"Only because you were with me. I can't just go around telling people I'm dating Brogan Six."

"We'll tell them together." I pull out my phone. "I'll post it."

"Hold up." She flings a hand out between us. "You want to post on your very public social media that you're dating me?"

"You can post and tag me if you prefer."

Laughter slips from her lips. It starts quiet but soon her body is shaking with it and she can't seem to stop.

"Don't worry. My ego isn't hurt at all," I say wryly. I honestly didn't think it'd be so hard to convince her to do this. It seems like the perfect solution to both our problems.

"I'm sorry," she says through more laughter. "It's just…this is crazy."

"Maybe, but it's a quick, easy fix."

"One social media post isn't going to convince anyone."

"When is the engagement party?"

She shakes her head. "Oh no. You can't show up to my sister's engagement party."

"Why not?"

"Because…" She trails off. "So many reasons."

"I like parties and weddings, and Chris already thinks I'm the guy you're dating."

"But my entire family will be there."

"Do they think you're dating someone too?"

She doesn't need to answer for me to read it on her face. She went to a lot of trouble to avoid telling Chris she's single.

"Would any of your teammates truly believe you're suddenly dating someone?" she asks.

"Sure." I think they would anyway. Archer is the only one that would question it, but I'd have to tell him the truth anyway. "I'm gonna grab another drink. You want anything?"

She shakes her head, and I leave her at the table to go to the bar. Cody steps up beside me as I order another beer. "Who's that?"

"That is the girl that handed him his ass at the club." Archer smirks.

Cody's eyes widen. "I thought she looked familiar. The one with your old mailbox?"

"Yep." I accept the beer with a thanks to the bartender. "We've been talking since then. She came to the game tonight."

"That's…" As he trails off as if he's unsure what to think about the situation, I wait in suspense. Maybe she was right. They won't buy it.

"Surprising. You need someone like that who can keep you in line," Cody finally finishes, wearing an amused smile. The worry I had at selling the idea that I had a girlfriend is quickly forgotten. Sure, they'd be suspicious if I continued hooking up with other girls at the bar or parties, but if I don't and instead she were there…

"I gotta go," I say to him quickly. "Don't want to keep her waiting."

I'm mentally preparing how I'm going to convince her to do this, but when I slide into the chair across from her, she looks up at me with a steely resolve.

"How do we do this?"

"Really? You're in?" My relief is so swift and immediate that it takes me by surprise.

"On several conditions."

"What conditions?" I sit taller, leg bouncing with excitement.

"Number one: no hooking up. Not with other people and not with each other." She gives me a pointed stare like she's sure I'm going to cave on that point.

"Fine. Me and my hand for the foreseeable future."

"Not an image I needed." She winces. What the hell? My

dick is a sight to behold. Or at least I like to behold it quite often. "But along those lines, the foreseeable future is how long? I think through the wedding should be fine. After that, I can tell them we broke up or whatever."

"When is the wedding?"

"The last Saturday in October."

"That's not that far away." Two months. We'll be smack dab in the middle of the season. "How about December?"

Her eyes widen. Before she can argue, I add, "A two-month relationship isn't that long. It doesn't really sell me as a changed guy." I've had casual flings last longer than that. "I know it's a lot to ask. You're a beautiful woman and giving up that amount of time to pretend to date me when there are lots of dudes wanting to take you out for real is not ideal for you."

She snorts. "That's not the issue. It's just…four months is a long time."

"I'm gonna be busy. We have games nearly every weekend and practices and meetings…"

"What kind of things would you need me to do? Parties and bar hangs?" She glances around.

"We also have some team events. There's a community health and wellness day coming up."

She looks visibly nervous. "And I'd go with you as your girlfriend?"

"Mhmm." Picturing it, I smile. This could be cool. I'll get to hang with her while easing the minds of my coach and teammates.

She blows out a breath that puffs out her cheeks. "Oh god, I feel like I'm going to regret this."

"Nah. It's going to be great," I tell her. "For both of us."

CHAPTER TWELVE
London

The following Wednesday night, I'm in the apartment alone while working on an illustration for a client. I get up to take a short break. Carrying my phone with me to the kitchen, I pull down a glass and pour myself some wine. I drink it in sips, stretching my neck from side to side and marching in place while I scroll social media. I sat for too long, and my body is tense from the inactivity.

Finishing off the wine, I set the glass in the sink and start back for my room. My phone rings in my hand. Who even calls anymore except spam numbers? Even my grandma knows to text first, but I freeze when I see the name on the screen. *Brogan.*

Why is he calling me?! Since our agreement, I haven't talked to him. I kind of hoped he'd wake up the next morning and change his mind. I don't think I have the acting skills to pull this sort of thing off.

The phone continues to ring. I have no idea what I'm going to say to him so I swipe to hit ignore, but accidentally hit accept instead.

"Oh shit," I whisper-hiss, still staring down at the phone. I watch the seconds tick across the screen. I expect him to hang up. Maybe he didn't really mean to call me. Maybe it's a butt-dial?

I pick up the phone tentatively and put it to my ear. There's faint music in the background.

"Hello?" I ask quietly. I don't want to say it too loud in case he doesn't realize he called me.

"Hey, London." That voice. A shiver skates down my spine.

My heart rate picks up and I open my mouth to reply, but I can't seem to come up with anything.

"You there?" he asks.

"Sorry, uhh, who is this?" I ask, playing dumb while I pull myself together.

"It's Brogan." He lets out a low chuckle. "I'll try not to be too disappointed that you didn't save your new pretend boyfriend as a contact in your phone."

"Hi."

There's a pause that feels painful, at least from my end.

"Why are you calling me?" I ask. Oops. I guess I've lost my tact along with my ability to speak coherently.

Another deep laugh rolls through the phone. "Damn, girl. You really know how to make a guy feel special."

"Sorry. It's just that no one calls me except telemarketers and my mom when she wants to guilt trip me."

"I'm too tired to text," he says, like that explains everything.

"O-kay."

"I'm bored, was thinking about you, thought I'd call so we can work out the details for this weekend." I'm still quiet and he adds, "That cool?"

Back in my room, I sit in the chair in front of my desk. "Yeah, it's fine. Creepy, but fine."

"Talking on the phone is creepy?" There's a hint of humor in his voice and I can almost see the playful smirk on his face.

"Uhh…yeah," I say defensively. "Nobody calls anymore."

"I'm bringing it back," he says. "Old school, just like the letters I wrote you."

This call, just like him sending me letters, feels like something I dreamt up instead of real life.

"What are you up to tonight?" he asks.

I consider lying because saying I'm sitting home alone by myself drinking wine and working feels kind of pathetic, but then I remember where the last lie got me.

"I'm home. I just poured my second glass of wine, and I'm about to watch Survivor while I finish up a work project."

"Nice," he says. "With your roommate?"

"No, he had a date tonight."

"Mine too. My brother left me alone, and I don't know what to do with myself." He sounds so despondent. I bet this man spends very few nights alone.

"You're home alone on a Wednesday night?" I gasp dramatically in mock shock.

"Eh, it's fine," he says. "I have practice in the morning anyway."

"I wouldn't have pictured you home by yourself even with practice the next morning. Your brother certainly didn't think he needed to stay in."

"I'm trying something new," he says. "And now that my teammates think I have a girlfriend, I can't exactly hit up the bars like before."

"You told them?"

"Just a few of the guys that were at the bar and saw us together. The others will have heard by the end of the week, I'm sure."

Oh god. I'm going to have to tell people we're dating. Sierra. *My parents*. A rush of panic shoots through me and I close my eyes and concentrate on breathing.

"Sorry to hinder your social life," I say dryly, trying to keep the panic from seeping into my voice.

My sarcasm is lost on him or maybe he just doesn't know what to say. The line goes quiet. This is the strangest phone call of my life. I'm talking on the phone to Brogan Six. My fake boyfriend.

"How is your week?" he asks, like we're old friends playing catch-up.

"My week is fine," I say. And because it seems like the polite thing, I add, "Yours?"

"Not too bad. Practices have been killer as we gear up to play Dallas Monday night."

I don't even know how to relate to that. *Yeah, my days sitting at a desk and creating graphics for a website refresh have been brutal.*

"What are you working on tonight? Another drawing of me?"

"Didn't you say you wanted to work out details for this weekend?" I ask, pulling his attention back to the point of the phone call.

"Yeah, but first show me something you've done recently. I'm curious now."

With a small laugh, I set the phone down and put him on speaker. Then I pull up a character illustration I did for one of my author clients. It's an early draft that didn't make the final cut, so I don't think she'd mind me sharing.

After I fire it off to him, I say, "Now, let's talk—"

He cuts me off mid-sentence. "Whoa. You made this. No jokes?"

A small laugh slips free. "No jokes."

"This is incredible. You're really talented."

"Thanks." The compliment is so simple but sounds so genuine. Then I remember who I'm dealing with. Brogan knows just what to say or do when it comes to making women fall at his feet. "So, this weekend…"

We talk logistics for a few minutes. There isn't really that much to work out. We decide to meet at the restaurant since he has practice just before and I give him an overview of everyone that will be there.

"Chris, you've already met," I say. "My sister, Sierra, and her fiancé, Ben. Plus our parents. A few of their close friends maybe too."

"Cool. Sounds fun."

Is he for real? "Going to dinner with a group of complete strangers sounds fun?"

"I know you, and me and Chris are practically BFFs."

"Ha!" I bark, and then uneasy laughter follows.

"I'll be fine. I can talk to anyone."

"Somehow that doesn't surprise me."

"Can I see more of your work?"

Thrown by the request, I hesitate. "Why?"

"Because I think it's interesting. What if your family asks if I've seen your work?"

I scoff. "They won't."They never ask about my freelance projects. But I send him over another design anyway, this one completed.

"Badass," he says when he receives it. "Is this for a cover?"

"No, I think he's using it for some marketing materials to promote the book." I'm pretty proud of this particular design. It's a vampire hunter with magical abilities, and the pose is of her staring off into the distance with a look of determination and purpose. Knives strapped to her pants and blood on her hands.

"I love it. Wait, is your job the reason you have the PO Box? For your legions of fans? Do art fans send panties too?"

"Yes, I have it for work, and no. It's so I can use it as my business address, mostly." I can't help but laugh at the thought of people sending *me* panties.

"You have such a cool job."

"That feels like a weird compliment from someone who gets paid to play football."

"You think my job is cool?" he asks.

"Doesn't everyone?"

"You didn't seem that impressed the other night."

"You obviously put a lot of hard work into what you do, and I think that in itself is impressive."

"Thanks," he says, then asks, "Highlight of the week?"

"What?"

"What has been the highlight of your week? Totally fine if you want to say this conversation." He says it in a way that I know he's teasing, but god is he cocky.

"I had a really great club sandwich for lunch today."

He snorts. "Fine, fine. I see how it is. And low point?"

"Wait, you didn't say what your highlight has been."

He goes quiet for a moment and then says decisively, "I had a nice video chat with my brothers."

"How many brothers do you have?"

"Four."

"Four?!"

"Yeah. Do you just have the one sibling?"

"Yep. Just me and Sierra."

"That's nice." He hits the FaceTime video request button.

"Seriously?" I ask. "I thought we were doing this old school?"

"Super old school. Like back when people didn't have technology and had to talk face-to-face…just through the phone."

I still don't accept it.

"Come on, London." He always uses my full name, and I like the way it sounds when he says it.

"Fine, but if you're naked or sniffing panties or something, I'm hanging up and then blocking your ass." I hit accept and his amused face fills the screen.

Shit. I almost wish he were doing something gross because he's just so hot.

"I question the guys you've been talking to," he says. He holds the phone out in front of him. He's wearing a gray T-shirt with the Mavericks logo and his jaw is lined with stubble. I can see a little behind him. I think he's on a leather couch.

"You mean you?" I fidget, wishing I had another glass of wine to take the edge off. I feel a little self-conscious with him staring at me. My hair is up in a messy bun and I have on an old T-shirt from a vacation with my family to San Diego years ago. It's faded and worn thin. Not exactly the kind of thing women wear to impress a guy like him.

"You talk to other guys, don't lie. Look at you. You probably have a line at your door right now."

An unladylike snort erupts from me. "Yep, they're about to break it down. Help me!"

He laughs lightly, mouth pulling into a big smile. "I know you're fucking with me, but I promise you, there's a line even if you don't think there is."

I don't know what to make of that, so I change the topic. "Four brothers, really? That sounds chaotic."

"In the best way." He nods. "What has been the low point in your week?"

"I had to do a three-hour training at work on how to avoid phishing schemes," I say quickly, trying to cruise right by any other questions. "Yours?"

"It's been a pretty good week," he says. "But I did have a run-in with Marissa that left me wishing for a quick death."

"Is Marissa an ex?"

Smiling, he shakes his head. "Masseuse. That deep tissue shit hurts."

"Somehow I don't feel sorry for you." I roll my shoulders instinctively. I could use a good massage.

"Fair." His smile doesn't falter. "So, anything else you want me to know for Saturday, *girlfriend*?"

A lump forms in my throat. Good god, are we really going to do this? I consider telling him not to worry about it, but then I picture walking in alone and facing Chris and having to admit I made it all up.

I'm never lying again. Nothing good comes from it.

I hear the front door of the apartment open, and then Alec's voice calls out, "Are you home?"

"I gotta go. My roommate just got home, which means his date must have been a disaster. I think we're good for this weekend. I'll text you the details."

"Ah, gossip time. All right."

I stand, carrying my phone with me. "You'll be able to keep yourself occupied until your brother gets home?"

"Yeah, I'll find something to do."

"Call the next girl on your list and ask her if it's creepy to call without texting."

He laughs. "Can't. I'm a one-woman man now."

I groan and his laughter continues.

"Later, London."

"Sorry. Practice ran late." Brogan buttons the black dress shirt as he comes to a stop in front of me outside of the restaurant.

We're standing out of view from anyone inside, namely my family. I spotted my parents' vehicle, as well as Ben's, so I know they're all here already.

"It's okay," I say. Nerves make my voice sound strained and tight. I've spent every day since agreeing to this questioning my sanity. I cannot believe we're going through with this. I can't believe *he's* going through with this. I really expected him to bail at the last minute.

"You look stressed. Anything else I should know before we go in?" he asks.

"No." I shake my head and try to clear out my anxiety. "They know it's new, so they aren't going to grill you or expect you to remember their names or anything."

"Mom is Renee. Dad is Wes. She's a middle school principal and he's a lawyer." He grins. "I remember."

"Sierra is two years younger than me. She's starting law school this fall. Following in my father's footsteps. Her fiancé, Ben, is a zookeeper."

"Got it." He finishes buttoning his shirt and then starts to unroll the sleeves.

"Leave them rolled up," I say. "What about you?"

"Me?"

"Your family? I should probably know something about them."

He gets a blank expression on his face like he hadn't considered that, then shrugs it off.

"They won't come up. And if they do, just say you haven't met them yet."

"Okay."

"We've got this." He takes my hand and gives it a reassuring squeeze. Unfortunately, his touch elicits a whole other kind of anxiety. I'm so aware of him and how good he looks and how good he smells and how nice he's being. It's too much.

He drops my hand and fixes the sleeves on both arms. "Better?"

Dammit, his muscular and veiny forearms scream professional athlete. "Let's see one rolled down."

He doesn't question my request, just pushes one sleeve down and buttons it at the wrist. When he looks up at me, it's with one brow arched in question.

My gaze trails up his arm to where his bicep pushes at the material. The man is broad and muscular and there's really no way to hide it. "Either way is fine."

"Which does my fake girlfriend prefer?" he asks with one side of his mouth kicked up in a smile. "I think I'd be the kind of boyfriend that would consider those things."

A snort escapes me before I can stop it. "I prefer anything that makes you blend in." I wave a hand in front of him. "No one is going to buy this."

"Your ex did." He rolls the sleeves back up. The look suits him and what little I know about his personality. He still looks nice, but casual and relaxed.

"In a dimly lit bar for a few minutes." This suddenly feels like the worst idea I've ever had. Does the man have to look so much like a superstar? Maybe my family would believe that I was dating some unknown, unheard of local athlete, but the Mavericks' hot new rookie?

"We got this," he says. "No one will know." He steps toward the restaurant, but I don't budge.

I don't believe him, but it's too late now. "Wait. We should go over our story one more time."

He cocks a brow. "You're overthinking this."

"I just want to be prepared."

"Or maybe you're just stalling."

I start to deny it, but he's right. We're here, it's not going to get any easier, so we might as well get this over with. Anyway, tonight is about Sierra and Ben. Hopefully we can fly under the radar. I didn't tell anyone Brogan was my date, so there's a chance they might not even recognize him. I didn't.

The hostess leads us to the back of the restaurant. My stomach is in knots as I spot our group. In addition to our families, a few of Sierra and Ben's closest friends have joined, and they're at a long table.

My mother spots us first, followed by my dad. I feel their heavy stares move from me to my date. I did warn them I was bringing someone, but Brogan is...well, he's clearly not what they were expecting.

I break their gaze and scan the rest of the table. Chris and Gretchen are cuddled up together, seated next to his parents. Sierra and Ben are at the very end, surrounded by their friends, but when my sister sees me, her face lights up and she points to the two empty seats in front of her.

"Hi, everyone," I say as I stand behind one of the empty chairs, as far away from Chris as I can manage.

"Oh, thank goodness. They wouldn't take our orders until the entire party was here," Sierra says. "I'm starving."

"I'm afraid that's my fault." Brogan steps up behind me, warmth radiating off him. "I was running late, and London was kind enough to wait for me."

Sierra's eyes widen almost comically, and her mouth drops open. I feel a twinge of guilt that I didn't warn her, but there's really no way to prepare for Brogan Six. He's a lot to take in. "That's... wow....Hi." She squeaks out the last word.

Several awkward seconds pass by while everyone at the table quiets and then just stares at him. I'd be amused if I weren't also freaking out. Even more so when a big, beefy arm drapes around my waist. "Hi. Good to meet you all."

That's when I realize I need to introduce him. Ben notices too and is the first to cut the silence. He stands and extends a hand. "Excuse my fiancée, I think she's in shock. I'm Ben. You're Brogan Six."

"I am. Hi. Congrats on the engagement." Brogan's body presses into mine as he leans closer to shake with Ben. Sierra snaps out of it, then lobs a wobbly smile from me to my date. I read the *What the hell, Lo Lo?* written on her face, but I ignore it.

"Everyone, this is Brogan." I angle my body to him and say, "You met Ben, that's my sister, Sierra, and our parents."

Sierra takes over introducing her and Ben's friends. A few more people get up to shake his hand, including my dad.

"Wes," he says. "Glad you could join us."

"Likewise," Brogan says. He aims a charming smile at the entire group.

When the formalities are done, I pull out my chair. Brogan takes the last vacant one beside me. He drops a hand to my knee and I jump like someone took a cattle prod to my back. When I glance over, my date gives me a reassuring smile. He leans in and pretends to kiss my temple.

"Relax, we got this," he says quietly.

CHAPTER THIRTEEN
Brogan

've never been to a dinner with parents before. Not like this. Two families with both parents, everyone happy and laughing, having a good time. The only one not having fun is London. She sits next to me, quiet and pushing her food around her plate.

The parents are in a conversation about a new pickleball court; Sierra and Ben's friends are talking animatedly and laughing, and Sierra is watching me with her sister carefully. I'm not sure she's totally buying us together because London looks miserable.

"So how did you two meet?" Ben asks, draping one arm around the back of his fiancée's chair.

"Ooooh. Yeah, I want to know too." Sierra sits taller.

I reach for my water glass and take a drink while I wait to see how London is going to react. A flash of panic crosses her face and I drop one hand to her thigh under the table. I meant it to be reassuring, but she jolts in her seat at my touch.

"Do you want to tell them or should I, baby?"

Her eye twitches a little at the endearment. "Go ahead, *pookie.*"

I can see we're going to have to workshop some better nicknames. London shifts in her seat, reminding me I still have my hand on her bare thigh. Her green dress is just a few shades lighter than her eyes.

She's close with her family. I can tell that, even if she's barely spoken to them tonight. It's a peculiar thing, watching them all interact. I don't think I ever went out to dinner with my parents. Not once. Not even to McDonalds or some other cheap fast-food place. And while I shared plenty of meals with the Holland brothers and their mom before she passed, the dynamic here is different.

When we all sat down I expected some Hallmark-style dinner where everyone talked and shared stories, and while for the first twenty minutes or so it was sort of like that, there's a nuance to how it's evolved as the dinner has continued.

The parents are having their own conversations and we're having ours. I think it must take a certain kind of security that I'm unfamiliar with. London and Sierra don't worry about engaging the parents or fight for their attention; they're content to just sit at the other end of the table and be together.

"We met at a club," I say finally.

"You went to a club?!" Sierra asks her sister, and it's clear that's out of character for my girlfriend. Interesting.

"With Alec," London clarifies, perking up slightly.

"Ah. I should have guessed." Sierra nods, then waits for me to continue.

"I took one look at her and knew I had to get her number." I glance over at London.

Her lips press together like she's fighting a physical reaction that'll give us away.

"That's a bit of a stretch," she says. "He had a line of women vying for his attention. It took me almost five minutes to approach him."

"You approached him?" Sierra is even more surprised by this piece of information.

London stills like she realizes she's made an error. I doubt she wants to tell them the truth—that she was coming over to yell at me because she was getting my mail, including other women's panties, which by the way—still weird.

I cut in to save her. "She thought I was someone else."

"Who?" Sierra is hanging on every word.

London hesitates for only a second before she decides how to answer.

"I thought he was this guy I know from work." A slow smile lifts one corner of her mouth.

"She was calling out, 'Dave! Dave!' and waving at me." I do a dramatic reenactment that has Ben and Sierra laughing.

"Only you wouldn't recognize Brogan Six," Ben says, giving his head a shake and me an apologetic smile.

I catch the wary gaze Chris is shooting us. Ignoring him, I shift my chair closer to his ex-girlfriend.

I like that she didn't know who I was. I got to see unfiltered London in a way I don't always get from people who know that I'm a professional football player.

"What'd you do?" her sister finally asks me.

"I was confused at first, but I wasn't letting her go without buying her a drink."

"You mean the drink you spilled on me?"

My smile hitches up as London finally comes alive. There's a spark in her eyes that's been missing all night long. She's getting into the story, weaving a tale that's part truth and part fiction.

"I'm a lot of things, but clumsy isn't one of them," I say, looking into her eyes. The dark green color continues to remind me of four-leaf clovers and the bright green of grass in the spring.

"Someone must have bumped your arm, then." She doesn't break my stare.

"Must have."

We're only about a foot apart and both leaning in. I don't know if she's acting or not, but I'm happy to play my part. My gaze drops to her lips. Tonight they're painted a pinkish-red that makes them look poutier than ever.

"Then what happened?" Sierra's question finally drags my attention away from London.

Suddenly everyone at the table is listening in, enthralled. Me too. Chris is the only one that doesn't look happy to hear the story of how we met. I don't know if it's because he's jealous or just annoyed by me. Either way, I do my best to ignore him and focus on London.

"We spent the whole night talking and dancing, getting to know each other. We closed the place down and then I took her to breakfast."

"London doesn't like breakfast food." Chris pauses with his glass up to his lips.

Well, shit. I said too much.

"I like *some* breakfast food," London says with a little grit in her tone. "And besides, I would have agreed to anything to spend more time with him." She places a hand on my forearm.

I stare down at her fingers. Her nails scrape against my skin as she pulls back and I feel a tingle roll down my spine.

"Awwww." Sierra's voice brings me back to reality—the one where we're only faking. I pretend to be smitten, but it's not all that hard honestly. I smile at London's sister, and we share a nice moment. I like her. I like how happy she is for her sister. She lets her head fall over onto Ben's shoulder as she says, "That's so sweet."

The rest of dinner goes by without any more questions for us. Conversation turns to Sierra and Ben, people asking about details for the wedding: has she picked out her dress, what kind of reception are they having, what color scheme is she using, and on and on.

Most of the questions are fielded by Sierra, and eventually Ben turns back to me to talk football. Turns out, he's been a fan of the Mavericks a long time, and by the end of the dinner, the only person in London and Ben's families that I don't like is Chris. Even his girlfriend seems cool.

We stand from the table and I shake hands with Ben while London hugs her sister. Chris and Gretchen stand off to the side. Even if I don't like the guy, it isn't in me to be rude, so I go over to him and extend a hand. "Good to see you again."

He eyes my hand for a moment like he's trying to figure out how to politely tell me to fuck off, then grasps mine with more force than necessary. What a prick. I smile at his girlfriend as I step back. "It was nice seeing you again too."

"Bye," she chirps, completely oblivious to the glare Chris is shooting in my direction.

I guide London through the restaurant with a hand at her back. When we're outside, I say, "Well, I'd say that went pretty well."

She hurries down the sidewalk, heels clicking with her short, quick steps. Once she's a good twenty feet away, she glances back like she's checking to make sure we're alone and then exhales.

"Thank you," she says.

"For what?"

"I don't know...being convincing. Although I feel terrible lying to my sister. I could tell she likes you." She fidgets with her hands in front of her and her mouth twists into a concerned pout.

"I like her too." We reach my truck parked next to her car. I walk her to the driver's side door of her car and open it. "Not bad for our first fake date. Although I almost blew it there by saying too much. What kind of person doesn't like breakfast food?"

A short laugh accompanies her smile. "It isn't that I don't like it, exactly. I just prefer other foods. I like French toast!"

Leaning against the frame of her door, I smile back at her.

"And croissants."

"You like sweet breakfast food then?"

"But not cereal or pancakes or waffles or..." She trails off with a shy smile.

"No, keep going. I'm making a list in my head."

"What's your favorite breakfast food?" she asks me instead of continuing with her likes and dislikes.

"I'm not picky about food. Most mornings I have a protein drink with oatmeal and peanut butter in it."

She wrinkles up her nose.

"It's good." That might be overselling it, so I tip my head to the side and say, "Okay, maybe not good, but it's an efficient way to get protein, carbs, and fats, and I can drink it on the drive to the stadium."

The breeze blows her hair into her face, and she pushes it back with one finger, still smiling at me. "I like my coffee for the same reason. I get my essentials, caffeine and sugar, in one delicious mug."

Our laughter drifts off and we continue to stare at each other over the top of the door.

"So…" she says finally.

I'm finding I don't really want to leave. I enjoyed hanging with her tonight, even if the circumstances were odd. We don't have any other fake dates set up to see each other again and though I hadn't planned on it, I find myself asking, "Do you want to come back to my place?"

Her lips part, then she closes them again. "As your fake girlfriend?"

"Just to hang. Nothing official."

"Thank you for that." She waves a hand toward the restaurant. "You were great. My sister and Ben loved you, and I appreciate that you were so chill about everything. Especially considering I was so nervous."

"But?" I know she's not coming home with me by the look on her face, but I still want to hear why. Maybe I can change her mind.

"I'm exhausted and tomorrow I promised to help Sierra with flowers for the wedding."

"Ah," I say, shoving my hands in my pockets. She's blowing me off, which can only mean that she's just not interested. Major bummer.

"When is your next team event?" she asks.

"A week from today. I'll send you the details."

"Great," she says, but she looks nervous. "Do all your friends and teammates know about us now?"

"Archer is the only one that knows the truth."

"Your brother and roommate?"

I nod. "Yeah. I tell him everything."

"And everyone else?"

"Most of my teammates have heard through the rumor mill at this point."

She presses her lips together to stifle another laugh. "I wouldn't have thought football players liked to gossip."

"Oh, they're the worst," I tell her. "Big fucking mouths, all of them. Especially my buddy Tripp."

More of that sweet laughter trickles out of her.

I finally move away from her car and step back toward my truck. "Later, lover."

"Oh, god no. That's worse than baby." She shakes her head as she ducks into the car. "Good night, *honey*."

CHAPTER FOURTEEN
Brogan

HOLLAND BROTHER LOVE HOTLINE

ME

Yo, Knox, are flowers overkill for a day date?

KNOX

I need more information.

HENDRICK

Flowers are never overkill. Also, why are you asking Knox instead of me?

KNOX

Because I'm a better boyfriend, duh.

HENDRICK

I'm the only one that's actually married, so I don't think that line of logic works.

ME

You're both pretty. Now stop fighting and help me.

KNOX

Not knowing any of the details, I say Henny's probably right.

HENDRICK

See? Should have just asked me.

ME

Thank you.

HENDRICK

Who's the girl?

ARCHER

I'll give you one clue: "her eyes are like a four-leaf clover" ●

KNOX

The one that yelled at you? Ha! Yeah, definitely flowers. But no roses, those things have thorns and if she throws them at you, it could hurt.

ME

So noted. Also, Arch 👆

FLYNN

> Bringing flowers to a day date feels a little desperate, bro.

"Not bad," Coach says, pacing in front of us. "Not bad at all."

He never says anything is good so "not bad" feels like high praise.

"Rams tomorrow. Their defense is one of the best in the league and they're still pissed we knocked them out of the playoffs last year."

Tripp says, "Hell yeah, we did."

"Not bad isn't going to cut it." Coach stops and looks at us in a slow scan so that his serious stare bleeds into each of us.

Excitement and anticipation hum under my skin. We had our usual Saturday morning walk-through and review, the last practice before tomorrow's first official game of the season. I played well during the pre-season games, but I know teams will be pushing harder now. I need to show Coach and everyone else what I can do tomorrow and secure my spot on this team.

It won't be easy. We're facing one of the best teams and they're out for blood and redemption. But I'm ready. I've been working hard on the field and soaking up every piece of advice Cody and the coaches have given me. I'm ready to show everyone that I can compete against the best in the league.

Football isn't the only thing in my life. I have friends and a pseudo family, but my relationship with the sport is simple and pure. It's always been there for me, which is more than I can say about almost anyone else.

"All right. That's it." Coach's hands go to his hips. "Be back here this afternoon for the wellness event. Rookies, this is your first big community event, don't embarrass me." I swear he looks right at me. "I expect you to be here on time, showered, jerseys on, and smiles in place. And no funny business. You represent the Mavericks today, the same way you do when you step onto this field. No fighting, no cussing, and dear god, no hooking up with anyone."

Someone coughs and says, "Six."

Everyone busts up laughing. Even one of the assistant coaches has a smirk on his face.

"Actually, I'm bringing my girlfriend," I say, smiling as I watch the news hit them.

The field goes quiet, and I bite back a laugh at the shocked looks on their faces.

Coach's brows lift but his mouth falls into a pleased smile. "That's all, gentlemen."

When Coach dismisses us, Archer falls into step next to me with a slight limp on his right side. His ankle has been a constant nag and I know he's worried about his spot while he recovers.

"Are you going home before the event?" he asks. "Some of the guys are going out to lunch." We rode together today, so my plans impact him. He rubs a hand over his head and blows out a breath. "Damn, I need a nap just thinking about spending all day smiling and signing autographs."

Tents were already set up in the parking lot this morning when we got to practice and now there are dozens of people unloading supplies from trucks and vans.

I don't mind the required press junkets and community service that goes along with being part of the team, but going home and taking a nap does sound nice. Or it would if the other option didn't include a certain woman. I know this kind of stuff stresses Archer out, though. Not because he doesn't like people, he does, but because it's hard for him in crowds with lots of noise and people coming at him from all directions.

"Yeah, I gotta pick up London, so I was going to head home and shower and eat, I can give you a ride if you want to meet up with the guys."

"I'm sure I can get a lift with someone else," he says, brows tugging together. "You're really going through with it then?"

When I told him London and I had agreed to help each other by pretending to be a couple, he laughed. I think he thought I'd been kidding. Or maybe he hoped I was.

"Of course. Did you see Coach's reaction in there?" I shake my head. *"He was stunned speechless."*

"Yo, Six." Cody jogs up on my other side. He leans forward and nods to Archer, making sure his face is visible before he continues. Archer wears hearing aids but it's helpful if he can read lips as well. "Anthony wants to know if you can stop by the dunk tank today."

The head of the Mavericks PR is good at keeping us in line at events and convincing us to do all kinds of things.

"Sure," I say slowly. I nudge my buddy. *"Arch and I love a good dunk tank."*

"Speak for yourself," he says. "I hate getting soaked with my clothes on. Any chance I can go in my boxers?"

"Anthony specifically requested you," Cody says to me.

When I stare at him blankly, he continues, "It's a big attraction at the event each year and he likes to make sure he has the players people are most excited about there."

Archer chuckles and then whistles. "Brogan Six is a hot commodity."

"*Shut up,*" I say as he doesn't even try to hide the giant smirk on his face.

"People are excited about you. You're a big fucking deal, bro." His words are half tease and half pride. That pretty much sums up our entire friendship.

"*Yeah, they're so excited that they want to watch me freefall into a tank of water.*" I arch a brow at him as he continues laughing.

"Your new girlfriend will be *super* impressed with the wet dog look. I can't wait. What time will he be up? I don't want to miss it."

Cody ignores Archer's question and focuses on me.

"So you weren't joking back there, then. You and that girl from the bar are a thing? It's been a couple of weeks, I figured you'd already moved on."

"Nope. You'll meet her today."

He continues to stare at me with the same skeptical expression Archer had. "*You* have a girlfriend?"

I'd like to be insulted, but I get it. I'm not exactly boyfriend material. I think that's what makes me such a great fake boyfriend. No feelings, no messy entanglements. It's purely business.

London's green eyes flash in my mind, followed by a picture of her last weekend in that green dress. My fake girlfriend is gorgeous, so that's also a bonus.

I debate whether or not I should be honest with him. Archer is the keeper of so many of my secrets that hiding it from him never crossed my mind. But I haven't known Cody that long. I don't trust easily, but something tells me my new teammate will keep this to himself. At the end of the day, I'm doing it for myself but the team benefits. And if I know one thing about Cody St. James, it's that he's always doing what's best for the team. I guess a part of me wants him to know that I've heard his advice and I'm heeding it in my own way.

"We have an arrangement," I say finally.

Cody stops in his tracks and narrows his gaze on me. "You didn't hire a girl to be your date, did you? Because I swear to God if the next headline is about you paying escorts and bringing them to events with children, I'll kick your ass."

"No money is exchanging hands," I promise.

He crosses both arms over his chest. We're about the same height, but he's bigger and years of training at an elite level have sculpted him into a powerhouse. "What the hell did you get yourself into, Six?"

CHAPTER FIFTEEN
London

"**D**o you think this is okay?" I face Alec with a tentative smile and arms held out to my sides.

He gives me a slow, bored once-over as he shovels another bite of Lucky Charms into his mouth. It's almost noon, but he just woke up and is now getting to witness my meltdown.

"This event is outside, right?"

"Yeah," I say slowly.

"You don't think black pants might be hot?"

I glance down at the freshly-ironed material. "I was trying to look professional. I wore these when I interviewed at Channel 3."

My roommate chuckles as he drops the spoon to the bowl. "It's an outdoor community event, I don't think business attire is how you want to show up if you're trying to convince people you're Brogan Six's new girlfriend."

I glare at him. I kind of wish I hadn't told him, but I never would have been able to keep it from him. He thinks it's hilarious and awesome, but he did make me promise to share my location with him just in case Brogan turns out to be a total creep.

I throw my hands up. I know he's right, but I spent all morning going through my closet trying to find something to wear, and it turns out I don't have anything suited for mingling with professional football players. Also, I'm nervous.

My palms are sweaty and it's not because it's a hundred degrees outside. Brogan is going to be here soon, and I'm not ready.

"Help me," I whine. "I'm so far out of my depth here."

"Lo, you're a beautiful woman. Put on a pair of shorts and a plain T-shirt and call it a day. And don't take this the wrong way, but no one is going to be looking at you if you're standing next to the Mavericks' players. They may not even be able to see you. You could hide behind one of their biceps."

That does make me feel slightly better. But then I picture Brogan and the nerves ramp back up. He'll notice. He doesn't miss anything. And he was such a trooper at Sierra's engagement dinner. He showed up looking amazing and played the part of my new boyfriend so well. I want to do a good job for him in return.

The trouble is I have no idea what is expected of me. Brogan wasn't very explicit in the details. Just that we'd work some booths and mingle with people. Mingling as myself would be no big deal. I can blend in and chat about the weather or random things to pass the time. But mingling as Brogan Six's girlfriend is a completely different story. My family didn't question our relationship, but will his teammates? And oh god, what if they ask me about football? What position does Brogan even play?

"I have an idea." Alec disappears down the hall toward his

bedroom and returns a few moments later with a wad of navy material. He tosses it at me. "Here you go."

Holding it out in front of me, I smile at the large Mavericks shirt. It's going to be big on me, but it's better than the stiff button-down I'm wearing.

Five minutes before he's supposed to arrive, there's a hard knock on the door. My eyes widen and Alec smirks as he watches me tie the T-shirt into a knot on one side so it doesn't look like I'm pantless.

At Alec's suggestion I put on shorts and sneakers. The shoes are much more comfortable so that was a good idea since I imagine I'll be standing or walking a lot. And the shirt is a nice touch, I hope. Go team, go, or whatever.

It's very possible I've overthought this to an embarrassing degree, but here we are.

"You want me to get that?" Alec asks.

"No," I say quickly then take a big breath and exhale slowly. I get to the door just as another knock comes. I open it and find Brogan on the other side with one hand lifted in a fist.

He does the usual once-over in that slow sweep like he's more curious than checking me out. His lips were already curved up in a smile, but now both corners inch higher. "Hey."

"Hi." My skin feels tight and itchy as we stare at each other, then I remember my manners. Stepping back, I open the door wider. "Do you want to come in?"

He nods as he moves forward. His gaze automatically scans the apartment, taking in the small living room and then my roommate standing in the kitchen. While he scopes out my apartment, I scope him out.

He's in black athletic shorts and his jersey. It looks different without all the padding underneath, but his biceps still pull at the sleeves. He's got a jacket and keys in one hand.

"What's up, man?" Alec asks, giving Brogan a chin nod.

"You remember my roommate, Alec?" I ask.

"Of course." Brogan's smile turns into that usual playful smirk as he walks closer and offers his hand. "Nice to see you again."

He and Alec shake hands and my roommate says, "You too."

Brogan continues looking around the place, stepping from the kitchen into the living room. He walks over to a framed print of the Mavericks' stadium. Alec's, not mine.

"This is a great apartment."

"Thanks." Alec and I share an amused look. It's nice, sure, but not what I'd expect Brogan Six to consider nice. It's small and has a retro style with the exposed brick and original windows that are drafty in the winter. I've always loved the charm of this apartment, but it's still surprising that he seems so enchanted with it.

"Should we get going?" I ask. I am wavering between wanting to hurry up and leave so we get this over with, and wanting to hide in my room and fake a sudden stomach bug.

"Yeah, uh, but first." He extends his arm toward me. I thought he was holding a jacket earlier because it's so big, but upon closer inspection it's just a very large T-shirt. Even bigger than the one I'm wearing. No, not a shirt. A jersey. Oh my freaking go—

"Is it okay?" Brogan asks. "I have to wear mine and I know some of the other guys' girlfriends and wives are wearing matching jerseys."

Matching jerseys? My ears ring and my face flames hot and I just know that if I looked up at Alec right now, he'd be grinning so big.

"Of course. That makes total sense," I say in a voice that sounds nothing like my own. "Just, uh, give me two seconds."

I head into my room and close the door, then lean my back against it. What in the hell have I gotten myself into?

CHAPTER SIXTEEN
London

The event spans the parking lot of the Mavericks' stadium. Tents are set up along the front and people are everywhere.

Brogan leads me through a private entrance where we're handed VIP lanyards. It's weird seeing my name printed on the badge. Somehow that little detail makes it all seem too real.

My date doesn't seem to notice that I'm in my head, freaking out. Brogan chatters away, pointing out people he knows, introducing me to some, waving to others. He's well-liked, which isn't all that surprising. He has some inside joke or camaraderie with everyone from the parking attendant to the coaches. And I feel all their questioning gazes on me like the force of a thousand suns.

But none of that prepared me for the moment we stepped into a group of his teammates.

"Six!" They yell in unison. A couple of them look familiar from the club or the bar, but all together they look so big and intimidating that it's hard to focus on any one for too long.

Each of the guys is wearing their jersey, showing off wide chests and thick arms. The closer we get, the smaller I feel.

The largest guy steps forward and I gulp as he bear-hugs Brogan, lifting him off the ground and shaking him like a ragdoll. The others laugh it off, so I guess he's not going to die, but ouch. My bones hurt just watching the interaction. Brogan is six foot three, broad and muscular, and he's being tossed around like he weighs nothing. It's impressive really.

I catch one of his teammates staring at me with a curious expression on his face. It's not disbelief exactly, but he does look surprised. I'm not sure if it's because Brogan brought a girl or if it's specifically because he brought someone like me who so clearly doesn't fit in. The few other women in players' jerseys have that look. Perfect hair, perfect bodies, perfect smile. I'm not insecure normally, but this is all just a lot.

"Okay. Okay. Down, boy." Brogan's voice is tight and he inhales deeply as his feet are returned to the ground. He sounds like he ran a mile…or had the air forced out of his lungs.

"You commanding me like I'm a dog, Six?" the giant asks with a lift of one brow. He has an easygoing smile, but I think he could crush Brogan's head between his colossal hands if he wanted to.

Brogan obviously doesn't value his life because he pats him on the head and says, "Good boy."

That has the guys all laughing again, and Brogan steps back to my side. If he's going to die, I guess he's taking me along with him.

Slowly, each of their gazes slides to me. I don't usually blush, but I can feel my face warming and I have to fight the urge to use Brogan as a shield.

"This must be her," the giant says. "I thought you were putting us on. Damn, she's beautiful. What's she doing with your ugly ass?"

Brogan scoffs. "I'm a fucking catch. Right, London?"

My eyes widen and I open my mouth to speak but I have no clue what to say. Luckily, it doesn't seem like he's really expecting an answer.

He continues, unfazed, "But you're not wrong, she is gorgeous."

My face is officially on fire.

"These are my teammates," Brogan says, bringing a hand to my lower back. The light touch keeps me from bolting, but just barely.

"I could have guessed," I say with a small laugh. I smile and let my stare travel quickly over all of them. "Hi."

The giant is the first to approach.

"I'm Slade," he says. "Nice to meet you. Sorry I roughed up your boy."

"I'm sure he deserved it," I say, surprising myself with how easily the words tumble out. Then second-guess myself. Maybe I should be quicker to defend my fake boyfriend.

Slade lets his head fall back and he lets out a laugh that makes my insides shake.

"I like her." He winks at me and smiles at Brogan.

Another guy edges in front of him. "Tripp. Glad to see the rookie here finally screwed his head on right."

I have no idea what that means so I just keep smiling and lean into Brogan a bit like I'm snuggling up to him, but actually I'm just trying to keep myself upright. These guys are a lot.

"We better get to our spots before the head of PR comes looking for us," another guy says. "Nice to meet you, London. I'm Cody. Let me know if the rookie needs to be kept in line."

"Will do," I promise.

Brogan takes it all in stride. A few of them cuff him on the shoulder as they head off.

One player hangs back. He's the one that had the curious expression earlier. He has dark brown hair that has a reddish tint in the sunlight and hazel eyes that seem to see through me. He isn't as tall or as broad as Brogan, but he's still both of those things.

"London, this is my brother, Archer," Brogan says with more affection in his tone than earlier.

"Oh." I glance between them. They don't look that much alike, though they are both handsome in their own ways. Brogan has a more playful air about him while Archer appears more serious, almost broody. Though he smiles at me now, and I'm rethinking my initial assessment. Charm must run in the family. "Hi! It's so nice to meet you. I didn't realize you played for the Mavericks too. That's rare, right? Two brothers on the same team?"

Archer glances at Brogan and then me. I feel like I'm missing something, but I don't know what.

"Well, I'm not doing a whole lot of playing lately." Archer glances toward his right leg and when he does, I notice the hearing aid. When he looks back up, his hair falls back over it. "I've been struggling with an ankle injury," he says. His smile falls and then reappears, though not as believable. "You two were pretty convincing walking in here. I don't think anyone will suspect it isn't for real."

A flare of panic rises, but as quickly as it comes, it goes. Brogan said he told Archer, and it is nice to have one more person I don't have to pretend in front of.

"Of course not," Brogan says. "I told you we could pull this off."

I wonder what those conversations were like between the

brothers. Does Archer think this is a terrible idea? If he does, he doesn't say so now.

"Ready?" Brogan asks, and he looks almost giddy about spending the day pretending to be my boyfriend in front of all these strangers.

"I guess so." I am not nearly as giddy. Brogan is great, but I am way, way out of my element.

The three of us walk toward the event together, but we're stopped by a man in crisp black dress pants and a red polo shirt with the Mavericks logo on the left side of his chest, and a lanyard like the ones we were given. He has that frantic energy about him of someone in charge. The clipboard in his hands also is a telltale sign.

"Archer, Brogan," he greets them and then scans the paper attached to the clipboard. "Archer, you are in the autograph tent, and Brogan..." He looks up and from Brogan to me. "You are in the autograph tent at eleven. Until then, you and your partner can help in the free health evaluation tent. Cody talked to you about the dunk tank?"

"Yep." Brogan gives the man a nod.

"Perfect. We'll slot you in there after you finish signing."

"Thanks, Anthony." Brogan claps him on the shoulder, and the guy startles a little and stumbles to regain his footing.

"Mingle and have fun!" he calls after us.

"I'll catch you two later." Archer turns, walking backward away from us. "Might want to hold hands or at least walk a little closer."

Brogan's laughter dies off as his brother gets out of hearing distance. I wipe my palm on my shorts in case he decides to take my hand. He steps maybe an inch closer, but keeps his hands to himself. We talked easily on the drive over, but now that we're alone again and on display, I can't find a single thing to say to Brogan as we cross the parking lot.

People are starting to walk around the large circle of tents and activities set up. I have to guess by the sheer space allotted for it that many more people will be coming today. A crowd has already formed at the autograph tent when we pass by it. Young kids are grinning as they get the jerseys on their backs signed, plus hats and footballs, and other miscellaneous items. Some adults are waiting too. They shake hands with the players and pose for pictures.

A local radio station has music going and it provides a euphoric background to the warm summer day.

"What do you want to do first?" Brogan asks like we're out on a real first date with no agenda instead of on a tight schedule run by the polo-shirt-wearing Anthony. He's wearing a big grin and looking more excited than his teammates had. "Are you hungry?"

He points at a snow cone truck. Next to it is a food tent with long cafeteria-style tables set up. The scent of hot dogs and hamburgers fills the air as we pass it.

I shake my head and bring my hands up in front of me. While twisting my fingers together, I glance over at him. He looks so comfortable in his own skin. I get that we're on his turf, so to speak, but there isn't any environment yet that I've seen him look any other way.

And I'm still nervous. I can't put my finger on exactly why. No one is watching us and his teammates seemed to accept me easily enough, but this feels like a big deal, and I'm wondering if we can really pull it off.

"I have a surprise for you." That boyish grin of his widens as he turns to face me.

I can't help but smile back. He has that kind of pull, causing me to mimic his actions without being conscious of it.

"What?" I ask.

"I wasn't sure how into the whole hanging out with strangers thing you'd be. Or hanging with me for that matter."

"I'm fine," I say quickly, hoping to reassure him. The last thing I want is for him to worry about me when he should be working. "I can hold my own and I promise I won't embarrass you or anything like that."

One of his dark brows arches and his smile twists into an amused smirk. "You think I'm worried about *you* embarrassing *me*."

"You're not?"

"That's funny. Seriously. It's endearing that you think you could possibly embarrass me when anyone who knows me would say there's no way you could embarrass me more than I embarrass myself on a daily basis."

A little of the tension I've been holding eases. Brogan's gaze dips down over me and lingers on his jersey. "You look incredible, and after the way you handled my teammates, I don't think I need to worry about you junk-punching anyone that gets out of line."

I arch a brow. He expected people to get out of line? I thought this was a community event.

"No one will mess with you," he says as if realizing where my thoughts had strayed. "But I feel better about leaving you alone now."

"Leaving me alone? Where are you going?" The questions come out in a panicked squeak.

We're standing just past the food tent and my anxiety spikes at being left to fend for myself. Despite his faith in me, I don't know if I can handle that. What if I say the wrong thing to someone? I don't know that much about Brogan and his time with the Mavericks.

"I'm not going far. I'll be right there." He tips his dark head toward a large white tent in front of us. Signs indicate free health evaluations, and I can see a line of kids waiting to have their hearing and vision tested, and some older folks having their blood pressure taken.

"And where will I be?" Hopefully not in the dunk tank.

He turns then and I do the same. Two women sit at either end of a table with children seated in front of them. Paints and brushes are scattered on top of the table. A little boy has half the Mavericks logo painted on one chubby cheek, and the girl on the other side is going for a pink heart.

"I signed you up to face paint," Brogan says, stepping closer. It's hot out, but I enjoy the extra warmth radiating off him. "Is that okay? If you're not into it, I can tell Anthony that we're so in love you can't stand to be away from me for that long."

I tear my gaze from the table to him. Something about his expression tells me he isn't kidding. And I can see where a girl might fall for him hard enough for that sentiment to be true.

My mouth opens to reply with some witty, cutting remark, but I can't find the words. I'm oddly touched that he considered how I might want to spend my time at this event even though I'm here for him.

And the other thing…I think I'm disappointed that I won't be spending the day with him. Weird. Then again, I doubt any of the children waiting in line are going to ask me about Brogan's latest stats so that's a plus.

He's still waiting for me to say something, so I shake the thoughts from my head. "It's perfect, actually. Thank you."

The proud smile on his face makes my stomach flip.

"I've never painted anyone's face, but hopefully it's not that complicated."

"I have no doubt that you'll be awesome at it. Maybe later you can do me."

Does my mind go straight to the gutter? Yes, yes it does.

"Maybe," I squeak out, and I could swear by the way he fights to keep his laughter in check that he knows exactly where my thoughts went.

"Jenna." He looks around me and the woman sitting closest to us lifts her gaze from her work and smiles at him in the way I'm noticing all women do. Even ones that don't consciously realize they want to sleep with him still are affected by him.

"This is my girlfriend, London."

His girlfriend. I wonder if I'll ever get used to him saying it. Likely not before this whole thing is over.

"Hi." She turns her attention to me and waves a paint brush. She has long blonde hair and a friendly smile. "It's nice to meet you."

"You too."

Brogan leans in and his scent of cedar and citrus comes with him. "I'll be in there if you need me," he says and points again at the tent. "Good luck."

"Are you sure you don't want your face painted first?" I ask him, raising my voice over the noise as he moves away from me. Frankly, the practice sounds nice. Also, each of his big steps away from me has me wanting to run after him and attach myself to his side. I stop myself. I am a smart and independent woman, dammit.

But I am not exactly a kid wrangler. Sierra got all the maternal instincts. Kids kinda freak me out if I'm honest.

"You mean do I want you to do me?" He winks. Damn him. He knows exactly what he's saying, and my face is getting hot again. "Later, sweetheart."

Blowing out a breath, I watch him disappear into the tent across from me.

Jenna gives me a quick rundown of the brushes and paints, plus a handy sheet with different art pieces the kids can pick. Most of them are pretty basic—footballs, the Mavericks logo that I've already seen several little boys and girls proudly wearing, unicorns, hearts, and a variety of other adorable animals.

I'm feeling as confident as one could expect until the first little girl sits down in front of me and demands I make her into a butterfly. She looks to be around four or five, but she has a whole lot of sass and determination in her little body. When I ask if she wants it on the right or left cheek, she corrects me, and that's how I end up spending way too much time doing a full-face paint. The end result is pretty great, if I do say so myself, but the line has grown exponentially. And one full-face paint turns into another and then another. I get faster with each one, but I'm damn near sweating as I try to keep up with the other two women painting faces.

The kids are bouncing in place impatiently and some of the parents look annoyed.

I stand between customers to wash out my brushes and walk closer to Jenna. She gives me a knowing smirk and I shoot her what I hope is an apologetic one.

"I'm so sorry. I couldn't tell her no and now they're all asking for it."

"Are you kidding? It's amazing. Look at that line."

Yeah, that's what I'm worried about. "I'm going as fast as I can."

"Don't sweat it." She waves me off. "You're working for free and there are lots of other things they can go do if they're tired of waiting."

"Thank you."

Her smile widens. "You're good at this. Have you done it before?"

"No. Never."

"Brogan said you are an artist though, right?"

I don't know how Brogan knows her so it's hard to speculate what else he might have told her. Maybe she's also aware we're not really dating. Whatever the scenario, I'm filled with pride that he chose to add that piece of information about me when talking to people. It's silly, but with so many others in my life not believing in my work, Brogan so easily calling me an artist means something. Which is why I don't give her any of my usual canned responses that I just do freelance work.

"That's right. Graphic design, mostly illustrations."

"And now face painting." She holds up a paint brush with flair.

"My turn! My turn!" A little boy plops into the seat in front of my chair and bounces excitedly.

"I guess I better get back to it."

She blows out a breath that sends her blonde bangs up into the air. "They're cute, but demanding."

After two hours of painting the faces of mostly adorable small children, my time slot is over. I offer to stay since the line has only gotten longer, but Jenna thanks me profusely and then shoos me toward the tent that Brogan disappeared into earlier to "spend time with my man." I guess maybe he didn't tell her that it's all an act.

The health evaluation tent is packed, but I find Brogan easily. He's in the back right corner surrounded by kids. The only reason I am able to see him is that he's several feet taller than all of them.

My smile inches higher as I navigate through the crowd toward him. I just knew he'd be wherever the most people are. While one of his teammates is standing behind a table with inflatable footballs and other free swag, looking uncomfortable every time someone approaches, Brogan is laughing and chatting away with a little boy wearing red headphones over his ears at the front of the hearing test line. The boy is sitting in a chair and behind him a man presses buttons. The little boy raises his right arm, then his left in response to the test.

The line for the test rivals the one for face painting, and my guess is that has more to do with the Maverick player helping out than a wave of interest in having their hearing evaluated. My steps slow as I get closer to him. Brogan helps the boy remove the headphones and then holds out his hand for a high-five.

The glee on the boy's face is so sweet as he smacks his tiny palm against Brogan's much larger one. I can see now why the Mavericks do this for the community and I have newfound respect for the organization and the players.

Brogan reaches for a roll of stickers on a folding table that blocks off one side of the test area. When the boy stands from the test, Brogan takes one and presses it to the kid's shirt.

"Nice job, little man."

"It was just like you said." The boy grins, showing off two missing front teeth. "It didn't hurt at all."

"You were amazing and so brave."

He bounces off and Brogan turns slightly. His gaze scans over me and the line of waiting kids to my right, then he does a double take back to me as if just realizing who he saw.

As the kid at the front bounds forward and into the chair, Brogan's smile widens on me. "Hey. How was face painting?"

"It was fun." I move toward him and then hesitate. "Am I allowed to be in here?"

"Yeah, of course." He wraps an arm casually around my waist and gives me a little squeeze. "I saw several of your pieces walking around. They look good. No shock there."

"My pieces?"

He points toward a girl in line with the Mavericks logo on her face.

"Oh. Thanks. I was kind of slow and the others were way better at it, but I enjoyed it."

"Take the compliment, sweetheart."

It's the second time he's called me that today and my stomach does this weird flip. I like it. I think if this were for real, it would fit us.

He keeps smiling at me and we are in a stare-off until the kid in the chair singsongs, "Can I have a sticker?"

Brogan's stare holds on me for another moment before he turns back around and drops his arm.

"As soon as you're done with the test," Brogan promises.

I stick close and try to offer the kid a reassuring smile as the woman giving the test explains that he'll wear headphones and she'll play a series of sounds and he'll raise his right or left hand depending on which side he hears it. The kid looks a little nervous now despite being so eager and confident before.

"It's a piece of cake," Brogan says as he places the headphones over the boy's ears with care. "Ready?"

"I don't know…" He glances around. "What if I don't pass? Sometimes I listen to the TV too loud and my mom says I'm going to hurt my ears."

Most people, myself included, would probably blow off this kid's concern and promise that everything is okay. But Brogan doesn't do either of those things.

He squats down in front of him. "This isn't a pass or fail test. It's just to get more information."

"But what if I can't hear?" He puts both hands over the headphones protectively.

"You know what? My brother is deaf. He can't hear well, and he's still the coolest guy I know."

"He can't?" The boy's eyes widen.

"He wears a special device on both ears to help, but without them, you could be shouting behind him, and he wouldn't know. Being hard of hearing or deaf doesn't mean you can't do the things you want. He plays football, watches TV…and he uses his hands to communicate. What's your name?"

"Michael."

Brogan signs something then says, "I just said 'It's nice to meet you, Michael. My name is Brogan.'"

"That's so cool. It's like a secret handshake. Can you teach me?"

"I'd love to, but this nice lady has a line of kids waiting. Think you're ready now?"

The boy nods and his face grows serious as he wiggles in his seat to sit straighter.

Brogan chuckles, pats the kid on the knee, and stands.

My heart melts to the floor.

It goes on like that for a while. Some of the kids are eager; others are nervous. I stand next to Brogan, observing more than helping. He's good with the kids. He knows what to say or do to put them at ease. He's funny and goofy, which most of the kids love, but the ones that need more reassurance get that from him too.

About twenty minutes before his turn at the autograph tent, another player arrives to take his place. Brogan leads me outside and we're immediately engulfed in people. The sun is high in the sky and it's a perfect blue-sky day without a cloud in sight. Which also means it's hot.

In the food area, we grab lunch. I get a hot dog and chips, and Brogan gets two hot dogs, a hamburger, chips, and a large pickle. We sit in the shade next to a couple of misters. There are a few other football players also eating, but they're scattered around among everyone else.

I'm surprised to notice that nobody approaches the players, even though they're mere feet away from them. They all seem to want to respect their time while they eat. That doesn't stop them from staring though.

"I don't know how you ever get used to this," I say as I open my bag of chips and do my best to pretend people aren't watching us. Him, really, but me by extension.

"What?" he asks, completely oblivious. He takes a huge bite of the hot dog while he waits for my response.

"Everyone staring all the time. Is it always like this?"

He nods while he chews, then takes a drink of his water before saying, "Yeah, I guess so. But it's all pretty new. No one was doing much staring before I was drafted, so I don't mind. It's a novelty that'll wear off, I'm sure."

The shrug that accompanies that answer is so him. So casual and unaffected by being the center of attention. It's not like I don't think he enjoys it. He obviously does. But he seems to have a good awareness that it's this fleeting, amazing thing instead of it being his entire personality and reason for existing.

It makes me like him even more. He could easily let it all go to his head, but he hasn't, and I hope he never does. He's a really cool guy—words I am shocked to think.

"Your brother...Archer. He's the one you were talking about with the little kid, right?" I ask, then add, "I noticed the hearing aid when you introduced me earlier."

"Yeah. That's right. He'd probably kill me for sharing so much, but he really is the best guy I know, and I don't want kids to be freaked out by people that are different than them. People find out someone is deaf or has some other disability and that becomes their entire personality. I've seen it happen to Arch, seen the way he's fought against it since we were kids. He learned to read lips because so few people around him knew ASL. He compensates a million different ways so that people don't feel like they need to give him special treatment."

"I get that."

"Me too, but it's bullshit. We should be happy to make simple alterations to accommodate people that need it. Everyone should learn sign language. At least the basics. And..." He stops. "Clearly I could go on and on about this. Sorry." He offers a sheepish smile and then takes a huge bite to finish off one hot dog.

"No, you're right. The world would be a much better place if we all had a little more empathy."

He grins at me, mouth still full. We finish our food with neither of us mentioning Archer again, but I'm still thinking about what Brogan said as I watch him sign jerseys and hats for adoring fans and after when we head over to the dunk tank.

His brother is there and when he spots us, his smile widens.

"Shouldn't you be doing something useful?" Brogan asks him as we stop in front of him. They have this teasing banter, but it's easy to see how much they care about one another just in the easy smiles and goofiness they both slip into.

"And miss this?" Archer shakes his head. "Not a chance."

Brogan sighs and glances at me. "I'll be back in thirty minutes. If I don't see you when I'm done, I'll shoot you a text."

My brows tug together.

"In case you want to walk around or whatever."

"And miss this?" I ask, parroting Archer's words.

Brogan lets his chin fall to his chest and chuckles. "Perfect. Only our second date and my girl is going to watch me make a fool of myself."

"She might as well get used to it," Archer says.

Brogan punches him in the arm as he walks away. Archer moves to stand beside me, still laughing quietly. "Are you having a good time?"

I remember what Brogan said about Archer reading lips so I angle myself so it's easier for him. "I am actually. It's obvious a lot of time and consideration went into planning it. Do you do a lot of big community events like this?"

"This is only the second one we've had to attend since we joined the team, but I think the Mavericks front office does a lot more."

"Do you guys hate doing them?"

"It's not that. I think it's a great idea. It's just…being forced to do anything makes it a little less fun."

Brogan is getting into the tank now and sitting on a ledge with his feet dangling into the water. His grin is so wide you would never know that a minute ago he was worried about making a fool of himself.

"Does he know that?" I ask as I tip my head toward where the first kid is about to toss a mini football toward a target.

"He doesn't know how to not have fun. In case you haven't already realized that." Archer's smile speaks of a fondness and bond that cements what I already knew—they're close.

"I think I'm starting to get that," I say with a small laugh.

Archer's face goes serious, still smiling but there's a warning too. "Don't let him fool you, though. He acts like everything is great even when it's not."

"Oh." I glance back at Brogan. I feel like there's more he wants to say, but doesn't. "Is there something I should know?"

"No. You already know he's struggling with his reputation."

I nod because I do. Seeing him in action today, I'd forgotten. It's easy to be with him and lose sight of our reasons for doing this.

"I'm glad you two are helping each other," Archer says. "But I hope when it's all over, this fake relationship won't have caused more damage than it fixed. For both of you."

"Me too. I promise to keep that in mind."

He offers me a smile, and I can feel the weight of his relief. He cares about his brother a lot. I guess I'd feel the same if it were

Sierra in my shoes.

"Speaking of helping…" I motion toward Brogan. I've been hanging back all day, not fully committing to this whole act. But the reminder of what's at stake for him, has me moving toward the table where they're selling chances to toss a ball at the target. "Want to help me dunk my boyfriend into a tank of water?"

One side of his mouth lifts. "Definitely."

CHAPTER SEVENTEEN
London

O n Wednesday I'm drinking my third cup of coffee and trying not to fall asleep at my desk when Alec stops by.

"What are you doing here?" I ask. He's a long way from the broadcasting floor.

He's ditched his suit jacket and his tie is loosened. "Heading out. Thought I'd swing by on my way and make sure you were alive."

"Barely."

"Another late night being the girlfriend of a star athlete?" His sly grin widens as he leans against my desk.

I glance around to see if anyone is eavesdropping. The last thing I want is for my coworkers to find out about Brogan.

"Did you see this?" He holds his phone out for me to see the screen.

It's a picture of me and Brogan at the Mavericks event last weekend right after Archer helped me dunk him. I'm not named, which is good. Brogan has an arm around me, pulling me against his wet chest, and he's aiming a big smile at the camera. We look like a couple in our matching jerseys. My insides warm as I think about that entire day. I had fun with him.

"I've seen it." I take another sip of my coffee.

"You look good." He slides his phone into his pants pocket. "Happy."

"I'm supposed to. That's kind of the whole point."

He leans in with a smile and whispers, "You're not that good of an actress."

I haven't heard from Brogan since he dropped me off after the event on Saturday. He asked me to hang out again that night, but I couldn't get Archer's words out of my head. Are we going to somehow cause more damage by pretending to date? I can't imagine that, but I figured the less amount of time we are together when we don't need to be, the less likely it is possible.

They had an away game this weekend. They won and Brogan had another great game according to every article I've read. I almost sent him a text to congratulate him, but that felt strangely intimate, like I was overstepping some unspoken line of our agreement.

"So, where'd he take you last night? The new Italian restaurant opening? Trivia night at Rockwells? Dancing at Gaga?"

"I was here," I say before he can continue guessing. It doesn't escape my notice that he knows every possible date location in the city on any given night. "Wayne needed me to redo some graphics."

"All night?"

"Until ten or so. They were going out this morning."

"And let me guess, someone else did the first draft, management didn't like them, and he dropped them in your lap at the last minute?" Alec's mouth pulls into a straight line and his brows lift.

That is basically what happened, but for some reason I don't want to admit it. I feel a sense of loyalty to Wayne despite everything. He hired me and gave me this opportunity.

"What did you do?" I ask him.

"Nothing much. Ordered takeout, went to bed early. When are you seeing him again?"

I toss a pencil from my desk at him. "Why are you so interested in this?"

"Are you kidding? You're dating—" He lowers his voice after I widen my eyes in warning at him. "Brogan Six."

"You know it's not like that."

"Uh-huh." He stands, cocky grin still plastered to his face.

It's not. But I'm starting to wish it were.

I go to Sierra's apartment after work to help her make a final decision on wedding invitations.

"You must really like this guy." Sierra's smile widens as she catches me scrolling the Mavericks website. She decided on a simple but elegant white invitation with black engraved type an hour ago, but has kept on looking just in case she finds another she likes better.

I'd given up on invites and had been searching for details on the team event schedule to know when Brogan might need me to be his fake date again, but got distracted when I saw a picture of him from today's practice. Ever since Alec's interrogation earlier, I can't stop thinking about him.

"I told you, it's new." I really hate keeping things from Sierra, but

I'm afraid she might lose her shit if I tell her I made an agreement with Brogan so I didn't have to suffer seeing Chris alone at all the wedding festivities.

"God, I still can't believe you're dating a Maverick." Her grin widens and she looks at me with such awe.

"Yeah, you and the rest of the city." Probably the country. Not that I imagine myself important enough that the entire country knows who I am. There were a few photos of us together from the community wellness event that popped up, including the one Alec was flashing around earlier, but I think people are used to seeing him with different women, so maybe they assumed I was just the girl of the night.

Brogan keeps mentioning the idea of posting a photo of us on his social media but that feels big and scary. I rarely post anything myself, so it isn't like I have a lot of followers or anything. I have separate pages for my art, and I've gotten to where I really only check those.

"Why didn't you tell me about him?"

"Because…" I trail off. Because it's a sham?

"What's it like going out with him? Where does he take you? Are women just like pawing at him everywhere you go? Have you met Cody St. James?" She fires questions at me, fully abandoning her search for invitations.

"He's busy a lot so we haven't gone out on a lot of real dates, but he's fun and sweet." I realize as I say the last part, it's true. He is a sweet guy, considerate too. "Yes, he gets plenty of attention from people everywhere. And I have met him. Briefly."

"Cody St. James is my free pass."

"I'm going to have a hard time not imagining that now every

time I see him." I scrunch up my nose. He's a good-looking guy though, so I get it. He has a whole serious, fuck anyone who gets in my way vibe going on that shouldn't be hot, but it is. He was nice and polite the few times we spoke so maybe I'm projecting and he's just intimidating as fuck.

"I'll be sure not to bring him around so Ben is safe," I tease.

She laughs. Me too. But somehow the idea of it isn't as far-fetched as it was a few weeks ago.

"That reminds me, Grandma wants you to bring him to Mom and Dad's house next Sunday for a late afternoon pool hang."

Panic blooms in my chest, but then I remember... "I'm pretty sure he has a game that day."

"The game is early."

Dammit, how does she know his schedule better than me?

Another laugh escapes from my lips. She must really love Ben if she's let him convert her into a hardcore football fan. "And you expect him to head over to our house afterward?"

If I had spent three hours running and being tackled to the ground, the only thing I'd want to do afterward would be move into my bed and order takeout.

She shrugs. "He has to eat. Besides, he'll probably want to see you. This way he can eat, see you, and Grandma can scope him out."

I groan.

"Just ask." She nudges my knee with hers. "We want to get to know him. You haven't dated anyone seriously since Chris. I think this guy could be good for you."

"You think dating a professional football player would be good for me?" I scoff. "This from the same girl who told me not to date Ken Reynolds because he was captain of the basketball team."

"This is different. Ken slept with half the school."

I don't point out that I'm pretty sure Brogan has slept with at least that many women since he joined the Mavericks. It doesn't matter anyway. It isn't real.

"Bring him and I'll let you choose your own maid of honor dress."

"Oh, now that's cruel," I tell her.

She beams proudly, knowing she has me.

"Fine. I'll ask, but I'm not making any promises."

On Friday, I finally get my opportunity to ask when he texts me.

BROGAN
Hey! How's your week been?

ME
Good. Yours?

BROGAN
Not bad. Better if you say you're free tonight?

ME
I'm free.

I purposely didn't make plans in case he needed a date for something, but now I realize how pathetic that sounds.

BROGAN
Great. I'll pick you up in fifteen minutes.

ME

Wait. Fifteen? Where are we
going? What do I need to wear?

BROGAN

A party and whatever you want.

Only after I race to my room to take the quickest shower I've ever taken in my life do I realize that I didn't ask him about coming to my parents' house next Sunday.

He arrives as I'm putting on a second coat of mascara. My hair is still wet, but I managed to put on my favorite black dress and paired it with sneakers, hoping I'm dressed casually but dressy enough to get by in any scenario.

When I swing the door open, his gaze immediately tracks down my body.

"Wow." He runs a hand over his jaw. "You look great."

My stomach flips and it feels exactly like a first date with a guy you really like.

"Thanks. You too." And he does. He's in jeans and a gray T-shirt but the way they hug his body is unbelievable.

He leads me to his truck and opens the door for me. I try to banish all my thoughts about this feeling like a date, but he is not making it easy.

"Where are we going?" I ask again.

"A teammate is having a party at his place tonight."

I want to ask why he couldn't go alone. Not that I don't want to go, because I kind of do regardless of whether I have to pretend to be his girlfriend all night, but it seems like he could have easily just gone without me and made excuses that I had plans.

"Wait until you see his place. Slade lives in this sick penthouse with city and mountain views. He's got a hot tub and pool on his rooftop."

That makes my stomach swirl with nerves. I am so out of my league. A penthouse? A private rooftop? Hanging with pro football players?

My only saving grace, and the reason I don't jump out of the truck, is that Brogan seems as in awe of that kind of luxury as I do. I guess he hasn't quite gotten used to the fact that his new job can lead to that kind of life. It's odd to think of him being a rookie professional football player as a new job, but it is. I make a vow to remember that.

The penthouse is as nice as I imagined. I try to keep my jaw from dropping as Brogan leads me through the massive space, but I don't think I quite come off as unaffected.

He takes my hand and squeezes. "Crazy, right?"

My heart skips a few beats. Crazy is exactly what this is.

He doesn't let go of my hand and I find I'm grateful because if I got lost in here, I don't know if I could find my way out.

We stop in the kitchen. Archer is there with a beer in hand. When he sees us, he smiles.

"Hi." I lift my hand in a wave and then smile at the blonde woman at his side.

"Nice to see you again, London," he says. He wraps an arm around the woman's waist. "This is Wren."

"Hi. Good to meet you," I say to her.

"You too. I love that dress." Her gaze drops to my shoes. She's in heels, as are most of the other women.

"What do you want to drink, sweetheart?" Brogan asks, pulling my attention back to him.

He holds open the fridge door. The inside is filled with rows of beers and hard seltzers, even boxed wine. It seems to contradict the bottles of champagne on the counter, but I suppose it's fitting for a bunch of football players. They can obviously afford the expensive booze, but they seem to be drinking a lot more of the other.

I opt for a glass of the cheap wine, and he grabs a beer for himself. Once we have our drinks in hand, Brogan takes my free hand and pulls me farther into the apartment. I can just make out the large floor-to-ceiling windows when Brogan comes to an abrupt stop and I run into the back of him. Our hands break apart as I attempt to save my drink. Half of the sweet wine splashes onto him, but when I go to apologize, I discover the reason for the sudden halt.

She's tall, blonde, and the dress she's wearing hugs her hourglass figure to perfection. She also has her mouth pressed against Brogan's.

"I was wondering when I would run into you again." She swats at him playfully as she pulls back, but only slightly. Her mouth still hovers an inch from his. "You never called after that amazing night in Sedona."

"Yeah, uh, I've been busy. Practice and the team…" He takes a small step back so he's standing next to me. He clears his throat. "Tiffany, this is London."

Her gaze slides to me. I'm not sure what I expect her reaction to be, given she's obviously slept with him and was expecting him to call her again so they could recreate an "amazing" night together, but she doesn't seem at all surprised about my presence.

She smiles and not in a fake way, or if it is fake, it's very convincing. "Nice to meet you."

"Yeah, you too," I say, shock making me polite even when I

should probably be acting jealous and possessive of my date. Isn't that what a real girlfriend would do? I do actually feel a little peeved.

Her stare lifts over my head and then back to Brogan. "Excuse me, my friends just got here." She moves past us but not before tossing out one more comment. "Call me sometime. You still owe me tiramisu."

When she's gone, I turn to face him. "Sedona? Tiramisu?"

"It's a long story." He rubs at his jaw with two fingers.

"It doesn't seem that long. You slept with her and then never called again. Am I right?"

His lips part but it's a moment before he replies. "Something like that. It was a long time ago. When I first moved here."

"Two whole months ago?"

"Three and a half." He grins.

I find myself laughing even though the whole thing is ridiculous and I'm slightly appalled.

"Any other women here tonight I need to worry about?"

"You don't need to worry about Tiffany."

"Yeah, well, tell that to the red lipstick all over you." I step closer and run my thumb along the mark she left on him.

He has nice lips. They're full and softer than I expected. My hand lingers there a beat, and he reaches up and closes his fingers around my wrist.

"I'm sorry."

The sincerity of those words surprises me.

"It's okay," I say quickly because it is. It has to be. We aren't really together and this whole thing is about fixing the problems he created for himself before he met me. I should expect more moments like that and probably be thankful she was as nice as she was.

We make it around the apartment and then head up to the rooftop. It's somehow even more packed up here. Brogan pulls me with him, stopping to say hello to some of his teammates and a few more women. Luckily, none of them try to kiss him or mention seeing him naked.

I keep a tight hold on his hand as I play the part of adoring new girlfriend. It's an easy gig, really. And Brogan is a good date. He notices when my drink is getting low, he pulls me into conversations, and he leans in close and whispers to tell me the dirt on several occasions. Once to warn me about a teammate whose breath is always terrible. That warning came too little, too late as I had just leaned in to shake his hand and nearly fell backward as he shouted a greeting that brought a wall of stench with it. And another time to point out an author in case I wanted to pitch my book cover designs to her. I didn't, but I appreciate that he thought to mention it all the same.

Eventually we settle onto an outdoor loveseat. His teammate Cody is across from us, sitting with his legs wide and a beer bottle resting loosely in his grip. He looks bored, which seems impossible given the sheer amount of people and the incredible view up here. Other teammates come and go. Archer and his date stop by before getting into the hot tub.

"Are they a couple?" I ask Brogan, nodding my head toward them. I can't get a read on them. He's affectionate toward her, but she's either playing it really cool or not into being all touchy in public.

"It's new," he says with a shrug. "I don't think they've defined it, but they're spending a lot of time together."

I don't push for more, but I enjoy watching the various couples around the rooftop. Some are in the pool and others take their turn in the hot tub. It's big enough for at least ten people, but at one point I count fifteen. A few others are sitting around like us, talking or making out.

The heat of the day still lingers in the air, but darkness has brought a cool breeze that whips over the tall building. My hair is kept in place by the arm Brogan rests behind me. The fingers draped at my shoulder slowly stroke up and down my upper arm, and his thigh presses against mine. The logical and practical part of my brain realizes that we're putting on a show, but my hormones do not. My stomach flutters and my pulse races and a shiver rolls down my spine.

He uses the hand at my shoulder to pull me into him. "Are you cold?"

"Just a little." I'm too embarrassed to admit that the goosebumps don't have anything to do with the temperature out here.

"Do you want to go back downstairs?"

"No way." I cuddle closer to him. "I may never have this opportunity again and I want to enjoy it."

He looks at me with humor in his gaze.

"What? It's not every day a girl like me gets invited to a penthouse with a rooftop hot tub. It's like an episode of some cheesy reality dating show, complete with champagne and other women who want to sleep with you."

"Other women meaning you included?"

My cheeks heat. "Well, that's what we want everyone to think, right?"

One corner of his mouth quirks up. "I have an idea."

He removes his arm from around me. The body heat he was sharing, as well as the wind barrier his large body provided, leaves me cooler immediately when he stands. Now I really am wishing I'd worn something warmer.

"I'll be right back," he says before I can follow him.

I feel suddenly bashful sitting around with his teammates when he's gone.

Cody offers me what I think is meant as a smile. He's got this permanent look of displeasure on his face that makes the action seem painful. If Sierra could see me right now.

"Can I…" I start and then hesitate.

He arches a brow.

Fuck it.

"Can I take a photo with you? My sister is a huge fan."

Slowly his mouth pulls into a real smile. "You want a photo with *me*?"

"Mhmm." I nod. "Is that okay? I know you probably hate doing that. Especially at a party."

"Yeah, but it'll be worth it when I tell your boyfriend that you were fangirling over me."

I can tell he's teasing, but I still clarify. "For my sister."

I quickly snap two pictures. He looks nicer in the photos than he does in real life. Sierra is going to freak out.

"Thanks," I say again.

He nods in reply, then says, "Six seems more chill around you. I think I see why."

"This is him chill?" I ask with a small laugh.

"Aside from Archer, you're the only person I've seen him sit and relax with for longer than twenty minutes. He's always bouncing from one thing to the next. Always the center of the party. But not with you."

I can't decide if it's a compliment or insult.

"I guess maybe he's just comfortable with me like he is with his brother." As soon as I say the words it feels wrong. I don't have a ton of relationship experience, but I know it shouldn't feel like you're dating your sibling.

His brows furrow and his head tilts to the side. It's too late to take it back so I sip my wine instead.

"His brother?"

"Yeah, Archer."

"Archer isn't his brother."

I open my mouth and then close it. Oh shit. Did I just fuck up? I know Brogan called Archer his brother on more than one occasion.

Cody lifts his beer bottle in one hand and takes a long swig. Then he says, "Well, not by blood, but I guess they are attached at the hip most of the time."

I force a brighter smile. "Right. That's what I meant."

Hopefully I play it off well enough that he doesn't see right through me. I take another sip of my wine, finishing off my third glass, and look away. The alcohol is starting to make my head light. I want to blame my misstep on that, but I know that's not it.

Why would Brogan refer to him as his brother? I suppose he could have meant that they were close, but the way he said it...it didn't seem like he was referring to a friend.

I don't have too long to ponder it before he reappears. He's wearing a proud, boyish grin that immediately erases all my concerns. Holding a bottle of champagne in one hand and two blue and white striped towels in the other he says, "What d'you say, sweetheart?"

CHAPTER EIGHTEEN
Brogan

London looks up at me with those big green eyes, then stands.

"What do I say to what?" she asks, looking slightly terrified at my possible reply.

"Pool or hot tub, your choice."

"I don't have a suit."

"You have on something under that, I presume," I say as I let my gaze slide over the black dress that molds to her perfect body.

"Yeah, but…that's not a swimsuit."

I step closer and drop a hand to her waist. "It'll be fun. I snagged us a whole bottle of champagne."

She still doesn't look convinced.

"When else are you going to have the chance to swim on this rooftop while drinking champagne?" The answer, I hope, is many more times. Slade has parties here pretty frequently, but she doesn't know that.

I can tell she still wants to object, but she's considering it too.

"All right, well, I'm gonna take a swim. I hope no beautiful women get the wrong idea and think I'm single. A guy in the pool alone with a bottle of champagne is like a homing beacon."

I start to turn away, walking slowly to let her easily catch me. She does two steps later.

"Fine, but I am not getting in that hot tub. My boobs are about two cup sizes too small."

A laugh loosens from my chest. Her tits are perfect, but I also noticed the average cup size in the hot tub is a DD.

There are people in the pool, too, but it's bigger so it doesn't seem so crowded. I lead her to the shallow end. I pull off my T-shirt and then kick off my shoes. She watches me, not undressing.

"What's wrong?"

"Have you looked around? These women are…perfect."

"So are you. You're stunning. You have nothing to be nervous about."

She scoffs. "You should have had your vision checked last weekend."

"I see 20/20, baby, and you're a rock solid ten. Now stop down-talking my gorgeous girlfriend and take off that dress." Another laugh leaves my lips. "Now those are words I never imagined saying unless I was about to get laid."

"Store it up for the next time you talk some innocent woman into dating you."

She pulls the black dress over her head, leaving her in red panties and a matching bra. My mouth goes dry, and I have to swallow several times before I can speak. It's the first time in weeks I've really thought about the fact sex has been off the table with other women. Weirdly, I haven't really missed it. I mean, I miss sex, of course, but the only person I've been fantasizing about is standing in front of me.

"You're not that innocent," I say, gaze locked on her lingerie. She is full of surprises. I did not have her pegged for the matching lingerie set type, but I have never been happier to be wrong.

"No, I'm not." She tosses her dress at my face. It's warm from her tight little body and smells of her shampoo.

My dick is real interested all of a sudden, and I have to remind myself that I'm not actually going to get to fuck this woman tonight. It's a real bummer.

Unless…

I set the champagne by the side of the pool and wade in until it comes up to my chest. London follows, looking more than a little uncomfortable. Wrapping an arm around her waist, I pull her toward me. All that smooth skin under my touch is like silk. Her stomach rests against my hip and her legs tangle with mine. The ends of her dark hair are wet and stick to her shoulders and chest. Damn, she's beautiful.

"What now?"

Laughing, I shake my head and move us so my back is resting against the side of the pool and she's basically sitting on my lap.

"Do you need an agenda, sweetheart?"

"Not usually. My sister is more the planner, but I don't know what I'm supposed to do here."

"You've dated before."

"Not like this." She lifts one arm from the water and waves it around.

"Same premise." I reach for the champagne. "Better booze."

After taking a long drink, I hand it to her.

"I probably shouldn't. I'm about half a glass of wine away from making friends with everyone around and telling them my life story."

"Now that I'd like to see," I tease.

"I bet you would." She grins. "Plus, I don't want you to have to take care of me or anything."

"Drink or don't, but I've got you. I won't let you do anything I wouldn't do."

"Oh, great. I'm really relieved," she says with a laugh, swiping the bottle from me and taking a small sip. "As if you will be in any condition to look out for anyone."

"I can handle myself," I say. "I don't actually like to get wasted. A happy buzz does me just fine. What fun are nights like this if you can't remember them?"

I set the bottle back on the edge and we settle in to watch the people around us. Or she does. I can't take my eyes off her.

"I like the red. Surprising, but it suits you."

She glances back at me, confusion marring her brow at first, and then when she realizes what I mean she blushes. "I wasn't planning on anyone seeing it."

"That would have been the real tragedy of the night."

Shit. I might need to stop staring at her before my dick makes her seat a little less comfortable.

"You are full of charm, aren't you? It's like you just can't help it."

I know she thinks I'm full of shit, but really, I'm just being honest.

"I get it now," she says, surveying my face like she's really taking me in. I wonder what she sees. Just another cocky football player?

Does she still think I'm just a fuck boy?

"Get what?"

"Why women are sending you their panties in the mail and lining up for a chance to let you break their heart."

"I haven't broken anyone's heart."

"Tiffany inside might disagree."

Using my arm at her waist, I pull her back to my chest. The position has her perfect ass sitting right on my crotch and I hold back a groan.

"What—" The question dies on her lips as I lift an arm and point toward where Tiffany is in the hot tub making out with one of my teammates.

"Ooooh." London stares in that direction for a few more seconds before adding, "Wow. They're really going at it."

"You were saying?" I take another drink of champagne and offer it to her.

She drinks it, eyes still locked on them as Tripp cups Tiffany's breasts over her tiny bikini top.

"Are you sure you don't want to take a turn in the hot tub?" I ask, sliding the hand at her hip up to rest just under the band of her bra in the front.

Her stomach sucks in with a sudden breath. I've caught her staring at me enough to know there's some level of attraction there, but I can't get a good read on her. Have her feelings changed?

"That would be a terrible idea." She moves off my lap, taking her tight body and the champagne with her.

When she's put two feet of distance between us, she faces me, then takes another drink.

"Why?"

"Seriously?"

When I nod, she laughs. "So many reasons."

"Lay 'em on me." I want to hear all her excuses so then I can tell her why they don't matter.

"You want me to tell you why we…" She cuts the distance between us in half. "Shouldn't make out in front of three hundred people?"

"So it's the people watching that's a problem for you? Because I know some spots that are a lot more private if that's the only thing keeping you from kissing me."

Her gaze drops to my mouth, then quickly up. "It's not the only reason."

"Give me one more."

"I'll give you two." She smiles smugly. "Tiffany and tiramisu."

"We've already established that she meant nothing."

"And that is exactly the point." She's getting more comfortable around me, but instead of being glad, *I'm* feeling uneasy. "Have you ever dated anyone for real?"

"What does that even mean? What makes it real?"

"Have you ever had a girlfriend?"

"Once. In high school."

Her smile widens like that tells her everything she needs to know about me.

"Relationships take a lot of time and effort. I didn't have the capacity for that then…or now."

"I thought all high school boys wanted was to date a lot of girls. Or maybe I'm confusing date with sex." Her empty hand skims across the water.

"Yeah, well, you're not wrong about that." I hesitate, not sure how much I want to say. "But when your home life is rocky, it's harder to navigate all that and keep certain things private."

Her brows pinch together like she's trying to make sense of what I'm saying. Fuck, I really didn't want to go there.

"My childhood was tricky," I tell her. "My parents weren't really present, and I bounced around crashing with friends. I moved in with Archer and his brothers when I was in junior high."

The change on her face is immediate. It's sympathetic and sorrowful. I hate talking about it, but I want her to understand that it wasn't a choice I made lightly. I couldn't bring girls home when I didn't really have one. My friendship with Archer saved my life. That's not an exaggeration. Even before I moved in with them, I spent as much time as I could there. His family gave me a safe place, any time I needed, no questions asked, and the family dynamic I craved. I had older brothers to look up to and a younger one to set an example for. That changed me.

"The Hollands took me in, and I am so grateful for that, but it still wasn't *my* home. You know? Girls had too many questions, and as soon as I answered them, they looked at me differently. It was easier to keep things casual."

"I'm sorry. I can't imagine what that was like."

I nod, ready to move away from that depressing topic. "What about you? How long ago did you and Chris break up?"

I want to drop-kick myself for the hurt that flashes across her expression before she quickly masks it. "Two years ago."

"Any other boyfriends since then?" I ask.

"No, nothing serious." She shrugs it off, but I can feel her holding back.

"When I met Chris, I thought you might still be hung up on

him, but I'm not so sure anymore."

"I'm not," she says quickly in a tone that sounds believable. "He just…"

She trails off and it hits me that the reason has much more to do with the damage he inflicted on her than wishing she could have him back.

"I feel you," I say.

"You do?"

"Don't look so surprised." I wrap my hand on top of hers on the bottle of champagne, but don't make any move to take it. I might not have that much experience with dating, but I know what it's like to have people disappoint you in a way that fucks you up.

"Come on then, sweetheart." I bring the bottle to my lips with her hand still under mine and take a slow drink. She tracks the motion, staring hard at my mouth and then my throat as I swallow. It takes everything in me not to ignore all her reservations and kiss her to prove to her how good we could be.

I push the bottle back to her, and then stand up tall in the water and scan the party for ideas. My voice is low and filled with gravel when I speak. "If we aren't going to make out, then let's find some other ways to make this night memorable for you."

Archer stands in the kitchen of our apartment fighting a laugh as I try to wake up London. She crashed on the couch last night. She wasn't kidding about not being able to hold her booze. She didn't get sick or anything, but I didn't feel right about dropping her off at her apartment. Especially when she told me Alec was gone for the weekend.

She has one arm thrown over her face and she's clutching the T-shirt I gave her last night to change into to her chest. She didn't change and the black dress has inched up high on her thighs during the night.

I've been trying to wake her up for a few minutes now, and she's fighting me even in sleep.

"London, sweetheart," I say softly, trying to take the pillow. "I just want to make sure you don't need to be anywhere and then you are free to go back to dreaming of me."

Archer snickers loudly.

Her body stills and then she shoots upright. It's followed with a wince, and she closes her eyes and rubs her forehead.

Laughing, I take a seat next to her on the couch. She crosses her legs and then realizes she's flashing me.

"Oh god." She quickly uncrosses her legs and yanks on the hem of her dress, then looks down at the old Valley U T-shirt I lent her and groans. "*Oh god.*"

"That's exactly what you were moaning all last night."

Her eyes widen in panic.

"Kidding. I slept in my bed."

Her body relaxes. "So we didn't..." She points her pinky finger at me. "Nothing happened, right? I remember getting here, but not much after."

"Nope. Nothing happened," I reassure her. "I tried to get you to take my room, but you kept saying, 'I am not sleeping in your sex sheets.'"

"Right." She nods, eyes fluttering closed. "I remember now. And to be fair, when I asked when the last time you washed them was, you couldn't remember."

Another chuckle shakes my chest. "How are you feeling?"

"Like I drank too much." She runs a hand through her hair. "How do you look so chipper?"

"I've been up for a while. Went for a run and did some mobility stretches."

She stares at me like she's waiting for me to say I'm only kidding, then says, "Athletes are weird."

"You're not wrong there."

"Here." She hands me my T-shirt back. "Sorry you had to take care of me."

"It was nothing." I wave her off. "Did you have a good time?"

"I did." The laugh that follows is light and airy.

"Me too." It's the first time that I hung out with a girl like that. Like we were really dating, minus all the making out. Do couples make out as much as people not in relationships? I've been thinking on that. I sure hope the answer is yes. Someday I might want to be one of those and I can't imagine hours and hours of talking and hanging out without it. I'm in blue-ball hell from one night of it.

"I should get home."

"No need to rush off. You said last night you didn't have any plans today."

"Then why did you wake me?"

One side of my mouth inches higher. "I was getting bored and impatient for you to wake up. Want to grab breakfast?"

"Don't you have things to do?"

"Not really. Practice isn't for a few hours."

"I don't think I can go out in public like this." She looks down at her wrinkled dress.

I hold out the T-shirt again.

"Unless you have a matching pair of pants that'll fit me, that won't work either." She stands. "It's fine. I am going to grab an Uber and get out of your hair."

Like I'd let her take an Uber looking like a sexy, rumpled goddess.

"Stay." I stand and block her path to the door. "We'll eat in. I'll make us breakfast and then I can drop you at your place on my way to practice."

"You cook?" She arches a brow.

"Yeah. What do you want?" I start for the kitchen.

She doesn't respond. In fact she still looks like she's about to jet for the door.

"Tiramisu okay?" I toss her a wink.

Her eyes narrow in a playful glare, but she follows me. She takes a seat on one of the stools in front of the island and puts her head in her hands. I should have made sure she took some Advil last night. I had no idea she was going to hurt so much today.

"Kidding. I only make one thing. Luckily, I'm terrific at it."

"Toast?" Her voice is still raspy from sleep, but her sarcastic humor is alive and well.

"Close." I waggle my brows. "*French* toast."

The smile she rewards me with makes me feel like I'm the king of the world.

Archer is leaned back against the counter watching us like we're entertaining as hell.

I feel like I missed a few things last night, he signs, gaze sliding to London and then back to me in question.

Just making my fake girlfriend French toast, I sign back.

"Right," he says quietly. Then signs, *Are you sure it's still fake?*

CHAPTER NINETEEN
London

"**Y**ou really didn't have to do this," I say for what is probably the hundredth time in the span of the twenty minutes since Brogan arrived at my parents' house.

It's been a week since I saw him last, but we've talked almost every day. Stupid things, a text to tell me about something one of his teammates did or to ask me to show him my work or a funny reel. I hate to admit it, but I kind of missed him.

"Are you kidding? I love family get-togethers." He's grinning so big that I believe he's one hundred percent telling the truth.

I lead him through the kitchen and outside where most everyone has gathered. Sierra and Ben are in the pool, as is my aunt Corinne. Grandma is kicked back on a lounge chair with a big sun hat covering most of her face.

"Want to swim?" I ask him. He has on red swim trunks that show off his thick, muscular thighs.

"Yep. Are you wearing that sexy red lingerie again?"

"I have a suit," I say, not bothering to mention, let alone think about, that night in the pool with him.

At the sound of the back door slamming shut, everyone turns. My steps slow. I can feel their gazes. Neither of my parents said much about me dating Brogan. I think they were too shocked and didn't really know what to say.

"Too late to turn back now, sweetheart," Brogan whispers, that cocky smirk never leaving his face. "They've seen me. Better act like you like me."

"I do like you," I say. Over the course of hanging out the past few weeks, I've come to realize what a good guy he is. A helpless flirt and an unapologetic playboy? Yes. But he's hard not to like.

At my admission his features light up.

"I'm still not sleeping with you," I add because I can read the look on his face. "But being your fake girlfriend isn't so bad."

He smacks my ass, trying to play it off as cheeky flirting, but the shock on my face makes it a little less believable.

"What the hell?" I whisper-screech. "What was that for?"

"For saying that being my fake girlfriend 'isn't so bad.'" He shakes his head. "I'm a fucking great fake boyfriend."

"And so humble too." A small laugh leaves my lips.

He winks. "Now be a good girl, sweetheart, or I'll have to put you over my knee later."

"You wouldn't dare." I narrow my gaze on him.

The look he gives me—he would. He *so* would.

By the time we reach the table where my parents are sitting with my uncle Steve, my face is poised back in a smile, and Brogan and I are holding hands.

"Hi," I say as they stare shamelessly at him. "Uncle Steve, this is Brogan."

"No shit," he says. "Your parents told me you were seeing each other, but I thought they were joking."

He laughs and my dad joins in too. My uncle stands and extends a hand across the table. "Nice to meet you. Hell of a game today."

"Yes, sir, it was."

Oh shit. I totally forgot to ask him about it.

"Did you win?" I look over at Brogan.

My family's laughter makes heat bloom in my cheeks. Brogan's smile widens, but he doesn't look offended that I didn't keep tabs on him. I was too busy freaking out about him hanging out all afternoon with my family.

"By a landslide," Uncle Steve says. "That run you made in the third quarter was a thing of beauty."

"Thank you, sir." He almost looks embarrassed by the compliment. A look I wasn't sure he was capable of.

"I'm going to go put on my suit," I say, needing to extract myself from the questioning gaze my mother is shooting me and the hero worship on everyone else's face. The man walked right into a houseful of his biggest fans.

"Want me to come with you?" Brogan asks with a wink. "I can help."

"I think I can manage," I say, wanting to murder his ass. Doesn't he know you don't basically proposition a girl in front of her parents? My face grows warmer. Oh my god. Does my dad think Brogan has seen me naked? Of course he does, because he thinks I'm really dating him. *Groan.*

I hightail it away from them, leaving Brogan to fend for himself.

Something tells me he isn't going to have any trouble managing on his own.

In the kitchen, I grab a glass and fill it with water. Sierra hurries in after me. A towel is wrapped around her wet body and she's dripping on the floor.

"Oh my gosh. You two are so cute together," she gushes.

"I cannot believe you blackmailed me into bringing him. Did you see Uncle Steve? He's probably getting his arm signed so he can tattoo it."

"No, but I wouldn't put it past Grandma." Sierra motions with her head out the window where our grandmother has a hand on my boyfriend's bicep. Even from this far away I can tell she's flirting with him.

"Dear god, no wonder I don't date." I catch myself. "Didn't date."

"I think it's sweet."

"You would."

The sound of car doors shutting out front draws my attention.

"Who else is coming?"

She pulls her bottom lip behind her teeth looking guilty as hell. Panic flares even before I know why I'm panicking.

"Don't be mad, but Ben invited Chris and Gretchen."

"Sierra!" How many times am I going to be blindsided by my ex? Two years without running into him and now he's freaking everywhere.

"I know. I know. I'm sorry. He really wants you two to bury the hatchet before the wedding."

"We're fine," I say, waving her off. "We don't need to bury anything."

She's not having it. "You can't even be in the same room together."

"Which is why we're fine. As long as we don't have to see each other, everything is great."

Sierra tilts her head to the side and gives me a sympathetic smile. "Do you want me to tell him to get lost?"

I'm fairly certain she would if I asked her to, but then that puts her in a tough spot with Ben.

"No." I sigh.

"If you change your mind, say the word."

I won't but the offer is nice.

"Look at it this way, he gets to see how happy you are, and you get to rub it in his face. I mean, you're dating a freaking professional football player."

"Right," I say, not trusting myself to say more. Even if it weren't all fake, Chris is too full of himself to be bothered by me dating anyone.

I shake off my irritation. Today, and until the wedding is over, at least, I am going to be the bigger person. After that, I can go back to loathing him and hopefully never seeing him.

"I love you, Lo Lo." She throws her arms around me and squeezes me tight as the front door opens.

I meet Chris's gaze through the headlock she has me in. His brows inch higher in amusement that speaks of a familiarity with Sierra's and my bond. Sierra steps back and then lifts a hand. "Hey! So glad you two could make it."

While she rushes forward to properly greet Chris and Gretchen, I empty my water glass and set it in the sink.

I take a cleansing breath before I attempt to play nice.

"Hi." The bubbly word comes out a little too forced.

"I love this neighborhood." Gretchen scans the living room with a smile. "Baby, we should totally look at houses over here."

Luckily, I know how much Chris detests the traditional southwestern style houses in this neighborhood, because if he moved in nearby, I'd have to spend my weeknights egging his house.

"Yeah, maybe," he says.

I want to snort at the dismissive way he plays it off.

"Excuse me," I say, leaving them in Sierra's much politer presence.

In my old bedroom, I go to the dresser and pull out my swimsuits. I keep them all here since my apartment doesn't have a pool. None of the options feel appropriate. Too-small bikinis I bought because they were good for tanning, and old ones that are too tight in the butt since it got bigger after the rest of me stopped growing.

I have to remind myself that it doesn't matter. Brogan isn't some guy I'm interested in. There's absolutely no reason to try to impress him.

I pick a black one-piece that I bought to do water aerobics with Grandma last summer. I mistakenly thought I needed something more appropriate than a string-tie bikini. But I only wore it once because when I showed up the first day, half the old ladies were rocking bikinis and tankinis. Plus, I figured if I was going to brave the heat, I should at least get a decent tan.

When I walk back out into the kitchen, I pause at the window. Brogan is sitting at the table with my parents while everyone else is in the pool.

Perfect. I let out a long breath. I guess it's showtime.

Outside, I head straight for Brogan. His mouth curves up when he spots me. I slide into an empty seat next to him.

"Nice day," my dad says, turning his face up to the sky. It *is* a beautiful day. I love the fall in Arizona when the temperatures start to drop from unbearable to just hot.

"What's Alec up to today?" Mom asks. "I'm surprised he didn't tag along."

My mom loves Alec. He lets her fawn over him like a mother hen, something Sierra and I stopped allowing years ago. And he's completely himself around her, giving her all the gossip and insight into his dating life.

"He's at a company picnic."

"For Channel 3?" Her brows knit in confusion.

My anxiety arises at the mention of my job. Me and my big mouth. "Yeah."

"Why didn't you go?" she asks, leaning forward in that way that tells me she has an opinion about me skipping a company function.

"Because I'm here spending time with my family." And because I didn't want to see everyone in the stupid shirts I designed. My attempt to play it off like it's not a big deal isn't working.

Dad shifts in his seat. "Social events are a great way to rub elbows with the executives, network and make connections. It shows loyalty and initiative."

"It's just a picnic." Irritation slips into my tone. He wants to believe that all companies and managers treat their employees with respect and loyalty but that's just not true.

Dad's gaze quickly darts to Brogan and then back to me. Whatever he wants to say, he's tempering his words for my boyfriend's benefit.

"How can you expect to move up in the company when you don't make an effort? Your generation thinks things are just going to be handed to you. That isn't how it works."

"I know, Dad. I do. I work really hard at my job and I'm thankful for it, but I'm not even sure I want to move up. I think I'd rather work for myself."

Both of my parents sigh, quietly, but their disapproval is so loud.

"You want to spend the next thirty years scraping by and worrying about getting work? Being your own boss is nonstop. The job doesn't end."

Mom is never as vocal as Dad in her disapproval, but they are a united front. She has this downturned mouth, worried expression every time we talk about it. "Very few artists are able to support themselves," she says.

Dad jumps right back in. "You have to get your own health benefits and keep track of your finances, do your own taxes—"

"I know," I cut him off. My face heats. The last thing I want is to have this conversation in front of Brogan.

When I glance over at him, he's got a sort of shell-shocked expression like he's trying to figure out what's happening. I rest my hand on his. "Want to take a dip with me?"

"Yeah." He's quick to agree. I can't blame him. I want to get far away from this conversation too.

CHAPTER TWENTY
Brogan

London splashes me from across the net. We're in an epic game of pool volleyball. Me and her uncle Steve against her and Ben.

"Don't need to splash me to distract me, sweetheart."

I can tell she wants so badly to roll her eyes at me. She thinks I'm kidding. The one-piece she put on might not show as much skin as the lingerie she wore the last time we were in a pool together, but I have that memory etched into my brain forever.

"Game point." Ben rolls the ball in his hands and then serves it over the net. It's closer to Steve than me so I let him have it. He hits it up, but not over. I chance a quick look at London as I move into position to spike it. She looks so damn sexy. She's a competitive thing too. The concentration on her face is almost enough to make me hesitate from spiking it over.

Almost.

She and Ben move to stop it at the same time, diving toward each other and knocking heads as the ball falls just in front of them.

"Hell yeah!" Steve calls. He holds up a hand for me. I slap it as I watch London come up out of the water, rubbing her head.

"Are you all right?" I ask.

"You have a hard head," she tells Ben. "Yeah, I'm fine."

I duck under the net and inspect her, running my fingers over the spot. "You've got a bump."

"I'm fine, really."

"We should get some ice on it."

"No way. I want a redo."

Chuckling, I look down into her fiery green eyes.

"I need to grab a beer anyway," Steve says. "Brogan?"

"Yeah. That'd be great."

"I'll come with you," Ben says, wading toward the ladder to get out and leaving me alone with London.

"Are you okay, honey?" Her mom asks from where she sits at a table under a large umbrella blocking the sun. "That looked bad."

"Fine," she calls quietly. I get the feeling even if she was hurt, her ego wouldn't dare let anyone know it.

"I got her, Renee."

"Sports were never London's thing," her dad adds. "You should have seen her the time we signed her up for basketball."

Laughter follows the statement.

London blushes and ducks her head so I can't see her eyes.

Steve reappears with a beer, handing it to me from the edge.

"Thanks," I tell him and then lead her by the elbow. "Come on. You don't want it to get any worse."

She follows and I lift her up onto the edge of the pool in

the shallow end farthest from her family. London watches in amusement as I put the cold can gently on the bump.

She takes over holding it there. "Laying it on a little thick, aren't you?"

"Not at all. This is how I take care of all my fake girlfriends."

I place my hands on either side of her and then dip down into the water in front of her. Those sexy legs of hers graze my chest. I take in some water and then when I pop back up, spit it at her.

Her smile finally makes an appearance. "My family likes you."

"Yeah?" I ask, running a hand over my wet hair.

She nods.

"I like them too." Her family is legit. They've all been nice and welcoming. I can see there is a lot of love there, and London and her sister are obviously tight.

"What's your family like?" she asks, tilting her head so she can more comfortably hold the beer can there.

"I got it," I say, stepping back up to her and taking over to give her arm a rest.

She looks like she wants to fight me for a moment, but then relaxes.

"My family is…chaos." I grin thinking of the small house in Valley where I lived with the Holland brothers.

She searches my face for…something. I can't read her expression.

"I think it's okay." She reaches for the can and neither of us lets go for a moment. She smells like coconuts, and I have the overwhelming desire to lean in and lick her face.

"Mind if we join?" Chris's deep voice cuts through the nice moment.

London takes the can from me and I slowly turn in time to see

Chris step down into the pool with his girlfriend next to him.

"Sure," I say, moving beside London but staying close. I don't like the way he looks at her. Or the way she seems to stiffen every time he's around.

"London, I love your suit." Gretchen smiles at her and moves closer with a floatie. Chris doesn't have a lot of options but to follow. Though he had the option of not coming today.

"Thanks." London's reply has a hint of uncertainty in it like she isn't sure if she's messing with her. Probably because the suit Gretchen is wearing is basically floss. London's suit could be ripped apart and make five of hers. No judgment but I'm afraid to look at Gretchen too closely because I'm pretty sure I can see part of a nipple.

I don't think Gretchen's being petty, though, maybe just a smidge oblivious to the situation. Or, fuck, maybe this is perfectly normal behavior for two girls who have dated the same guy. What the hell do I know?

"I heard the Mavericks won today," Chris says. "Congrats. I think you guys are going to have a great season."

"Appreciate you saying so."

He comes up behind his girlfriend and slides both hands up the back of her thighs and onto her ass. My brows rise.

I keep watching, even though I feel like maybe I shouldn't. It's nothing I haven't seen before—or, hell, probably done at a party—but the atmosphere just feels wrong for that kind of PDA...so wrong.

I glance over at London. She's trying really hard to look anywhere but at where her ex has his hands.

I try to put myself in his position. If London really was my girlfriend, I wouldn't be able to keep my hands off her. Maybe it's my bad for assuming that feeling up a girl in front of her dad was probably crossing a line. Again, what the hell do I know?

I'm gonna have to call Knox or Hendrick for relationship advice—words I cannot believe I'm saying.

Am I playing it too cool to convince this prick I'm her boyfriend? Maybe a little butt-squeeze would really sell it. Before I can decide on how to work that in while my girl sits on the edge of the pool, Ben yells for his brother and Gretchen to swim to the other end.

Fuck it. I come up on her, wrapping my arms around her waist and hoisting her up over my shoulder. That puts her ass right at my shoulder. I smack that perfect, round ass and then keep my hand there. Well, damn, that is nice.

"What are you doing?" London screeches. "Put me down."

"Or what?"

"Brogan Six!"

"Love it when you say my name like that, sweetheart."

I had no idea what to expect from today, but London's family hang is fun. There's food and drinks, lazy naps on lounge chairs, and nice conversations with London's family. The whole thing is like nothing I've ever been a part of. I had no idea families could function like this. I latch on to a little tension between London and her parents over her job situation, but the fact that they're spending the day together despite their differences just reinforces all the ways in which what I had from the man and woman who gave me my DNA was wildly different.

I'm just finishing another game of volleyball in the pool when

I get out and look for London. She disappeared sometime while I was playing and missed the awesome victory dance me and her grandma made up. I don't want to spoil it, but it involved a lot of hip bumping and spirit fingers.

I finally find her inside in the kitchen.

"Hey," I say, standing on the rug so I don't get the floor wet. "Whatcha doing?"

"Nothing."

"Liar. You're hiding. What's wrong?"

She huffs a short laugh. "How are you so certain that I'm lying?"

I pad across the room to her. "I'm an expert on all things London, like any good boyfriend."

She smirks.

"You get this cute little wrinkle right here." I press my finger gently to the spot between her eyes.

"I do not."

She totally does.

"Is everything okay?" I try another tactic to get her to tell me what's up.

"Yeah." She lets a little of her irritation bleed into her tone. "It's dumb."

"Tell me anyway. I say dumb shit all the time."

Another small laugh leaves her lips and she twists her hands in front of her like she isn't sure she wants to confide in me. "I hate him and I hate how he still gets under my skin after all this time."

"Chris," I say, nodding. "Yeah, he seems like a real peach. Why'd you break up?" What I really want to ask is why were you ever with him? He so doesn't seem like the guy for her.

"He cheated on me. Like a *lot*. Basically the entire time we dated. Two years of lies." She shakes her head and looks annoyed. At him and a little at herself, I think.

"We went to high school together but didn't start dating until sophomore year of college. He went to Stanford and I stayed here. He was visiting for Christmas and we ran into each other one night out at a bar…that was it. We were inseparable until he left, then we texted nonstop and took turns going to see the other."

I hook my pointer finger around hers and then run my thumb along the top of her hand.

"We made all these plans for the future. Marriage and kids. We even picked out names. Emily and Jackson." She wrinkles up her nose like the names are ruined for her now. "He let me believe that we were going to have this happily ever after all the while lying and sleeping around behind my back."

What a fucking asswipe. I grind my back teeth.

"I don't get what kind of game he was playing. What was the point of stringing me along? Seems like a lot of effort for sex a few times a month."

"I'm sorry," I say. What I mean is I'd like to punch him for her. I doubt she'd find that romantic. "How'd you find out he was lying?"

"I surprised him. A terrible idea, in hindsight. I showed up at his dorm and he was with another girl. One of many I found out later. You know what was the most infuriating?"

"What?"

"He had the gall to act like I was overreacting. He didn't really think it was cheating since we were at different schools."

"Ah, the different area codes excuse," I say dryly.

"Yeah. Funny how he never mentioned that as a stipulation in our relationship before. I could have been sleeping my way through the frat boys and jocks."

"I can still help you with that last one," I joke, trying to ease some of the hurt I can tell talking about it brings up for her.

She lets out a short laugh. "Anyway. That was two years ago, and I guess I still haven't really gotten over it. I'm over him, just not what he did. I was so naïve."

"You trusted him. That's nothing to be ashamed of." Though I get how hard it is to let people in after you've been jerked around.

She lets out a long breath and attempts to smile. "Let's go back outside. It's getting late and I know you need to leave soon. I'm not letting him ruin a perfectly good pool day."

Nodding slowly, I intertwine our fingers as we walk outside together. I swing our hands lightly between us. "Hey, want to come shopping with me later?"

"Shopping?"

"Yeah, we need some more furniture for the apartment."

Whether the amused expression is over my need for furniture or asking her to help, I'm not sure, but I'm glad when she agrees.

"Sure." She shrugs.

I spot Chris out of the corner of my eye. He's in the pool while his girlfriend lies on a towel at the edge on the opposite end. He glances up at London and me, then moves quickly toward Gretchen and pulls himself up next to her. He leans over and presses a kiss tenderly to her shoulder.

What an asshole. I really want to punch him.

For the next hour I notice a trend. Any time London is nearby, Chris is all over Gretchen. When she's got her back turned or goes inside, he seems to forget he even has a girlfriend.

It's the most bizarre thing I've ever witnessed. And I start to get a better understanding why London was feeling strange earlier. Her ex-boyfriend is dry-humping his new girl right under her nose like it's a sport. It's so obvious to me that he's either trying to make her jealous because he's an asshole, which pisses me off, or because he wants her, which for some reason pisses me off even more.

London and Sierra went to get popsicles from the freezer and when she steps out laughing with her sister, Chris picks that exact moment to kiss Gretchen. The grip on my water bottle tightens. This motherfucker.

I move without thinking.

She's got an orange popsicle in one hand and in the other has another still in the wrapper. One for me, I'd bet my next paycheck on it. That makes something warm spread in my chest. I don't think anyone's ever brought me a popsicle before. And yes, I know it's just a popsicle, but it's more too. It's considerate and thoughtful.

When I'm about six feet away, she notices me heading in her direction. The smile on her face falls away and her lips part in confusion. Sierra is still talking, but I don't think London is listening anymore.

She stops when I'm right in front of her. Sierra's voice trails off. I lean down, brushing her hair back as I whisper in her ear, "Sorry about this."

"What—"

I cut off the question when I drop my mouth to hers. There's a sharp inhale of breath and a second where I'm not sure if she's going to kiss me back or shove me away. I thought I was doing this for her, but the moment I feel her lips against mine, it's just us. I sweep my tongue in her mouth. She tastes like oranges and sugar. I want more. So much fucking more.

I thread one hand through her wet hair and deepen the kiss. Slowly her body slackens against mine. I capture a soft little hum that escapes. I want to hear it again, but then a voice of warning starts to go off in my head. *She's not yours, dickwad. You proved your point, now step away.*

So I do, reluctantly.

Her lashes flutter open slowly. My hands are shaking as I bring them back down to my sides.

Sierra is gone and it's just the two of us on display for her entire family.

"What was that for?" she asks, voice wavering.

I run my tongue over my bottom lip and then clear the lust from my head enough to move to the side and incline my head to where Chris had been before.

"Is he still watching?"

She scans the yard and then brings her gaze back to me. "Yeah."

I clear my throat. I'm struggling not to ask her if she just wants to kick this party and go make out. She's made her interest in pursuing anything with me pretty clear though. As in, she's not at all.

So I shoot her the playful smile she expects from me. I'm not letting my penis ruin a nice gesture. Maybe.

"He's been doing that shit to you all day. Every time you're around he's handsy and shit but when you're not looking, he couldn't care less."

She doesn't look convinced.

"I'm serious."

"That could just be a coincidence."

"Maybe." It's not. I don't believe that for one second. Especially after everything she told me earlier. He gets off on fucking with her.

Her stare drops to my lips then she holds up the still-wrapped popsicle. "Want one?"

"What flavor?" I ask. "Because I have a sudden craving for oranges."

CHAPTER TWENTY-ONE

"**L**ondon?"

I nearly collide with Brogan's back as he stops walking and glances over his shoulder at me. The look on his face is a mixture of amusement and concern.

It's a good look for him. Although right now he could look like an ogre and I might not notice.

"Yeah." I blink several times and move my focus from the way his biceps strain against the white T-shirt to his face. He's still in his red swim trunks and he pulled a ball cap on over his damp hair. The ends have dried and curled up. I desperately want to reach up and run my fingers through it.

I've been following him around the giant furniture store for half an hour while he picks out...I don't even know because all I can think about is that kiss.

That *kiss*.

My stomach flips at the memory.

"I made it weird, didn't I?" he asks, then curses under his breath.

"Huh?" My brain still isn't functioning normally.

He takes off the hat and runs a hand through his hair because apparently he can read minds and wants to mess with me. "Fuck, I'm sorry I kissed you. I just couldn't stand the thought of your asshole ex playing you like that after he was such a jerk while you were together. Who the fuck cheats on a woman like you?"

"It's not weird," I say too quickly. It totally is.

And judging by the "the fuck it isn't" expression on his face, he knows it is as well as I do.

"Can we go back to before? I don't want to lose the best fake girlfriend I've ever had. I can keep my lips to myself." He winks. "Probably."

His concern is sweet, but unwarranted. I'm not mad or even freaked out. I just…want to do it again. Is it possible it's just been so long since I kissed someone new that I'd forgotten how great first kisses are? Or is he really that good? I know the answer to that with zero consideration. Of course he's a great kisser, he's had a lot of practice.

I know that asking my fake boyfriend to kiss me again so I can test a theory I'm working is a terrible idea. Do I consider it? Absolutely. But what I say is, "Yeah, definitely."

"Cool." His lopsided grin reappears. He takes my hand like it's the most natural thing. While I replay what those long fingers felt like tangled in my hair.

"So, what are we looking for?" I ask, stepping away from him and breaking contact but trying to play it off like nothing is wrong. The only thing that's wrong is I haven't had sex in too long, and thanks to Mr. Great Kisser here, my body is all primed for some action. Even hand-holding feels like too much contact right now. It's hormone overload inside me.

"A bed."

"A bed?" I'm sure I misheard him. That's my hormones wishing he'd pull me onto one and kiss the crap out of me. I stop and look around. Sure enough, we're in the section where dozens of king-size beds are made up in cozy, tempting displays.

The universe must be fucking with me. My fake boyfriend didn't kiss me, make me all hot and bothered, and then bring me to pick out a bed, right?

"Yeah, I figured it's time to say goodbye to the old beer pong table and get a proper guest bed."

I'm still staring at him blankly.

"You know, for when my fake girlfriend gets drunk and crashes at my place but refuses to take my bed."

"You're buying me a bed?"

"I mean…" He tilts his head to the side and shuffles uncomfortably. "Not just you."

Right. Of course. It's totally normal to buy a bed for a guest room. But the idea that he's doing it specifically because I slept on his couch is so considerate, I'm a little taken aback.

But not really. Brogan is always considerate. I mean, the guy just kissed me because he was trying to piss off my ex-boyfriend for my benefit. I just…I didn't expect him to be like this.

"So…" One side of his mouth quirks up. "See any you like?"

I shake my thoughts free and force myself to look around. "I'm not so picky."

"Says the woman who wouldn't sleep in *my* bed."

"I wasn't going to kick you out of your own bed."

"Could have just joined me. It's big enough for company." With a cocky grin, he heads through the showroom.

"Right about now I'm wishing I had," I mutter so quietly he doesn't hear me.

Brogan stops next to a low platform bed. "What do you think of this one?"

I shake my head. "You might as well just get a mattress and toss it onto the floor."

He chuckles. "Okay. What about this?"

"You're kidding." I side-eye the futon.

"Yeah. I just wanted to see your face."

We keep going. There are many of the same simple bed with upholstered headboards in varying colors. He skips by all those and heads toward a massive four-poster canopy bed. It looks like something out of a Victorian-era movie but with modern furnishings. The headboard is large with intricate details. The mattress rests on a low-profile platform similar to the first bed, but this one has dark navy posts at each corner that connect at the top. A flowy, gauzy material hangs above it. The whole thing screams sex.

"It's a big bed," I say.

He rests one of his big hands on the posts and then wraps his fingers around it. After giving it a shake, he says, "Sturdy, too."

Heat surges from head to toe as I imagine him naked and on top of me, shaking the whole bed with the force of how hard he fucks me.

"I don't know. It might be too big for that room. I remember the realtor saying something about the third room being smaller than the other two," he says like his brain didn't go down the sex rabbit hole that mine did.

I can't do anything but stare at him. If I speak, there's no telling what will come out.

"What do you think? Too much?" He takes my silence as boredom. "Yeah, you're right. Let's keep looking."

He starts to walk off, but my feet won't move. Brogan stops and looks back. "Everything okay?"

Beside the pulsing between my legs, sure.

"Lo?"

He hardly ever calls me by my nickname, always using my full name instead. I never really thought about it until now.

"Are you all right? You look a little flushed." He closes the distance between us and brings a hand up to cup my cheek. His dark eyes survey my face with such concern.

"I think I want to kiss you again."

His brows lift and his eyes widen.

"I'm so sorry." I squeeze my eyes closed. "That's a terrible idea. We're not really dating. It would complicate things and…It's just been a while since I fooled around with anyone and then you kissed me, and wow, you're a good kisser. My body is on fire. Like literally all I can think about right now is your lips…" I bring a hand to mine and I swear I can still feel the remnants of that first kiss. I realize what I'm doing and drop my hand. Oh my god. I want to disappear into the floor. I just propositioned my fake boyfriend in the furniture store. Does it get any lower than that?

"You know, that first bed wasn't bad. What's so wrong with waking up every morning and rolling out—"

His giant hands frame my face and his thumb sweeps over my

bottom lip. "Why the hell are we still talking about beds?"

I all but goaded him into it, but a surprised squeak still escapes from me as his mouth crashes down onto mine. I throw my arms immediately around his neck and press my body against his—things I've been wishing I'd done the first time.

The second his lips touch mine I forget why I thought this was such a bad idea. Nothing that feels so good could possibly be wrong. Said every woman about to make a huge mistake.

Brogan kisses me like he's dying and I've drunk the antidote that will save him. He devours me. His tongue sweeps into my mouth and he groans. I'm not sure who pulls the other onto the mattress, but my back hits the soft cushion of the giant four-poster bed, and Brogan pins me in place with one giant thigh thrown over my hips. One hand is behind my lower back and the other is in my hair.

I have died and gone to heaven. No one has ever kissed me like this. I'm not sure *I've* ever kissed anyone like this. I'm clinging to him and pulling him tighter against me.

"Excuse me?" We're interrupted by a sales guy who looks like he doesn't get paid enough to deal with customers like us.

I hide behind Brogan's shoulder as he rolls off me.

"Sorry, man," he says, sounding anything but sorry.

"You can't make out on the beds," the guy says. "I'm gonna have to ask you and your girlfriend to leave."

I am mortified.

"Of course." Brogan stands and gives me a wicked grin as he takes my hand to help me up. "This one wasn't for us anyway. Too soft. We like a firm mattress. Right, sweetheart?"

I shoot him a murderous look, but he just wraps an arm around me and leads me out of the store like he isn't sporting a hard-on and I don't have sex hair that gives us away.

Brogan's apartment is only a few blocks from the store. We're quiet for the drive, but as soon as we get inside, his mouth is back on me and our hands are everywhere. He kisses me while leading me through the quiet space. Both of our shirts are gone and my shorts are undone seconds after we make it to the bedroom.

For the second time today, we fall onto a bed together. This one is in fact much firmer. And it smells like him.

He pulls back a fraction and his dark stare darts from my mouth to my eyes. "Are you sure you want to do this?"

I had the entire drive to reconsider. Maybe it's the dumbest idea I've ever had, but I want to do this. Besides, how much worse could we make it at this point? It's not like I'm going to forget how good a kisser he is anytime soon. It's too late. We crossed the line and there's no going back. I lift my head in invitation and Brogan must decide that's confirmation enough because he's kissing me again and I never want him to stop.

My shorts come off next and then his hand slides up and down the curve of my waist as he sucks on my tongue. Long fingers make their way up between the valley of my cleavage and dip under the band of my bra and he flicks open the front clasp.

The cool air hits my pebbled nipples and a rush of warmth floods my lower stomach.

He rolls over onto his back and then pulls me on top of him. My hair falls around his face and he uses both hands to push it back. Only the thin material of my panties and his trunks separate us. I can feel how much he wants me as he lifts his hips and my body rocks against his long, hard dick.

My eyes fall closed and my head tips back. Brogan groans as he moves his hands to cup my breasts.

"I have died and gone to heaven." He sits up and licks a slow circle over one tight bud.

His hands cup and squeeze, and his mouth works me over until I'm arching into him for more and grinding against his dick.

"More." The one word is all I can manage to articulate.

"Tell me what you need, sweetheart." His teeth graze up my neck and his hands go around my back. He draws me against his chest, fingers tangling in my hair and pulling my head back to give him better access to the sensitive column.

"You're wearing too many clothes."

He lifts his hips to tease me with the hard length I'm sitting on. "So are you."

"You have on more than me," I argue.

"I need to taste every inch of you before I'm ready to fuck you."

A jolt of pleasure rolls down my spine at the promise of his words, but I'm needy and impatient.

"I never thought it'd be so hard to get you naked," I grumble, to which he laughs. His warm breath tickles my skin. He brushes his mouth over mine and then freezes.

"Don't freak out."

It takes me a second to realize why he'd issue such a warning. Footsteps sound in the apartment, and before I've quite figured out what to do, Archer appears in the doorway.

Brogan has my chest pressed to his and his knees are blocking my ass, I think, but it's still clear what the hell we're doing.

Archer takes in the scene, eyes wide, then turns to face the other way.

"Sorry. Didn't realize we had company," he shouts, then holds up an envelope in one hand. "This came for you. Looked important, but now it feels awkward. Fuck…" While keeping his eyes averted, he walks closer and sets the envelope on the edge of the bed. "Okay, then. I'm gonna go to my room now. Good to see you, London."

Brogan keeps laughing as I bury my face in his chest.

"You too." I hold a hand up over my head in an awkward wave.

"He's gone," Brogan says, loosening his grip on me.

No sooner has he said the words than Archer's voice comes closer again. "Oh, and uh…some of the guys are on their way over."

CHAPTER TWENTY-TWO
Brogan

London is muttering into my chest, something about jumping out a window.

Chuckling, I drop a kiss to her forehead. "Still want me to take off my shorts?"

She groans and climbs off me. As she stands in front of me in nothing but her panties, I seriously consider shutting and locking us in for the foreseeable future. She is stunning. Her long brown hair hangs over her shoulders, perfect tits peeking out at me. Her panties aren't as sexy as the red ones she had on the other night, but she's the kind of girl that doesn't need any of that to be sexy as fuck.

I get out of bed and stand in front of her, running my hands up and down her arms. "Second-guessing coming home with me?"

"No," she says with a shake of her head. Then a sheepish smile. "Maybe a little, but not because I don't want to finish what we started."

"You don't have to go."

"It's fine. I should get home anyway. This was..." She trails off. "An interesting day."

"We could go to your place, and I could show you just how much more interesting it can get." I wrap my arms around her, holding her hostage.

"Alec is home, and I don't think I can sneak you in without answering a hundred questions first." She wiggles out of my hold and quickly gets dressed.

"It looks like you should have been shopping for more than a bed." She motions with her head toward my makeshift nightstand. A moving box propped up next to the bed.

"Why? This one works just fine." I reach into the box and pull out a strip of condoms.

She laughs. "Oh my god. That's the most bachelor thing I've ever seen."

I give her a sheepish smile before I drop them back inside. Yeah, she's right. I probably do need a proper nightstand, but picking out all that shit is exhausting.

I reluctantly pull on my T-shirt and adjust my dick, hoping he'll get the message this isn't happening today.

I hug her again when we're both fully clothed. "Don't go."

The front door closes, and the house gets louder immediately. I recognize Tripp and Merrick's voices through the walls.

"Your teammates are going to think we were in here having sex."

"We would have been if they'd waited another fifteen minutes."

"This is probably a bad idea," she says.

"Probably." I suck her bottom lip into my mouth. Her arms go around my neck and it's several seconds of kissing each other like it might be the last time before she pulls back. She looks beautiful with puffy lips and flushed cheeks, and I get off on the fact I did that to her.

She puts a foot of distance between us, then her gaze drops to the bed. "More fan mail?"

I forgot about the envelope Archer dropped off. I step forward and pick it up. My brows furrow. My name and address are handwritten on the front, but it's the return name that makes me pause. Sabrina Whitlock. *Sabrina.* It's probably a coincidence. I haven't had another text from her in a week or so. But my stomach swirls with unease anyway.

"Brogan?" London says my name, head dipping to catch my gaze.

"Sorry." I shake my head and shove the letter into my pocket. "Nah. Just junk mail. I don't give out this address."

"Maybe a stalker fan then."

I snag her arm and tug her back to me. I really don't want her to go. I press my lips against hers. "I hope she's cute like you."

"I am not a stalker," she says.

"Just a fan who once sent me her panties."

"Those weren't mine."

I gasp like I'm shocked. "No? Say it isn't so. I'll have to dig through my collection and toss those out."

She makes a deep hum of disapproval, and I get more than a little enjoyment out of the possible jealousy I detect.

She pulls back again, this time moving toward the door. "Walk me out?"

"Duh," I say, stepping into my shoes before joining her. "What kind of boyfriend do you think I am?"

"The kind that isn't real," she says quietly as we walk hand in hand down the hall and into the living room where Archer is chilling with Tripp and Merrick.

I slap her on the ass. "My dick is *really* hard. That real enough for you?"

Her mouth parts in shock and then a surprised laugh escapes her lips. The guys in the living room glance up as we come into view. Archer's smirking but the rest don't give the fact that London and I were just in my room together a second thought. Why would they? They already thought we were sleeping together. Something I hope to make a reality very, very soon.

"Six!" Tripp says.

"What's up, guys?" I squeeze London's hand a little tighter so she can't flee like I'm sure she's considering.

"Archer says you're unbeatable on the new Street Fighter and I want to test that theory."

I laugh. "You got it, but first I'm gonna take London home." I glance at my girl. I really want her to stay, even if it's not to make out. "Unless... you changed your mind and can stay a little longer?"

Maybe now that she's faced everyone and seen it's no big deal, she'll hang. Although, who am I kidding? If she does, I'm probably dragging her right back to my room.

"Actually, I already called an Uber," she says and lifts a hand. "Bye, guys."

To everyone else it probably doesn't look it, but I can tell she's rushing out. I walk her out to the car waiting at the curb.

We stop a foot away and I take her hand. "Damn. I was really hoping to drive you home so we could make out some more. My truck has plenty of room in the back."

She giggles. "A selling point I'm sure you've tested on many occasions."

I have, but I don't know if I've ever wanted to as badly as I do now. "What are you doing tomorrow?"

"Working."

"Right."

She seems amused as she watches me try to figure out when I can see her next.

"Tomorrow night. Some of us are going to Tripp's place to watch Monday Night Football."

"Wouldn't that be weird?"

"No. Not at all. There'll be other people too." I squeeze her hand. "Come with me. Please?" I'm not above begging.

"Yeah." She nods. "All right."

She steps away from me. I hold open the door for her as she ducks into the car. Then shut her in and watch as she leaves.

Inside, I find Archer in the kitchen while our guests are playing video games. His smirk grows as I get closer.

"Interesting day," he says quietly, also signing.

"You're telling me." I take a seat at the island and the envelope in my shorts digs into my thigh, reminding me of the letter.

I take it out as Archer fires off the obvious question I expected. *"So, I guess things aren't so fake anymore?"* He shakes his head.

I grin, drop the envelope on the counter, and drum my fingers on it excitedly as he adds, *"I never thought I'd see the day, you with a real girlfriend."*

"Why?" I ask, a little defensively.

"Maybe because you've said time and again that you don't want

one and that these are the years to have fun and not take anything too seriously."

I have said that. Many times. *"She's cool as fuck and I hope there's a lot more making out, but it's not like that. We're just having fun…and kissing her is the most fun I've had in a long time."*

God, it's been so long I don't even know what it'd be like to date someone for real anymore. I don't think I'd be sacrificing fun with her, but the idea still gives me pause.

He laughs, then tips his head toward the envelope on the counter. *"Junk?"*

"Where'd you find this?"

"With the rest of our mail." He glances at the stack of junk magazines and marketing brochures. *"Who's Sabrina Whitlock?"*

"I'm not sure."

"You're acting funny. What aren't you saying?"

"Nothing."

"Okay. Then just open it."

I do, and that uneasy feeling I had at seeing her name spreads and intensifies.

> Brogan,
> My name is Sabrina. I've been trying to contact you via text, but I must have the wrong number. I think I'm your sister.

CHAPTER TWENTY-THREE
Brogan

Archer looks up from the letter to gauge my reaction. I think I'm too much in shock to feel anything else.

"This has to be a joke, right?" He tosses the paper to the counter. He looks...mad.

I shrug, not trusting my voice yet. The guys are still carrying on in the other room, fifteen feet away.

He picks up his phone and while staring down at the letter, taps out something on the screen.

"What are you doing?"

"I'm calling her. I want to tell this lying piece of shit that it's not fucking funny to—"

I jump up and take the phone from him, hitting end before he finishes that sentence or calls some random person. Not random... my sister. Maybe.

"You don't know that she's lying."

It doesn't seem possible, but I can't outright dismiss the possibility.

"It's too much of a coincidence. Now that you're a professional football player with some success and notoriety she pops up out of the blue?" He shakes his head, face made of stone.

"She's not just popping up." I let out a breath. *"For the past few months, I've been getting texts."* I pull out my phone and show him. *"There were more, but I deleted the first couple."*

He's quiet as he reads through them. *"Why didn't you say anything?"*

His mask falls, and I see the surprise and pain that I kept it to myself.

"Because…" I run a hand over my hair. *"The stuff with my parents had just happened and I didn't want you to get worked up all over again. I thought it was just another scam."*

The words taste bitter. Another scam like my parents loving me and suddenly wanting to be in my life.

"Do you think they're behind it?"

I shrug. I didn't until now. It would make more sense than a sister suddenly appearing. *"What do you think?"*

"I think that if you really had a sister out there, you would have heard from her before now."

"Yeah." It makes sense. The timing is suspicious.

Archer takes the letter and crumples it up. *"If she contacts you again, we can go talk to a lawyer. We'll file a restraining order if we have to."*

I nod, knowing he's probably right. The lengths people will go to take advantage of others astounds me. How low do you have to be?

"You hungry?" Archer asks, back to his light, cheery self. Though his brow is still furrowed. *"I was going to order some pizza."*

"Yeah. I'm just gonna take a shower. London and I were out in the sun all day."

"All right." He watches me closely, then comes over and hugs me. *"Love you, brother."*

The following night, I pick up London and we go to Tripp's house.

"I thought you said there were just going to be a few people," she says as we walk through the packed living room.

"Compared to the last party you went to, this is small."

Her light laughter loosens some of the tension I've been carrying around all day. The letter from Sabrina has continued to haunt me. Archer's been hovering and I know he means well, but it takes me back to when we were kids and he first started inviting me over to his house.

We were already good friends so of course I wanted to hang with him, but I also knew there was some small part of him that was doing it out of pity.

London and I grab drinks and find an open spot on the couch in front of Tripp's huge TV.

It's a tight spot, so London is practically sitting on my lap. I drop a palm to her bare thigh.

"I missed you."

Her eyes light up with amusement. "You saw me yesterday."

"Twenty-five hours and fifteen minutes, but who's counting?"

Her gaze darts from my eyes to my mouth. I lean in and brush my lips against hers.

She sighs into me, then pulls back. "We should talk about it."

"Mhmmm." I take her mouth a little harder.

She kisses me back, then presses on my chest. "That's not talking."

"We're using our mouths. It's basically the same thing."

She laughs, but wraps her arms around my neck and then she's the one initiating contact with her lips.

"Yo, Six!" Tripp calls.

"Ignore him," I say to her when she stops kissing me.

Tripp yells again, louder this time.

Reluctantly, I pull back and look at him. "What?"

He grins like he knows he was taking me from a very nice moment with my girl. "I need to borrow your girl."

"Excuse me?" My grip tightens instinctively around London.

"You too. Come on. It'll be fun."

"What have you gotten me into?" she asks, not seeming the least bit annoyed by the fact we were interrupted.

"I actually have no idea." I stand with her and place her on the ground next to me, quickly lacing my fingers through hers.

We head toward Tripp in the kitchen and when we get closer I can see a few of the guys have started a game of Phase 10.

"What exactly do you need us for?" I ask, arching a brow in question. Normally, I'd be up for just about anything, but not when the other option is making out with London.

Tripp pulls a chair out next to him. "London, girl, have a seat."

She glances briefly at me, but then moves toward him. "Oh, I love this game. My family used to play it all the time."

"Brogan, I grabbed you a seat over there." He points across the table.

"No," I say, unmoving. A quick scan of the table and they aren't even playing pairs. "Fuck off. You can't steal my date just because you can't find one."

He flips me off. "I can find plenty, but don't want one. Remember what that was like?" He smirks at me.

Of course I remember, it was only a few weeks ago. Now though... I'm having fun with London.

"I'm colorblind. I need her eyes."

I glance at the table where the multi-colored cards are laid out. Fuck. I know he is. The guy showed up to practice one day talking about his new blue shirt. It was purple. Like *super* purple.

"Fine," I relent and put a table's worth of distance between us. At least now I can look at her.

Except watching Tripp whisper into her ear isn't exactly doing it for me. I glare hard at him. He looks over and smiles all smug-like. What the hell are they whispering about? And why is she smiling and nodding along?

Cody keeps his voice low as he speaks next to me. "Seems like your *arrangement* is working out well."

"Yeah." I pull my stare away from Tripp and London.

Cody looks at me like he's waiting for me to deny my very real interest in London.

"Going to give me another lecture?" I ask.

"Not at all. I like London for you. You've been more focused than ever, playing well, and she doesn't seem too caught up in the lifestyle."

"She's not." Although I don't think she'd turn down another swim in the rooftop pool at Slade's. I smile at her across the table. Tripp is saying something, and she laughs easily at him.

"Keep doing what you're doing, Six, and you'll be breaking my records."

I'm glad that our arrangement has helped everyone else's focus return to my performance on the field, but right now it's the least of my concerns. I want her. All my focus is on that.

Tripp and London wipe the table with the rest of us for the first two games.

"My good luck charm." He wraps an arm around her and squeezes.

London beams at his words, but then her gaze flits to me. I wonder if she remembers that's what I called her.

For the next half hour, I spend as much time watching Tripp cuddle up to London as I do paying attention to the cards. London is as charmed by him as Tripp is with her. They high-five and talk smack to everyone else every time they win. I concentrate on not tossing the table at him.

"It'll be hard to run when I take out your kneecaps," I mumble as he wraps an arm around London's shoulders. I swear he lets it linger there a little longer than necessary.

Merrick chuckles next to me. "You all right, rookie?"

"Peachy."

We finish another game and I stand up quickly from the table, sending my chair flying backward. "Okay. Time to switch it up. Give me back my girl."

"One more round," Tripp says.

"Fine, but she's with me."

"No way. London and I are a team." He scoots closer to her. "A fucking great team. We are smoking you guys."

"Aww, rookie, calm down." Cody tips his head toward London

and Tripp. "I think they're kinda cute together."

"What? I— They're not fucking cute together. Take it back. *They're* not even together. She's *my* girlfriend." Wasn't he just saying she was good for me? What the fuck? My chest is tight, and frantic energy courses through me. Somewhere deep down I know this is an overreaction to my fake girlfriend, but all I can think is *mine*.

London's mouth falls open and then she smiles at me. Fuck, she's so beautiful.

Tripp's face goes from surprise to blank to laughing so fast I don't know what's happening. But then the rest of the guys around us join in.

"Pay up." Cody holds out his hand. The guys at the table all hand over cash.

"You cheated," Merrick says. "Calling them cute together. You were clearly baiting him."

"And it worked like I knew it would." Cody arranges his money and then folds it in half, stands, and cuffs me on the shoulder as he walks off. "Thanks, rookie."

"You fucking played me." I shake my head at them.

"Sorry," Tripp says. "The game is boring. Have to get our kicks somewhere."

He holds up his hand to London. "Nice work, Lo. That laugh was perfection. Every time you did it, your boy looked like he wanted to toss the table at my face."

"You were in on it too?!" I ask my not-so-innocent girlfriend.

She walks over, looking guilty, but still as beautiful as ever. "I'm sorry. I didn't think you'd be so easily fooled by a little flirting."

I grab a fistful of her T-shirt and tug her to me. "You don't look very sorry, sweetheart."

She drapes her arms over my shoulders and then lifts up on her toes, bringing her lips an inch away from mine. "I have an idea of how to make it up to you."

My brows rise with interest and a little surprise. I don't speak girlfriend well, but I speak sex and that was a clear invitation.

I lean down and take her legs out from under her, then toss her over my shoulder.

"Oh my god, Brogan. Put me down."

"In time, sweetheart." I jut my chin at Tripp. "Borrowing your room. Payback's a bitch."

He just chuckles as I head toward the stairs that lead to the bedrooms in his place.

"You did not just announce to the whole party that we're going to have sex in his room." She wriggles in my hold to get free.

"Well, I hadn't, but if that's what you want." I raise my voice. "I'm going to take my girlfriend upstairs and we're gonna—"

She smacks my ass before I finish the statement. "No, we're not. We're just going to talk."

The noise of the party dies off as we get to the top of the stairs. Tripp's room is open. I walk in and set her down, then kick the door behind us closed.

She smooths her hair down. "You're a very convincing fake boyfriend."

"I'm not playing, sweetheart." I take her mouth and walk her back to the bed.

She kisses me back as frantic and needy as I feel, but then pauses. "Wait. We need to talk."

My fingers slide under the hem of her T-shirt. "Okay. Let's talk."

Her laugh is tight as she sits on the bed and puts more distance between us. "I'm serious."

"Me too."

"What are we doing?" she asks. "We are pretending to date, but now kissing for real...I don't want this to screw up everything else."

"It won't. I like you. We're just enjoying the benefits of our arrangement."

She wrinkles her nose.

"Yeah, that sounds way too businesslike for the dirty things I want to do to you."

Her eyes spark with heat. "Are you sure? I like you too, but what if we start messing around and then you get bored of me or decide you want to sleep with someone else? I don't think I could keep pretending to be your girlfriend."

"I am not going to get bored of you. And the only person I want to sleep with right now is you."

"You're just saying that because you want to sleep with me. You don't know how you'll feel after."

"I promise to keep being your awesome boyfriend through the wedding and end of the regular season, just like we planned. My penis belongs to you." I tilt my head to the side. "That sounded weird. I won't hook up with anyone else. It's just me and you."

It suddenly hits me that she might say no. I know she wants me, but she's much more levelheaded than me. What if she decides I'm not worth it? That this arrangement isn't what she wants anymore?

My heart races while I wait for her to say something. She hesitates another moment, then nods slowly. "Okay."

"Yeah, we're doing this?" I say, unable to hide my excitement.

"Yes. Your penis belongs to me." She grins. "Bring it over here."

"Not here." It suddenly hits me that I don't want her to think of Tripp in any capacity when I'm fucking her. I want her in my bed only.

"But I thought…"

"Stay with me tonight."

"I have work in the morning."

"What time?" We have the day off so my usual Monday night plans include staying up late and sleeping in, but I'm flexible if it means waking up to her.

"I have to be there by nine."

I do some fast math. "Then that gives us ten hours."

CHAPTER TWENTY-FOUR

London

"**F**or a guy who says he enjoys casual sex, we seem to be struggling to accomplish it," I say to Brogan as the two of us carry Archer into their apartment.

While we were busy flirting and kissing at the party, Archer was playing beer pong. And losing terribly, apparently.

"You two still haven't had sex?" Archer asks, slurring the words together. He stumbles over…absolutely nothing, and Brogan quickly grabs him around the middle and moves in front of him.

"All right, buddy. *Couch or bedroom?*" Brogan asks.

"*You're not staying up and having a beer?*"

"*I think you've had enough for the both of us tonight.*" Brogan navigates Archer to the couch and drops him onto it. I am exhausted and I was barely contributing to the effort. Drunk football players are heavy.

"K. Go have sex now. I'm just gonna rest here a minute and

then go to bed." He takes his hearing aids out and tosses them on the coffee table.

Brogan's smirking as he grabs a throw blanket and pillow and basically tucks in Archer, who already has his eyes closed.

I watch on, a little amused and a lot endeared.

He taps Archer on the leg. "Hey."

"Hmm?"

"If you need anything," he starts and then taps him again. Archer's eyes finally open. This time when he starts again, he signs as he speaks, *"If you need anything, holler."*

Archer nods and then curls up on his side.

Brogan shakes his head as he finally turns to me.

"Sorry about that." One side of his mouth pulls up into a half smile.

"It's okay." A bout of nerves takes root in my stomach. There's nothing stopping us from finally getting naked and I'm suddenly nervous.

He stalks toward me slowly, then takes my hand. "Still want to stay?"

"Yeah."

"Good. I don't have to hold you here against your will." He takes my legs out from under me and carries me like a child down the hall and into his room.

Brogan doesn't bother turning on the lights or shutting the door as he lays me down on his bed in the dark room.

"What about Archer?" I ask as he takes off my shoes and tosses them to the floor. "Will he be okay?"

"He's most likely passed out until noon tomorrow." His big hands glide up my legs. "What time do you need to wake up?"

"I'll need to go by my place to shower and change, so seven-ish."

"How about seven thirty? You can shower here." He drops a kiss just above my knee, then follows it with a light bite on my inner thigh. "Seven forty-five and I'll even make you breakfast."

I sit up and run my fingers through his hair. It's thick and a little long and soft to the touch. "How can I say no to that?"

He kisses me then, pushing me back onto the bed. His hands seem like they're everywhere, but he doesn't immediately try to get me naked.

"Much better," he murmurs against my lips.

"What?"

"You in my bed. I couldn't stand the thought of fucking you anywhere else. My sheets. My scent. My dick making you feel so good."

A shiver rolls down my body. "Promises, promises."

He grinds into me. The hard ridge of his cock rubs against the aching spot between my legs.

"Patience, sweetheart."

Who would have thought I'd be the one trying to speed things up? Not me, but here I am panting and so ready that I feel like I might die at this rate.

"Maybe I just want you more than you want me."

He stills and looks down at me, one brow cocked and a dark expression on his face. He sits back and takes my hand in his, then guides it to the front of his jeans. "You feel that? I've been walking around hard like this for weeks."

"For weeks?"

He moves my hand up and down him slowly. His jaw tightens

and his words come out clipped. "Every time you're around. Seeing you in my jersey or that black swimsuit, those red heels, the little black dress, even your laugh does this to me."

"I haven't worn those red heels since the first night I met you."

"I know." He lunges for me then, kissing me harder than he had been before and with more urgency.

My hands fumble to get his pants undone and he lets me slide my hand down until my fingers are wrapped around his hard cock. He groans as I squeeze him. His reaction makes me want him even more. I love that every reaction from him is so genuine. He doesn't hold back, so neither do I.

Pushing him back, I move so I'm hovering over him and drop my head into his lap. He pushes his pants down his thighs as I take him into my mouth.

"Oh fuck," he groans. He abandons the task of getting his pants all the way off and, instead, cups the back of my head with one hand. His thumb strokes over my head as I slowly glide down until he hits the back of my throat. He's long and thick, just like the rest of his body.

"That feels so good." He gathers my hair in his hands, so it's out of my face. "Want to watch you take me, sweetheart."

My pulse quickens and warmth spreads all over my body as I feel his heated gaze. My stare lifts to him. His lids are hooded and jaw tight.

A moan escapes my lips, and he shudders under me. Before I know what's happening, he's shifted us again so I'm flat on my back. He stands next to the bed and removes his pants, then his shirt. I swallow thickly as I take him in, in all his naked glory. Large muscles and thick ridges that showcase how hard he pushes his body regularly for football. His shoulders are broad and his thighs are impressive. He's big everywhere. I was not prepared.

"Come here." He takes my hand and helps me off the bed. My legs are wobbly and the pulse between them won't be ignored.

Slowly, he lifts my shirt up over my head. My bra goes next. He takes a moment to appreciate the view and even drops a kiss between the valley of my breasts before he continues. He undoes the side zipper on my skirt and pushes it down. He squats in front of me, lifts one foot for me to step out, then the other. It's the most sensual way anyone has ever undressed me and so unexpected, given we almost had sex in his teammate's bedroom earlier.

"Look at you," he says, staring up at me. The only barrier between us is my black panties and he guides those down past my hips like he's unwrapping a present that he never wants to end. When they're gone, he just keeps staring and my skin prickles with excitement and nerves.

I've seen some of the women he's been with, but surprisingly— the way he's looking at me—I can't find a self-conscious bone in my body.

As he stands, his hands glide up my legs to my waist and then around to my back. The tips of his fingers brush the top of my ass. With one hand, he reaches over to the box acting as his nightstand and grabs a strip of condoms. I count at least three and I hope that's him planning ahead.

"So many things I want to do with you. I don't know where to start."

Before I can offer a few suggestions —namely fucking me so hard I get a concussion from my head banging against the headboard—he lifts me up into his arms and walks in the opposite direction of the bed.

"Where are we—"

My question is cut off when my back hits the wall. His grin is mischievous, and his voice is all sex when he says, "Wrap your legs around me."

I comply happily. Brogan somehow manages to open the foil and cover himself while keeping me from falling. And quickly too. I'm aware somewhere in the back of my mind that this is not the first time he's pulled this move, but I don't care. His past doesn't concern me. This night is all I want to focus on. This night and this man. Morning will come, as it always does, and I'll worry about everything else then.

My shoulder blades dig into the wall behind me, and my hands rest on his shoulders. He takes one hand and kisses the top before draping it around his neck. I move the other instinctively, and he turns his head to press his lips into the crook of my arm. "I'm not even inside you yet and I know I'm never going to want to leave."

My stomach flips and my heart rate speeds up.

"Ready, sweetheart?"

My throat is thick with emotion and excitement, so I nod.

"I want to hear you say the words."

"Need an ego boost even now?" I ask, voice breathy. "Isn't my being naked and wrapped around you enough confirmation that I want you?"

His smile grows at the last two words. "Maybe I just like hearing it."

"I want you, Brogan Six."

"Say it again." His mouth meets mine, stealing a quick kiss before he rests his forehead against mine.

The tip of his cock nudges my entrance, thick and hard.

I open my mouth to speak, but a groan comes out instead.

His smirk is so satisfied, and I guess it should be. I'm on the edge and he's not even inside me yet.

"I want," I say, and he pushes the tip in. My eyes fall closed.

"What's that?" he teases, running his lips down the column of my neck.

"I want," I start again, and he rewards me the same way but giving me more of him. "Oh god, I need you."

He lets out a low groan as he buries himself completely. My legs quiver as all the muscles in my core clench around him.

"Never leaving this pussy," he grits out, jaw tight as he begins to move. The look of raw, unfiltered emotion and pleasure on his face is such a turn-on. There's no mask with Brogan. This is him, wanting me, being in this moment with me. I'm not sure I've ever felt more cherished by someone.

I want to erase those thoughts from my mind and just focus on the way my body feels, but my heartstrings are being tugged without my permission. I like him. I like how he makes me feel when I'm with him.

My thoughts are finally chased away when he repositions us and carries me back to the bed. Every step jolts us together and I'm so close that I know it won't take long before I'm falling apart.

He lays me down on the mattress, then presses a kiss to my hip. "Turn over, sweetheart."

My body shivers with excitement as I roll onto my stomach. He can't seem to decide how he wants me, or maybe he wants me the same way I want him—every way possible.

He smacks my ass lightly, but with enough sting that I cry out.

"Oh, fuck."

"You like that?"

I nod.

Without warning, he does it again. My pussy clenches as the pain rockets through my body. His warm mouth covers the spot, and he kisses me tenderly.

Then he wraps an arm around my waist and pushes into me. The angle is different, but no less divine. His mouth continues to press kisses into my back as his cock thrusts in and out at a slow, rhythmic pace. He's unhurried, but possessing my body in a way that there's no denying his reverence.

Seconds pass with us both panting. I can't hold off the spike of pleasure, even though I want to so that I can keep living in this moment. I don't want it to end.

"It feels too good," I say, almost delirious.

"Not yet," he groans. "I want to watch you come with my dick buried inside you."

He pulls out and I whimper at the lost sensation, but when I move onto my back, he wastes no time climbing onto the bed with me and giving me exactly what I want. *Him.*

My eyes flutter closed. My orgasm is right there and I'm no longer able to do anything but let it pulse over me in waves. I cry out, back arching from the bed. When I open my eyes, he's staring back at me with a look of awe.

"So pretty." His voice is barely restrained. "I wish you could see yourself right now."

My pussy clenches around him as my orgasm continues so long that I'm pretty sure it's triggered another.

He lets out a growl as his pace increases and then he's coming with a loud groan that vibrates in his chest.

We cling to each other, continuing to fuck even after we're both too tired and limp, and we've already come. It feels too good to stop.

A delirious giggle escapes from my lips.

"Told you I was never leaving." He swipes his mouth over mine and then slows to a stop. I know it's coming, but the second he pulls out, it's still a shock.

My body is one big nerve, and I just lie there feeling exposed and wonderful and terrified and wondering how long until we can do that again.

"Maybe you should just quit your job so we can stay in bed forever," he says nearly mirroring my thoughts. He gets rid of the condom and then flops onto his back.

Laughing, I curl up on my side and rest a hand on his bare chest. "Don't tempt me."

For several minutes we lie there, unspeaking and catching our breath.

He props his head up with a hand and turns toward me. "Can I ask you something?"

His breaths are still labored, but he has that energetic spark back in his eyes.

"Sure," I say hesitantly, unsure where he's going with a lead like that.

"What's the deal with your parents and your job?"

"You want to talk about my parents right now?" I ask, glancing down at his dick, which is only about halfway deflated.

"We could talk about anything right now. It's not going to change the fact I'm going to fuck you again as soon as I can."

I laugh, but then say, "What do you want to know?"

"Everything, but let's start with your job."

"You mean the one at the station or my little drawing hobby?" Another short laugh leaves my mouth.

"They call it that?" Brogan's brows disappear under the floppy piece of hair on his forehead. "That's bullshit."

"Originally, I was going to follow in my dad's footsteps and be a lawyer, like Sierra."

"Why didn't you?"

"I took an art class my sophomore year and fell in love with it. They weren't happy but when I got the job at Channel 3 they were excited that I had a stable, steady paycheck." I take a breath. "Eventually, I want to be my own boss, set my own hours, and pick the projects I work on. Every time I bring it up, they freak out. Sierra says my dad worries that I'm not going to be able to support myself, but I've never once asked them to help me, and the illustration jobs, when I book them, pay better than my regular job at the news station."

I hadn't meant to unload on him or get fired up about it. I try my best not to think about it anymore than I have to. It's not like I'm going to change it. Dad's made his stance very clear. Supporting myself by being an artist isn't a real job to him.

"I'm sorry." Brogan's fingers trail over my head into my hair.

"I've accepted that they're never going to be on board with it." I shrug.

"Is that why you haven't quit to pursue it full time?"

I start to say no but have to admit that there is some small part of me that might be holding back for that very reason. "Partly. But also...what if it doesn't work out?" There are a lot of people trying to make a full-time job out of the thing they love and not succeeding.

"What if it does?"

"You are a hopeless optimist." I lean forward and kiss him.

"Good people deserve good things. Plus, you're really fucking talented."

"You've only seen like two things I've done."

"So show me more."

"No." I laugh as I roll away from him.

He moves on top of me, holding himself up so he isn't crushing me, but instead he's like a weighted blanket that I want to stay under for a very long time. "Why not?"

"I don't know." I continue laughing at the earnest look in his eye.

"You're really good. I'm not just saying that to get in your pants." He waggles his brows.

"No?" I run my fingers up and down his back.

"No," he confirms. "But if it helps keep you naked, I will spend all night telling you how fucking incredible I think you are."

"Wow. That's really convincing." My body shakes with more laughter.

"You're smart." He kisses my lips, then scoots lower. "And kind." His mouth brushes over my neck. "And sexy." He licks one nipple. "And you are good at what you do. The best illustrator I know." He kisses my stomach just below my belly button, then looks up at me.

"I'm the only illustrator you know."

"Doesn't make you any less."

My heart squeezes at his words. So sincere, even if it's an outrageous claim.

"You're not so bad yourself," I say. Those aren't the right words for what he is. He's kind and smart and talented—all those things he said about me, but he's also just good. He wants the best for everyone around him, but I never hear him talk about what he wants outside of football.

"Not bad, huh?" He moves lower, using his broad shoulders to widen my legs so I'm open to him. Heat pools in my stomach again as he runs one long finger down my slit.

I'm still so sensitive and his light touch has me pressing against him for more.

"Are you sure you're not misremembering?" he asks, continuing to tease me with just the drag of his calloused fingers against my swollen flesh. "I think your exact words were 'it feels too good.'"

"I think your memory is bad." I tease him back with my words. We're playing a game right now, and admitting just how much I like him feels like losing.

"I don't think so." He drops an open-mouthed kiss to the inside of my thigh, and my hips lift off the bed of their own accord. His deep chuckle ghosts across my pussy, and I want to give in. I want to say all the things I'm thinking, yell at the top of my lungs, kiss him until he knows without a doubt no one has ever made me feel better than him. But I know I'll regret it when this thing is over between us.

I gave so much of myself in my relationship with Chris, and when it was over, I felt empty. And the way Brogan makes me feel right now—I don't ever want that to end.

CHAPTER TWENTY-FIVE
London

"**G**od, I'm so jealous."

"Says the girl who spent the last few weeks on the beach with her new husband drinking cocktails with little umbrellas." I roll my eyes at Paige as I fill another goody bag with bachelorette essentials like hand sanitizer, breath mints, lip balm, Tylenol, and of course a beaded necklace with little penises. They go perfectly with the penis straws and naked men figurines to freeze inside the ice cubes I bought for the pre-outing cocktail hour I'm hosting before we head out on the town.

Sierra and Ben wanted to do a dual bachelor and bachelorette night, but I talked her into a girls-only hour before a night out.

My best friend just got back from her honeymoon and is keeping me company while I prepare for the big event.

She picks up one of the penis straws and holds it up. "I don't know. It sounds like you got dicked-down better than me."

My face flushes as memories of last night pervade my mind.

"You should see your face right now." She laughs.

"Am I as red as I feel?"

"Like a tomato." Her grin widens. "I assumed a guy like Brogan Six would be memorable in bed, but it must have been sensational. Your glow rivals mine, and I worked hard on this tan the past three weeks."

"He's just…" I struggle to figure out how to accurately describe him or just…any of it. "I don't know. I've either been with some real duds or he's exceptional."

"I think you know the answer to that."

"It isn't just the sex," I say. "He's different than I expected. Deeper. More considerate, more thoughtful, just…more."

Her dark auburn hair falls forward as she tips her head down and studies me carefully, making me self-conscious with the admission. I know Paige would never judge me, but I still feel a flash of panic that I've opened myself up in a way that I can't take back. I know holding in the words won't keep me safer, but it feels that way sometimes.

"You like him."

"Of course I do. He's Brogan Six. Everyone likes him." My tone is light-hearted with a tinge of vulnerability.

"Everyone doesn't know him. They just think they do."

"I guess, but it's still hard to wrap my mind around whatever we're doing, knowing that he quite literally has a line of women waiting for us to break up. To fake break up." I finish another goody bag and set it with the others. "You should see the way they come up to him at parties like they don't even see me."

"I will destroy them," she says automatically, always wanting to have my back. God, I love her for that.

"No, it's not even them. They're just reacting to the lifestyle he's crafted, which screams that the women he's with are disposable." My throat tightens on the last word.

"He doesn't think you're disposable."

"No, of course he would never say that. He's a good, decent guy, but that is quite literally the terms of our relationship. He made sure we had an expiration date from the very beginning."

The look she gives me is bordering on pity.

"And somehow I still let myself get in over my head." I drop my chin to my chest and groan.

"Honey, you can't blame yourself for that. You're not a robot. You're a woman with real feelings. Sometimes we make plans and then things change."

That's the problem, though. Things haven't changed, not really. I bought a one-way ticket to heartbreak.

"Being a robot might be easier." I look up at my best friend, wishing she could solve it all for me.

She considers that for a moment like it might be possible to turn ourselves into mechanical beings. "Robot sex probably isn't as much fun."

"It was really, *really* fun," I admit.

"So are you going to keep enjoying the benefits of your not-so-fake relationship, then?"

My phone pings with a text and I glance over to see Brogan's name on the screen. My stomach flips and my insides turn to mush.

"Is it him?" she asks.

I nod. "He wants me to go to a dinner thing tonight."

"And?"

"Help me pick out something to wear?"

Brogan picks me up an hour later. I meet him downstairs because we're running late, but he still gets out of the truck to come around and greet me.

"Hey." His smile is so big and genuine that I can feel my own growing wider as he envelops me in a hug. He rocks us back and forth, continuing to squeeze me like he hasn't seen me in days or weeks.

"How was your day off?" I ask when he pulls back. His hands remain wrapped around my lower back.

"Good. How was work?"

"Fine." I shrug. "Kind of boring."

"Should have stayed in my bed." He uses his hold on me to press our bodies together. His cedar and citrus scent and the warmth of his body makes my head spin.

Before I can come up with some witty reply, he steps back and takes my hand. "Come on. Let's see if we can't turn your day around."

At the restaurant, a hostess leads us to a back room where some of his teammates are already seated. Just teammates, around eight of them. I don't see any girlfriends or wives. And the guys are dressed casually, some in shorts and T-shirts, others in jeans, but the whole atmosphere is low-key.

Brogan and I take the two empty seats at one end. No one bats an eye at me being here. Archer tips his head, and Tripp smiles and winks.

I lean over to whisper as soon as it seems like people have gone back to their conversations and aren't looking at us. "I thought this was a team dinner?"

"It is. Well, sort of. Cody played his hundredth game with the Mavericks last weekend and we're celebrating. This is his favorite place."

Well, that's nice, but I still feel awkward. "Should *I* be here?"

Brogan's brows pinch together, and he glances around the table like he's just now noticing what I did the second we walked in—I'm the only non-football player. "Huh. Weird."

"I can go." I start to push my chair back, but he puts a hand on my thigh under the table.

"No, don't leave."

"It's okay. Really."

He keeps his hand glued to my skin. "Not for me. I missed you all day."

I tilt my head and let out a small laugh. It isn't that I think he's lying. It's just too bizarre to be true.

"I did," he says, angling his body toward me. "I like spending time with you. You're fun, and smart, and gorgeous." His gaze scans over my face and his fingers come up to rest on my cheek, then stroke down to my chin. "These guys might have left their women at home, but that's not my style."

"You're a very good fake boyfriend," I tell him, keeping my voice low enough that no one can overhear.

He beams with the compliment. "You make it easy."

We keep staring at each other for a beat, then I ask, "Are you sure?"

"Positive." His fingers push back into my hair. "Just one question."

"Okay?"

"What's this?" He moves the hand that was in my hair into view and between his thumb and forefinger is a tiny little metallic blue penis.

My face heats. "Oh god."

I run my hands over the rest of my hair, searching for any more penis confetti. I knew it was a bad idea. I'm going to be finding it in the apartment for weeks…and I guess on me as well.

"I'm starting to wonder if work was so boring after all." He still has the offending confetti in hand and he's smirking at me.

"I was putting together the goody bags for Sierra's bachelorette party."

"A penis-themed goody bag, huh? Why wasn't I invited? I love a good theme." He finally sets the confetti on the table but shakes his head at it like he's never seen anything quite like it.

"You want to come?"

He looks at me like I just asked the dumbest question ever. "Absolutely. Am I allowed or is it girls only? Maybe I could crash it later when you're all tipsy and handsy."

I blush at the reminder that he knows firsthand how I am when I drink too much. Although to be fair, I've never been as handsy with anyone else, drunk or not.

"They're actually having a joint party, so if you want to come, I'm sure Ben would be thrilled."

He nods and then his smile pulls the corners of his lips higher. "When is it?"

"Next weekend. Saturday. We're just going to hit up the bars and clubs downtown." I don't want him to think we've got VIP access or private rooms like he's probably used to. We'll be out in the main areas and very visible, which means he'll be very visible.

"Joint party…" He trails off. "I thought the whole point of those parties was one last night of living the single life."

"Probably for some people," I say.

"But not them."

"No. They seem pretty excited about getting married."

"So I can be your date?" he asks, looking hopeful and adorable.

"If you want."

"I literally can't think of anything I want more than seeing you in action at a bachelorette party. Are you going to wear a sexy little dress and one of those sash things girls wear out?"

I hold in a laugh. "I think those are a requirement of bachelorette parties."

"God bless them." He leans in and takes my mouth.

I forget we're sitting at a table with his teammates until someone tosses a balled-up napkin at us. "No making out at the table."

Brogan drapes his arm along the back of my chair and scoots closer. "Don't be jealous because I'm the only one that was smart enough to bring my girl to dinner."

"Rookie's not wrong," Cody says begrudgingly. "For once."

They all commiserate in nods and grunts of acknowledgment.

I realize then how well we're selling it. People think we're really a couple.

And so does my freaking heart.

CHAPTER TWENTY-SIX
Brogan

I love the sounds on the field during a game. Everything from the crowd yelling and cheering to the snap of the football, and everything in between. There's magic in the air. It seeps under my skin and makes it hard to stand still.

Taking a long drink of water, I scan the stadium behind me while our defensive team is on the field.

My gaze is drawn to the spot where London sits with Alec and her best friend Paige. I can't make out their expressions, but I can feel London looking this way.

I waggle my fingers at her, feeling a shot of adrenaline when she returns the gesture.

It feels so good having her here, but I wish I were out there playing instead of standing on the sideline.

Turning back around, I walk over to Coach.

He side-eyes me, keeping his attention mostly on the field.

"How are you feeling, Six?"

I dislocated my thumb during warmups. I caught a ball at just the right spot and that was that. I'm fine. The trainers wrapped it and I took some throws to make sure I'm solid. Still, Coach has been playing me sparingly to give me more rest and to not risk injuring it further.

We've had a lot of injuries already this season. Football is a tough sport. Two of our top defensive tackles got injured in last week's game and then both Archer and Merrick were given sit out orders for today from the team doc. Arch with his nagging ankle sprain that seems to flare-up every time he's cleared, and Merrick with the flu so bad he's been in bed for two days.

It's early in the season and no one wants to risk a setback that will put our playoffs chances in jeopardy, but the result is we're moving people around and not meshing like we should.

I bounce on the balls of my feet, hands resting at the neck of my jersey and pads. "Good. Ready."

It's the fourth quarter and we're down by thirteen. It kills me not to be out there contributing.

"You look like you have ants in your pants." One of his gray brows rises.

"I want to play. Put me in. I'm fine." There's so much tape on my hand, nothing is moving. Not even if a three-hundred-pound defensive tackle lands on it.

"There's only a few minutes left. There's no reason to risk it."

"Come on, Coach. My girlfriend's here. She's gonna think I'm a bench warmer."

His mouth curves. "Oh well, since your girlfriend's here…"

For a second, I don't realize he's fucking with me.

"Put me in. I'll get us within six."

A timeout is called by San Francisco.

"I admire your determination," he says. "You've been playing well, and you seem to be finding a groove and staying out of trouble. But for tonight, your girlfriend is going to have to admire your handsome face more than your skills on the field."

"Fine." I huff. "You're lucky I have such a handsome face though."

He shakes his head as his smile turns back to a thin line and he focuses on the game.

I dress quickly and head out to the family waiting area. Guys with wives and kids or other family in attendance fill the room. I watch moms and dads embrace their sons. The atmosphere is somber, probably because of the loss, but it's plain to see how much these parents love them regardless of the outcome of the game.

Sometimes it just hits me how much of that I missed out on. I don't think my parents have watched me play a single game and if they did, there weren't after-game hugs or words of encouragement.

A little girl wearing a Mavericks jersey nearly takes me out as she darts in front of me for her father. My teammate, Slade, scoops her up and nuzzles into her little neck. I smile at them, wondering what that would be like. It seems nice.

At the back of the room, I finally spot London. Her friends are still with her. London steps forward slowly as I approach. She seems to hesitate like she isn't sure what to do, but as soon as I wrap my arms around her, she does the same.

"I'm sorry about the game," she says when we pull apart. "How's your thumb?"

"Fine. Disappointed like the rest of me. Glad you guys came though. Sorry we didn't get you a win." I nod my head to Alec. "Hey, good to see you again."

He dips his chin back. "You too. Tough loss."

I finally let my stare linger on the woman I know is London's best friend.

"You must be Paige."

"One and only." She lifts a hand in a wave as she studies me closely. She seems to take in every detail from the hand I have resting on London's back to the way her friend glances between us.

I smile at her. She has this hard-ass exterior that reminds me of London. "I've heard a lot about you. I'm glad to finally meet you."

"Likewise."

"Do you all have plans? Some of the guys were talking about going to a friend's house to hang. Just a few people."

London laughs. "I don't believe that for a second."

"Fewer than usual." I glide my hand around her waist and pull her against me.

"I wish." Alec looks genuinely apologetic as he speaks to me. "I promised some buddies I'd meet up with them."

"I need to get home too," Paige says. "I have to be in Chandler at seven tomorrow for an estate sale. Too bad. I'll have to grill you another time." One corner of her mouth lifts, but I have a feeling she means it.

"Absolutely. I'll be ready."

"What about you?" I ask London.

"I should probably go too. I need to work in the morning."

"Are you sure?" I really hoped we'd get to spend the night

together again.

"Yeah."

Her friends step away, giving us a little privacy. I circle both arms around her, pulling her against me.

"We don't have to go to the party. You could just come to my house."

Her smile makes my pulse kick up a notch. "That is tempting, but I have a feeling I'll sleep more at my house."

She's not wrong there. But I'm still disappointed.

"We could just sleep."

A soft laugh leaves her lips. "It's okay. Go have fun. I'll text you tomorrow."

Reluctantly, I let her free. "What am I supposed to do until then?"

She laughs again, louder this time, like she thinks I'm kidding.

"Did you let London know about tonight?" Archer asks the next day as we get dressed after practice.

Today was brutal. Coach tacked on a mandatory film review later.

"No, we didn't have plans."

Archer's brows lift and he can't hide the surprised look that crosses his face.

"What?" I ask, sitting down on the bench and putting on my shoes.

"Nothing." He goes back to staring into his locker like he thinks I'm going to let it go.

"Just say whatever it is you want to say." I stand and grab my wallet and keys, then shut my locker.

I wait while he grabs his stuff too and we head out together. He doesn't say anything until we're walking out the back door to the parking lot.

"You like her."

"Wow. Congratulations on figuring that out." I chuckle and shake my head.

"You know what I mean." He stops at his truck. We rode together today, but neither of us makes a move to get in yet.

"No, I don't think I do."

"You're spending time with her that has nothing to do with making people believe you're a guy in a serious relationship."

I resist rolling my eyes, but an uncomfortable sensation works its way up my spine anyway. "We're having fun and enjoying the perks of the situation."

"The perks? You mean that your pretend girlfriend is smoking hot and you want to sleep with her every chance you get?"

"Exactly." I finally open the door to the passenger side and get in. Arch does the same, situating himself behind the wheel and starting up the engine.

"Why can't you just admit that you like her? This is more than sex."

"I like her. She is a really cool chick."

"And…"

"It's not as serious as you're making it out to be." Another rough chuckle scrapes up my throat.

"You know, I thought after watching Hendrick and Knox go through this, you of all people would be more insightful."

"What in the hell do they have to do with this?"

My best friend groans and lets his head fall back onto the truck's headrest.

I swat at his arm to make sure he's looking at me as I speak. *"I like her, I do. She's great and if I were the type of guy that could be in a relationship with anyone for real, then London is exactly who I'd want. But I'm not that guy. I don't know the first thing about how to love and support someone in that way. She knows that."* Until a few weeks ago, she thought I was a total jerk who slept with women for sport. I doubt she's ready to go all in with someone like me just because she's decided kissing me is fun. A whole lot of fun.

"Why not? You're the best guy I know. And I've seen how you are with her. How the two of you are together. You treat her like a goddamn queen, and she looks at you like you are the only guy on the planet."

I know he means it, but he's biased. He sees the good in everyone, especially me. *"We're pretending half the time."*

"No." He shakes his head. "I can tell when you're putting on a show for everyone else and that stopped weeks ago."

He's wrong. Sure, it's easy to be together and we've gotten comfortable with each other and the chemistry is off the charts, but it's all centered around being caught up in this thing together. Isn't it?

I'm still thinking about it after our late film review is over. I head to her place instead of home.

She opens the door wearing an oversized T-shirt and her hair up in a ponytail.

"What are you doing here?" Her grin is pleased even if the rest of her is clearly shocked by the late-night drop by.

"I was thinking about you. Thought maybe we could have a

sleepover."

"I have work tomorrow and I have to be there earlier than normal for a big corporate meeting." She looks as bummed as I feel.

"Why are you up so late then?"

"Finishing an illustration for a client."

"Lo?" Alec's voice calls from somewhere in the apartment.

"Sorry. It's just Brogan." She motions with her hand for me to follow her. I do...into a small bedroom. She closes the door behind us and with a low voice says, "He has to get up really early during the week."

"Right." I'm suddenly feeling a little like an ass for interrupting her normal routine, but then my gaze drops to her computer and I find myself walking closer. "This is the piece you're working on?"

"Yeah. It's not done." She fidgets next to me, looking uncomfortable as I take in her work in progress. It's a couple embracing. A blue alien with boobs spilling out of her space suit and a human man holding a sword at his side. It's like nothing I've ever seen before and could have never dreamed up, but it's awesome.

"You're so talented," I tell her when I can manage to pry my gaze away from it. "It's amazing to me that you can come up with that in your head and then draw it."

"Well, the client usually gives me some guidelines and descriptions."

"Take the compliment, sweetheart." I turn to face her. With her hair pulled up like that, her neck looks about a mile long. All that smooth, delicate skin. I bring a hand up to one side and glide my thumb over her pulse point.

"Thank you. I've been getting a lot more business lately and some very interesting projects. I sketched like a dozen poses before

I came up with this one."

"Aliens, I dig it. We could do a little role-play later. You're the sexy alien and I'm defending the galaxy."

"He's an alien hunter who falls in love with the enemy."

"Oooh." My eyes widen. "Even better."

She laughs, leaning into my touch.

"I won't stay since you're busy and have to get up early."

"Okay." A flicker of something like disappointment flashes in her eyes.

I sit on the edge of her bed. It has a white comforter. The walls are decorated with art and photos. My gaze lands on a framed photo of her and Sierra when they were younger. London looks to be about twelve or thirteen. She has braces and hair that's shoulder-length.

"How was your day?"

"Good." She says the word slowly as she leans against the desk, facing me. Laughter spills out of her, all airy and light.

"What's funny?"

"You in my room."

"Is funny?" I arch a brow.

"Funny because if someone had asked me a month ago what the odds were, I would have said impossible."

"Nothing is impossible." I take her hand and tug her to me. She stands between my legs and I run my hands up the back of her bare thighs. Her shorts are hidden by the big, baggy T-shirt, but mold to her slim curves.

"So it seems." Another small laugh escapes her, but when I cup her ass in both palms she quiets.

"I like your room." I think what I really mean is *I like you*, but she either understands or doesn't care.

"I like yours too. Bigger bed."

"The bed is optional." I wink, remembering how I fucked her up against the wall last time. So many more things to explore with her. We've barely scratched the surface.

I let my fingers drift up to the hem of her shorts and then I slowly pull the material down, along with her panties. She steps out of them, hands on my shoulder, never breaking my gaze. This time when my hands trail up her smooth legs, there's no barrier. I can't see her because of the shirt, but I have every last inch of her burned into my memory. She's perfection.

Standing, I pull up the hem of her shirt and hold it in one hand above her belly button. I walk us forward a step to the desk, then brush my mouth over hers. "Turn around for me, sweetheart."

She does, the movement twisting the shirt around her, hugging her tighter. Gently, I push her back down so that the front of her rests on top of the desk, then I nudge her feet farther apart. Kissing her neck, I glance over at her laptop screen, still open.

"So talented," I murmur. "Don't you think so?"

She doesn't reply, just moans as I drop one hand between her legs from behind. My fingers slide over her slick heat.

"So talented. So beautiful. So perfect." I dip two fingers into her tight pussy. Her muscles contract around me and she whimpers.

My pace is lazy and unhurried, which just seems to drive her wilder. I'd like to think it's the time apart that has her frantic with need, but we're so deep into this thing…whatever it is…I can't even begin to guess the reason for any of it anymore. Maybe, we're just good together.

CHAPTER TWENTY-SEVEN
London

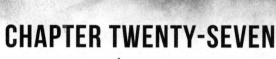

We pile out of my apartment. Eight women, happy and tipsy, and ready to hit the town. I follow behind, making sure we have everyone and everything for the night. Tylenol and water for the ride to the bar, plus snacks and wet wipes. I threw it all into my purse, determined to be the mother hen for the night so my sister can cut loose.

"Oh, Lo Lo." Sierra walks back through the group of her friends to me. "I forgot to grab my tiara in your apartment."

"Got it right here." I pat the side of my giant leather bag.

"Thank you." Her eyes shine with a mixture of glee and alcohol. "You're the best sister ever."

"Not possible. You've already claimed that title."

She throws her arms around me, nearly knocking me off-balance. "Love you, Lo Lo."

"I love you too." I squeeze her back.

We break apart at the sound of squeals and laughter. A giant Hummer limo pulls up to the curb. It's black and sleek.

"You got a limo!" My sister's happy screech amps up another level when the door opens and her fiancé appears.

My confusion is quickly replaced with humor as I realize the guys rented the ostentatious vehicle.

The girls climb in, giddy and excited. I spot Chris when Gretchen climbs in next to him. No matter how much I don't want his presence to bug me, it still does.

Brogan gets out when I'm the only one left. His brows lift as his gaze travels slowly down over my legs and then back up. "Whoa. Sweetheart. You look…" He rubs a hand over his jaw.

"You like?" I ask, spinning in my very short black dress and the red high heels he likes so much. I grab my sash out of my purse and pull it on, then hold up my penis-shaped necklace. "I wanted to make sure I checked all your bachelorette party attire boxes."

"You check all my boxes all right." He steps to me and buries his head in the crook of my neck. He groans.

"Did you have fun with the guys?" While we had drinks at my place, they gathered at Ben and Sierra's apartment for cigars and whiskey. I can smell both on my date.

"Yeah, Ben's a cool guy."

My future brother-in-law would probably have a stroke if he heard Brogan say those words.

"You are making his night by being here. Thank you."

"No need to thank me. I've got all the thanks I need with you in that sexy fucking dress. I can't decide if I want to rip you out of it later or fuck you in it. Complete with the sash."

My skin pricks with goosebumps and my pulse races. "You

should be so lucky."

I trail a hand over his chest and pass by him. I'm pretty sure he mutters, "Don't I fucking know it."

We take the limo for a short five-minute drive to the first bar on our stop for the night. I hang back with my supplies while everyone else goes straight to the bar to get drinks. It's still early so it's not too crowded.

I pull out the checklist for the night. Sierra had only a few requirements to make this the best night ever, and I'm going to ensure we do all of them. Starting with a cheesy group photo.

Once everyone has a drink in hand, I get out my phone.

"Crowd together," I yell, holding up my phone to indicate I am going to take a picture.

Guys and girls alike shuffle closer to each other. All except Brogan.

"Let me take it," he says.

"I got it."

"Yeah, but you should be in the photo."

"Yes, get in!" Sierra yells at me.

Reluctantly, I hand over my phone to him and go stand next to my sister. We do a regular photo, then silly faces.

Someone ordered a round of shots and those come, breaking up our photo session. Sierra hands me a small glass of pink liquid with a grin.

"What is it?" I ask.

"Pink Starburst."

It smells good. Too good. The kind of shot that you take two or three of before you remember it is alcohol.

"Somebody has to keep us all in line tonight." I shake my head and try to hand it back.

"No! I want you to have fun."

"I don't need to drink to have fun. My baby sister is getting married and wearing penises around her neck." I laugh. "Tonight is about you. I've got everything covered. Let me be the responsible one for once in our lives."

"You have been looking out for me my whole life. Maybe I got the responsible genes, but you have always had my back."

"And I always will," I tell her.

"I know." She laughs, then glances over at her fiancé. "I really love him, Lo."

"I know you do." I take her hand and squeeze. I still can't believe my little sister is getting married. Her whole life is changing and I'm fake-dating a guy to avoid my ex. Or I was…now I'm sleeping with him and trying to avoid my feelings.

"And you and Brogan…you really love him too, don't you?"

"Love?" I try to play it off with a laugh, but it's strained even to my own ears.

"The way you two look at each other, I can tell you love him."

"Sierra," I start. How do you tell the most important person in the world that you've been lying to them? "We aren't really together. Not like you think."

She rolls her eyes. "Situationship, dating, whatever you want to call it…you're not fooling anyone."

"No. I mean…" I trail off. Telling her the truth tonight feels selfish.

My chest tightens and not only because I feel bad from keeping that from her, but because admitting we aren't a couple out loud feels like finally admitting to myself that I've gotten in over my head.

"And anyway," Sierra adds, "it doesn't matter if it wasn't serious when it started. You love him now?"

"Yes." God, I really do. I tried not to fall for him, but he's so easy to love. And the way he makes me feel is beyond anything I've ever felt.

Her smile is so wide, and she squeals happily.

"I already regret telling you."

She laughs and tears shine in her eyes. "I'm so happy for you."

I don't have the heart to tell her that I'm walking the plank alone.

"No tears!" I point a finger at her, then to her friends. "Go. Have fun, drink too much, and make out with your future husband in public."

She blushes but then heads off toward the group. I watch her, feeling lighter having admitted my feelings. Now I just have to figure out how to tell him.

"Hey." Chris appears at my side. He has one hand in his pants pocket and the other wrapped around a glass of whiskey.

"Hi," I say with as little emotion as I can manage.

"We need to talk."

My brows shoot up. "Excuse me?"

"About wedding stuff."

I still don't follow.

"You're the maid of honor. I'm the best man." He grins all sly-like. I'm sure I used to find him attractive, but right now all I feel is disgust. I try to remember that he's my sister's future brother-in-law.

"Right," I say. "What do we need to go over?"

I thought most of it was already done, but if I've forgotten something, Sierra might kill me.

"Ben wants everything to be perfect."

Yeah, no kidding. I catch Brogan's eye across the bar. He takes in the situation with a furrowed brow.

"Can we talk about this later?" I ask Chris.

"Of course. Is your number still the same?"

"Yes."

"Great. I'll text you."

I'll have to unblock him first.

Brogan comes to stand in front of us. Chris looks up and nods. "Hey, man. Good of you to show up tonight. I know Ben is thrilled to have his favorite Mavericks player here."

I shoot daggers out of my eyeballs at my ex. There's something snotty and demeaning about his tone, like the fact that he's a professional football player is the only reason anyone wants Brogan around.

"Not as thrilled as I am." I sidle up next to him, clutching his arm.

Brogan's eyes dance with mischief and he drops his mouth down to mine. I lift up on my toes to press my lips harder against his.

"I'm gonna…" Chris's words trail off. I don't know or care if he finishes that statement because when Brogan's lips capture mine, I am a goner.

"Everything okay?" The man holding my heart in his oversized hands asks when I drop back down on my heels.

"Wedding planning stuff." We move toward the bar where my shot still remains. The smell of it wafts over even from a foot away.

"And that smells like trouble."

He plucks the glass up between his thumb and forefinger and tosses it back with only the slightest grimace.

He leans against the bar with one hip. "So, what's on the agenda?"

"Oh, you know, shots, strip club, the usual."

His brows lift.

"I'm kidding. No strippers tonight, unless you're offering."

"Only for you." His eyes crinkle as he laughs. "Why are you standing over here hovering like an overbearing parent and leaving perfectly good shots on the table?"

"I'm running this ship tonight. Gotta be responsible."

"Good god, why?" he asks like he can't think of a single thing worse than responsibility. Honestly, that's on brand for him.

"Because…" I trail off. "What if someone needs something?"

One brow quirks up. "Everyone here is an adult. I think you can relax."

"It has to be perfect."

"Oh good. I'm glad we're keeping our expectations in check." He lets his head fall back and laughs loudly. The way his throat works with the sound makes my stomach dip.

I swat at him playfully. "Tonight is important."

"Yeah, of course it is." He takes my hand and smiles at me gently. "You're a good sister. It makes sense that you want to make sure it all goes smoothly, but I think if Sierra had to choose between perfect and having fun with her sister, she'd pick the latter."

I think of the words she said no more than five minutes ago. She did say that, but if things don't go well, I'll feel like the maid of dishonor.

"How about you let me be the responsible one?" He motions to the bartender, who immediately pours two more of the pink shots. Brogan holds one out to me.

"You're kidding, right?" I almost burst out laughing at the thought.

"Give me all the details and I will run this night like the party planner extraordinaire you didn't know you wanted."

I realize he's serious. "I don't think so."

"You don't think I can do it," he says more than asks.

I mean, I didn't, but looking at him now I'm wondering if I misjudged him.

"I specialize in parties. You're in good hands. Drink this."

I don't know why, but I do, then cough. "Oh god. That is good."

He grins. "Is there a schedule of bars and things?"

My face gives him his answer.

"Of course there is. Hit me with it."

I tell him my exact plans for the night, leaving nothing out. He doesn't even blink when I mention the checklist of mostly-girly things that I'm certain the guys will think is dumb. He writes it all down in his phone.

"That's it?"

"If we make it through all the bars still standing, I thought we could try to get into Gaga." I've only ever been with Alec so I have zero expectations that we'll get in, but it'll be fun to try regardless, and by that point everyone will hopefully be too drunk and happy to care.

"Got it," he says, then reads the schedule back to me. "Anything else to make this night perfect?"

I shake my head even though I have a few visions of us making out running through my head. He looks good tonight. Gray slacks, white button-up, sleeves rolled, white tennis shoes. He has this knack for always looking completely casual even when he's dressed up a bit. It all seems so effortless for him. From fashion to just existing in any situation. He looks like he could walk into the nicest club in the city or attend a frat party.

"Consider it done." He picks up the second shot and hands it to me. "Have fun, sweetheart. I got you."

Inexplicably, I believe him. I toss back the shot and he orders another round for everyone.

For the next two hours, we drink and bar hop. I veer away from shots and stick with sipping on drinks and water in between, but the alcohol in my system makes me happy and free to let loose with my sister. Nobody even notices that Brogan is barely drinking.

When we crowd into the limo to go to a bar about fifteen minutes away, I find myself smushed between Brogan and Chris. Happily, I've been able to mostly avoid my ex tonight since he cornered me about wedding plans. He's facing Gretchen on the other side of him, but our legs are touching and his fingers rest on his thigh, therefore grazing mine as well, making me squirm to get away.

"For a small thing, you sure do move around a lot." Brogan lifts me onto his lap and holds my knees in the opposite direction so no part of me is in any danger of touching my ex. If he realizes why I was so squirmy, he doesn't say.

"You smell nice," I say as his familiar cologne wafts around me. His body is big and warm and I'm still just tipsy enough to snuggle up to him with no inhibition.

His head dips down and he brushes his lips over mine. "So do you."

My gaze falls from his face to his chest. The button-down is open at his neck and I bring a hand up and trail my fingers over the area. Tonight he has on a necklace, and I lift it between my thumb and forefinger. The gold rose charm is dainty, barely discernible without looking closely.

"This is pretty."

"It was Archer's mom's," he says quietly. The rest of the party is talking loudly and laughing, so it feels like we're in our own little bubble.

"She gave it to you?" I ask carefully. He's said very little about his family and I'm afraid to seem too interested and spook him.

"He gave it to me when she passed away," he says. "She was more of a mom to me than my own and he thought I might want to hold on to it."

My heart squeezes in my chest. Deep down I think I assumed there was a reason he didn't say much about his family, but I wasn't expecting the deep hurt in his confession. "I'm so sorry."

"Thanks." He threads a hand through my hair and holds the back of my neck.

I don't know what else to say, but I feel awful. For all the ways my parents frustrate me, they're alive.

"What about your dad?"

His eyes drop from mine. "Never really had a dad."

"I'm really sorry." It feels like such a lame reply, so I do the only other thing I can think and wrap myself around him. He hesitates but a moment later, his muscular arms tighten around me.

Eventually, I tilt my head back and look up at him. We just stare at each other while my heart hammers in my chest and all the emotions I've been trying to hold back seem like they'll explode if I don't let them free.

"I like you." I love him, too, but tonight I just want him to know that I'm in this way more than for some fake arrangement.

One side of his mouth pulls up at the corner. "I like you too."

The limo comes to a stop and everyone piles out, including the driver. I stay where I'm at on Brogan's lap. I shift, and the movement puts my ass sitting directly on his dick.

"Don't look at me like that, sweetheart." His voice is low as he drops a hand high on my thigh.

"Like what?"

"Like you want me to slide this hand under your dress." He squeezes my leg and a shiver dances up my spine.

I grab his wrist and glide his hand up under the skirt until his fingertips graze the lacy material of my panties.

"I'm leading the ship tonight, remember?" His voice is hoarse and strained.

"They're all adults. They'll figure it out."

A rough chuckle rumbles in his chest. He groans as he slips a finger underneath and then gently inside me. My lashes flutter closed and I widen my legs to give him better access. He continues pumping in and out of me, then brings his thumb to rub circles over my clit. I palm his cock through his pants.

The door of the limo is still open and the wind and noise filter in, reminding us we aren't alone. Not that I care. The pulse between my legs thrums as he works me over with his fingers.

"I didn't realize fucking in the limo was on your checklist."

"Me neither."

"You want to though, don't you? You want me to take out my

cock and fuck you right here where anyone could see."

I don't know how to tell him it isn't that I want people to see, it's that I want him too badly to care.

"Please." I'm so close. He adds a finger and my pussy clenches around him.

"Come for me, sweetheart, and I'll give you what you want."

I grab on to his shoulder as my orgasm rockets through me. My body shakes and laughter bubbles up and then escapes as I gasp for air. I'm giddy and ready for more.

But Brogan is straightening my panties and pulling my skirt down.

"Ready?" he asks, sliding us over toward the open door.

"What about…"

He grins all mischievous and smug. "I'm being responsible, temptress. Come on. I've got the limo all night."

CHAPTER TWENTY-EIGHT
Brogan

"**Y**ou rented the limo?" London asks as we file into the bar. Shit. I did not mean to let that slip. I don't want her to think I'm flashing around my money.

"It's no big deal." When Ben suggested we get a couple Ubers for the night, I knew I needed to intervene. I've only been to a few bachelor parties, but I know that it's all about extravagance and fun. Two things I do very well.

"Thank you." She looks up at me with those stunning green eyes all soft. Her bottom lip has an indent from where her teeth were biting into it earlier as I fingered her in the limo. "I should have thought of that."

"You've done a great job." I scan the group. "Everyone is having a blast."

London beams with pride. "That's because you're such a good party planner."

"I am, aren't I?" I wink at her. "And I think it's time for you and me to dance."

"Dance?" She laughs and looks around. It's a small bar, crowded with twenty-somethings. The only way we're getting a drink is to push and shove our way with everyone else and I'm much more interested in her.

"One dance. I love this song," I say, leading her through the middle of the bar to one side where a guy with a guitar is crooning into the microphone. It's a cover of a popular 90s rock song, slowed down but still with a nice beat.

I wrap one arm around her waist and with my free hand, lace our fingers together. We hold our joined hands up at chest level and she drapes her right hand on my bicep.

Her cheeks are flushed from the alcohol or maybe the orgasm, but I think some of her tipsiness has worn off. She's been chugging water more than booze. Probably a smart choice honestly, but I'd take care of her either way.

It turns out I don't mind not being the center of the party as long as I can be the center of her attention.

She looks up at me, features soft and dreamy like she's happy. Me too.

"Hey, I have a question," she says.

"Yes, I definitely plan to fuck you in that limo later."

"Not that." She laughs. "But good to know."

I wait for her to continue. It takes her a beat, so I know whatever it is she wants to ask is more serious than fucking.

"When you said you never really had a dad and that Archer's mom was more of one than your own, what did you mean? Where were your parents?"

I still for a second. A small part of me wants to open myself up and show her all of it. The good. The bad. The really ugly.

"You don't want to hear my sad story tonight."

She keeps staring at me, like maybe she does.

"I think if we're going to try to get into Gaga, we should go sooner rather than later. Your sister's friends look like they're a couple drinks shy of crying in the bathroom."

It takes her a moment, but she lets me off the hook, glances over at the group and nods. "It's okay. Gaga was a long shot anyway."

"I can get us in."

One of her dark brows lifts. "Oh, you can, can you?"

"I know a guy." I shrug. I don't like to use my name or the team for myself, but I have no problem doing it to make sure London has the night she hoped for.

"Are you sure? If it's weird, we can just hit up a Jack in the Box drive-thru on the way home and I'm sure everyone will be just as happy."

I bark out a laugh. "Consider that added to the schedule afterward."

Her smile widens, and fuck does it hit me right in the chest. "Okay. If you're sure it's not too much. I know Sierra would love it."

"Let's do it then."

It's embarrassingly easy to get us in at Gaga. The bouncer recognizes me, and I thank him as he holds the rope open for all of us, no questions asked.

I didn't think or I would have called ahead to see about VIP, but as it is the group rushes toward the dance floor. London and I head to the bar where I order a round for when they're ready to take a break.

"What do you want, sweetheart?" I ask London while we have the bartender's attention.

"Umm…" She thinks, leaning over the bar. While she gives him her drink order, two women approach me on the other side.

One has long, almost white, blonde hair and the other is a brunette with a headband that pulls her hair back in a way that accentuates her sharp features and heavy makeup. She's pretty. They both are. A month ago I might have even tried to take one or both of them home. Fuck, maybe I did. I squint. No. *Maybe*. Nah.

"You're Brogan Six, aren't you?" the blonde asks.

"Yeah," I say relieved that I didn't sleep with her and forgot, but suddenly nervous and not sure why.

"I knew it!" The other girl steps closer and places a hand on my arm. "You are the hottest professional athlete in the state of Arizona. I've been saying it for months. Haven't I been saying it for months?" She looks back at her friend.

"She has. We've been coming here every Saturday since we heard it's your favorite spot in town."

The girl laughs. "We've been trying to run into you for months."

They introduce themselves but their names go in one ear and out the other.

My gaze slides over to London. She's oblivious to the wide *help me* eyes I'm giving her, and instead her stare is locked on the hand draped over my forearm. I try to sort of wiggle out of the woman's hold, but there's nowhere to go and she's latched on tight. I don't want to be a jerk, but I'd like her to stop touching me. The last thing I want is for London to get the wrong idea or feel uncomfortable. I just want to hang with her and pretend we're the only two people in this club.

"Hi." London steps forward, voice sugary sweet. Alarm bells go off in my head. My girl is friendly and kind, sweet even, but this is something else, and I'm suddenly nervous she's about to tell me to have fun and leave me with my new stalker friends.

"Hello," the girls say back in unison, then dismiss her by turning their gazes back to me. Except she sidesteps, blocking me. Well, sort of. I'm still almost a foot taller than her, even in her sexy heels, so I can see the confused reactions of the women in front of her.

"Ummm…" The blonde turns to the brunette and they exchange a look before their stares return to London. "Excuse us. We were talking to *him*."

"I know, and now you're not."

They scoff and then share a laugh. I'm still not sure what's happening, but London crosses her arms and straightens, giving her maybe another half inch in height.

"Who are you?" one asks.

"His girlfriend. And I'd appreciate it if you kept your hands off him."

"Girlfriend?" Their stares lift to mine. I don't mean to grin, but it's hard not to right now.

"Yes," London chirps back. And if I didn't know better, I'd say she sounds a little smug.

"Sorry, we didn't know," the blonde says.

"Well, now you do."

They hesitate, give me one last longing look like I might stop them from going, then start to walk off.

"Oh, and by the way…" London's words trail off until the women pause and give her their attention. "He's not *just* the hottest professional athlete in Arizona. He's a good guy who cares about his friends and being a decent human."

"Ummm...okay."

"And he's the hottest professional athlete anywhere, not just in Arizona."

The girls finally shuffle away awkwardly and London swivels around to face me. Her expression is timid like she's scared of my reaction. "What was that?" I ask, laughing. My chest is light and a giddy feeling spreads through me.

"I'm sorry. I probably shouldn't have done that." Her face scrunches up. "She was touching you and I just lost it."

"Oh my god, I think I'm in love with you."

"What?" Her pupils blow up and she recoils like she's in shock.

"You looked like you were seconds away from clawing her eyes out or throwing a punch. Do you even know how to throw a punch?" I'm real interested in knowing the answer to that and maybe seeing it in action.

"She put her hands on my man. I mean, at least as far as everyone else knows you're my man. You were right, we should take a photo and post it on your social media."

I get my phone out immediately and snap one of us, then post it without bothering with a caption.

"Just like that? I didn't even get to check it to make sure I look okay."

"You look beautiful. Trust me." I pocket my phone. "So, not the kind of girlfriend who lets other women hit on your man, huh? I like it."

She rolls her eyes at me, but I am serious. I want that look of fiery possession on her face and aimed at me always.

"Is there a whole list of women you've scared off from hitting on ex-boyfriends? Maybe a support group you could offer them, because frankly they look like they might need a safe place to express their feelings."

"No." She laughs and crosses her arms over her chest. "I'm not the jealous type."

"No?" She's kidding, right? If that wasn't jealousy, I don't know what it was.

"Random strangers shouldn't just walk up to you and put their hands on you. Guy or girl. It's rude."

It is, but I guess I never minded much before. Now I just want London's hands on me, and I think she feels the same.

"So, if it wasn't a stranger, say it was someone I knew, then it'd be okay?" I step closer until our chests brush. She has to tilt her head back to look up at me, and I bring a hand up to the back of her neck.

"Theoretically."

"I'd like to test that theory, but I'm too turned on and I need to be inside you." I take her hand and lead us back through the club to the exit.

"Where are we going?" she asks, voice strained with laughter as she takes little quick steps to keep up with me. I slow down so she doesn't have to hurry, but everything in me wants to rush.

Outside, the limo driver is standing at the front of the vehicle smoking a cigarette.

"Hey, man," I say when he spots us and pushes off like he's preparing to get back in to drive us. "I need to talk to my girl. Mind if we sit in the car for a few minutes?"

He hesitates. He knows exactly what I want to do in his back seat, and it isn't talk.

"I'll pay you double for tonight."

A smile slowly curves his lips. "It's all yours."

I open the back door and help London in before following and shutting us in. It's dark with only a little of the light from outside getting in through the tinted windows.

"You're incredible. You know that?" I frame her face with both hands and kiss her with an urgency that steals my breath.

"You're pretty incredible yourself." She kisses me back with a desperation that I feel to my core. Maybe we're not the same in a lot of ways but right now we want each other with the same voracity. "Every woman in this city thinks so."

I've got her in my lap, sitting on my dick as I slide my hands up the hem of her dress. Her skin is like velvet and she shudders as the tips of my fingers reach the apex of her thighs.

"Wait. There's something I've always wanted to do in a limo."

Before I can question her, she slides off my lap to the seat next to me.

There's a spark in her eyes as she goes for the button on my pants.

"I think I like where this is going," I say, voice rough with need for her.

God, the way she smiles at me while getting my pants undone and pulling my dick out is like she's unwrapping a present.

"I think you lied about the sock."

"The what?" My mind can't make sense of much right now, but I'm pretty sure I wouldn't follow that sentence even if she wasn't wrapping her fingers around the base of my cock.

"You told me in one of your letters that you had a sock in your underwear for the model campaign." She wraps her lips around the head and takes me into her mouth.

My head falls back against the headrest as she glides so slowly down until I'm hitting the back of her throat. She moves off just as slowly, releasing me with a pop.

There's a satisfied smirk on her face when she looks up at me. "You don't need any help in that department."

"Better look a little closer just to be sure." I guide her head back down over me while she giggles, teeth lightly scraping me. I'm so turned on. So close. So totally and completely gone. Everything she does is sexy as fuck.

"Damn, London. That's so good. I don't want you to stop."

"I wasn't planning on it," she says, around my mouthful.

With a tortured groan, I pull her back onto my lap. "I made you a promise, and I'm dangerously close to not being able to fulfill it."

Kissing her, I pull her hair to one side so I can trail my lips down over the slender column of her neck.

"So sexy," I whisper, nipping at the skin. "So beautiful."

She grinds over me, making my dick twitch.

"Slide those panties off, sweetheart."

While she does, I grab a condom from my wallet and cover myself. I take the balled-up panties in her hand and shove them in my pocket, then guide her back down on my lap. The head of my cock slides against her sensitive skin and she lets out a little moan, head dropping to my shoulder.

I take her chin with my thumb and pointer finger, bringing her mouth to mine and kissing her hard and deep. The same way I plan to fuck her.

When I can't wait any longer, I gently lift her, guiding her back down on me slowly. With my hands on either side of her waist, I move her up and down.

"I love it when you do that," she says. Her hands press against the window behind me while I drive into her.

"Oh god." She slaps the window, and I increase the pace.

"Brogan." The way she says my name, frantic and loud like she doesn't give a shit who hears her, makes a heady possessiveness take hold of me. Mine. It's all I can think. This girl is mine and I want everyone to know it.

She comes still screaming my name and banging the window. She finally pushes against me, bouncing in my lap like she can't help herself. I grab her by the sash and bring her mouth to mine as my orgasm splinters through me.

Mine. "Fucking mine."

We come down from the high of our post-orgasm bliss slowly. I run my hand down the back of her head, keeping her against my chest where I can feel her heart beating.

I glance back at the window behind me and chuckle. Her handprints are all over it.

She glances up to see why I'm laughing and gives me a rueful smile. "Now everyone knows you're a taken man."

"I don't care who else knows as long as you do." My heart does a funny leap thing in my chest. "I'm yours, sweetheart. In case that wasn't obvious, I'm telling you outright. I don't want anyone else but you."

"Good. Because I was so jealous at the thought of you hooking up with those women inside that I think my blood pressure is still too high."

I already knew it, but hearing her confirm it sends another rush of pleasure through me.

"Let's do this for real. Me and you."

She studies me, lips parting, and chest rising and falling as she catches her breath. I'm not sure if she understands the full weight of my words. I'm not sure I do. I just know I need her like I've never needed anyone.

"If we're half as good together as we are when we're faking it, then we'll be the happiest couple I know," I say in case she still needs convincing.

"I thought," she starts and then stops herself. "What about everything you said about not wanting anything serious during your rookie year, enjoying being single, and all that?"

Maybe Archer was right. I can be in this with her for real. The thought scares and excites me in equal measure. "Things change."

She says nothing, just smiles and lets her teeth graze over her bottom lip. Then ever so slightly, she nods.

"Yeah? We're doing this for real?" I ask, maybe just a tad too eagerly. I want to fist-pump or scream. Fuck it. I tip my head back to the ceiling of the limo. "Fuck yeah."

CHAPTER TWENTY-NINE
London

"**T**onight was perfect." My sister's eyes are barely open as she leans forward to hug me. "I love you so much. You're the best big sis ever."

"I love you too," I say, laughing softly. I think this is the drunkest I've ever seen my baby sister. "Take some Advil before you go to bed and call me in the morning. We can grab coffee or something if you feel up to it."

"Yeah, that sounds great." She pulls back and stumbles into her fiancé. He's not nearly as bad off as her, and I'm thankful she has someone to look after her.

They start up the sidewalk to their apartment and I turn to face Brogan. The limo is still idling at the curb and it's just the two of us.

"So…" he says with a wicked grin. "Wanna have a sleepover?"

We go back to my place because it's closer. There's an awkward moment as soon as we step into the dark, silent apartment.

"Alec is visiting his parents in Tucson this weekend," I say, in case he doesn't realize that we are alone all night.

"Good." He gets a devilish glint in his eye. "We don't have to worry about being quiet."

Brogan scoops me up and carries me to my bedroom. He leaves the door open and sets me on the bed. The way he looks at me makes my skin tingle and my pulse race. He has this way of making me feel like the most special person in the world.

I thought I got it when I first met him—the charisma, the good looks, it all made sense why women and just people in general flock to him. He is still all those things. He's funny and goofy and so hot that it takes my breath away, but it's also the way he makes others feel. The way he makes me feel. He drowns out the noise and all the critical things I've heard or thought.

He undresses me like it's a sacred act, kissing me and telling me how beautiful I am. I answer in moans and murmurs. When I'm naked beneath him, he takes me in with a low growl of approval.

"I'm the luckiest guy in the whole world." His fingers graze tenderly down my side.

Taking off his clothes is a much more frantic endeavor. I loop my arms around his back and clutch him to me. The head of his dick nudges my entrance and I still, then push down onto him.

"One sec, sweetheart. I need to get a condom."

I don't release him. "It's okay. I'm on birth control and I haven't been with anyone but you since the last time I was at the doctor."

His brows pinch together like he's not certain.

"I mean if it's okay with you," I add.

"I was tested right after we started this arrangement. I'm good and I haven't been with anyone else. You trust me?"

There's something in his voice, like he still isn't sure it's a good idea.

"We don't have to. I have condoms." I move to roll off the bed, but he stops me.

"No, I want to. God, do I want to. I just can't believe you're real sometimes." He grins. "You're more than I deserve."

"That's not true."

"It is, but I'm gonna do my best to make it up to you with multiple orgasms." He pushes into me slowly. My eyes close and my body tenses as he fills me. He's big and thick and the sensation of him inside me with no barrier is so good that I already feel like I'm on the brink of coming.

He takes both of my hands in one of his and holds them over my head, pinned against the mattress as he thrusts in and out. Our mouths are inches apart. His ragged breaths mix with mine as he fucks me hard and fast.

"Sweetheart," he grits out. "Fuck, London."

My name on his lips in such a tortured tone sends me over the edge. It's too fast. I don't want it to be over.

I'm still coming down from the high of it when he flips me over. He wraps one hand around my stomach to hold me up as he takes me from behind. I cry out again, another orgasm building on the brink of the last. His lips graze my back, placing tender kisses as he slams into me. It's so Brogan. Tender and passionate even when he's destroying my body.

"Oh fuck," he says, and then groans with his cock buried to the hilt. He pulls out and turns me back over. He sits back on the bed and then pulls me onto his lap. I love that he can never make up his mind which way he wants me. Sex with Brogan is an adventure.

"Ride my dick, sweetheart."

"Only because you asked so nicely," I taunt. Or I try to. The eager way I scramble to impale myself on him probably doesn't make it very believable.

We both still as I sit on him. He's buried so deep, the walls of my pussy clenching around him. My heart hammers in my chest, and my skin is slick with a thin coat of sweat. My body is on fire.

"You feel too good," I say as I slowly move.

"Like heaven." His hands go to my hips. He doesn't try to take over, but his fingers dig into my flesh as I glide up and down, gaining speed with each bounce.

I can tell he's close, but trying to hold off, and that just makes me want to push him over the edge more. Watching him come undone is my favorite thing. This gorgeous guy, who could have any girl he wants, wants me.

My hands move to his shoulders and I push my tits out into his face. He wastes no time giving them attention. He takes one nipple into his mouth and sucks, then the other. I roll my hips and move faster. I don't give him any chance to try to hold back. I fuck him until he's too delirious with lust to worry about getting me off.

He comes with a growl that vibrates in his chest. One of his big hands moves down between us and his thumb circles over my clit, sending me careening into ecstasy right along with him.

After my three orgasms, we go to the kitchen to look for snacks. I'm sitting on the countertop, legs dangling and wearing only Brogan's button-down shirt from earlier. He stands between my legs in his boxer briefs.

I grab another handful of grapes. He parts his lips and I bring two up and pop them into his mouth, then eat the other two myself.

"You've never had a pet...ever?" My brows lift in question. I don't remember how we got on the topic at this point, but after I told Brogan about all the animals Sierra and I convinced our parents to get us growing up, he admitted he'd never had one.

"No." He shakes his head and reaches over to the bowl for more grapes.

"What about a fish or a pet rock?"

One side of his mouth lifts into a smile. "Oh, wait. Once in third grade, I got to bring home the class hamster for a night."

"That doesn't count."

We share a grin.

"Do you like animals?"

"Sure." He shrugs.

"What's your favorite animal?"

He thinks for a moment and while he does, he runs his palms up and down my thighs. "Pet animal or any?"

"Both."

"Dog, probably. I like that you can train them to do cool stuff. But my favorite of all animals is probably a rabbit."

"Rabbit," I repeat. "Why?"

I expected him to say lion or cheetah or something big and strong. A rabbit??

"Yeah, they're soft and fast and they have those big floppy ears." He reads my surprised expression and adds, "And at Easter they bring all kinds of candy."

I burst out laughing. The movement makes me tilt forward and I rest my head on his shoulder.

"Rabbits are awesome. Don't laugh at my favorite animal."

"No. I'm not," I say, but I can't seem to stop.

His hands move up under the shirt and he starts to tickle my sides. I'm not normally this ticklish, but my skin is oversensitive from the night and him and the giddy bubble that we seem to be floating inside.

His hands stop and flatten against my side and my laughter dies off. I look up at him into his dark eyes.

"You never stop surprising me," I tell him.

"I'm not sure if that's a good thing or not."

"It's very good. Never a dull moment."

"Dull doesn't sound so bad as long as you're around."

"Are you calling me dull?" I ask. I know he isn't, but I just want to stretch out the moment.

"Definitely not." He brushes his lips over mine in a quick kiss, then rests his forehead against mine. "But when you're around, I don't think I'd notice or care what was happening. I sort of lose track of everything else."

My heart rate picks up speed and my lungs struggle to pull in air. "Yeah, me too."

I know it's the moment that I need to lay my cards on the table.

"I'm glad we're doing this for real. Me and you, Saturday night out, and then going home together. It feels good and right and fun."

He stares at me intently, but says nothing.

"I lose track of everything too. Or maybe I don't, but I choose to ignore it because you're the most amazing, kind, generous, and sexiest person in every room."

"That's a lot of adjectives."

"And not the full list." I want him to know that I can see how much more he is than he gives himself credit for. He feeds into the sexy, professional football player role like he's hiding behind it. But he doesn't need to.

"I think…" he starts, bringing a hand up to my face and stroking my cheek. I stop breathing as I wait for his response. "You might still be drunk."

Disappointment settles in my gut. I'm not. I haven't felt drunk since before we went to the club. And something about him blaming my feelings on booze makes me feel silly and small.

"I'm not," I say. "Or maybe I am, but I still mean it."

He studies me, then nods. "All right."

I'm not exactly sure what he's agreeing to until his lips curve into a smile. "Me and you, sweetheart. Let's lose track of everything else together."

CHAPTER THIRTY
Brogan

I laugh at the current name of our group text thread and then
read through the messages that came in while I was in the shower.

KNOX

> Flynn, it's been a whole week without
> a text back, little brother. Send proof
> of life or I'm showing up to campus
> tomorrow.

ARCHER

> Oh, he'll do it too. One time he dropped
> in at a high school party to yell at me
> and Brogan for staying out all night and
> not calling to tell him where we were.

KNOX

It was three days, you missed school, and the principal was calling around to check. I had to do something.

HENDRICK

No word from Flynn still? Should we call campus security? Maybe his coach?

ARCHER

I was thinking we should start a social media crusade.

HENDRICK

Ooooh. Good call. That way all his friends can help us piece together his last whereabouts.

FLYNN

For the love of...I'm alive. I was sleeping.

KNOX

For six days? How do I know it's you and not someone else?

Flynn sends a selfie, his reddish-brown hair a mess on his head and his eyes droopy with sleep, flipping-off the camera.

FLYNN

That good enough?

KNOX

No. Where the hell have you been?

HENDRICK

I think what he meant to say was, we're glad you're okay. We've missed you. Could you please check in more frequently? We worry about you.

KNOX

No, I said exactly what I meant.

FLYNN

It's too early for this much dysfunction. I'm going back to bed.

KNOX

Yo, Brogan. You were right.

ME

Always. What specifically are you referring to?

KNOX

Her eyes really are the color of grass.

He sends the picture I posted of me and London at the bachelor party. Seeing us together and her smiling makes me smile.

ME

Right?

HENDRICK

This is the girl, huh? I'd like to meet her.

ME

We'll see.

KNOX

What does that mean?

ME

I don't want to scare her off so soon.

KNOX

If she's dating you I don't think that's possible.

I head out into the living room where Archer is kicked back on the couch, his feet on the ottoman, watching TV. He glances over when I plop down next to him.

"Hey," I say, gaze flicking to the screen. The TV is muted, but subtitles are on. They're showing highlights from this week's games and doing predictions for the coming weekend. We had a bye this weekend, but next Sunday we play Baltimore and they're undefeated so far this season.

"When'd you get home?"

"Not long ago," I say and sign. *"Next weekend is going to be tough. Any word from the docs if you'll be able to play?"*

"They think so." The relief on his face is palpable.

"Hell yeah. Finally." It's not been the same playing without him. We've been on the same team since we were eight years old. When I look up the field and he's not there it just feels wrong. And I know he hates not being able to contribute to the team. It's different when it's your job. Teams are businesses and make decisions to help the bottom line. I know Archer is good for the team, but that's because I've spent years watching him. The Mavericks don't have that kind of history to rely on.

"What are you doing tonight? I was thinking about having some people over."

I nod. "Yeah. That's perfect. I can invite London."

He grins. "How's that going?"

"Good. Great actually. We're legit. No more pretending."

His brows rise. "You're *together* together?"

"Mhmm." My smile doesn't falter.

"I don't know what to say. Congrats?"

A rough chuckle escapes. *"Congratulations will do. I was thinking maybe I'd take her down to Valley to meet everyone."*

I get up and go into the kitchen and he follows. I pull out some leftovers from two nights ago and sniff the container, then toss it in the microwave. Archer's got that pensive, constipated look on his face still.

"What?" I prompt, knowing he has something he wants to say.

"Nothing."

"Bullshit. You've got something to say, so say it. You were right. Is that what you want me to say? Fine. You were right. She's great, and I really like her."

"That's not it. It just seems like you changed your mind really fast. A week ago you were sure you weren't ready and now you want to take her home to meet the family? I like London. I like her for you. But you don't need to rush things."

I tamp down the unsettling feeling of being the problem child of the relationship so early. Am I already fucking this up?

"I've never felt like this about anyone."

"I believe you and I'm stoked, but taking her to Valley is a big step…"

"You don't think I'm good enough for her?" I ask the question I've asked myself about a dozen times since last night.

"The fuck I don't." He stands a little taller. *"You're the best guy I know. Hands down. No contest."*

"Then what?" I ask, not sure I want the answer, but needing to hear it anyway.

"Have you told her anything about your parents?"

"She doesn't need to hear about that bullshit." I scowl at him. *"Have you told Wren all your family drama?"*

He makes a face that confirms my suspicions that he hasn't. His jaw flexes and he briefly looks away.

"We aren't defined by our parents," I tell him. *"Except your mom. The rest don't have any bearing on who we turned out to be."*

"Don't you think we should be able to share that stuff with someone though? Don't you want to?"

"No." I don't even have to think about it. *"It's in the past."*

"Is it? What about Sabrina?"

"I haven't heard from her since the letter," I admit. *"And the last thing London wants to hear is that I have some fucked-up person claiming to be my sister so she can get paid."* The idea makes shame and anger swirl in my gut.

Archer's voice drops. *"Like it or not, our experiences have made us who we are. You're a great fucking guy. You shouldn't need to hide any of that from her."*

Easier said than done. Talking about it puts me right back in that place. I don't want to hide it from her as much as I just want to forget about all of it.

I do also hate the look of pity when people know my situation. Luckily, I've been able to keep it mostly to my small circle. When I say that the Hollands are my family, I mean it and people don't question it. I know I'll never be to them what they are to me, but that's okay. They have each other, real brothers, and I'll never be that. How could I?

The bonds between family, real family, are different. I believe that even if my own experience proved otherwise. But Archer and his brothers have been there for me every time I've needed them. That's enough for me.

I'm still thinking about it when London gets to the apartment. She's holding a bottle of champagne and looking sexy in jeans and a black tank top. And just like that, the last thing I feel like doing is talking about deadbeat parents and family dynamics.

"You're late."

"I brought booze." She holds up the champagne.

I take it from her and then loop an arm around her waist and drag her into the apartment. I drop my mouth to hers and kiss her hard.

She's breathless when I pull back. "Wow. Maybe I should have mentioned it's cheap booze."

Laughing, I take her hand in mine. "Around here, it gets drunk the same way."

I stop in the kitchen and drop off the bottle before leading her down the hall. "I want to show you something."

"Is that something, you naked?" Her laughter tinkles and echoes in the narrow space.

"Make that two things I want to show you." I walk to my room and step in, flipping on the light.

"Oh my gosh." Her eyes widen as she steps in behind me. "What happened to your bed and the box you were using as a nightstand?"

"Gone and gone."

I shove my hands in my pockets as she moves toward the bed.

It's the one we made out on in the store. I went back to pick one out for the spare room, but I kept being drawn to this one.

"Do you like it?"

"It's gorgeous."

I beam inside and out. "Recognize the bed?"

She swivels her head and looks at me over her shoulder, then back at the bed. "Oh my gosh. Is this…"

"Yep." I step to her. "The location of our first kiss."

"Technically, it was our second."

My lips press to hers, but before I can get carried away, I stop. "There's more."

I walk over to the wall and incline my head to the framed illustration. It's the one she drew of me in my uniform holding red lacy panties. I had it printed and found a nice frame.

Her jaw drops and she walks toward it with a look of pure disbelief. "You kept it?"

"Of course. It's the coolest thing anyone has ever given me."

"I drew it in like five minutes," she says as she runs her fingers along the edge of the frame. "If I'd known you were going to put it up on your wall I might have spent a little more time on it."

"It's perfect." She's perfect.

She shakes her head and turns in a circle to take in the entire room. Besides the bed, I got a nightstand, a dresser, and a mirror that hangs over it. The saleslady said it all went together. I didn't think I cared much about the room, but now seeing her approval makes me glad I did.

"I thought you were picking out a bed for the spare room." She faces me, hands going to her hips.

"I did that too. Moved my old bed frame into the spare, got a couple of nightstands and a lamp."

"I hope you don't expect me to sleep in there."

"Hell no. You belong in here."

She leans up on her toes to kiss me. Noise in the hallway interrupts us.

"Sorry," Tripp says, covering his eyes, but then peeks through them. "I'm going to do a beer run. You need anything?"

"Stay. We'll go," I tell him.

"You sure? I've got a whole list."

"Yeah. Text it to me."

"Cool." He raps his knuckles against the doorframe.

"What if I want to stay?" London asks when he's gone.

"Nope." I scoop her up and put her on my shoulder, stopping only to grab my keys on the way out. "You're coming with me, sweetheart."

The drive is nice. I'm not really in the mood to party and I like having London all to myself. We go to the liquor mart and I grab a cart.

I hand her my phone. "Read it off to me."

We wander down aisles picking out everyone's special requests. By the time we're finished, we've got more alcohol than could possibly be drunk in one night.

My phone pings with a text while she's still holding it in the checkout line.

"Oh, sorry." She averts her gaze and tries to hand it back to me.

"Who is it?"

"Uhhh…" She looks at me like she's gauging whether or not I really want her to check my phone before she glances back at the screen. "Joey is calling."

"That's my agent. I'll call him back later."

She silences it and then holds it out to me again.

"Put it in my pocket for me," I say as I load up the counter with our purchases.

She does, grinning as she slides the device into my front pocket. I take the opportunity to lean forward and kiss her.

Once we've paid and gotten everything in the truck, we start back for the apartment.

"Pick a song." I hand her my phone again.

"You are very free with this thing tonight," she says, taking it.

"Why wouldn't I be?"

"I don't know. Aren't you worried I'm going to snoop around and find all your secrets?"

"Have at it. Just avoid the folder labeled blackmail."

Her brows rise. "Well, now I have to look."

"I wouldn't if I were you."

A second later I know when she's not heeded my warning.

"Oh my god. Are those…balls?"

"Yep. Slade."

"I so did not need to see that."

"I did try to warn you."

"Why do you have this? How did you get this?"

"He took my phone and snapped some pictures of his balls thinking it was funny and probably assuming I was going to delete them."

"Why didn't you?"

"Was the folder name not clear enough for you?" I ask.

"You wouldn't blackmail anyone."

"Nah, probably not, but it's good to have leverage."

"Boys are very odd," she says, then continues to look through my phone.

I'm not at all worried. Okay, I'm not too worried. If she looked back far enough, I'm sure there's some sexting with other women or dirty photos, but she's the only one I've been talking to since we made our agreement.

"How old are you here?" she asks after a few minutes. She holds the phone up to show a picture of me and Archer in our junior high football uniforms.

"Seventh grade," I say. "That was the last game of the season."

"Did you win?"

"I don't know," I say, realizing it's true. I think we did. I remember taking the photo and I remember it all feeling strange because it was the first game where Rosie wasn't in the stands cheering us on. The reminder of her makes me reconsider Archer's words from earlier.

"That was right after Archer's mom died," I say. "She'd been sick with cancer for a while so it wasn't exactly a surprise, but we were still wrecked."

"I'll bet," she says, a hint of sympathy lacing her tone. "That's so young to lose a parent."

I lift the rose necklace up with a finger. I told her last night that it belonged to Archer's mom but remembering what Archer said, I decide to give her a little more truth. "Her name was Rosie. I gave it to her one year for Christmas. I mowed lawns and did landscaping jobs for a month to save up for it. I thought I was clever getting her a rose charm because of her name. When she died, we found like three other necklaces that were similar. Guess I wasn't so clever after all."

"I bet she loved it anyway."

I nod. "She pretended to for me. I think she knew how bad it was for me at home. She always made me feel special and wanted."

The truck goes quiet. London puts the phone in the cup holder and then scoots over and takes my hand.

"She sounds really wonderful. I'm glad you had her."

"Yeah, me too." I huff a short, brittle laugh. "I don't know where I'd be if it weren't for her."

London looks up at me with a thousand questions in her eyes. "I want to ask, but I know it's probably hard to talk about."

I nod in reply.

"Just…you know that you can always talk to me, right?"

I squeeze her hand. "Yeah. I know."

She doesn't question me or push me to talk more and I'm grateful. Talking about Rosie feels like a lance to the heart. I often think about how if it still hurts me this badly, how much worse it has to be for Archer and his brothers.

I clear my throat and attempt to lighten the mood. "Have you talked to Sierra today?"

"Yes." She laughs softly. "She was nursing a pretty wicked hangover."

"I'll bet."

"But she had a blast last night. Thank you."

"It was nothing. You planned it all."

"Maybe, but the limo and the club were the cherry on top."

I open my mouth to say something dirty but her hand flies to cover it before I can. "Don't ruin this very nice moment."

I chuckle around her hand. "Anything you say, sweetheart."

CHAPTER THIRTY-ONE
London

On Sunday after another home game, I go with Brogan to the bar. The same one we went to the night our fake dating arrangement started. It feels like years ago instead of months.

The team is in great spirits. They beat Baltimore and even with my lack of football knowledge, I know they outplayed them. Brogan had another touchdown, and I screamed my head off with Alec in our seats close to the field.

"You want something to drink?" he asks as we make our way to the bar.

I place a hand to my throat. It's dry from yelling at the game. "Yes. I'm so thirsty."

He grins like he knows exactly why I'm parched, but doesn't comment as he leads me to an open spot with two fingers on my lower back.

The bartender looks our way instantly. Ah, what it must be like to get this kind of service everywhere you go.

"What can I get you?" the guy asks.

"Usual for me and she'll have…" He looks down at me.

"Diet Coke."

The guy nods and gets started pouring our drinks.

"I'm laying off alcohol for a very long time," I say by way of explanation. Ever since the bachelorette party, hard alcohol makes my stomach churn.

"Mhmm…until someone breaks out the champagne."

My mouth goes suddenly much drier. The cheap champagne I brought to his party was opened and drunk…mostly by us in his new amazing bed…and let's just say that a cheap champagne hangover is not on my list of things to repeat. Sex in that gigantic bed though…yes, please, forever.

With our drinks in hand, we go to a table where some of his teammates are sitting.

Tripp lifts his chin in greeting as Brogan pulls a chair out for me. "Hey there, gorgeous."

The man behind me growls, and I look back in time to see him glaring at his friend.

Tripp chuckles. "What? You don't think your girl is gorgeous or don't like that every other guy in here is looking at her? It's kind of hard not to notice how pretty she is. Especially when she's standing next to your ugly ass."

"I think…" He sits next to me and drags my chair closer to him and farther from Tripp. "She's the hottest woman in the universe, but I'm not letting you, or any of these other fuckers, steal her away from me."

He grins and holds up his hands. "Wouldn't dream of it. You

lose this one and it's all on you, Six."

"I'm dumb, but I'm not that dumb." Brogan drapes an arm around the back of my chair, and I lean into him.

In the time we've been hanging out with his teammates at parties and events, I've gotten to know a little about their personal lives and they don't ignore me or talk around me. I feel like one of the guys around them. I chat with Merrick about his recent adventures in dating apps – he's been matched with some real losers but since half his profile is a lie, it's hard to feel sorry for him. I force Slade out of his shell by asking him about the game even though I understand very little of what he says in return, and I help Tripp look for women in the crowded bar when Brogan gets up to get the table another round.

While I'm scanning the bar for "his type," which is very vague and basically includes all women between the ages of twenty-five and forty, I see a woman stepping up next to Brogan at the bar.

He's oblivious to her until she invades his space. I watch in amusement as he takes a step away from her. His mouth moves so I know he says something to her, but as soon as the bartender sets the drinks down in front of him, Brogan practically runs away from her.

When he gets to the table, I smirk at him. "Trouble at the bar?"

"You saw that, huh?" His grin is wobbly and nervous. "I told her I was happily in a relationship and that my girlfriend didn't like it when people put their hands on me without permission. Except in football, although it's the rules of the game so it's sort of like they have permission."

I bite my lip to keep from laughing.

"Are you mad?" he asks. "I'm sorry. See, this is why you need to come with me everywhere I go. I need a bodyguard."

"You called me your girlfriend."

"Yeah," he says slowly. "Is that okay?"

"I've just never heard you say it since it's been true. I like it." I like it a lot.

"Oh yeah?" He leans in and my stomach flips around as his dark eyes glitter with mischief. His lips ghost across mine. "Girlfriend."

A thrill shoots through me. I am totally in love with this man. Ridiculously, hopelessly in love with him.

"Boyfriend," I whisper back.

"Ooooh. That is nice," he replies before kissing me harder.

A moment later we're being catcalled and whistled at. I pull away, blushing as his teammates stare and cheer us on.

"Want to come with me to the bathroom?" Brogan asks.

"Excuse me?"

"For protection," he adds.

"I think you'll be safe. Be quick."

He shoots me that boyish grin and hurries off. He glances back before he disappears around the corner to the bathroom and mimics wiping his forehead with the back of his hand.

I laugh out loud and then take a sip of my Diet Coke.

"You two are cute," Tripp says.

"Thanks."

"I gotta say, when he told us he was dating someone, I thought for sure he was making it up. Then I met you and I thought, 'Now I know he's making this up.' You're not at all what I expected."

"Smaller boobs?" I ask as I feel a little self-doubt creep in.

"I mean that you're not with him just for the glitz and lifestyle. A lot of women, men too, latch on to guys in the league because of what it can do for them. Money, party invites, status…" He trails off. "And you show up to the bar in jeans and a T-shirt, drinking a soda, and not trying to steal him away to some bigger, better event."

A rush of sympathy hits me that these are the standards. Being a decent person shouldn't be such a rare trait in the women he comes across.

"You really care about him." He doesn't ask it as a question, but I can tell he's curious.

"I really do," I admit.

He holds his fist out to me and I bump my much smaller one against his. "If he fucks it up, I'll bust his kneecaps."

A laugh leaves my lips and warmth fills my chest. "Thanks, Tripp."

"Now…tell me what you think of the redhead at the bar."

I swivel around and scan the area in front of the bar until I place a woman with beautiful strawberry-blonde hair standing alone. It's hard to tell how old she is. Twenty-one. Maybe twenty-two. She's on the taller side and wears a dress that shows off her long legs and curves. Her face is round and has a sweetness to it. Guys around her have noticed her but so far no one has approached her. She's glancing around like she's looking for someone and doesn't look entirely comfortable being alone.

"She's really pretty, but I don't think she's twenty-five."

His lip curls. "I can't date anyone more than ten years younger than me. It's too weird. They don't get any of my jokes or pop culture references."

I laugh. "Well, maybe she just has a young face."

She steps away from the bar like a woman who has just found her friends in the crowd.

"Maybe we'll be able to tell by her friends," I suggest.

"Knowing my luck, she's here to meet her boyfriend."

We keep staring at her like we're two detectives cracking a case. She struts across the bar with a confidence that reminds me of Brogan.

No sooner have I had the thought than she steps in front of my boyfriend coming back from the bathroom. Brogan pauses and starts to go around her. I love that he's so determined not to let women touch him. God, I love him.

He tries to dodge her, but she must say something because he looks up at her, steps slowing.

"Ah, they always go after the rookies," Tripp says. "Better go claim your man."

I laugh it off, knowing Brogan can take care of himself, but also already enjoying how he's going to tease me about it when he gets back to the table. The man really does get hit on more than anyone I've ever met. It's hard to blame them though.

I watch as Brogan's expression changes from mild discomfort to confusion to something I can't read at all. He glances up at the table and I give him a reassuring smile that he doesn't return. Instead, he ducks his head to speak to the woman and then the two of them move through the crowd together toward the front door. I sit taller in my chair and can just make out his head as they exit the bar.

Tripp has already stopped paying attention to them and is in conversation with the other guys at the table. An unsettling feeling takes over me.

The whole thing is odd, but I know there are a million different explanations. I tell myself that for the next few minutes while I wait for Brogan to return. When he slides back into the seat next to me, my relief is palpable.

"Hey," I say. "Get stopped by a jilted ex-lover?"

I hope my tone is playful, even though my heart is still racing. He doesn't have the same happy, carefree expression on his face as he usually does.

But before I can go into full panic mode, his features shift, and he smiles. "You know me. The ladies can't get enough. I'm gonna get another drink. You want anything?"

He's already out of his chair and moving toward the bar before I say no.

I chalk it up to my own uneasiness reading too much into his actions, but when he returns to the table with a tray of shots and proceeds to take three in a row, I start to worry.

What the hell is going on?

"Are you okay?" I ask him as he lets out a whoop and chases the liquor with his beer.

"I'm great," he says, but he doesn't quite meet my eye.

CHAPTER THIRTY-TWO
Brogan

I t feels like someone is sitting on my face. And not in the good way.

In the head-throbbing, brain feeling like it's being squeezed, afraid to open my eyes kind of way. "I drank too much last night" is probably the understatement of the century.

London. My eyes fly open when I remember my girlfriend and brief visions of her helping me into bed last night. Fuck. I squeeze my eyes shut after I realize I'm in bed alone.

I rub two fingers along my forehead as I try to think of what happened after. Did I tell her?

"Hey." Her soft voice is like music to my ears. My lashes lift tentatively, and she smiles at me from the doorway. She's wearing my shirt over her jeans and it hangs down almost to her knees. I must not have fucked things up too badly if she's here.

"How are you feeling?" she asks.

"Better now." I glance down at myself, still dressed in the jeans I wore last night. "I'm sorry about last night."

"It's okay. You had a good game. I'd say that's cause for celebrating."

Is that what I told her I was doing last night? I guess that answers the question of if I told her. Fuck. How do you even bring something like that up?

I aim as much of a smile as I'm capable of at her and get out of bed. I'm nauseous and stumbling as I walk to her.

"What time is it?"

"Just after ten."

"You don't have work?"

"I called in sick." She grins. "I thought you might need someone to hold your hair back this morning."

"I'll be all right after I get some food in me."

"I got bagels from the place down the street."

"You're a goddess." I wrap myself around her and breathe her in. My mind is spinning and my heart feels like it's going to leap out of my chest. I squeeze her like I never want to let her go because I don't. "You should come back to bed with me."

"Come on." She takes my hand with a small laugh and starts out of the room. "Let's feed you and then we can nap."

I think I agree, but I feel like I'm wading through mud. Everything sounds far away, like I'm not really present.

My phone rings as I'm taking a seat on a barstool in front of the island. I must have left it there last night when we got home.

"Are you gonna get that?" London asks. She sets the bag of bagels in front of me.

"No. It's probably spam."

The call ends and a second later it starts up again.

"Want me to check?" she asks.

"Yeah. Please."

It's only when she's stepping over to get closer to see the screen that I remember another key detail from last night. Oh shit.

I hop up from the stool as London says, "It's Sabrina."

My head sways, so does the rest of me.

"I should…" Fuck. I need to answer it, but this is going to be awkward.

"Who's Sabrina?" she asks.

"She's the girl from the bar last night."

"O-kay. Why is she calling?" Her brows are marred in confusion.

A totally reasonable question, but I can't think of how to explain.

"I'm sorry," I say to her. "I forgot. I thought you'd be at work."

Not the right thing to say.

"Oh my god." The color drains from her face. "Is she someone you're interested in? Are you seeing her? Or planning to see her after you and I are done?" The hurt on her face makes me think of Chris and how he jerked her around. Of course, I'd never do that to her. But I can't seem to make my brain function enough to figure out what to say or how to explain.

"Brogan?" London's voice is filled with that fire I love.

"No," I say. "It's not like that."

The ringing starts up again. London glances at the screen, and by her expression I know it's Sabrina calling back.

London walks over to the couch where her purse is lying, picks it up, and puts it on one shoulder. She's assuming the worst and honestly, I can't blame her. Nothing I'm saying or doing is right.

"Please don't go," I tell her.

I blow out a breath and then my feet move toward her without thought. Thank fuck, because my thoughts suck.

I'm barefoot as I hurry after her down the stairs and outside. The sidewalk is cool from the morning.

"Wait, London."

She pauses and glances back at me.

"I'm sorry. I need to explain. Just give me one second."

She turns to me and waits.

"Last night at the bar I got drunk because Sabrina showed up. I wasn't expecting to see her. She's been texting me and trying to contact me for months, but I thought…" I trail off. A lump has lodged in my throat. "Sabrina isn't someone I'm interested in like that."

"Does she know that? Because she's pretty eager to talk to you."

"Yes, she is. At first, I thought it was a scam or she was just making shit up, but then she showed up at the bar last night."

"What are you trying to say?" London asks. "Is she someone you hooked up with in the past? Is she pregnant? What? Just say it."

Pregnant? Whoa. Wait. I shake my head.

"She's my sister," I blurt out.

London rears back like that is more surprising than some random woman calling me up and saying she's pregnant. Her mouth falls open.

"Yeah." I nod. "Or she says she is. I don't know for sure yet, but her story adds up."

"How would you not know if you had a sister?"

"That is a complicated answer." I run a hand over my head. "I told you my family was shit and I meant it. I moved in with the Hollands when I was a kid, and I haven't seen them since. The only time they've bothered to reach out since then was for money after I got drafted."

Her eyes take on a pitying, soft edge. "Brogan."

"I don't want your sympathy."

She wraps her arms around my middle and places her head against my chest. "I'm so sorry."

My throat tightens with emotion as she hugs me. "It's fine. I've accepted it, but then Sabrina started contacting me and I didn't know what to do. I've ignored her for months. I had no idea about her. I don't even know if she's telling the truth. Archer thinks it could be my parents using some random girl to get more money."

"But you don't?"

"I don't know what to think." I shake my head. "She looks like my mom."

Fuck, maybe it's all in my head.

"So, she tracked you down at the bar last night because you've been avoiding her texts?"

"Yeah." I let out a short laugh. "She's as relentless as I am."

The thought sobers me. I have a sister. Maybe. A part of me wants it to be true and the other part is afraid anyone who shares my blood can't possibly have pure intentions.

"I should get back. She's probably going to call back until I answer. I don't have any idea what to say to her."

"I think you just...talk to her. Be you. Sweet, open-minded Brogan Six."

I don't think it will be that easy, but I can't keep going without knowing the truth.

"Yeah. All right." I blow out a long breath, then voice that fear that's been picking at me since last night. "What if she isn't really my sister?"

What if I let myself hope and then it turns out she's just another person who doesn't give a shit about me?

"Either way, you'll know." She studies me. "Do you want me to come back up with you while you talk to her?"

Absolutely, I do. I want to wrap London around me like a security blanket, but this isn't her mess and I've already dropped one bomb on her today. If she sits through this conversation with Sabrina, she'll know just how fucked up my parents are. How could they never mention that I have a sister?

"That's all right. I should talk to her alone. It's going to be awkward as fuck."

"Will you call me later?" she asks. "Let me know how it goes?"

"Of course. We have dinner with your parents, right?"

"Brogan, you don't have to come to that. I'll cover for you. This is a lot. You should take time to sit with it."

"Nah, it's fine. I want to come. I'll be there."

She searches my face. I wonder if I look as wrecked as I feel.

"Okay," she says finally, lingering a little longer. "Text me if you need anything or just want to talk. I can stop back by if you want."

"I don't deserve you." I hug her and breathe her in one last time.

"You do, and I'm yours."

CHAPTER THIRTY-THREE
Brogan

Archer's face gives nothing away. I just gave him a play-by-play of the last twenty-four hours. I didn't leave anything out, including how I drank so much that London had to put me to bed.

"What do you think?" I ask when I can't take it any longer. I need his opinion because my brain is too cluttered. I've used it more in the past twenty-four hours than in my entire life.

"You know what I think, but I didn't talk to her. Is she willing to do a DNA test?" His face is still guarded.

"I don't know," I say. *"We only talked for a few minutes. She told me how her parents adopted her at birth, and she always knew, but she only started looking for her birth parents earlier this year. She obviously didn't know about me either, but when she started researching them..."*

"She found you."

I nod.

"Did she ask for money?"

"No. She said she just wanted to meet me."

He makes a gruff, disbelieving sound deep in his throat. *"She could still be making the whole thing up."*

"I know." He's not wrong. It's just a story. *"But Arch...I don't think she is. It feels like she could be the real deal. I can't explain it. Something about her..."* I trail off, feeling silly. *"Maybe I'm just gullible."*

His scowl turns into a sympathetic smile. *"You're not gullible. You just see the best in people and some people are assholes."*

"Will you meet her? I know you're skeptical and I understand why, but I need someone else to help me figure this out because I can't see straight." He knows what my parents were like, so I don't have to worry about him feeling any differently about me. He saw me at my most broken and he's never held it against me.

"Of course I will."

"And not yell at her."

"No promises."

My body relaxes knowing he has my back on this.

"Where were you last night anyway?" I ask, desperate to change the conversation.

"I went to Wren's house after the game." He grimaces. *"We ended things."*

"Oh, shit. *I'm sorry.*" I drop what's left of my sandwich onto my plate and wipe my hand on a napkin. *"You let me go on and on for the past hour and said nothing until now?"*

His masked expression gives way to a small smirk. *"I don't think my relationship status competes with a potential secret sister."*

Secret sister. Fuck. My brain is going to explode.

"What happened?" I ask, pushing thoughts of Sabrina away for

now. I went twenty-three years without thinking about her, another hour or so won't make a difference.

"Eh…" He lifts a hand and waves it around, diverting his gaze. *"It wasn't really going anywhere. I knew it. She knew it."*

"So? I thought you were just having fun and not looking for anything serious."

"I'm not."

"Then why stop seeing her?"

He lets out a long breath. *"I just wasn't feeling it."*

There's something he's not telling me, but I can't figure out what. *"Did she dump you?"*

"It was mutual," he replies dryly.

"I don't get it then. She's hot. You two seem to get along. It's uncomplicated. And the sex sounds like it's fun."

I get another look at that comment, but come on, our bedrooms are close.

"You're deaf. I am not," I remind him.

He flips me off in reply.

"What is the actual problem?" It's cheering me up focusing on his life instead of mine.

"She talks a lot."

"O-kay." One side of my mouth lifts. Of course, I've noticed that Wren likes to hear herself talk, but I didn't realize this was a dealbreaker for him. *"And that's a problem? Because it doesn't sound like a problem when she's yelling your name. 'Archer! Oh, Archer!'"*

He looks like he wants to strangle me, but I feel better so, whatever.

"No, but…" He hesitates like he doesn't want to admit whatever it is to me.

"She always forgets to look at me while she's jabbering on," he says finally. *"Or she covers her mouth with her hand."* He demonstrates, resting a hand over his mouth so it's impossible to read his lips.

He lets his hand drop and shakes his head. *"It's dumb, I know. I've dated plenty of women that I've struggled to communicate with at times. I think that's just to be expected, but Wren treats my hearing loss like it's an urban myth. I'm constantly having to ask her to repeat herself or just smiling and nodding and pretending like I understood and hoping I didn't agree to something crazy. It's exhausting and I'm always on edge. Sex is the only time we manage to communicate just fine."*

Sympathy for him and anger at her duel for my primary emotional state. What an inconsiderate asshole. I guess anger won out.

I think back on the times I've been around them, seeing it all differently now. I thought he was just tuning her out. I should have known better. Fuck.

"I'm sorry," I say. And I am. Sorry I wasn't there when he ended things. I'm sure he was way too nice about it.

"It's whatever. Dating is too complicated right now anyway. Sex, parties, and fun only from now on. The Brogan Six playbook so to speak. Pre-London, that is."

I know he's deflecting, but I let him off the hook. Lord knows I have done enough of that lately. *"Let's hope I'm not Post-London."* Thinking of my girlfriend makes my chest tighten.

"I thought you said she was great about everything."

"She was, but I'm supposed to see her tonight and she's going to have questions..." I trail off. *"How do I explain it?"*

"What?"

"All of it. My parents. That the people who are supposed to love me

more than anyone or anything in this world could give a shit less about me. Or that the thought of having another one of me was so awful they gave my sister up for adoption and never bothered to tell me. I was barely two when she was born, so it's not like I expect to remember much from that timeframe, but it still seems like something I should have known. I guess it's on par for them. The only time they've contacted me in the past ten years was to ask for money. Not even a fucking 'Hey, how are you? Congrats on the job!' 'Proud of you, son!'"

"Fuck them. It's their loss."

God, I wish I could write them off as easily as he does, or at least write off their actions as having nothing to do with me. What the hell did I do to make them hate me so much? I wasn't a bad kid, I don't think. I tried my best to stay quiet and not need them for anything. No matter how small I made myself, they weren't happy with me.

They didn't care if I got good grades at school or if I played a good game. They didn't care about me, period. And they didn't want me around. They were only interested in going out and hanging with friends. At least as best I remember it. If they were home, they were sleeping, or our house was filled with people I didn't know. They weren't addicts, I don't think, though they did plenty of partying. It just seemed like they weren't interested in being parents. Sometimes I think it'd be easier if they were. I know that's fucked-up, but if I could blame it on anything other than myself, I would. Otherwise, it just feels like it was my fault they didn't love me.

Seeing Sabrina put me back in that place. If she is my sister and they gave her away, why didn't they do the same for me? Was there some time they did want me, and I fucked it all up? I know what Archer would say if I asked him, but I can't help but wonder. Was

I the problem?

We eat the rest of our lunch in silence, but when we get up to leave, Archer says, *"I'm sorry I wasn't there last night or this morning."*

"Probably better this way. You might have tossed her out before I had a chance to talk to her."

"If she's as hot as Tripp says, I doubt it."

I stop and glare at him.

"He doesn't know she's your sister, but I put it together. The hot redhead from the bar you were talking to..." He trails off. *"He texted me last night because he was worried you were fucking around on London."*

"What the fuck?"

"I told him you weren't."

"You weren't even there."

"I don't need to have been there. I know you," he says firmly.

I relax, thankful the rest of the team doesn't know who Sabrina is yet. And then I remember he just called her hot. Twice. *"That's my sister you're talking about."*

He chuckles. "Maybe."

Later that night, I swing by London's apartment to pick her up for dinner with her parents. I gave myself a pep talk on the way over. I spent the day spiraling and wondering what the fuck I should do.

"Hi." Her smile is bright, and she searches my face with a hint of worry in her eyes. "How are you?"

"Good." I let my gaze fall over her. She's wearing a short black dress. It's simple, but hugs her curves, and she has on red lipstick that makes the green in her eyes stand out. "You look great."

"Thanks. You too."

"Sleeves down?" I ask, smiling a little as I think about the first time we went out with her family. God, that feels like a million years ago, but also like no time has passed since I met her.

"Your choice. They've all seen your forearms, unfortunately."

Chuckling, I put the truck in drive and pull away from the curb. I turn the radio up a notch. My shirt feels tight around my neck as London continues to glance over from her seat.

"How did things go with Sabrina?"

Her name alone has my anxiety climbing. "Fine. I don't really want to talk about it. If that's okay?"

"Of course," she says, smiling, but I can see the underlying concern in her expression. "We don't have to go tonight if you don't feel up to it."

"Nah, I'm good." I force my smile to inch higher.

We drive to the restaurant with our fingers intertwined and the radio loud enough to drown out some of my thoughts.

The day has been weird and I'm not feeling like myself, but I can do this for her. I'd do anything for her. The realization doesn't freak me out like I always thought it would.

Her parents are already seated in the back with her sister and Ben. London groans when she spots them.

"Why are they always here?"

I look closer to the subject of her frustration. Chris and Gretchen. A few other members of the wedding party are here too, so it isn't that odd, but I wrap my arm around the back of her waist and drop a kiss to her forehead. "Ignore him."

We're seated and food is brought out not long after. I find myself in a daze more often than not. It's hard to follow the conversation around me, and London keeps glancing at me like she's checking in.

I take a long drink of water, wishing it was something stronger.

The conversation has turned to work and I perk up when London's parents ask how things are going at Channel 3.

"It's fine," she says, looking down at where her fingers rest on the bottom of a water glass. "I've actually been thinking about moving to part-time or maybe seeing if they'd let me freelance."

A smile lights up my face. "Really?"

She gives me one of her own smiles back and hesitantly nods.

"You want to quit your job?" London's dad asks, breaking the moment. His tone has my hackles rising.

"Well, no," she says. "I'd still work. I've been getting more side projects, and I could take on even more if I had extra hours."

The silence at the table says more than her parents' matching disapproving looks.

"What about benefits?" her mom asks. "Healthcare? 401k? Do you have savings?"

London opens her mouth to answer, but her dad speaks first.

"It's great if you want to do your arts and crafts on the weekends, but quitting your job to draw cartoons for people?" His tone softens like it makes his words any less cutting. "That's not a real job, honey."

"It is a real job," I butt in without thinking about it. "And she's really, really talented."

"Of course. We're so proud of you," her mom says.

"Are you?" London asks.

I hear the uncertainty in her tone, the hurt that is buried so deep that she's questioning everything right now. Is she good enough? Can she succeed without their approval? Do they love her? Why don't they want her? I know exactly how that feels.

My head spins and my body feels like it's not my own.

I'm vibrating with anger when I speak. "She's worked really hard, and you all should be congratulating her, not dismissing her accomplishments like they're nothing."

"We're just looking out for her. London knows we love and support her no matter what." Her mom's face is filled with shock, like she can't imagine how I jumped to that conclusion.

"Does she?" I glance at my girlfriend. I know how much guts it took for her to bring it up to them. She was excited and shared something with them and now she looks defeated.

"I'm fine," London says in the same tone I've been using all fucking day. She's not fine and neither am I.

"Being her parents doesn't give you a free pass to make her feel bad. Don't you want her to feel loved and appreciated? The world is hard enough, but you're her safe space. She cares about you more than anyone else in the world, and this is how you repay her?" My temper rages on. "London is smart and talented, and she just wants you to love her for who she is instead of whoever you think she should be. Do you know she works twelve- and thirteen-hour days just to do the thing she loves? Or that she designed the cover of a book that hit the *New York Times* list?"

They say nothing, but I can't seem to stop.

"She deserves more from the people who are supposed to care about her the most."

"Really, Brogan." London places a hand on my forearm. "I'm okay."

"We didn't mean anything by it. We only want to make sure she's thought through everything before she makes any rash decisions." Her dad's voice has a hard edge, but I can see he means the words coming out of his mouth. He's completely oblivious to how his words cut her down. God, why do we as people have no ability to limit our damage to only hurting ourselves instead of everyone around us?

"Your parents must like to give you a hard time sometimes," Chris says patronizingly. "You know what it's like."

"No. I don't, actually. The last time I spoke to my dad, I was thirteen years old, and he was kicking me out of the house because I accidentally spilled orange juice on the counter and ruined his cigarettes." One of many times he kicked me out, but that was the final straw. I was so tired of being yelled at every time I made a mistake. I moved out the next day on my fourteenth birthday.

The shock on their faces is immediate and no one says anything for too long. *Fuck.*

"If this is what it's like to have your parents be a presence in your life, then I don't think I missed out on much." I stand, my chair screeching back along the floor. "Excuse me."

My hands are clenched into tight fists as I step out into the night air and gulp it in. I let my head fall back so I can stare up at the dark sky.

Footsteps click behind me. I could pick hers out anywhere. I drop my chin to face her.

"Brogan." Her voice is soft.

"I'm sorry." I run a hand through my hair. "I can't stand the way they dismiss you and your art like that. You work so hard, and it's like they can't see that not accepting it only hurts you."

Her lips pull into a thin line.

I'm suddenly very aware that I've overstepped a pretty big boundary. The parents' approval is usually a pretty big thing in relationships, I think.

"Thank you for having my back and for coming tonight when I know you have other things going on, but whatever just happened back there wasn't just about me."

My brow furrows.

"You are pissed at your parents, and I understand why." She steps forward and runs her hands up the side of my arms. "Or I want to, but you have to talk to me. Tell me what's going on with you."

"I'm sorry," I say. My emotions are jumping between rage and guilt. I overstepped. Fuck did I overstep.

"Talk to me," she says again.

"What do you want me to say?" I have a barely contained leash on my anger. "My parents didn't love me." The words feel like nails and the pressure on my chest intensifies. "They didn't fucking love me and I don't know why." I tip my head up to the sky and all but yell, "What the fuck did I ever do to make them hate me so much?"

She coils herself around me, squeezing me like she thinks she can take away all the pain.

Letting out a breath and feeling more tired than I have in years, I drop my stare to her face. She's so beautiful. So perfect.

"I don't know why either," she says, offering me a sympathetic smile. "But you didn't do anything."

I look away from her, but she reaches up and tugs my chin down until I meet her gaze again. "I can't tell you why they didn't, but I'd venture it has everything to do with them and nothing to do with you. You are the most wonderful man I have ever met. You bring so much happiness to everyone in your life. You are funny and considerate, hard-working, talented, sweet." She drops her hand to my chest. "The way that you make people feel says so much about your character. Anyone who doesn't love you just hasn't gotten to know you."

Silence falls between us, but she continues to hold on to me and pierce me with those stunning green eyes. The need to flee is so strong but fuck, I don't want to leave her either. She's the best thing that's happened to me since the Holland family.

"I should go. I'm in a shit mood and I don't think anyone wants me back inside."

"I do."

I try to smile at her, but I don't know if I manage it. "Can you catch a ride home with your sister?"

"Yeah."

I pull back slowly.

"Brogan." The plea in her tone almost undoes me as we break apart. "Are you going to be okay?"

"Fine. I'm really sorry." I'm so ashamed that I made this whole night about me and embarrassed her in front of her family.

She steps forward, wrapping her arms around me again. "Text me tomorrow?"

I don't say anything. I want to, but then what? I need... something. I don't even know what. All I want to do is slam my fist into a wall repeatedly.

"I need a couple of days. Is that okay?" I ask.

A flicker of hurt passes over her expression, but she nods. "Of course it is."

She steps away this time and my chest feels hollow.

"Hey," I say quietly.

She glances over her shoulder at me. I don't say anything, just smile the best I can.

"I'm here if you need anything," she says.

"Yeah." I nod. "I just need to clear my head for a day or two."

Her mirroring nod is the only reply I get before she disappears back into the restaurant.

God, she's so understanding. I love her for that. I love her, period. And it's just about the worst fucking time to have that realization.

I let out a long breath, already wishing I could run after her. But fuck, she deserves so much better. If my own fucking parents don't want me, why would anyone else?

CHAPTER THIRTY-FOUR
London

I invite Paige over the following day so I can unload and get another opinion. I'm having a hard time wrapping my head around everything that's happened the last twenty-four hours.

"I'd like to buy him a drink. God, I wish I could have seen your dad's face. Did that vein in his forehead bulge?" Paige's eyes light up with excitement at the visual.

"I don't know. Brogan ran off and then I followed…" I groan and fall over onto the couch, burying my head in a throw pillow. "I pushed him too hard."

"He said he was fine."

"But I knew he wasn't. I could tell he was faking it and I dragged him into my family drama while he was still reeling from his own."

"You couldn't have known that it was going to end with him yelling at your dad."

"No, I definitely never imagined that."

"What are you going to do?"

"Nothing. He said he needed some time."

She gives me a sympathetic smile, then comes to sit next to me and lets me rest my head in her lap. She strokes my hair, and I close my eyes and let all the sadness wash over me.

"What if he never lets me in?"

"Then we'll get Pat to recruit some friends to jump him."

The image makes me laugh. "They'd probably fangirl instead."

She joins in with my laughter. "My hubby's got my back."

She's just stating facts, but it twists the knife in my gut. Brogan has my back, but he won't let me have his. Or maybe he just can't. I don't know what to do. But I miss him.

Over the next week, I do my best to not hover or worry about Brogan. I fail miserably, but I keep busy. There is an endless list of wedding to-do's now that the wedding is only weeks away.

Today I'm distracting myself at Sierra's apartment where I am inundated with little name cards. Her calligrapher bailed at the last minute and what good is an artsy sister if she won't handwrite a few names? That was her pitch, which was only convincing because I need the distraction. And for the record, a few turned out to be a hundred. Twice as many, really, since nearly a third of them are quickly placed in the redo pile.

"Have you talked to Dad?" she asks only when I'm on the last stack of twenty cards.

"No." I glance up after I finish writing *Gretchen*. The G is a little wonky, but I'm not redoing it. "Have you?"

"No. I'm on your side."

"I don't want there to be sides." Especially right before the big day. Especially after comparing it to what Brogan is going through. I'm still hurt that my parents don't support me, but it doesn't feel as important as it did. "Everything is such a mess."

"Look, I'm not thrilled you and Dad aren't speaking thirteen days before the wedding, but it was bound to happen eventually. And bad timing aside, I'm glad Brogan said something. You never would have, and Dad needed to hear it."

I avert my stare back to the next name on the list. Sierra reaches out and places a hand over mine, stopping me from my task.

"I'm sorry that it wasn't me. It should have been."

"No." I look up, surprised that she's trying to take it on. "I don't blame you at all. If anyone was going to say something, it should have been *me*."

"I have listened to Dad dismiss and disregard your art since we were kids. Little jabs or acting like it wasn't as impressive as me winning a trophy in whatever sport I was playing. I liked that he was proud of me and I think I was afraid that if I did speak up, I'd lose that special bond with him. You are so brave for following your dreams."

I drop the pen and place my other hand on top of hers. "It was a fucked situation. I would have probably done the same if I were you."

She gives me a thankful smile, her blue eyes glistening with unshed tears. "Let's promise each other that we'll stand up for ourselves from now on. Okay? And for each other."

"I promise."

She nods, satisfied with our promise, and I go back to writing names while she stacks them neatly in order of table.

"How is Brogan?" she asks, her voice regaining some of her usual bubbliness. "Is he nervous about the game tonight?" She stops and looks up at the ceiling. "Do they get nervous?"

"I don't know," I say, smiling at her.

"Ben is nervous enough for the both of them. Kansas City's offensive unit is meshing really well right now and their zone defense is the best in the league."

I stare at her a beat, trying to make sense of the words that just came out of her mouth. "You've been watching too much SportsCenter."

She laughs it off but a second later, she asks, "So how is he?"

"I don't know." I'm careful not to look at her but to keep my voice even. For some reason, I don't want her to know how sad I am. There has been enough drama right before her wedding and she doesn't need any more. Plus, she'll probably give me some happily ever after nonsense, and I don't think I can stomach it today. "We haven't talked much. He's dealing with some family stuff."

"Yeah, I gathered that from his outburst about his dad. I know you probably don't want to say, but is everything there okay? There's family drama and there's family *drama,* and it sounds like he might have the latter."

"I really don't know."

Her brows furrow.

"He won't talk to me about it. I have tried, but he always shuts down." I sit back and drop the pen to the table. "I don't want to force him to talk to me, but I don't know how else to be there for him."

"Sometimes people keep secrets because they don't want to admit it to themselves, much less to you or me. If his situation is as bad as I think it must have been, then I doubt it's easy to talk about, even if he cares about you. Which we both know he does. He's crazy about you."

"So, what do I do?"

"You just show up for him. Let him know you're a safe space and when he's ready, you'll be there."

"You make it sound so simple."

"Isn't it?"

I consider it for a minute. It's not the worst advice I've ever been given.

"When did you get so much smarter than me?"

"Oh, about fourth grade." She grins.

I toss my pen at her without the cap on it and it lands ink side first on one of the name cards.

"Ah, no. You crossed out Chris." She holds it up to show me.

"If only it were that easy. He's been texting me about wedding things." I make a face.

"Really?" Her brows shoot up. "And you're replying?"

"Yes." Begrudgingly. "We have planned the rehearsal dinner and the toasts."

"And he's still alive." She grins. "You really do love me."

After I finish the name cards, I head home. On my way I go by to check my mail. The time with Sierra did wonders for my mood. I don't have a clue how to fix any of it—the stuff with my dad or Brogan—but I feel less helpless than I did earlier.

I pull out the envelopes and shove them under one arm while I lock the box and shove the key in my purse. As I'm walking out,

I rifle through to see if there's anything aside from junk. I stop in my tracks when I see the letter addressed to #6. Complete with pink pen and little red hearts. No perfume or lipstick, so that's something.

Whoever sorted the mail wouldn't have realized this was meant for Brogan without his name clearly written out, so it didn't get forwarded with the rest of his mail. I smile at the envelope.

I consider texting him. Maybe I could take a picture of it, break the ice that way? I snap a pic but delete the text before I send it. He wanted space, and I want to honor that.

Sierra's words are still floating around in my head though. Show up for him. Make sure he knows I'll be there for him when he's ready.

I tap my thumb on the envelope and then an idea hits me.

As soon as I get home, I run into Alec in the kitchen. He looks at me with wide eyes that tell me I must look like a woman on a mission. I am. A mission to show the man I love just how much he means to me.

"I need a favor."

CHAPTER THIRTY-FIVE
Brogan

"Thanks for coming." I get to my feet as Sabrina stands in front of the outdoor table. I decided meeting outside of the apartment might be easier and less awkward.

"Of course." She clutches her purse to her side and takes a seat across from Archer. My best friend is glaring at my maybe sister.

"This is my friend, Archer," I tell her. "Archer, this is Sabrina."

"His brother," Archer corrects me. He doesn't usually care what I call him: friend, brother, teammate, but he's staking a claim right now and while I find it mildly amusing, Sabrina looks confused.

"Wait, did they put you up for adoption too?" She looks at me for answers and my throat tightens.

"No, they didn't, but I went to live with Archer and his family when I was fourteen. He and his brothers took me in because things were bad at home."

I take a drink of my water. This is going to be harder than I thought. I haven't talked about my family in years, and of course she's going to have questions.

"Do you want something to drink?" I ask, tipping my head to the inside café.

"Yeah, I think I'll grab a coffee." She starts to get up, but Archer pushes back and stands first.

"I got it," he says tersely. Fuck. I hope he doesn't spit in it. He pauses and it looks like it physically hurts him to ask, "Cream and sugar?"

"Yeah. Please."

With a nod, he goes back inside, and Sabrina and I settle into our chairs.

"So…" My leg bounces under the table.

She places her hands on the table and taps her fingers. "So…"

Sabrina breaks first, smiling and then laughing. "This is awkward."

"So awkward," I agree.

"Look, I didn't badger you for months because I thought we'd be automatic besties. I know this is a lot and you must be surprised to see me or to know I exist. I wasn't sure until I started trying to contact you if you were even aware you had a sister, but I'm guessing now you didn't know?"

"Definitely not. How'd you find out?"

"My parents never kept it a secret from me that I was adopted, but it wasn't until about six months ago that I started feeling like I might want to find my birth mom and dad."

"Did you find them?" I ask. Maybe she hasn't reached out to them yet and I can save her the heartache.

"I haven't been in contact with them if that's what you mean."

I don't know what I mean. This whole conversation is so bizarre.

"I sent a letter, but never heard back." She shrugs. "Then I found you and I realized I cared less about them and more about knowing you. Maybe we didn't grow up together or have the same circumstances, but I felt like I had to meet you. My parents are my parents, ya know, but a brother…" She trails off. "My parents didn't have other kids, so I guess I liked the idea of having a sibling. I'm sorry. I'm not explaining it all very well. It just felt important that I meet you."

Archer reappears and sets her coffee down on the table in front of her.

"Thanks," she says.

"You look like our mom," I tell her, then wonder if that's a weird thing to say. Fuck, it's all weird.

"I do?"

I nod. "She has red hair too and the eyes are Dad." Hers are brown like mine.

"Does anyone else have asthma?"

"Not that I know of. Do you?" Am I allowed to ask that? I guess it's too late to worry about it now.

"Yeah, it's pretty bad. My doctor said it was probably genetic."

"Maybe our grandparents did. I never met any of them. Mom's parents died when she was young, and Dad didn't talk to his family."

"Seems like a common theme."

I don't know if she means it as a dig, but I feel a little judged. I guess it's her family too so if she's judging me, then she's judging herself as well.

"Where did you grow up?" I ask.

"Flagstaff."

All this time she's been so close, and I had no idea.

"What do you do?" Archer asks. I'd forgotten he was here, but his hard tone reminds me that he is and he's still not on board.

"I'm a dance teacher. Or I was. I really want to open up my own studio but first I have to figure out where I want to settle."

"That's cool. You dance?" A sister that's a dancer. Each new detail feels like this secret puzzle.

"All my life." She nods. "I played some other sports too. Never football though."

That makes me grin, and the awkwardness between us starts to dissipate.

"I've been working at a night club as a cage girl while I'm here. Lilac Lounge. Do you know it?"

Archer nudges me and then signs. *Did your secret sister just say she's a stripper?*

No. I glare at him as I sign.

"Sorry," I say to Sabrina. "He was just making sure he understood what you were saying. Archer is deaf but he's pretty good at reading lips."

She looks at my best friend in the whole world. "I dance with my clothes on, but stripping is honest work and nothing to be ashamed of."

My jaw drops, and Arch and I both stare at her in surprise.

"What? I know ASL." Then she stops speaking and signs, *If you are going to talk shit about me, you will have to find another way.*

A rough chuckle escapes my mouth. "Ignore him. He's just overprotective."

"I get it. My friends weren't thrilled about me meeting up with some guy who might be my brother either, but I had to know."

"I'm glad you did," I say, and once the words are out, I know they're true. It might have been a lot less lonely growing up if she'd been around. Maybe that can still be true.

"I'm driving back to Flagstaff this afternoon, but I'll be back next week. I know I dumped a lot on you, so I'll let you think about all of it and get back to me." She smiles. "I promise not to pop up out of nowhere again, but I do think it'd be cool to spend some more time together, if you want."

I scan the crowd as Archer and I walk out onto the field for the game. It's early still. Only the hardcore fans are in their seats while the teams warm up.

My stomach churns when I don't see her. I knew London wouldn't be here. I asked for space and she's given it to me, but it still hurts not to see her in her usual spot.

"The guys are here." Archer turns and points toward a section where we often get seats for family and friends. Hendrick, Knox, and even Flynn are sitting side by side. When they see us looking, they all wave in unison. Flynn even sort of smiles.

I wave back, shocked.

"Did you tell them about Sabrina?" I ask, turning back to Archer and signing the question too.

"No way. That's not my place. You can tell them when you're ready."

I'm relieved, though I can't say why.

"I don't understand then," I say.

"What?"

"You're not playing today, they don't know about Sabrina...why are they all here?" I realize that sounds like I don't want them here, which is never true. It's just…it's the first time we've all been in one spot since Flynn left for college. How is he even here? That's a long-ass trip for a weekend visit.

"To cheer for you," Archer says slowly like the answer is beyond obvious.

I can't think of what to say. I know they all care about me, and maybe they just planned to come to a game anyway and decided not to cancel even though Arch isn't on the field.

"Dude." He grabs hold of my shoulder and squeezes. "They're here for you. They love you. I love you."

"I know and I appreciate it, but they should have waited until they could watch you play too. You are their brother." I try to shrug out of his hold, but he won't let me.

"Stop it. Stop acting like you aren't just as important to them."

I cock my head to the side. I'm not trying to play the pity card, but I'm not as important. I'm just not and that's okay.

"This is what you do. You let people in but only to a point. Even me. You don't have to be the happy, carefree guy all the time. You act like nothing ever bothers you, but I know better. I know shit with your family sucked and that you've done your best to bury it and never think of it, but it will eat you alive if you don't. Let us be there for you. You are our brother. You're one of us. You always have been, and you always will be."

"I know what you're saying, but I'm not. As much as I joke about being a Holland brother, as much as I have wished for it to be true my whole life, we're not blood. It's not the same."

"No, it's not. And thank god for that."

"You don't get what I mean." I try to think how to phrase it.

"I do though. My dad walked out on my family and your parents suck. Fuck blood. Fuck all that. Family is a hell of a lot more than DNA. You are one of us. If you're not a Holland, then neither am I, because we are the same here." He removes his hand from my shoulder and places it in a fist over his heart.

I swallow thickly and the back of my eyes burn.

I love you. He signs the words. *You are my brother always.*

He's said similar things before, but the intensity in his face, the way they're all here, the way they're always here when I need them…it finally hits me how deeply he means the words.

"I love you too." I grab him around the neck and hug him. I feel him relax under my embrace and then he squeezes me back.

"Fuck," he mutters. "I thought I was going to have to punch you."

I laugh, a real honest to god laugh that makes my entire body feel lighter. When I pull back, I shove at his shoulder. "Try it and see what happens."

He chuckles, looking a whole lot less stressed than I've seen him in a while.

"I'm sorry," I say. I thought what he had with his brothers was different, but maybe that was just me keeping them at arm's length. Not intentionally, of course, but deep down I guess as much as I have always wanted family, I was scared too.

"No. None of that. We're good." He tips his head toward the field. "Now go and kick some ass for the both of us."

"Hold up." Everything is almost the way it should be.

He pauses and his brows rise in question.

"Can you do one thing for me first?"

"That depends." He squares off with me to hear what I have to say.

One word.

"London."

A slow smile spreads across his face. "Tell me what you need."

CHAPTER THIRTY-SIX
London

"**Y**ou know, the only time we hang out anymore is when you're dragging me to your boyfriend's games." Alec glances at me out of the corner of his eye as we shuffle down the row.

"Oh, please, don't act like you mind."

My roommate grins. "Could have at least sprung for better seats. I cancelled a date for this."

"You did not cancel, you told her you'd meet up with her later."

"Whatever. Same thing." His gaze is now locked on the field. "So is there a plan?"

"Showing up is the plan," I tell him as we settle into our seats. There's a pole blocking half my view, but the players are so little down there I'm not sure it matters.

"How is showing up and sitting so far up he can't even see you to know you're here *the plan*?"

I scowl at him. I thought a lot about what Sierra said, how showing up and being there was important, even if he hadn't asked me to be, and decided she was right. I want to support him, even if it means sitting in the nosebleed section at a game he's playing while he has no idea I'm here. When he's ready, tonight or weeks from now, I'll still be here. Hopefully, he's ready before playoffs because that's a whole lot of football in my future. Maybe I should learn some of the rules.

The game is close. Alec tells me the same things Sierra had about Kansas City. Or I think it's the same. I get the punchline: they're good. I'm not usually so anxious watching Brogan play, but my stomach is in knots from the second the ball is snapped.

I spend the first quarter drinking the foamy beer to calm my anxiety, then realize at this rate I'll be drunk before halftime so I switch to water.

The jumbotron zooms in on Brogan as he jogs out to his position after the huddle. His brown eyes have an intensity that he usually reserves for sex, and my lady parts tingle. I miss sex with him. I miss laughing with him. I miss *him*.

I don't think I've ever wanted someone this much. No, I know I haven't. I can't imagine not seeing him or talking to him. He's under my skin and I want to keep him there.

I hope when he's able to see through all the hurt his parents inflicted that he wants to be there too. And more than anything, I hope he knows that there's nothing he could share with me that would make me care about him less.

His parents not loving him makes me hate them with a fiery passion I wasn't sure I was capable of. It makes my hatred of Chris feel like a cute little grudge by comparison.

It breaks my heart. He's good and wonderful. Maybe it's because of what he's been through, maybe it's in spite of that.

I know he's lovable because I've never loved anyone more than I do him.

Suddenly, I feel like I can't sit still. Maybe it's not about being patient and waiting for him to need me, but about continually telling him all the amazing things I love about him until he has no choice but to believe it.

When people don't love us the way we want to be loved, we decide it's our own character flaw. It's not. It just means someone else is out there waiting for you, ready to love you in all the ways you deserve.

I want to be that person for him. Or at least one of them.

At halftime I clutch my phone in my hands, willing him to call or text like he did the night we met up at the bar after the game. That night changed my life, and I don't want to go back to before.

"Maybe I should text him," I say to Alec.

He's scrolling on his own phone, but looks up with one brow cocked. "No."

"Why not? He called me at halftime. Remember?"

"Yeah, it's sexy when a guy does it, but needy and demanding when girls do."

I scowl at him. "That's sexist!"

"I don't make the rules." He shrugs.

I don't text Brogan. Not because I think it's needy but because I don't want to distract him. He has enough going on and I don't know where his head is at.

The game is tied and there's a nervous energy in the stadium that's bled into me, making me more anxious than I was earlier. I guess I care about football now. Or at least a single football player, and I know he'll be disappointed if they lose.

The third and fourth quarters are back and forth. My fingers are red from where I've been clenching my hands into fists and then sitting on them to stop myself. The Mavericks are down by three with less than a minute to go. I feel helpless and sick to my stomach.

"God, you're antsier than me." Alec places a hand on my leg to stop it from bouncing.

"I think I'm gonna throw up."

"You are really not cut out to be a football wife."

"I just hope I'm still a football girlfriend," I mutter. "I'll worry about my iron stomach later."

The stadium is on their feet when the Mavericks get into position on the field. I go between watching on the big screen to staring down at the field, all the while watching Brogan. When the ball is snapped, he runs at a slant toward the sideline. Cody scans and steps back, then fires the ball toward Brogan. He's still running toward the end zone but somehow manages to catch the ball over his shoulder.

The crowd erupts and we all scream as Brogan sprints toward the end zone with defenders chasing after him. One defender gets close, and I hold my breath. Brogan holds out an arm, keeping the guy away from him and then somehow pushing him to the ground, all while running at an incredible speed.

When he crosses over and makes the touchdown it feels like the ground shakes with the excitement. Alec and I turn to each other, jumping and yelling, then I turn back to watch Brogan celebrate. His teammates on the field rush him, and the ones on the bench sprint onto the field. It's madness.

"We have to get down there," I say to Alec. If we don't start that way, we're going to be blocked by the thousands of people in front of us.

We jog down many, many flights of steps to the lowest area, then down to where people are going onto the field. Security is tight and there's no way we're going to be allowed on.

"Flash your press badge around or something," I say to Alec.

"I'm a weatherman."

"Doesn't that count for something?" I groan, then spot a familiar head and renewed excitement surges through me. "Wait, there's Archer."

He's at the edge of the field in a group, but it's definitely him. I can see his profile and he's grinning wide at the field where Brogan is still celebrating.

I start to yell for Archer, but it's so noisy in here I know he'll never hear me. And there is no pushing my way through.

"Holland!" I yell with everything I have. My throat burns. Someone taps him on the shoulder and points, and he turns.

I wave when he spots me. Then he starts for me.

"Hi." I lean closer to him as I scream the greeting, but I can't even hear myself.

Archer grins at me, then yells, "You're here?"

He looks confused, like maybe he thinks I shouldn't have come. I try not to let it deter me.

"I need to see him." I point to the field.

"You're here?" he asks again.

I wave a hand in front of me.

He's smiling bigger. "But you weren't home."

"What?" I'm not sure I'm hearing him right.

He leans over to the security guard and says something, then Alec and I are allowed to pass by.

"I went by your place to give you this." Archer pulls an envelope from his back pocket. I recognize Brogan's slanted penmanship. I take it, feeling my insides swirl. "Brogan wanted me to give it to you. I started to leave it under your door, but I wasn't sure what to do when you didn't answer."

"I must have already been on the way here."

He nods, then glances to the envelope.

My fingers shake as I open it up. It has the familiar style of the letters we exchanged when we first met. It's folded in thirds on white copy paper.

> London,
> Meet me after the game?
> x,
> Brogan

With the letter are two tickets for the game.

"You mean to tell me we could have been in a box?" Alec asks, looking over my shoulder. He curses under his breath.

"Where were you sitting?" Archer asks.

"Nosebleed section." I give him a sheepish smile, then notice the three other guys who were standing with him before have followed him over. And they're all looking at me.

Not just looking at me. They're grinning ear to ear and watching me like they know me.

"Uhh…" I start, and then it clicks. "Your brothers."

"Oh, right." Archer turns to them. "Guys, this is London, but I see you creepers have already figured that out."

"Nice to meet you." One of them steps forward. He has a nice smile that he continues to aim at me. He looks a little older than Archer and Brogan, dark hair, hazel eyes. He's wearing a Mavericks shirt under his jacket.

"You too." I take his hand. "You must be Hendrick."

His smile gets impossibly bigger. "That's right."

"The oldest."

The others laugh.

"And the reason Brogan wanted to be a football player when he was younger," I add.

I pick Flynn out by his unruly russet-colored hair and baby face.

"You must be the future major league baseball star." I nod at him, and he blushes.

"And that makes you...." I lock gazes with the third. He has the same hint of mischief about him as Brogan, but a harder edge. "Knox. The motocross rider."

"Also known as the biggest pain in the ass," Archer says.

Knox runs his tongue along his top teeth and tries to fight a grin.

"I thought you said he screwed things up," Knox says to Archer, signing as he speaks.

"He said that, not me." Archer locks gazes with me. "But I think he was mistaken."

The noise around us gets louder. The players have moved closer, and people are calling out to get their attention. I resist glaring at several women yelling for Brogan.

"Come on, I'll take you to him," Archer says.

I look to Alec, who is still standing behind me.

"Go, go," he says.

"Thank you." I hug him before turning to follow Archer.

"You owe me box seats," Alec calls after me.

Archer and his brothers flank me on all sides as we move through the crowd. I'm too short to see over them, so I trust we're making progress.

When we come to a stop, I can hear Brogan, but he still sounds like he's a little ways away.

Archer is in the front and he turns to me. "I can't get us any closer."

I lift onto my toes, but it's useless.

"Sorry about this." Archer steps closer and crouches in front of me, then pulls me up onto his shoulders.

"Oh," I yelp and grab on to his bicep with one arm and his head for balance, but his grip is locked on me. My fear lasts only a few seconds because I'm tall enough now I can spot Brogan.

I yell his name, but it gets lost in all the other shouts.

"We got you," Knox says to my right. He cups his hand around his mouth and yells, "Yo, Six!"

Then they all join in. People nearby start to notice and the five of us keep screaming Brogan's name.

I see the moment he hears us. He stills and then scans the crowd. Our eyes lock and I wave awkwardly.

His grin makes my insides light up. He cuffs one of his teammates on the shoulder and says something, then moves toward us. The crowd parts much more easily for him than us.

Before I have any idea what to say to him, he's in front of us.

Archer sets me down while his brothers congratulate Brogan.

"Thanks, guys. Appreciate you all being here."

"That was a great game. We're so proud of you." Hendrick hugs him, then they all step back to give us some room.

"I see you met my brothers," he says.

"Yeah." I laugh. "They're handy in a crowd."

His smile remains, but his eyes soften. "I wasn't sure if you'd come. I'm sorry I was such a wreck this week. I wanted to reach out, but after the way I acted, I wasn't sure you'd want to hear from me."

"I was never not coming. I'm here. Good and bad. Always. You're my guy." I open the front of my jacket to show him the Six jersey I'm wearing.

"I don't deserve you."

"Yes, you do. And I'm going to keep telling you that until you believe me. I wouldn't sit through a football game for just anyone."

"Good to know." One side of his mouth inches higher.

"I don't know a lot about the game, although I am a fan of you in football pants. Actually, the whole uniform really does it for me. Your arms, your chest, your butt…The way your hair curls out around the back of your helmet." I wave a hand in front of him, and he smirks.

"But my favorite things about you have nothing to do with your ability to catch a ball or even your rugged good looks." I hear his brothers snickering behind me. I turn to them. "Shocking, I know!"

I turn back to him. "I like how kind you are, how much fun you make the most mundane things. I admire your work ethic and how you make people feel loved and appreciated. People want to know you because they can sense how wonderful you are. I wonder if I made you feel half as adored as you made me feel the past couple of months. I hope so. And if not, I promise I will if you let me." I take one more step toward him. "There are so many more things I like about you. The list is endless. I guess you could say I'm your biggest fan."

He reaches forward and fists the material of my shirt, tugging me to him. Then, his mouth comes down onto mine and he kisses me hard.

When we come up for air, there's a camera in our faces. I glance up at the jumbotron and want to hide behind my giant boyfriend.

"Better get used to it." Brogan kisses my temple. "I plan on kissing you a lot more before we manage to make it out of here."

And he does.

CHAPTER THIRTY-SEVEN
Brogan

"**Y**ou look happy," Archer comments while we stand at the bar waiting for drinks.

"I am." My smile couldn't be any bigger.

"I'm happy for you. You deserve it, man. London is great."

I glance over to where she's sitting with Hendrick, Knox, and Flynn.

"It's not just her," I say. "It's everything. We have some pretty great brothers."

"That we do." His chest rises and falls with a quiet laugh, but then his face falls back to his somber expression.

I tap his shoulder with the back of my hand. "You'll be back before you know it. Your time is coming."

He nods, a hint of a smile erasing the worry that's been there all season, but especially the last couple of days after not being cleared for another game. "Our time."

We knock wrists and then someone clears their throat next to us.

Billy Boone watches us, gaze flicking from Archer to me. He nods his head in greeting.

"Nice game tonight," Billy says.

I lean forward. I swear he just complimented me. My mouth opens, then I close it. Every time I talk to this guy, I put my foot in it.

"Brogan's having a hell of a season," Archer says. "And he's just getting started."

He stares at Billy, daring him to disagree. I'm not surprised when he doesn't jump at the chance to shower me with praise, but he does lift his beer in what I choose to see as a silent peace treaty. "Best of luck with the rest of the season."

"Thank you," I say. "And if it's not too late to apologize, I am sorry."

"I appreciate that." He walks off, and I'm still staring after him, shocked, when our drinks come, and Archer reaches for them.

"That was…interesting," he says. "I'm proud of you."

"I'm still waiting for him to come back and yell at me. I don't think I like being on his good side. It's creepy."

Laughing, Archer leads me back to the table.

London looks at me as I slide into the chair next to her.

"Whatever they're saying, it's a lie." I give all the guys my meanest scowl. Not that they buy it. I'm too happy tonight to pull off the expression. My brothers are here, my girl.

My girl.

I know there's a lot we need to talk about, but I'm not scared anymore. If she can handle a secret sister and knowing I haven't spoken to my dad since I was a teenager, then I think chances are good she can handle anything.

"We were telling her how great you are," Knox says with an unconvincing smirk.

"Yeah, I bet." I wrap an arm around her shoulders, and she nuzzles into me, laughing.

"Jokes aside, you're pretty fucking great." Hendrick lifts his glass. "To Brogan. Love you, Brother."

Brother.

The word hits different tonight. They didn't do anything different. They've always shown up for me, always treated me like one of them. I guess I just feel it now. We're not blood, but we're family. The family you choose, the ones who choose you back, are so much harder to find.

We spend the next hour catching up. Flynn lets us pepper him with questions about school and baseball. Knox fills us in on how he plans to spend the off-season doing freestyle and hanging out every free second with Avery, Hendrick is all smiles and constantly turning the new wedding band on his left ring finger. It's nice. I missed them and I don't want to go this long without seeing each other again.

When the conversation comes to a lull, I take London's hand under the table for encouragement and then decide to tell them the news.

Releasing her hand so I can sign as I speak, I say, *"I, uh, have some news."*

"You already got married, didn't you?" Hendrick asks, looking between me and my girl.

"We just literally watched them get back together." Knox shakes

his head at our older brother then me. *"I'm betting there's a baby involved, or maybe you're a throuple instead of a couple."*

Archer starts coughing on his drink.

"Kiiiidding." Knox grins.

London's brows rise. "I'm not pregnant."

I glance at her. "That's more important to clarify than the fact you're not also sleeping with Arch?"

"I mean…" She shrugs. "You two are close and the three of us hang out a lot. I can see where people would think that."

"We're not a throuple." I glare at everyone around the table.

"Eh…" Knox keeps on smiling, the smug bastard. *"I took my best shots."*

"I'm pretty sure I have a sister," I say before they can come up with any other ridiculous ideas.

"A sister?" Hendrick leans forward. *"How?"*

I tell them what I know. How Sabrina was adopted as a baby and grew up in Flagstaff. And the letter and texts that I ignored, thinking it was another scam from someone just wanting money. London squeezes my fingers, silently supporting me. But the truth is it doesn't hit me with the same sort of pain that I thought it would.

Not with these five. They're my family, and family loves you no matter what.

I've always hesitated in planning things and instead let them come to me because I guess I felt like I was inconveniencing them in some way, but before they leave, I make sure we've got some solid dates for Christmas while Flynn is home and Archer and I have a few days off.

And if I had any reservations about them all liking London,

though the thought didn't even cross my mind honestly, it's obvious they do by the way they each hug her and then me on the way out the door.

The three of us, Archer, London, and myself, head back to my apartment. Archer gives us a salute and heads off to his bedroom, and then it's just me and the most gorgeous woman in the world.

"So…" I take both her hands and swing them between us. "What should we do now?"

"Hmm…" Smirking, she glances up as she thinks. "Maybe we should go to bed."

"Yeah, sure, we could do that." It's after midnight, but I'm wired. Totally fine though. I'll just stare at her while she sleeps. That's not strange, right?

She leans in and brushes her lips over mine then says, "I've been dying to really test out the sturdiness of the bed."

"I love you," I blurt out.

She startles, smiling.

I wince, but fuck it. "Not because you want me to fuck you hard enough to break a bed. Or not just because of that."

She laughs.

"Thank you for showing up for me tonight and for wanting to know all of me. I'm not good at opening up about my family, but I will if you still want to hear it."

"I want to know all of it. Every detail about you. I'm not going anywhere so there's no rush."

Some of it is going to be really hard to share, I know that, but I'll do it for her. Because I understand. I want to know every detail about her too.

"Did I mention I love you? Because I fucking love you." I don't think I'll ever get tired of saying it.

Her mouth curves, and the way my chest tightens I know she feels the same way even before she says it.

"I love you too." She stares at me a beat and then gets a sassy glint in her eye. "Also not just because I know you can fuck me hard enough to break a bed."

I lift her up and toss her over my shoulder. My hand automatically goes to her ass, giving it a little smack. "Can and plan to, sweetheart."

She squeals and giggles as I carry her to my bedroom. I set her down on the floor in front of me but keep my arms circled around her back. She looks up at me with those big green eyes the color of a four-leaf clover. My lucky charm.

Everything in my life is better with her by my side. She peels me out of my shirt, then I lift hers over her head. Her skin is like satin as I run my hands down her shoulders and arms to capture her hands. Threading our fingers together, I drop my forehead to hers and close my eyes. I just want to soak in this moment. She's here.

She chose me. I can't even begin to describe what that means to me. A strange sensation, something like contentment, fills my chest.

"Everything okay?" she asks quietly.

"Perfect," I say, pulling back so she can see my eyes and know that I'm being sincere. "I have never been better."

"Never?" She cocks a brow and then her hands go to my jeans, fingers working quick to pop the button and unzip me. I'm still in a haze of happiness and bliss as she drops to her knees and her intent finally becomes clear.

Her mouth feels so damn good. Our gazes remain locked as

she takes me slowly to the back of her throat then glides back to suck on the tip. She is a fucking goddess. I'm not sure I'll ever feel worthy, but I'll never take her for granted.

"I need to be inside you." I pull her back up to her feet and kiss her while I take off the rest of her clothes.

We tumble onto the bed in a tangled heap, kissing and laughing softly. Her body molds to mine, and I hold her against me like I thought about so many times over the past week. I swear I can breathe easier when she's around.

When I finally push inside her, we both still, mouths fused together but not moving. My heart races and a jolt of electricity courses through me.

"I love you." I'm not even sure I've said the words out loud until she says them back.

"I love you." She lifts her hips higher, taking me deeper. Her body quivers and she lets out a soft moan.

I capture all her sexy sounds, swallowing them as I continue to fuck her slowly. Hard but slow, dragging out every sensation with thinly contained control.

"Please," she whimpers. "I need to come."

I pull out, then grip my dick and tease her clit, stroking up and down over the sensitive bud until she cries out. I'm barely back inside her before my own orgasm splits through me. She clenches around me and stars dance in my vision.

We cling to each other as we come down from it, bodies shaking and breaths ragged. When I finally manage to shake the fog from my vision, her sweet smile is waiting for me.

"Sweetheart." The word comes out in a low gravel.

"You were right," she says. "I have never been better."

CHAPTER THIRTY-EIGHT
London

"There she is." Brogan stands as Sabrina walks through the restaurant to our table.

"Hey. You made it."

"Sorry I'm late," she says, taking her crossbody purse off and pulling out the chair across from me. "I still don't know my way around the city very well. All the one-way streets and…"

She stops, flustered, and takes her seat. Her red hair catches on the sunlight coming through the window. "How are you?"

"Good," Brogan says. "Did you get everything moved?"

"I'm in a month-to-month place for now until I decide where I want to live." She glances around the restaurant. "This place is cute."

"It's my sister's and my favorite brunch place. They have the best lemonade mimosas," I say as the server approaches our table.

"I'll have that." Sabrina smiles. "Thanks." Her smile widens. "It's so nice to meet you. Brogan has said such nice things."

"About you too," I tell her.

Sabrina agreed to do a DNA test and they confirmed she is his sister. Since then, they've been trying to get to know one another. He's taken her to lunch and another time she invited him to dinner with some of her friends. I can tell how hopeful it all makes him feel to have found this family he didn't know existed.

"So, Brogan tells me you're opening a dance studio." I'm so curious about his sister. I have my guard up, just in case, but so far, she hasn't raised any red flags.

The way her eyes light up at the question even reminds me a little of him. She's tall and graceful. Her features are softer, but she has that something about her that draws people in and makes them want to pay attention.

"Well, I'm trying, but you'd be amazed at how many building owners take one look at me and blow me off because they think I'm some young kid who's going to flake on them."

"I could help if you want," Brogan offers.

Quiet falls over the table, and I hold my breath while I wait for her answer. I think he's genuine in wanting to do whatever he can for her, but I hope that she doesn't see him as only that.

"No, it's okay," she says with a shake of her head. "I don't want to rent from someone who treats young women shitty anyway. And I have a lead on a place not too far from here."

I let out a sigh of relief.

"What kind of dance studio? Ballet?"

"And tap, lyrical, modern, hip hop."

"You're a dancer, then?"

"I was, but I have pretty bad asthma, so I do more teaching than dancing these days. It's fun and the kids are great."

I fire more questions at her, and so does Brogan. By the time brunch is finished, she's won me over. I'll still destroy her if she hurts him though.

"I hate to eat and run, but I've gotta go," she says. "I'm meeting a friend."

She opens her wallet, and Brogan waves her off. "I got it."

"No," she insists. "Please. I hounded you for months, the least you can do is let me grab food and drinks."

Brogan doesn't seem happy about it, but he gives in with a nod.

She sets some cash in the middle of the table and stands. Brogan gets to his feet as well.

"Archer and I are having some people over next weekend. Will you come?" he asks her.

"Uhh…maybe. Your buddy doesn't seem like my biggest fan."

"Archer's cool," Brogan says.

"He called me a stripper."

I cough as I take a drink of my mimosa. That doesn't sound like Archer, but then again, maybe it does. He's loyal and I know how much Brogan means to him.

"He was kidding." Brogan grins sheepishly. "Come. Bring some friends if you want, and I can introduce you to some of my teammates. I'll make sure they all know you are not a stripper."

"Or don't. I'll show up and tell them I'm the entertainment."

"I think I might have to beat up some teammates if you do that."

"Okay," she agrees with a laugh. "Thanks for letting me crash brunch. This was fun. It was nice to meet you, London."

"You too."

Brogan moves around to hug her. "Text me this week."

They embrace like two people who are still figuring out their relationship, but if I know Brogan—and I do—he'll do everything he can to make her feel special and welcome.

When she's gone, my boyfriend takes a seat next to me. He's grinning big and looks lighter and happier than I've ever seen him, which is saying something.

We've spent the past weeks talking a lot about his parents, how they were rarely around, so basic things like food and clothes weren't always available. He had to learn how to do his own laundry at a really early age and he forged their signatures so he could get things at school like free lunch. The stories were heartbreaking and hard to hear. He spent one whole week without water or electricity because they left him to go to a concert in California, and forgot to pay the utility bills. He was seven.

And when they were home, they treated him like his presence was a burden, often kicking him out if he made too much noise or got in the way.

Then Rosie Holland took him in, and Archer and his brothers looked out for him all these years. There's a lot of hurt there that he's ignored, but he has so many people that want only the best for him. I hope Sabrina can be one of those people too.

"I like her," I tell him. It's true. By all accounts, she truly wants to get to know her brother and doesn't have any ulterior motives. I hope I'm right. Even Archer can't find any flaws in her story, and he has definitely been looking for them.

"Me too." He shakes his head, eyes glinting with happiness. "It's weird having someone that's part of me. Blood family that doesn't suck. I never thought I'd have that."

I run a hand through his hair and rest my fingers at the nape of his neck.

"I know she didn't grow up the same way I did, but it's like she feels that same sense of loss that I do. I know I was lucky, don't get me wrong. I wouldn't change things if it meant not having the Hollands, but with her, I just feel like she gets it in a different way."

"That makes sense," I say. "Having a sister is a really unique and fun thing."

"A sister." He laughs. "She probably would have made my life hell growing up."

"Like any good sister." I bat my lashes.

He's grinning like he's still lost in the idea of Sabrina and what their life could have looked like together.

"You have lots of time for her to annoy and irritate you in all the ways sisters do."

He leans forward and presses his lips to mine. "Thank you."

"For what?"

"I don't know. Everything."

"You're welcome." I take another sip of my mimosa. "Did Archer really ask her if she was a stripper?"

"Not exactly, but he definitely put his foot in his mouth."

"He's protective of you."

He bobs his head in agreement. "I know, but once he gets to know her, he'll come around. I'm not worried."

"What did she say when he asked if she was a stripper?"

"He didn't ask her, he signed it to me."

My eyes widen. "And she knew?"

"Yeah." He laughs. "Turns out she knows ASL. Totally called him on it."

"I like her more and more."

"Hey," he says, angling his body toward mine and placing one knee between my legs. "I have an idea of how we can spend the rest of the day."

"You do, do you?" I ask, sounding genuinely intrigued by the possibility when I know very well it's going to include us being naked.

He takes both of my hands in his. "Let's go to your apartment."

I chuckle. "Mhmmm."

"And pack up all your stuff."

My brows furrow. Okay, this isn't going where I thought it was.

"And bring it to my place."

"You want me to stay at your place for the weekend?"

"Yes." He nods, placing a kiss on the inside of my elbow. My skin tingles. This man has made me insatiable.

"For the activities you have in mind, I don't think I'm going to need my entire apartment."

He chuckles softly and looks down at me with a soft expression that makes butterflies swarm in my stomach. "Move in with me."

"What?" There is no hiding the surprise in my voice.

"Move in with me. I already talked to Archer. He's cool with it so long as we shut the door while we're having sex and as long as you promise not to refer to us as a throuple."

I want to. God, do I want to. It hasn't been very long, but I've never been more sure of anything in my life. He is my guy. Forever. "I can't bail on Alec."

He scrunches up his face. "Can't I just buy him out of your lease? I really like waking up *and* falling asleep next to you."

I drape my arms over his shoulders. "Me too, but our lease ends in four months, which should be plenty of time for him to find someone else, and then…yes, absolutely. I have conditions of my own though."

"Oh yeah." His eyes light up. "Like what?"

"Ummm…." I kiss him while I try to come up with some. It turns out I don't have any conditions at all. I want him and all the fun and chaos that comes with him. The good times, the bad. All the dark parts he tries to hide so he never makes anyone feel anything but happy. I want those too. I want it all.

CHAPTER THIRTY-NINE

Brogan

Twinkle lights hang above us and a band plays a 90s ballad while people eat cake and mingle at the circular tables. Sierra and Ben's wedding was beautiful. The ceremony and reception were held at the zoo where Ben works. Dinner, dancing, and laughter. So much happiness and laughter.

The zoo has a cool vibe at night. All the greenery and random animal noises. After the vows, guests were able to walk around the park, although London had to stay for pictures so I didn't partake. The reception was a full sit-down dinner with toasts from friends and family. My girl cried as she wished her sister a lifetime of happiness. Not gonna lie, I teared up too.

It really is an amazing thing. Two people committing to love each other and having each other's back. The world is a bitch. Made harder by bad parents, personal fears and anxiety, and just the millions of ways we all fuck up every day. It's not an easy or simple thing to agree to do for another person.

The bride and groom have already left, and the last of the guests are clinging to the final hour of the magical night.

"This has got to be the coolest wedding I've ever been to," I say as London and I sway to the music. We're one of only a few other couples dancing. Most have given up and are sitting at tables, talking and covering yawns.

"It really was." She's had a dreamy smile on her face all night.

"And you look gorgeous, sweetheart."

"You mentioned that."

"And I'm gonna keep mentioning it."

She looks up at me, smiling, then rests her head on my chest.

"Where's your dream location for a wedding?" I ask. I've been to destination weddings, church weddings, backyard receptions, and everything in between. Hendrick and Jane did a Fiji wedding with just family and a few friends, and that was pretty awesome too. I don't know what I picture for my own. I always thought of weddings as just another party until London. Now I understand why there's all the fuss. A wedding should say something about the kind of life you want to have with another person. Or maybe I'm just getting sappy in my old age.

"I'm not sure." She tilts her head up, but keeps it leaned against me. "Small. Not a lot of frills. I don't care about place cards and flowers and all that."

"No?" I'm surprised she doesn't care about the details. She's an artist after all.

"No. After helping Sierra, I think I've had enough wedding planning for a lifetime."

"Leave it to me, then. I'll plan us the best wedding ever."

"Oh, we're getting married, are we?" she asks. We haven't talked about it, but I know I can't live without her and the thought of her having my last name makes me giddy.

"Hope so."

She hums and nuzzles back into me. "We'll see."

I smile, knowing it with every fiber of my being. She's my endgame.

"I'm gonna buy you a big diamond so everyone knows you're mine. You'll wave and blind anyone within a mile of you."

She chortles. "Not a bad idea. Maybe I should get you one too. My cousins are staring a little too hard." She glances over to a table of young women. They are in fact looking so I tip London's chin up and steal her mouth.

She tastes like champagne and forever. My forever.

"How about I just do that a whole lot?"

Her lashes flutter open slowly. "That would probably be okay too."

I steal one more and then wrap my arms around her and breathe a sigh of contentment.

Someone taps me on the shoulder and when I turn, Chris stands there.

"Mind if I cut in?" he asks. "It's tradition for the best man to dance with the maid of honor."

London says nothing, but one dark brow arches and she inches closer to me.

"Ah well, don't worry about it. You're not much of a *best* man anyway, right?" I cuff him on the shoulder and then give him my back.

London drapes her arms back over my shoulders with an

amused smile. "He and Gretchen broke up," she says.

"Shocker."

"Yeah, apparently she ended things with him because he's, and I quote, 'a terrible human who can't back up the big dick energy.'" Her smile widens.

"Aww, poor Chris," I say sarcastically. I don't feel the least bit sorry for the guy.

When the music ends, I take her hand and we walk through the fading reception. London's father steps in front of us.

"Hello," he says, nodding to me and then smiling at London.

We haven't talked all night, and although I have rehearsed a dozen apologies, at the end of the day, I'm not sorry about what I said, only that I let my own shit muddy the message I wanted to send him.

"Tonight turned out beautifully," he says.

"Yeah, it did." London leans into me, and I wrap an arm around her waist.

"I apologized to London, but I feel like I need to do the same to you," he says, locking eyes with me. "I let my fears and worries cloud my judgment. She's talented and hardworking, things I already knew, but you reminded me. Thank you. I don't know how long it would have taken me on my own, but I'm grateful I don't have to find out. You're a good man. She's lucky to have you."

"Not as lucky as I am," I tell him.

London steps forward and wraps her arms around her dad's neck. "Thank you."

When she pulls back, he clears his throat and then extends a hand to me. We shake and he excuses himself.

Neither London nor I say anything as we head out of the

reception and walk through the park toward an enclosure where bears sleep in caves that are too dark to see in at night. The final song of the night plays.

"You worked things out with your dad, huh?" I ask finally. I haven't pressed her on the family situation. All things considered, I didn't feel like I had any right. But she quit her job at the news station and we celebrated the hell out of that.

"We talked. It's a start. I'm pretty sure he still hates that I don't have a fallback career, but he did buy a copy of one of my book covers and brought it for me to sign."

"No way." For some reason the image makes me laugh. But also, damn, why didn't I think of that?

"Yep." Our steps slow and she swings our hands between us. "I think maybe we'll be okay. I can live with him thinking I'm making the wrong choices, and I can live with him saying I told you so if I fail."

"You won't fail."

"I know. I believe in myself and that's enough. Maybe that's the lesson." She turns her head and smiles at me. "Would you rather be a bear or a lion?"

My lips part on a smile at the question and topic change. "That depends."

"On what?" She stops walking and turns to face me.

"Are you a bear or a lion?"

"Female lions do all the hunting. I'm not sure I'm cut out for that."

"So a bear then?"

"They are cute, but I'm not a big fan of fish." She wrinkles her nose.

"You want to be a bear, I'll get all the best berries for you. And if you want to be a lion, we'll shuck social norms and I'll do the hunting."

Her grin widens like she thinks I'm kidding. There isn't a lot I wouldn't do for her.

"I want to be whatever and wherever you are."

"Me too." She wraps her arms around my neck. "Let's be us. That seems to be working pretty well."

Better than pretty well. I'm having the time of my life.

EPILOGUE
Brogan

The club is packed, and I apologize to people as I weave through couples and groups to get to the bar. I scan the familiar space until I spot her.

"Hey, man." A guy with dark, slicked-back hair, and shoulders broader than mine, steps in front of me. Something tickles in my brain. I can't place him right away but I know I should. "You're Brogan Six."

"Yeah. That's right. And you're…" I reach out my hand and then it hits me. "Jack Wyld. Fuck, what are you doing in Arizona?"

"Just visiting," he says as we shake hands. The man is a beast of a hockey player for the Wildcats in Minnesota. "You had a hell of a rookie season."

My jaw drops and I want to pinch myself. Jack fucking Wyld knows who I am. What even is this life?

"Thank you. You too."

"I'm just heading out to meet up with some friends, but it was really nice to meet you." He smiles at me. "Good luck next year. Maybe take it a little easier on my Vikings though, huh?"

"Yeah, sure. If you take it easier on the Coyotes."

Laughing, he walks off, and I shake my head to clear it. I just met one of the best hockey players of all time.

It's almost as exciting as the other person I'm about to meet. I continue to the bar where a pretty brunette is sitting.

"Excuse me?" I say when I'm standing behind her.

She swivels in her chair and gives me a surprised look. "Hi."

"Hey there, yourself. Can I buy you a drink?" I take in her long, slender legs and the low cut of her black dress. Her lips are painted a bright red that I plan to smudge just as soon as she lets me.

She cocks her head to the side. "Oh my gosh. Aren't you Brogan Six?"

She says it a little louder than I expected. We're doing a little role-play, recreating the night we first met—minus the leaving alone part. I rented out the VIP area in case she wants to fuck where we first met. That might be creepy instead of romantic. I'm not sure.

"I am. What's your name?" I slide into the space between her and the person next to her. She already ordered us both drinks. I take a sip of my beer and rest my hip against the bar.

"London," she says. "I am *such* a big fan."

"Is that right?"

"Oh yeah. That catch you made on the ten-yard line in last week's game against the Cowboys was incredible."

"God, I love it when you talk football," I whisper, breaking character. I can't help it. Tripp spent the off-season teaching her football in exchange for her help picking out women on dating sites. He's decided it's time to settle down with a nice woman. He went on zero successful dates, but London's got a real knack for remembering numbers and plays.

She blushes but then slips back into character. "Maybe we should get out of here, then. My place isn't far."

"I bet mine is closer." I lift my brows suggestively. She moved in months ago, and waking up to her every morning is even better than I imagined it would be.

Outside, she nearly laughs at the sight of the limo. We slide into the back. Neither of us says anything for a solid five seconds, and then we both break at the same time, turning to each other and lunging for the other.

"Fuck, I missed you," I say to her. It's the start of the pre-season and we had a two-day road trip. It turns out forty-eight hours without her is my breaking point.

"Me too. I'm sorry. I planned to drag that out longer, but I couldn't wait."

"And I planned to fuck you in VIP, but this will work."

"Oh, that's so sweet."

I chuckle into her mouth. Not creepy. So noted.

We make out in the back seat as the limo drives us to our next stop, which is sadly not our apartment. Not yet.

When the limo pulls up to the curb in front of my old mail place, I glide my hands out from under her skirt.

"Hey, look where we are," I say, nodding toward the window. "We should stop by and get your mail."

Despite it being kind of far from our place, she kept the PO Box for her work mail and comes by once a week or so. She says it's a good excuse to swing by and see Alec. But I think it's a sentimental place for her. Just like it is for me.

"You want to stop? Now?" she asks, then laughs like she thinks that's the worst idea I've ever had.

"Yeah. I haven't been in there in forever. It'll be fun." I scoot toward the door and open it before she can protest.

"It was more fun with your hand up my skirt," she mumbles, and I have to fight a laugh.

Inside, I take her hand and we walk through the maze of tiny metal boxes until we get to hers. She pulls out the key and then I start to get nervous. What if it's not here? What if I screwed this up?

She pulls out the mail and in it, the package from me. She grins knowingly when she sees the return name and address.

"This is why you wanted to stop? Did you mail me a pair of your boxers?" She grins and tears open the bubble mailer. She says nothing as she reaches in, but the second she pulls out the smaller box she freezes.

"What is this?" she asks, voice wavering.

I take it from her and flip it open, then turn so she can see.

"Are you crazy? You put this in the mail." She gapes at the diamond nuzzled in the black velvet box.

"Not exactly." I chuckle lightly. "I talked to a sweet lady named Beverly who works here, and she slipped it into your mailbox."

"Beverly helped you do this?"

"Mhmmm. Real helpful lady."

"Of course. For *you* she's helpful," London mutters under her breath.

I take the ring out and hold it between my thumb and pointer finger, then get down on one knee.

She shakes her head at me, but smiles. Tears glisten in her eyes. "This was in here all day?"

"A few hours. I had to keep you busy, so you didn't swing by on your own and ruin my brilliant plan."

"You never stop surprising me."

She shouldn't be surprised though. Doesn't she know I'd do anything to make her happy?

Her gaze drops to the diamond ring sparkling under the overhead lights. "Oh my god, is this really happening?"

"It's really happening, sweetheart." It's been almost a year since that first night at the bar where she told me off. I would have proposed months ago but she had this big project she's working on for a book publisher, and I had camp and the start of the season. I wanted it to be perfect. She deserves that at the very least.

"For the first time in a really long time, I've felt what it's like to have someone want and love *me*. I honestly never thought I'd have that outside of my brothers. And to have it from someone like you blows my mind every day. You're good and kind and talented and sexy. So fucking sexy."

Tears have started to fall down her cheeks, but she laughs at that.

"You always say you're my biggest fan, but I'm yours too. No one inspires or encourages me more than you. Marry me, London? Let me spend the rest of my life supporting you in whatever you choose to do, cheering you on as loud and as often as I can, and loving you better than anyone has ever loved another person."

My throat tightens as I think about all the things I want to say to her. I asked Hendrick for advice when I told my brothers I was going to propose, and he told me, keep it simple. I guess that's not bad advice. After all, I'm going to have the rest of our lives to tell her how much she means to me. Hopefully.

"Yes, Brogan Six. I'll marry you."

I slide the ring on her finger and then she jumps in my arms, wrapping herself around me and holding on tight. I never want her to let go.

Me and her.

Forever and always.

HOLLAND BROTHERS

HENDRICK

Well...?

ARCHER

Dude, we're sweating it. Did you ask her or what?

KNOX

Ask her before she wises up and she realizes she could do way better.

HENDRICK

Oh, like you're one to talk. Your fiancée is an Olympic athlete. People will refer to you as Mr. Avery Oliver.

KNOX:

Like I care. As long as they know she's mine and I'll break anyone who touches her, that's all that matters.

ARCHER

Wow. Okay. Brogan?? I'm dying over here. Do we have a new sister or what?

FLYNN

What's happening? Is he finally asking her today? I cannot keep up with the group texts. You all need to get a life.

KNOX

What? You get drafted to the big league and suddenly you're too good for us?

FLYNN

I was always too good for you ●

ARCHER

Daaaaamn. Nice one, little bro.

ME

She said YES! You can now refer to me as Mr. London Bennett, bitches!

ACKNOWLEDGMENTS

Thank you so much to everyone who picked up this book. I hope it brought you a few hours of joy and happiness wrapped up in a swoony escape. And if you got misty-eyed in a few parts, that's all Brogan's fault!

To my incredible team: Jamie, Devyn, JR, and Tori, I quite literally could not have finished this book without your help. I can't say thank you enough. I'm so fortunate that I get to work with each of you.

Sarah Jane, thanks again for the stunning cover illustration. You made all my pink, sporty dreams come true with this one. PINK STADIUM SEATS?! I adore you.

Lori, I know I can always count on you for the most stunning covers and this one was no exception.

Anelise, Becky, Jamie, Katie, Margo, and Sarah – this book is so much stronger for your suggestions and notes. Thank you for always treating my words with such care while still pushing me to be a better writer.

Lynette, your input was invaluable. Thank you so much!

Everyone at Valentine PR and my agent and publicist, Nina, thank you for all that you do.

Sahara – you claimed him first ☺

And lastly, to my husband. The reasons are too many to list. I love you.

ALSO BY REBECCA JENSHAK

ABOUT THE AUTHOR

Rebecca Jenshak is a USA Today bestselling author of new adult and sports romance. She lives in Arizona with her family. When she isn't writing, you can find her attending local sporting events, hanging out with family and friends, or with her nose buried in a book.

Sign up for her newsletter for book sales and release news.

Printed in Great Britain
by Amazon